catchlight

BROOKE ADAMS LAW

Catchlight, n.
The reflection of a light source in a photographic subject's eyes.

I will not return to a universe
of objects that don't know each other,
as if islands were not the lost children
of one great continent. The world
is flux, and light becomes what it touches . . .

—Lisel Mueller, "Monet Refuses the Operation"

Woodhall Press
81 Old Saugatuck Road, Norwalk, Connecticut, 06855
Woodhallpress.com

Distributed by INGRAM

Cover and Text Design: L.J. Mucci
Copyeditor: Paulette Baker
Author Photo: Daniel Silbert

Library of Congress Cataloging-in-Publication Data available.
ISBN 978-1-949116-18-2 (paperback)
ISBN 978-1-949116-19-9 (ebook)

First Edition

PART I

Chapter 1

Laura

Monday mornings were my favorite time of the week. All that possibility. Nothing had gone wrong yet.

And I was having a great Monday morning, until my sister called.

I knew it was her because I'd set "Wrecking Ball" as her ringtone. And she only called when there was an "emergency," like when her babysitter canceled.

All you ever did was wre-e-e-eck me. Yeah, you wre-e-e-eck me.

Maybe that song was a *little* too on the nose.

I let it go to voicemail. Izzy and Monday mornings were a bad mix, like tequila and red wine.

I'd just gotten to the clinic. I had three clients scheduled back-to-back, but there was still time to get coffee from the break room. Miley wailed from my phone again and I jumped. Against my better judgment, I picked up.

"Iz, what is it? I'm seeing a client in ten minutes. And no, I'm not saving a couple from getting divorced." My siblings liked to make bad jokes about the divorced therapist giving couples counseling.

Izzy took a shaky breath, which stopped me in my tracks.

"It's Mom," she said.

Panic flooded through me. "What's wrong? What happened?"

"Do you know Peggy Ramsey? She sits on the PTA board with me. She and her husband just bought a house on Lindsey Street—well, they haven't moved in yet, but she was there because they're having some work done on the kitchen, and—"

"Izzy. Focus. What happened to Mom?"

"Peggy saw an ambulance at Mom's house and saw Mom getting loaded into it."

"Did you talk to Bill?"

Long pause.

"Seriously? You didn't call him?"

"Can you just pop over to the hospital and see what's going on?"

I leaned my head on my hand. "Did you call Robert?"

"I'm sure he's busy."

"He *works at the hospital*."

I heard the doorbell ring through the phone. "Laur, someone's at the door. I have to run. Can you let me know what's going on?"

At the hospital I parked my baby-blue Caddy in the visitors' lot. Inside, the receptionist directed me to the fourth floor. Was it good or bad that Mom was already admitted? Was it a slow day in the ER, or what? Bill hadn't given me a lot of details, but when I asked him if I should come down, he hadn't said "no" right away. Which meant "yes."

I got off the elevator at the fourth floor and walked down the hall. The air smelled like disinfectant and feces.

I stopped at Room 412 and peered inside.

A woman I didn't know lay in the first bed, apparently asleep. *The View*, dubbed in Spanish, played on the TV.

I took a deep breath and walked around the curtain.

Mom looked worse than I'd feared. Her head was wrapped in gauze, blood seeping through the bandage at her temple. A bruise bloomed down the side of her face.

I'd never seen her look so small.

Her eyes were closed. I took two more steps into the room and sat down, trying to keep my breathing steady.

A rummaging sound from behind the curtain startled me. "Morning, Mrs. George," a male voice said.

"Screw you." The woman's voice was gravelly.

"That's not very nice." I could hear the Velcro of the blood pressure cuff being tightened.

"I can't understand a damn word they're saying," she said, turning up the volume. "And you're hurting me."

"You're watching the Spanish channel. And I'll be finished in a jiffy." Glass clinked against metal. The channel changed to *The View* in English.

"I'm going to complain about you, you know."

"About *me*? Why's that?" The charm in the man's voice made me smile.

"Just leave me alone."

"I'll be back later. I know you can't wait to see me!" The nurse ducked into Mom's side of the room. He had curly brown hair, green eyes, and a huge grin that showcased a crooked front tooth. "Hi."

I realized I was staring and broke my gaze. "Hi," I said. "Do you know what happened to my mom?" I stood up, overprotective.

He slid between me and the bed. "I'm just here to check on her. The doctor should be in shortly." He strapped the blood pressure cuff around Mom's thin bicep and pumped the bulb. The air hissed loudly. "140 / 85. Not *too* bad, it's starting to come down." He pulled the stethoscope out of his ears and hooked it around his neck.

"Do you—"

He clipped a small plastic contraption to Mom's finger. "Pulse is good too." He noted it on her chart. "Sorry, what were you saying?"

My chest felt tight, and I suddenly wasn't sure if it was due to anxiety about Mom or something else. "Have you seen my stepfather?"

"Oh, yeah. He went down to the cafeteria a little while ago."

"Thanks." I felt out of my body, as if my brain had been removed from my head and dunked in ice water. "Is she—" I swallowed hard, lowered my voice, even though Mom was still asleep. "Is she going to be okay?"

He looked me in the eye. "I don't know," he said gently. "You'll have to wait and talk to her doctor." He turned to go.

"Wait." I was at his elbow, holding his sleeve. We both looked at my hand. "What's your name?"

"Jonah." He waited a beat. "I have to go."

"Of course." I let go.

I went downstairs to the cafeteria, where it smelled like disinfectant and hot dogs. Bill was paying for a Coke at the register. He saw me and smiled, his tired face lighting up. "My girl," he said, hugging me tight. I pressed my face to the warm flannel of his shirt, inhaled the scent of his aftershave. "You want anything to drink?" I shook my head against his broad shoulder. My fear dissipated, if only for a moment. He popped the tab on his soda, and we walked back to the elevator bank.

"What happened?"

"She fell on the patio coming in from the garden." He took a long sip of Coke and jabbed the "Up" button with his fist. "They ruled out stroke, thank God. They think maybe she just slipped. They did a CAT scan to see if there's a fracture. Her doctor is supposed to come read it for us soon." Bill passed a hand over his face. "It was an accident," he said.

I squeezed his hand. "Of course it was."

An hour later we were all assembled. I usually had a week's warning to mentally prepare before seeing all my siblings in one room. All I could do this time was text my best friend, Amber, for support.

If you can keep your head when all about you are losing theirs and blaming it on you . . . , Amber texted back, referencing a Kipling poem.

Just pray I don't go apeshit, I wrote back.

Izzy was interrogating Robert in a low hiss about the possible causes for Mom's fall, and all the possible effects. He was sneaking glances at his iPhone. I inhaled surreptitiously as I kissed James's cheek. He'd shaved, and he smelled like Irish Spring, no trace of alcohol.

"Really, Laura? We're going to do this now?" he said.

"Do what?" I played dumb. "I was just breathing," I said, crossing my fingers behind my back. Ugh. Just being around them made me twelve years old again, superstitious and passive-aggressive.

Bill simply sat and stared at Mom, holding her hand in both of his.

I tried to remember the last time the six of us had been in a room together, without the diffusing elements of spouses or children or friends. It had to be dinner after my college graduation eleven years ago, before either Izzy or Robert was married.

Izzy was complaining to Robert about the price of visitor parking and trying to get him to validate her ticket.

James was on the phone, his back to us, muttering to someone.

Mrs. George shifted around and let out a barrage of curses: "Stupid bastards! I hate this goddamned place!"

A tense silence followed, and Mom stirred.

Izzy pressed the call button for the nurse.

"Hi, Mom," I said.

Mom opened her eyes and looked at Bill. "What happened?" Her voice was frail, a crackle of paper.

"You fell," Bill said, touching her unbruised cheek. "Coming in from the yard."

There was a pause as Jonah came in and checked her over. "Her doctor will be right down," he told us, nodding at me as he left.

"How do you feel, Mom?" I asked, moving closer to the bed to touch the scratchy blanket over her feet.

"Lousy," Mom croaked. She looked around at all of us. "I assume . . . since you're all here staring at me . . . that we're about to hear bad news."

Robert picked up her chart and flipped it open. "How's your breathing, Mom?" he asked.

"Robert, put that down," Bill said. His voice was quiet but authoritative.

Robert raised his eyebrows. "I'm just checking it over—"

"She's your mother, not one of your patients."

Izzy stepped up to the foot of the bed. "How's your memory been, Mom?"

Everyone tensed at her words. Because we'd all noticed—and ignored—the small signs. Losing her keys, forgetting her granddaughter's name, missing our cousin's bridal shower when she said she'd attend. And the time I'd gone to the house for Sunday brunch and Bill had been anxious; Mom hadn't come back from her ocean swim. We'd finally gone looking for her and found her wandering on the beach, as if she couldn't remember where the house was.

"God, Iz, lighten up," James said.

The doctor walked in then, a bustling Indian man who took the edge off the stress simply by being unrelated to us. "Hello, everyone," he said, picking up Mom's chart. "I am Dr. Pindar." He pulled a sheaf of brain scans from a large envelope under his arm. He stopped when he saw Robert. "Dr. Keene," he said.

Robert gestured to Mom. "My mother."

"Ah." Dr. Pindar nodded gravely. He turned his back on us, clipped the CAT scan to the board, and turned on the lights.

Robert sucked in a breath as he moved closer to the scan.

"There is a slight skull fracture here," Dr. Pindar indicated to Robert, "but of course I'm also looking at the enlargement of the lateral ventricle here. And a small cavity on the hippocampus—"

"Excuse me," Bill said, and we all turned to him. "My wife and I would like for you to speak to us directly."

"Of course." Dr. Pindar bobbed his head. He looked at Robert as if for permission to speak, and my brother nodded. "I'm afraid that Katherine is suffering from Alzheimer's disease."

The room was silent except for muted clapping from Mrs. George's TV.

"What's the prognosis?" Mom said. Her voice was quiet.

Dr. Pindar smiled slightly. "I find that a prognosis is often unhelpful in discussing Alzheimer's. The disease affects patients very differently."

"But?" Mom said, her voice steely.

"Well—" Dr. Pindar hesitated. "It's impossible to be certain, but a fall and a head injury often causes the disease to advance more . . . aggressively."

The next thirty minutes passed in a haze of medical talk. Dr. Pindar explained Mom's CAT scan to us, showing how it differed from the healthy brain scan he'd brought for comparison. Izzy argued with Dr. Pindar, then with Robert, insisting that Mom was too young (at seventy-two), then that a conclusive diagnosis could only be rendered during an autopsy. Robert's mouth grew thinner and thinner until his lips disappeared.

Dr. Pindar nodded, sighing. "And yet over five million people have been diagnosed this year." He took the scans down and placed them back in Mom's file. "I'm sorry. We will keep Mrs. Keene for a day or two until we can be sure that she doesn't have a concussion or other serious side effects from the fall, but you should begin to think about how you will want to proceed."

Dr. Pindar nodded to each of us then left, his feet making no noise on the scratched tile floor.

I felt removed, as if I were watching a movie during my clinical, preparing to offer therapy to the family of a recently diagnosed Alzheimer's patient. We all stared in different directions.

"Mom," I said, breaking the silence, "we can get you in to see someone, to talk about this—"

The change that came over Mom was more sudden than a car accident on the freeway. "For God's sake, Laura, not everything can be solved with a therapy session."

I blinked, startled, and was embarrassed to find tears in my eyes.

Robert stepped forward. "Mom—"

"Don't 'Mom' me, mister. You think you're so special just because you're a doctor. And you!" She glared at James. Her whole face was greenish, her features twisted in anger I'd never seen before, as if she were wearing a Halloween mask of her own face. "A drunk, just like your father!"

"Mom, stop it." Izzy's voice was firm, but her hands were clenched together so hard her knuckles were white.

"The perfect oldest child," Mom snarled. "You think you can do no wrong."

Bill stood up. "Everyone in the hall," he said. "Come back tomorrow."

None of us questioned him. But as we reached the door, I turned back. Mom's face was still mean. "You," she hissed at him. "Father of a bastard child!" Bill didn't flinch.

"Mom!" The tears were running down my face now. She swiveled her face to stare at me. I shut the door behind me.

"What did she say to him?" Izzy asked, her face bone-pale.

I pressed my tears back, covering my face, and the three of them moved in toward me, as if they could protect me. I was still the baby. "She called him the father of a bastard child."

There was an intake of breath. Bill had a grown son in Texas. He visited him once or twice a year.

"I can't stay here for this." Izzy turned and left without saying goodbye.

The three of us watched our sister walk away. We huddled in the hallway, trying to avoid nurses and doctors rushing from room to room. Robert's cell, holstered to his belt, rang. He looked miserable.

I grabbed his hand, and as he looked down at me from his eight-inch height advantage, I was five years old again and back at our father's funeral. The church had smelled of incense, and it tickled my nose. Robert, towering over me then as now, was crying. I had reached up and taken his left hand in my right and tugged on it until he looked down at me and tried to smile, tears dripping from his chin and plopping onto the tiled church floor.

Robert's face, angular and lined now, tried to smile down at me again. I blinked hard against the moisture in my eyes.

Finally it dawned on the three of us that there was nothing more to do. Kisses goodbye: Robert, James, and then I was alone in the hallway. I walked down the hall and ducked into a stairwell. One flight down I stopped and sat on a cold concrete step.

My fingers were freezing; I rubbed my palms together to warm them. My brain was stuck like a frozen computer screen, spinning on the image of Mom's twisted, angry face. I sat in the stairwell for a long time, my feet tapping against the lower step with anxiety, my fingers growing colder. I couldn't move.

The door above me opened and someone clattered down the flight of stairs above me. I leaned my head against the rusted railing and hoped they'd keep walking.

The person paused behind me. "Are you okay?" The nurse. Jonah.

I sighed. I wished he'd leave me alone. The requisite "Yes, fine" was on my lips, but instead what came out was, "No, I'm not."

He sat down on the step next to me. I could sense the heat of his body. "It's a tough diagnosis," he said. "I'm sorry."

"Thank you." My voice was froggy. I cleared my throat. I placed a hand on the step on either side of my body.

He laid his hand on top of mine for a moment and I felt a shiver of recognition. Then he got up and jogged down the rest of the steps.

"Wait," I said. The word was out of my mouth before I had time to think about what I was going to say after it.

He stopped and looked up at me, his hand on the doorknob of the third floor. A curl was falling in his eye.

I stood up and walked down the rest of the steps slowly, leaving my bag where it was. He raised his eyebrows, questioning. Instead of answering, I leaned forward and kissed him, pressing him against the door.

He kissed me back, his breath hot and minty in my mouth, my hands raking his hair, his stroking my lower back.

I pulled back suddenly. "I'm sorry," I said. "I don't know where that came from."

Jonah smiled. "Apology accepted. You never did tell me your name."

"Laura." I pushed some hair behind my ear. "Do you want to meet me for breakfast tomorrow?" My face heated up, as if I were in middle school asking a boy to dance.

His eyes shifted to the left.

"It's okay if you don't," I said. "God, I am so sorry. I don't know what got into me. Forget it." I turned and picked up my bag, slinging it over my shoulder.

Jonah touched my wrist. "Hang on. You're retracting your invitation that quickly?"

I could feel my face heating up. Embarrassed, I blushed even harder. "I'm out of practice."

"I can tell."

I knit my eyebrows together.

"Don't worry about it. I would love to have breakfast with you. I was just thinking."

I hitched my bag further up on my shoulder. "And now that you're done thinking?"

"Meet you at Murray's by the pier at seven."

My face split open in a smile. "See you then."

"It's a date."

Chapter 2

James

I leave the hospital and go directly to the bar. It's about noon. Gerry, the day bartender, uncaps a Bud for me as I take my usual stool. I sit. He plunks it down in front of me, exactly centered on a paper coaster.

"Double whiskey," I say, and watch him pour it. Gerry sometimes shorts you on the doubles.

Marty's on his third scotch and soda, by the look in his eye, and he raises his glass to me as I drain my whiskey. Albert's playing poker at the machine by the window. His seat is two stools down from me, marked by four empty pint glasses streaked with beer foam and a pack of Marlboros. Albert likes to see his empty glasses lined up. Helps him pace himself, he says.

"Another," I say.

"Listen," Gerry says.

No one ever starts a good conversation with the word "listen."

"Joe doesn't want me to let you run up your tab any higher," he says. He looks at the bar, twirling a coaster, instead of at me.

Thank God it's payday. I do some roofing for my cousin Benny and I picked up my pay envelope this morning. I pull out my wallet and put sixty dollars on the bar. Gerry pours me another double whiskey and I drain it. Gerry takes away my glass. He knows I like all evidence of my drinking to be removed as soon as possible. Helps me forget myself.

Albert comes back.

"Win anything?" I say.

"Up fifty dollars," he says. "Want a smoke?"

"Yeah." I follow him outside. The sun is bright, and heat rolls off the asphalt. My skin breaks out in a sweat everywhere: my face, my pits, the backs of my knees.

"What's up?" he says. "What's up" is Albert's way of saying, "You don't usually start out a Monday with two double shots of whiskey."

"My mom's in the hospital," I say.

Albert blows smoke in my face. "Sucks," he says.

Drunks are not the best sympathizers.

"I'll get your next round," he says.

"They think she has Alzheimer's," I say. The smoke from my cigarette is hot in my mouth. The sun is burning the top of my head. "She said something . . . I don't know, man. It was weird. She looked all crazy, you know?"

Albert grunts, stubs out his cigarette, goes back inside.

Mom has never called me a drunk before. She and Bill have done an intervention, she has kicked me out of the house, she has given me books and pamphlets on alcoholism, she has ignored my drinking, but she has never called me a drunk.

There's a sick feeling in the pit of my stomach—like my mother has finally seen the worst of me.

I go back inside, the A/C blessedly cool against my sweaty skin. My shirt's sticking to my back.

A woman comes in and sits on the stool next to mine. I hate when people do that. A goddamn forty-foot-long bar with twenty seats open, and she sits right next to me. Day drinkers like to have their space. She's not attractive, either—heavyset, late forties, wearing too much makeup. "Gin and tonic," she says to Gerry. Her voice is low and husky.

I can feel her looking at me out of the corner of her eye. Gerry slides the drink toward her and she plucks out the two red cocktail straws, inserts them into her mouth and pulls them out slowly. She puts the straws down on her coaster then picks up the glass and drinks it all down. "Another," she says. "I'm just going to the ladies' room."

I turn to watch her walk to the back of the bar. Her ass is big and round and her hips are fleshy, and she sways the whole thing from side to side as she walks, like she knows we're all watching.

Gerry sets her refill down next to me.

I drain the last of my beer. "Gotta take a leak," I say.

The bathrooms are in an alcove at the back of the bar. You take a left into a short hallway, and there's doors for the ladies' and men's rooms. The door to the ladies' room is open— it never is—and I can see her ass standing at the sink. She's smoothing her hair. Our eyes meet in the mirror. She doesn't turn around. She knows her ass is her best feature. "Well?" she says in that husky voice.

I'm in the bathroom with her, kicking the door shut, glad that it's early enough that it smells like Pine-Sol in here instead of like vomit and hairspray. I spin her around and pin her against the wall, grabbing that huge amazing ass, our mouths open in hot, sloppy kisses. My lips move to her neck, pull her shirt aside, bite her shoulder.

"Yeah," she breathes, and her voice is so goddamn sexy I feel my dick harden, no serious foreplay required.

She feels it against her thigh, undoes the button on my jeans, slides the zipper down. I reach into my left back pocket for the condom I always keep there, rip it open with my teeth, slide it on one-handed while I bite her ear, suck on her neck. Her sweat tastes salty and sweet on my tongue.

I hoist her up against the wall, her head against the long mirror. Thank God she's short, because she's heavy, but her ass fills my hands, and it's so hot I feel like I'm going to faint.

"Don't stop," she moans in that husky voice. She's got her legs wrapped around my waist.

It takes a while. All that booze. Finally I sag against her, panting.

"You can let me down now," she says, and I do. She kisses me again, pivoting me around so that I'm the one pinned against the wall, her tongue so deep in my throat she's probably licking my tonsils. She pulls back, and when I open my eyes she's gone, the door swinging shut behind her.

The taste of gin is strong in my mouth now, and I bolt into a stall and vomit. I haven't eaten anything today, so all that comes up is beer and whiskey, searing my throat.

I never drink gin. My father drank gin.

At Robert's eighth birthday party, I took a sip of Dad's drink when he wasn't looking. I thought it was Sprite—it was clear and bubbly—but it had this stringent metallic taste to it. Still, I swallowed it. And then spent the rest of the party sneaking drinks out of his glass. Robert started a game of Manhunt and relegated me to guarding the jail. I was chasing our cousin so he wouldn't set his team members free, and I vomited up everything

I'd eaten and drunk that day: birthday cake, penny candy from the piñata, a turkey sub, and all the gin. Mom was putting me to bed with a hot water bottle against my stomach when Dad flung open the door to my room, his silhouette dark against the brightness of the hallway, his face in shadow. He yanked me out of bed and dragged me to the basement, where he whipped me with his belt so that I couldn't sit down for two days.

And Mom thinks I'm turning out just like him.

I spend the rest of the week not going to the hospital. I think about going, think about how much it would mean to Mom, think about how badly my siblings will treat me if I don't go, think about how bad of a son I'm being. None of which motivates me to make the trip. In a way it's almost a relief to disappoint my family because that's what they expect from me. I so rarely meet expectations that this makes me feel marginally okay about myself.

Friday night I meet Dean and Eddie at Lazy Joe's. I pay for all my drinks in cash and give Joe another hundred dollars toward my tab. I don't bother to ask how much I owe. The answer will only depress me.

There's a girl across the room who's been staring at me all night. She's the same skinny-ass girl I always go for, attractive but not pretty: wild dark hair, eyeliner thick as my thumb, huge tat on her shoulder. After my Monday afternoon escapade I'm not interested, but when Joe brings me a beer and tells me the girl bought it for me, I have to at least talk to her. I buy her a Malibu and Sprite in return. I half-listen to her talk about her cosmetology classes while she twirls her hair and thrusts her small breasts toward my face. The game's starting again, but it occurs to me that the game gets boring when you always play the same hand: same bet, same risk, same win.

In the morning I wake up feeling like shit, but that's nothing new. I go into the bathroom and puke, my stomach heaving. I brush my teeth, avoiding my lower left molar.

I turn on the shower and wait until the water runs clean, then wait until it's hot. I get in and hold my face under the water. I can't remember the last time I woke up without a headache. I either drink too much or not enough.

The bathroom door opens and I groan inwardly. I wish the girls would just disappear by morning. I am fully aware that this makes me an asshole.

"Morning," she says, slipping into the shower with me. Her eyes are still ringed with eyeliner, now smudged; she looks like a raccoon. Her hair is a rat's nest. Where do I find these women? Even so, my cock rises of its own accord, and she smiles. "That's what I thought," she says.

As she sucks me, I put my face back under the water, wishing it could drown everything out.

My landline rings, loud and insistent. I'm nowhere close to coming, so I pull my dick from her mouth and hop out of the shower. "Hey!" she says, her small hands grabbing at me but sliding off my wet skin.

There are no towels in the bathroom. The only person who calls my landline is Ava. What the hell day is it? She won't call my cell because, she says, whenever I answer it I'm drunk. When I'm at home I'm either passed out and don't answer at all or semi-sober and able to carry on a conversation. She says.

I pick up at the same time my answering machine does.

"Ava?" I bellow over my own voice, drunkenly telling people to leave a message. The machine beeps.

"James," she says, the very calmness of her voice a warning.

"I, um, I lost track of time," I say. I'm dripping a puddle all over the wood floor. It's cold out here, man. Where the hell are all my towels?

"Good. I just wanted to make sure you were up. I'll meet you with Jeremiah in half an hour."

"Sure," I say, and she hangs up. The truth is, it's practically impossible to dress and drive out to Newport in half an hour. We meet at a Dunkin' Donuts, so at least there's breakfast on the horizon. So, get dressed. Doughnuts. Son.

"Can we pick up where we left off?" The girl is standing in the doorway to my bedroom, naked and dripping.

"No," I say. "You gotta go." I think about tacking on a "sorry," but I'm not.

I roll up to the Dunkin' Donuts six minutes late. Ava's already there. She's sitting on a bench on the narrow sidewalk, sipping coffee and smoking a cigarette. Jeremiah is in the front seat of her Mercedes, two cars over from me. The only thing Ava's ever done for me is agree not to smoke in her house or car. And I'm sure she would have done that anyway. She's a good mom.

I, on the other hand, am not a good father. I know it. Ava knows it. And Jeremiah knows it. I have no idea what we're supposed to do now that we all agree.

Ava stands and kisses my cheek in greeting. She's real affectionate now that we're not together. I inhale the scent of her: Marlboro Ultra-Light Menthols, coffee, and something vanilla that could be her body wash or maybe her perfume. She's shorter than I am, though her Afro almost makes up for the height difference. Today she's wearing a pink headband, making the Afro even taller. "I'm going to get my passport photo taken," she says, apropos of nothing. "Rick is taking me to Jamaica." She points to her head. "That's why the headband. You can't have any hair on your face." She smiles. God, she's beautiful.

"Can I bum a cigarette?"

She rolls her eyes but pulls a crumpled pack from her designer purse. She whacks the bottom of it against her palm a couple times, fishes out a cigarette, and hands it to me. She digs around for a lighter and I click it, the sharp crack that sparks the flame as satisfying as the first long pull.

"Did you bring me that photo?" she asks as we smoke.

My mind is totally blank, a chalkboard that's been erased. The door of the Dunkin' Donuts opens and closes, breathing in caffeine seekers and exhaling customers clutching waxy paper bags and Styrofoam cups.

Ava sighs, and I remember she asked me a question. "The photo Izzy had taken of the grandkids," she prompts. "You were supposed to bring me a copy at Christmas."

I nod. "Right."

"It's July," she says.

"Yes."

"I'm just going to call her myself," she says.

I haven't told her Mom is sick. I open my mouth, but no words come out. If she calls Izzy she'll find out from her and be pissed at me. "I'll bring it next time. Promise."

She rolls her eyes again; she's really perfected that gesture. "I'll believe it when I see it," she says. "Come on, 'Miah," she calls.

My son gets out of the car, slamming the door. He's taller every time I see him, but one thing stays the same: I always feel like I'm in a movie with the sullen kid. In movies there's always a teacher or a coach or somebody who straightens him out. But I'm sure as hell not capable of doing that. So I'm stuck with Sullen Kid, forever.

I pull him into a one-armed sideways hug. He shrugs me off. "I need breakfast," I say. "You want anything, J?"

He shakes his head. His neck is thin and scrawny, his back hunched under the weight of a giant backpack. He kisses his mom. Their skin is the same color.

I'm the darkest one in my family, the Lebanese on Mom's side coming out, but people who see me with Jeremiah assume he's adopted. Morons.

He gets in my battered Dodge Ram. I go inside and get a large coffee, a sausage egg and cheese, and two chocolate-frosted doughnuts. Hungry.

Ava kisses me goodbye. God, does she really have to kiss me twice in the space of ten minutes? That's just rubbing it in. "Have fun," she says. But I can tell by her troubled eyes that she knows her words are futile.

My truck smells like ass. I should really get that taken care of. The silence is thick and heavy. I never know what to say or do. My apartment is a mess; I didn't set up the futon. At least I know the girl is gone. Once I let one stay after I'd left and came home with my son to find her naked on the couch touching herself. That was a stellar fatherly moment right there. So, girls out before I leave. I guess a smarter guy would have figured that out without learning the hard way. Jeremiah had only been eight or nine at the time. He'd looked up at me, his eyes wide. "Is she a prostitute?" he'd asked. I'd gotten her out and sat him down and explained to him what a prostitute was, why I'd never hire one, and why he never should either.

"So," I say, starting the car. "What do you want to do?"

Chapter 3

Laura

I parked down the street from Murray's and texted Amber. *Going on my first post-divorce date.*

She wrote back immediately. *???!!! WTF tell me everything!*

I grinned. *Later. Late.*

She sent a string of celebratory emojis.

I took a deep breath. I was nervous.

And tired. I hadn't been sleeping well since Mom's fall. The hollows under my eyes felt as deep as thumbprints pressed in clay. I needed coffee.

The small diner was a maze of tables and chairs, with space carved out in the center for a deli case of meat and cheese and another stocked with pastries and doughnuts. The tables were plastic, painted to look like wood, and teetered against cheap diner chairs. A few booths lined up against the far wall with benches covered in powder-blue upholstery and plastic. The plate glass windows at the front showcased a spectacular view of the water.

The only patrons were blue-haired retirees—until I spotted Jonah sitting in the corner by the front window. His scrubs blended in perfectly with the booth. He saw me at the same time and stood up. "Hey," he said, waving me over and giving me a loose hug. "Have a seat."

I sat. And found myself tongue-tied. "You a regular?" was the only thing I could think to say.

He nodded. "I love this place. They have the best specials." He nodded to a chalkboard by the door.

"I bet they love you. You really bring down the age demographic."

The waitress, wearing a white apron over shorts and a polo shirt, came over and poured coffee without asking.

"Thank God," I said as I added a creamer and took a long sip.

"Seriously," Jonah said, adding three sugars and two creamers to his. "Oh, and sorry about the scrubs. Once upon a time I wore real clothes to go to work, until my favorite pair of jeans got stolen from my locker."

The waitress came back and took our order. Awkwardness descended.

Jonah took a long swallow of coffee. "So. What do you do?"

"I'm a therapist."

He nodded. "Tell me more."

"Ha. That's usually my line." I hooked my hand around the warm coffee mug. "I don't know where to start."

"At the beginning, I guess."

The early-morning sun poured in the window behind Jonah, glinting on gold streaks in his brown hair. His green eyes were flecked with brown, and they reminded me suddenly of my mother's eyes. I took a deep breath. "Well, I was a psych major at NYU, and I really wanted to be a therapist. So I went for my PhD at GW. I moved back to Eastville because my whole family is here." I took a sip of coffee. "I work at a clinic downtown."

Jonah was smiling.

"What?"

"Nothing." He shook his head.

"Tell me."

"Well, I asked about your work, and you gave me your résumé. Like a job interview."

"Isn't a first date kind of like a job interview?"

He shrugged. "You're the one who asked me out."

I bit the inside of my cheek. "I'm sorry; that was a stupid thing to say."

"Someone break your heart?" he asked, draining his coffee.

I traced the empty space on my left ring finger. "Yeah," I said. "Someone did."

The waitress clattered plates of eggs and home fries and bacon in front of us. Without a word she flounced off, returning with saucers piled with toast and a full pot of coffee to refill our mugs.

"How do you like being a nurse?" I asked.

Jonah folded his hands in front of him, a mock interviewee. "Well, ma'am, I did my undergraduate study and nursing school at the University of Rhode Island." He laughed, picked up a fork, and shoveled eggs into his mouth. "You can make any *Meet the Parents* joke you want. I had no interest in being a doctor. I didn't secretly ace the MCAT. I wanted to be a nurse. It's not really that weird."

"I'm sensing some defensiveness here," I said.

"Just trying to stay a step ahead."

"You didn't really answer my question, though." I cringed inwardly, but it was too late to take it back. "How do you like your job?"

"I enjoy taking care of people," he said. "Of course the hours are long, some of the patients can be really difficult, and there are no other men in my position." He laughed.

We ate in silence for a moment. The eggs were good.

"Are there rules about me being here with you?" I asked.

He looked at me steadily as he inhaled his eggs. "Yes. Rules that say I shouldn't be."

"And what do you think about those?"

"Well, I had no control over you kissing me, so I figured it was only polite to take you out for a meal."

"Point well taken."

"It must be nice to have such a big family," Jonah said. "I'm an only child, and my mom's remarried out in California."

I tried to picture my life as an only child. I couldn't.

"Why *did* you kiss me yesterday?" he said, his voice suddenly serious.

I picked up a plastic tub of strawberry jam, peeled back the film, and spread some on my toast. I leaned forward conspiratorially. "For your body."

He laughed appreciatively. "Good reason."

I couldn't answer him seriously because I didn't know.

I could walk to work from Murray's, so I did. The Oceanside Clinic was around the corner from the Main Street drag. The building was set back from the road behind a row of tall hedges. It looked like an office building masquerading as a beach cottage, with gray shingles and white-trimmed windows and pots of cattails on either side of the door. I loved the charm of the place, loved the sense of expansive possibility I felt when I walked through the door. My boss, Kevin, was a mentor and a friend. He and his wife, Elaine, had supported me through my divorce.

The lobby smelled like carpet and new paint. Plush, never-used armchairs lined the walls. In my office I breathed a sigh of relief. I'd taken more care decorating it than Ted's and my bedroom. The walls were painted a pastel yellow. I had a cream-colored sofa and a matching armchair opposite, with my desk set up kitty-corner to both. I felt safe here.

So when my first client of the day, Macy, arrived with her right eye swollen shut, I felt calm enough to deal with it.

When I'd done clinical work in southeast DC, many of my clients wore their problems on their bodies. Bruises. Track marks. Scars. In Eastville, Rhode Island, problems tended to be invisible from the outside.

Macy talked for fifteen minutes about her new job as an elementary music teacher. She'd started a few weeks ago with summer programs for the choir and band.

When she fell silent, I asked, "Macy, what happened to your eye?"

She didn't answer immediately, which was a good sign; she wasn't going to lie. In my office, silence bred truth.

"My boyfriend," she said.

I waited, trying to keep my face neutral. Scumbag.

"I opened a checking account," she said, "and signed up for direct deposit." Macy fidgeted with the hem of her T-shirt, pulled at a loose thread. "When I worked at Victoria's Secret, I cashed my checks near the mall," she said. "And he'd gamble with my money."

My blood was beating in my ears, but I nodded slowly. "You live with your boyfriend, right?"

Macy nodded, her brown eyes wide.

"If you wanted to move out, is there somewhere you could stay?"

Macy nodded again. "With my mom."

I leaned forward. "Macy, your safety is at risk. I think putting some physical distance between you and your boyfriend is a good idea."

She looked out the window, which was tinted so that we could see a view of the hedgerows but no one from the outside could see in.

"You have a few legal options," I said. "Do you want to hear them?"

Macy bobbed her head.

"You can go to family court to file a temporary restraining order, which would mean your boyfriend can't come near you without facing arrest. You can also file a domestic abuse claim with the district court." I folded my hands. "Are you still taking your medication?" Macy was on antidepressants, and her doctor had referred her to the clinic when he prescribed them.

Her eyes skittered to the left. "I stopped taking it," she said. "It made me feel . . . detached."

"When?"

Macy retreated into herself, curling her bony shoulders around her chest. Her head dropped forward on her neck.

My heart ached. I just wanted to help her, to take away her pain. But my job was to help her help herself. "Macy. I'm not yelling at you. But it's dangerous to stop taking medication without consulting your doctor."

"I stopped taking it on Wednesday." Her thin left hand lifted to cup her swollen eye. "He flushed the pills down the toilet. Because I never feel like having sex anymore."

I bit down on the inside of my lip. Macy was so sensitive that I couldn't push her very far. "How did that make you feel?"

Anger hardened her slight features. "Afraid."

"You look angry."

Her eyes widened. "I can't."

"Be angry?"

She nodded, three quick jerks of her head. She spoke to the floor, her voice barely above a whisper. "What should I do?"

"What do you want to do?"

"I don't know."

"You do," I said. "Just think about it." I glanced at the clock; we had five minutes. I let the seconds tick forward as I watched Macy. She was folded in on herself, her elbows propped on her knees, chin propped on both clenched fists, her head at a strange angle as she stared out the window. But as the silence swelled, her posture began to shift. First her head straightened on her neck, turning until she was facing me, staring at my foot. Her arms dropped to her sides. She uncrossed her ankles and tucked one foot under her.

With two minutes left, I said, "You've decided?"

Macy smiled, her eyes lighting up. "How did you know?"

"I had a feeling."

"I'm going to move back with my mom."

"If you'd like, I can call Dr. Sinclair and get an emergency refill for you. I'd recommend making an appointment with him soon to look into other types of antidepressants. He can help you find one that works better for you."

"Thanks, Laura." She hugged me on her way out the door.

I stood and stretched, smiling to myself. Macy had grown a lot in our six months together. I'd wanted to be a therapist to help people, and today I felt like I had. Sometimes, when I felt discouraged, it seemed that all I did was listen to people talk. On good days, I got them to talk about things that mattered. On very good days, I helped them begin to see the world in a different light.

On Saturday morning I couldn't wait to see Marisa.

Marisa was my own therapist. Kevin was such a strong believer in the therapeutic process that he not only encouraged his employees to be in therapy but actually paid for it. I'd been seeing Marisa since I started working for him two years ago.

Marisa's building was a mile or so from the stretch of downtown shops. I took the stairs to the fourth floor. The walls of her office were floor-to-ceiling glass on two sides. The carpet was a rich purple and the furniture gleaming black lacquer. Though it was ostensibly comfortable, I never felt at ease in this room. I wondered if my clients felt the same about my office.

"Laura," Marisa said. "Have a seat." Marisa was a few years older than I, with dark brown hair, perfect skin, and blue eyes always perfectly made up with gray shadow. Today she wore a tailored gray suit with a string of blue beads at her throat.

I felt like a little girl in my white cotton dress. I hadn't bothered to put on jewelry or makeup. I sat in my usual cream-colored armchair, the leather soft as silk. My outfit blended in with it.

Marisa stood from her desk and moved to sit opposite me in a matching armchair. "How's your week been?"

I told her briefly about Mom's accident and diagnosis.

"I'm so sorry," she said. "How are you doing with all of this?"

My sessions with Marisa felt like a chess game. She moved, I countered. She parried, I blocked. I couldn't stop thinking like a therapist. She had told me I had a problem embracing the role of the client.

"Laura?"

"Sorry," I said. "I'm anxious about my mom."

Marisa nodded, eyebrows raised. God, what a perfect "go on" face. When I didn't "go on," she smiled as if she knew what I was thinking. "Why are you anxious?"

The words I wanted to say about Mom didn't come. I swallowed. "I went on a date on Tuesday," I said, surprising myself. "A breakfast date."

Marisa smiled. "That sounds great. How did it go?"

"I'm not sure."

"Where did you meet the guy?"

I sighed. "He's one of my mother's nurses. Stupid, I know."

"Why is that stupid?"

"Oh, it's against hospital policy. There's all this potentially weird stuff with him as my mother's caretaker. And my brother would want to know why he didn't become a doctor."

"Do you care what your brother thinks?"

"No," I said defensively.

Marisa nodded. "Let's go back to your mom's diagnosis for a minute."

I didn't say anything.

"How did you feel when you heard?"

I thought of Mom's twisted face and the words she'd spit at me. *Not everything can be solved by a therapy session.* Did she really think that I thought therapy could solve everything?

That I thought I could solve this for her? Did she see me as that arrogant?

"Laura?"

My phone buzzed and I jumped, glad for the distraction. "Oh, sorry. I forgot to turn it off." I dug through my bag, the buzzing growing louder and louder. My fingers finally closed on the phone and I turned it over out of habit: Macy. Weird. "It's my patient," I said. "Let me just—" I stood up and answered the phone, walking to the window. "Macy? Can I call you back?"

"This is Macy's mother," said a woman's voice.

"Is everything okay?" I asked. My heart quickened for some reason.

Silence on the other end of the line.

"Mrs. Jackson?" I pulled my phone away from my ear to check that the call was still connected. "Hello? Can you hear me?"

The sound of a throat clearing. "Macy was found dead this morning."

I paced Marisa's office, my phone on speaker, dialing Kevin. "Pick up," I said. "Pick up, pick up, pick—"

"Hello?"

"Kevin, my patient Macy Jackson was murdered."

Silence. "Shit," he said.

"I'm wondering if I need to go to the police and make a statement." I glanced up at Marisa, who nodded once. "She had a black eye at our last appointment. She said it was her boyfriend."

"Yes," he said. "You need to go make a statement. Do you want me to go with you?"

Marisa tapped her own chest.

"I'm at Marisa's now," I said. "She'll go with me."

Marisa drove me to the police station. It was on the far side of town, near James's apartment. The street, which was lined with housing projects, was deserted. A few soda cans lolled in the gutters. The station was the best-kept building on the block, made of new brick. Its windows were clean and unbroken and its lawn was bright green.

Inside, Marisa and I sat on hard plastic chairs, my face numb with shock. The room was well lit, with plants flourishing in the corners. The carpet smelled new. A television mounted near the ceiling played the news on mute. Macy's face flashed on the screen and I recoiled.

A thirtyish man appeared in the doorway and beckoned to me. I followed him into a conference room. "You're here about Macy Jackson?" he said.

"Yes. I'm—I was—her therapist."

He was making notes on a yellow legal pad. "Tell me."

I told him about my last session with Macy. He sighed heavily. "Do you know his name?"

"No," I said. "But they lived in an apartment on First Street. West end."

"Thanks for coming in," he said. "I'll call if we need anything else."

In the waiting room, Marisa put her hand on my arm. "I'll take you to dinner, if you want."

"No," I said, my voice wooden. "No, it's okay. I'm just going to go home."

"I'll drive you."

"Hang on." My phone was buzzing. Jonah. "Hey," I said, answering.

"Hey yourself. Wondering if you're up for an impromptu dinner."

I met him at his apartment, which was only a few blocks from the police station.

He answered the door wearing cargo shorts and an orange Phish T-shirt. It occurred to me that this was the first time I'd seen him in something other than scrubs.

I was suddenly starving, and we dug into pizza and beer.

"So you like Phish," I said.

"Love them," he said. "I see them in concert at least three times a year."

"Wow," I said. I couldn't remember the last time I'd been to a concert. "That sounds . . . fun." Intense.

"My favorite year was '97," he said.

"You were . . ."

"Sixteen," he said promptly. "I hitchhiked to Maine, saw them two nights in a row."

"I don't even know what to say."

"I know, I take nerdiness to new heights," he said. "How was the rest of your week?"

I didn't want to talk. Suddenly, what I most wanted was sex.

I stood up slowly. "Want to show me the rest of your apartment?" I asked.

We ended the (very short) tour in his bedroom, where I let him make love to me as if it had been his idea.

Afterward he lay on his side facing me. I stayed on my back staring at the textured ceiling while Jonah traced circles around my belly button. Every time I closed my eyes I saw Macy's face at our last session, her eye swollen shut.

"What are you thinking about?" he asked. His voice was soft. I could feel his eyes on my face.

"I just remembered, I have to go," I said, untwisting myself from the sheets and climbing out of bed. I dropped my dress over my head and went into the living room. "I'll call you," I said. I grabbed my purse and let myself out of the apartment before he came out of the bedroom.

Kevin called me Sunday morning to check in. "How are you doing?" he said.

"Not good." I was still in bed at eleven o'clock, which was not typical.

"I saw on the news that the police arrested Macy's boyfriend."

I closed my eyes.

"You might have helped them catch a killer," Kevin said.

Three hours later, Bill called to tell me Mom was being released from the hospital. I banged the heel of my hand against my head. Too much. Too much. Too much.

"Robert is arranging for home aides in the evenings," Bill

was saying. "Come by the hospital and we can talk. It'll take them a while to process everything."

When I got to the hospital, Mom was asleep in her bed and Bill was sitting next to her, his head bowed in prayer over his rosary. I stood there watching them for a minute, wondering if I should go to the cafeteria and come back, when he looked up and smiled. "Come here," he said, standing and holding out his arms.

"I didn't know you prayed the rosary," I said, hugging him.

"You didn't?" he said, surprised. "I pray it every Sunday, usually. I've been praying for your mother."

"That she'll get well?"

"That she won't suffer unduly," he said. He coiled the rosary beads into a small leather pouch and put them back in his pocket. "I got them in Rome," he said. "Blessed by the pope."

He moved aside and offered me the chair. "Mind if I run downstairs for a soda?" His eyes looked tired.

"Sure." I scooted the chair closer to the bed. Mom looked shrunken. Her eyelids fluttered in her sleep. I wanted her to wake up, for her to tell me Macy's death wasn't my fault, to tell me I wasn't stupid for sleeping with Jonah after one date, to tell me everything would be okay. But even when she woke up she wouldn't be able to tell me those things. Her health problems aside, she had never been reassuring.

Grief pressed on my chest like the crushing sensation of being underwater too long.

I wondered whether she'd know me when she woke up. It had happened so suddenly. We'd celebrated Bill's birthday just three months ago, and she'd been vibrant and funny. They called it the long goodbye, but it felt awfully short to me—abrupt, irreversible, a cleaver separating the past from the present in one swift stroke.

I leaned forward and rested my forehead on the mattress edge.

"That doesn't look too comfortable."

I sat up. Jonah was standing at the gap between the curtain and the wall.

"Hey. Am I in your way?" I started to stand.

"No. I just came to see if you were here, actually."

"My mother is being released."

"I know."

Of course he knew. Idiot.

He came closer. "You ran out pretty quickly yesterday."

I looked at Mom, who was still sleeping. "I'm sorry," I said. "Is there somewhere we can talk?"

He turned on his heel and left the room. I followed him down the hall and into the stairwell, which was dark and dingy.

I stood by the door, just far enough away that it wouldn't hit me if someone barreled through it. Jonah retreated from me until his back was against the far wall of the landing.

"I found out yesterday that one of my patients was murdered," I said, forcing myself to meet his eyes. "I was upset."

Jonah's brow softened. "I'm sorry to hear that," he said. "Why didn't you tell me?"

"I don't know," I said.

Jonah crossed his arms. "You seem pretty self-aware. I think you probably do know."

Shit. "I guess you're not letting me off the hook with the easy answer," I said.

He waited.

"I was afraid to let you in," I said. "In that way. If I had told you, I might have started crying."

He gestured around him. "I see a lot of tears. Tears don't scare me."

"Not even in a woman you're seeing?"

"Not even then."

"Well okay," I said. "Let me take you out to dinner this week. Wednesday?"

"Deal," he said.

I stepped forward to kiss him, but he held up a hand. "No kissing at work," he said. "I really don't want to get fired." He walked toward me, reached past my hip to put his hand on the door handle. Then he leaned his shoulder into the door and pulled me toward him and pressed his lips to mine.

"I thought there was no kissing at work," I said.

"I'll see you on Wednesday," he said. He opened the door and was gone.

Mom was awake and watching *CSI: Miami*. She hushed me when I said hello.

"Excuse me?" A woman's voice called in the hallway. "Is Katherine Keene in there?"

"Yes," Jonah's voice said.

"Come on, girls, through here."

Robert's wife, Julia, appeared from behind the curtain, her shoulder-length brown hair looking like it had just been blown out, her skin luminous even under the fluorescent lights. "Oh," she said, seeing me. "Hi, Laura."

"Hey, Julia. Hi, girls!"

Athena, who was four, ran to hug me. Aurelia, two, clung to Julia's leg. Athena let go of me and climbed onto the chair by Mom's bed. I squatted down and held my arms out to Aurelia, who walked toward me slowly and allowed me to hug her. The smell of her shampoo set off the baby ache in my chest.

"Hi, Grandma," Athena said, patting Mom's hand.

"Don't get too close," Julia said. "Grandma is sick."

"Shh," Mom said, turning up the volume on the TV. She looked at me. "Let me know when Julia's gone, okay?"

There was a tense silence. I had just decided to pretend Mom hadn't said anything when Athena piped up: "Why does Grandma want Mom to leave?"

"She doesn't," I said.

"Can I sit on the bed with her?"

"Sure." I boosted her up. Mom put an arm around Athena.

I squatted down to hug Aurelia then stood and planted a kiss on Julia's cheek. "How are you?"

"Oh, fine. You?" She swept her hair back over her shoulder, dousing me in a cloud of Chanel No. 5. She kept talking without waiting for an answer. "We can't stay long," she said. "Just wanted to say hi and drop off this card." She brandished a heavy gold envelope. "And Laura, do me a favor, will you? Drop this in Robert's office for me?" She put the card and a manila envelope on Mom's tray table.

I frowned and took it. "Won't you see him later?"

She looked at me pityingly. "He didn't tell you?"

I didn't say anything, the suspicion of what Robert

hadn't told me dropping like a stone into my stomach.

"Well, I'm sure he will when he feels the time is right. Come on, girls, time to go." She swept from the room, not having said a word to Mom or even looked at her.

Mom turned up the volume on the TV as I sat down again. She narrowed her eyes. "Who are you?"

"Mom, it's me, Laura. Your daughter."

Mom laughed. "I don't have a daughter."

"You do. You have two daughters and two sons."

She guffawed. "Don't be ridiculous. I'm too young to have four children."

This was something we'd already begun to argue about: whether to play along or not. Bill always did. He became whoever Mom needed him to be. Izzy was adamant that we tell her the truth: Our father was dead, her parents were dead, and we children were grown. There was no use pretending otherwise. I sided with Izzy on principle, but in practice it was much harder to do. Today I just didn't have the strength. "How old are you?"

She grinned, preening. "Sixteen."

I smiled. "That's a good age."

Dr. Pindar walked in then, looking frazzled. "Hello, hello."

Mom surveyed him with wide, coquettish eyes. "Who are you?" she asked. Not quite demure enough to be flirty, but she was clearly trying.

"I'm your doctor," he said, smiling. "I have your release papers. I saw Mr. Norman in the hallway, and he'll be right down to take you home."

Bill walked in, whistling, pushing a wheelchair.

"You ready to go home, Mom?" I said.

Mom looked startled. "I'm not your mother," she said.

There was a beat of silence.

"I'm not your *mother*," she said again.

"Laura, why don't you go down and see Robert," Bill said.

"But—"

"I don't have any children," Mom said. Her voice was insistent, but her eyes were wide and fearful.

"Laura," Bill said, squeezing my hand. "I'll get her home and settled. Come see us tomorrow."

"Goddamn it all to hell!" Mrs. George yelled from behind the curtain.

I left the room, grateful for the cool hallway air on my face. I took the stairs to the basement level and found Robert's office. I stood in the doorway, which was as far as I could get. Every square inch of floor space and desk space was piled with manila folders. The fluorescent lights made my eyes glaze over. There were no windows. Robert was sitting at his desk, his back to me, gazing at five brain scans dangling from an illuminated board.

"Are those Mom's?"

He turned to look at me, his eyes bloodshot. "Hey." He looked back at the board, sighed, and turned off the light. The images became opaque.

I set the heavy envelope Julia had given me onto the desk in front of him, where it blended with all the other stationary.

"She's here?" he asked. He looked from it to me.

I nodded. "What's going on?"

He closed his eyes. I expected him to tell me to mind my own business. He opened his eyes again and looked at me. "I need a glass of wine. Can I take you to dinner?"

I raised my eyebrows. "Sure."

I followed him down Main Street to the fancy Italian restaurant where he and Julia had had their rehearsal dinner six years ago. I had been so glad that I was related to Robert and not to Julia; there had been no $250 hot-pink bridesmaid's dress for me. My only responsibility had been to read from 1 Corinthians 13 during the ceremony. *Love is patient, love is kind. It does not envy, it does not boast, it is not proud.* . . . I wondered if I had ever seen that kind of love. I thought of Julia's tendency to embarrass Robert in public. Of Izzy's constant nitpicking at Sam. Of Ted's habit of ignoring me when I wanted to talk about something important. Then I thought of Bill's impulse always to give my mother the rarest steak, to carry her sweater in case she got cold, to bend down and tie her shoelaces when they came undone as they walked on the beach. I thought of him telling us all to leave the room on Monday, even as she insulted him. *Love always protects, always trusts, always hopes, always perseveres. Love never fails.* I shivered.

Robert requested a table in the small dining room, which was quiet. Robert ordered a bottle of Chianti and appetizers. His chivalrous way of doing this had always made me feel cared for.

The mood at our table turned expectant, but I was determined not to intimidate him. When I'd started grad school, my siblings told me that my therapist demeanor made them never want to tell me anything. I was Robert's sister, not his therapist, and I would wait until he was ready to talk.

The bread came, warm and crusty, and Robert ripped off a hunk and dipped it in olive oil. He looked at me, and his face was the face of his nine-year-old self the day our father died. "Julia and I are divorcing," he said.

My first thought was simply, *Not you too*. But I wasn't surprised. "I'm sorry," I said, putting my hand over my brother's. I waited a beat. "Would you like to tell me about it?"

For the next forty-five minutes, through the appetizers and the entrée and the last of the wine, he told me about Julia. How she twisted their daughters' affections by telling them he worked so much because he didn't love them; how she'd accused him of cheating on her, though he never had; how she'd left with no warning: He'd simply come home at the end of a twelve-hour shift, and she and the girls were gone. No note. He'd called around, frantic, until his mother-in-law answered the phone and said Julia and the girls were safe; they were at the beach house on Cape Cod, and Julia didn't want to be bothered. How Robert had driven all the way to the Cape, after that long day, and she hadn't let him in; he'd had to stay at the Motel 6.

Finally he was spent. He insisted on paying for dinner, and I let him because I wanted him to feel like he could still take care of someone. As we got up to leave, he kissed me on the cheek. "Thanks, Laurlie," he said, and his words were so heartfelt and heartbreaking that they seemed to blot out every perfunctory thank-you I'd ever received from him.

"You're welcome," I said, squeezing his hand. "I love you."

Chapter 4

Laura

I took Wednesday off to go to Macy's funeral. Kevin offered to go with me, but I turned him down. I wanted to go alone.

It was hot, and the parking lot of the First Baptist Church of Kingstown was full. I finally parked three blocks away and dashed down the street. Humidity steamed from the uneven sidewalks. The ramshackle church overflowed with people. I squeezed into a back pew near an open stained-glass window that cast a red and blue shadow on my chest. The slight breeze on my face meant nothing: Within minutes sweat was trickling down the small of my back. My blonde hair and white blouse were conspicuous among the black church ladies in their dark suits and hats.

The casket was closed. I tried not to think of what the body looked like. I'd heard on the news that she'd been stabbed. Her boyfriend had been charged with first-degree murder.

As the service started, movement caught the corner of my eye: A white woman with bright red hair had just entered the church. It was Kevin's wife, Elaine. I motioned to her, and she came over to sit next to me. "What are you doing here?" I whispered under the hum of the organ.

"Came to support you," she said, squeezing my hand.

I swallowed against the lump in my throat.

The service lasted two hours, but I barely noticed the time passing. I'd been to a lot of funerals, but they were always Catholic: ritualistic, sometimes to the point of being formulaic. Pastor Riggs was a large black man in his sixties, his hair and beard going white. He stood before his congregation, lifted his hands up and said, "Lord, we are angry."

"Yes, Lord," the congregation chanted.

"Lord, we are angry, and we bring our anger before You today."

I had never known that anger had a place in church. I'd been taught that anger was unholy, sinful, and to hear the opposite made me so dizzy, I had to sit down while everyone around me remained standing.

Pastor Riggs spoke about Jesus instructing us to forgive seventy times seven times. He spoke about things I heard but couldn't understand: a thirst for mercy and justice, the fact that we lived in a Kingdom that was now-but-not-yet. He spoke about righteous anger, a phrase I'd thought was a contradiction in terms. I began to understand why a fifty-five-minute Mass couldn't always nourish the soul. Horrific things happened in the world, things that couldn't be addressed in a six-minute homily. In between the pastor's thundering speeches and hymns from the choir, women stood up to speak about Macy's life: the sweetness of her nature, her drive to work hard, her love for music. They talked of her devotion to her family, of how much she loved to sing in the choir. I hadn't known that she sang. I'd hardly known her at all.

Pastor Riggs gave a benediction, and Macy's sister Dina got up to sing. From the first resonant chord on the organ, my heart seemed to unfurl.

> *"I was standing by my window,*
> *On one cold and cloudy day*
> *When I saw that hearse come rolling*
> *For to carry my sister away*
>
> *Will the circle be unbroken*
> *By and by, Lord, by and by*
> *There's a better home a-waiting*
> *In the sky, Lord, in the sky ..."*

The space around me came alive with the prayers and murmurings of the women and the few men in the pews. "Yes, Lord," they whispered. "Amen," they sang. And after a few minutes, "Hallelujah. Hallelujah."

Will the circle be unbroken . . . I found myself suddenly sobbing, inconsolable, as the ladies stood and waved their arms heavenward, their faces etched with pain and longing. *By and by, Lord, by and by* . . . I hadn't brought tissues because I never cried in public. Elaine reached into her purse and handed me a whole travel pack of Kleenex. *There's a better home a-waiting* . . . I used up half the pack before the tears ebbed, the crumpled tissues piled on the pew next to me like melting snowballs. *In the sky, Lord, in the sky...*

At the end of the service, the family processed out behind the casket. Macy's mother stopped in front of me, and the line behind her halted. "You were Macy's therapist, weren't you?"

I nodded.

"I want you to come back to our house for lunch."

"Mrs. Jackson, I don't want to impose—"

She inclined her head regally. "You'll come," she said, "right after the burial," and kept walking.

I picked up directions and a funeral line flag for my car. I was so sweaty I wished I'd brought a second shirt.

On the sidewalk I turned to Elaine. "Thank you," I said, simply.

She squeezed my hand again. "You're welcome." She kissed my cheek. "I have to get to a meeting. Will you be alright?"

A light breeze stirred my hair. I took a deep breath. "Yes."

After the burial I followed the train of cars to the Jackson home, terrified. Was Macy's mother going to reprimand me? Embarrass me? And yet, in addition to being summoned, I also needed something I couldn't name, so I went. The house where Macy grew up was small and cramped, but the people jammed into its many tiny rooms didn't seem to mind. They were sprawled on the worn furniture, huddled in tight groups, talking about Macy's life.

During my clinical training, one of my patients had gone off her bipolar meds and jumped off the roof of her apartment building. I felt the same as I had then: nauseous with the *I-should-have-done-something*'s, helpless against the finality of death, angry with the futility of a life ended too soon.

The women around me were angry too, but their anger seemed veiled or muted by something greater, a forgiveness or a peace I wasn't sure I could ever access.

The house smelled like Thanksgiving: a cacophony of

scents, from roasting meat to sizzling vegetables to the burnt sweetness of caramelized marshmallows. The bright yellow kitchen was overflowing with trays of food on absolutely every surface, including a platter of rolls on top of the refrigerator. Mrs. Jackson wouldn't talk to me until I had a full plate: roast chicken and collard greens, mashed potatoes drowning in gravy, sweet potatoes topped with the gooey marshmallows I'd smelled, and cornbread dripping with honey. I looked at the plate doubtfully, sure that it was two days' worth of calories. Then I started eating, and felt suddenly as if I'd been starving myself for weeks or years. I ate until my reinforced paper plate was empty, puddles of gravy soaked into the first layer of absorbent paper. Someone took the plate from me and ushered me toward Mrs. Jackson, who was holding court in the front room.

I sat on an itchy paisley couch and waited. The room was covered with photographs of Macy and Dina, mostly as children. Toddler Macy precariously clutching the infant Dina. A posed Christmas shot, Macy with no front teeth. Dina's high school graduation, Macy looking as proud as if it were her own daughter.

That was the power of photography: to capture fleeting moments in time that would otherwise be swallowed up by our unreliable memories.

After ten minutes of suspense, Mrs. Jackson dismissed the woman with her and beckoned me forward. I sat down next to her on an identical paisley couch, but this one seemed more worn and less itchy.

"Ma'am," I began, "I am so sorry—"

She held up a hand, and the platitudes died on my lips. "Macy trusted you," she began. "I want to know what she told you about . . . him." Mrs. Jackson's face darkened.

I took a deep breath. "Mrs. Jackson, I am sorry for your loss. I liked Macy a lot. I wish I could tell you the things she talked about with me, but I can't. Anything told to a therapist is and remains confidential, unless we suspect someone's life is in danger."

Mrs. Jackson stuck her chin out and stared at me, her eyes hard and glittering.

"I'm sorry," I said again. I'd had this conversation before, with jealous spouses or concerned parents, but never with a grieving mother.

"You talked to the police," she said, an angry fiber hardening her voice.

"Yes," I said. "I told them exactly what Macy said about her boyfriend. I didn't even know his name. I won't ever reveal anything else."

To my surprise, Mrs. Jackson's face broke into a smile like a ripe piece of fruit, as if I'd passed a test. "Thank you," she said. "If you won't tell me about what she talked about with you, then you won't tell anyone." She nodded in satisfaction.

I stood up. "Mrs. Jackson, I'm sorry. I should have done more to keep her safe."

She nodded again, not letting me off the hook. "We all should have," she said.

As I gathered my purse, I looked around me. The women were practiced at the art of grieving. They emanated not helplessness or victimization but strength. They would weather this tragedy. They were a family, whether forged by blood or friendship, and they would endure.

It struck me then for the first time, as I got into my car alone, that my mother was going to die. Whether in six months or six years, she was going to die, and her mind would deteriorate until she did. And there was very little I could do to keep her safe. I wondered whether my family would endure our grief with anything resembling the grace and strength I'd just seen.

Back at my apartment I stripped naked in the entryway, ditching my sweat-soaked dress clothes. The main room had a living area with windows at the front and a kitchen at the back with a small oak dining table and chairs, a couch and TV in the middle.

When I left Ted I'd spent a few weeks at Mom and Bill's before finding a place of my own. This was the first place I'd ever lived by myself.

Before I moved in I'd spent a day alone painting the walls a deep red. Red repose, the shade was called. I'd seen it in a Behr catalog and liked both the name and the shade, imagining myself healing, wrapped in color.

The hallway ran along the side of the apartment into my bedroom, and the bathroom also connected my bedroom to the great room. I peed then dug out exercise clothes and laced up my running shoes.

Izzy had always teased me about this. Although my sister was meticulous about certain things, she shoved her shoes on her feet, usually breaking the heels in the process. I painstakingly laced and unlaced my shoes. I remembered, with a shocking jolt of decades-old anger that buzzed up my legs and arms like a bolt of lightning, the time Izzy had borrowed my new sneakers for a camping weekend with some boyfriend and his family. I had saved up from my high school waitressing job to buy them, and they came back ruined: muddy, wet on the inside from a night Izzy had left them out in the rain, and completely unsalvageable. I'd yelled at Izzy, who'd been watching *90210* and who said, "They're just shoes, Laur."

"They're not your shoes," I had muttered bitterly as I threw them in the trash can, then never said another word about it. Obviously, I didn't forgive and forget.

The thermometer on the side of my building read 90 degrees. The humidity was overpowering. I stretched my arms overhead and started running, my muscles creaking in protest. As I hit my stride, the turmoil in my mind grew rather than settled. I thought of Dina's haunting song at her sister's service. I thought of Mrs. Jackson's fierceness. I thought of the vacant stare that was already replacing the wry intelligence that had characterized my mother for my whole life. Grief and fear and anger fused into a single intense emotion, gaining strength, grabbing at my ankles. I ran and kept running.

That night I picked Jonah up at 7:30.

He got in the Caddy and kissed me. It was still awkward, our noses bumping. "Where are we going?"

I took him to the Seamus Pub, where Bill used to take me for lunch when I had a half day at school. It smelled smoky, even though smoking had been outlawed almost ten years ago, but the jukebox was playing Billy Joel and the place still felt like a neighborhood hangout where everyone knew each other. The walls were paneled in dark wood and hung with old business signs and other dust-coated tchotchkes.

We sat at a high-top table in the corner and ordered beers and fried oysters and burgers. We joked about the jukebox selections and the tourists, who were easily identifiable by their sunburned faces. It felt easy, and I was surprised. I'd forgotten dating could be easy.

He asked how my mom was without making too big a deal of the fact that she'd been his patient three days ago. I told him she was fine, my gut twisting with guilt. I hadn't been to the house to see her since she'd been home.

"So, what do you do for fun?" he asked as our burgers arrived.

I squirted a spiral of ketchup onto my bun. "I run," I said.

Jonah grinned. "Like an antelope?"

"What?"

"Nothing. Favorite Phish song. That's very healthy. What else?"

I arranged the tomato, lettuce, and onion so they overlapped evenly, then put the bun on top and took a bite. Did I *have* fun? "I don't know. Get coffee with my friend Amber. Go to the beach."

He nodded.

"What about you? Besides dating the relatives of your patients."

Jonah snorted. "Well played. You're the only one." He grinned. "I like to travel. Indoor rock climbing. I like art."

"What kind of art?"

"Photography," he said, and I felt a little hiccup of excitement in my chest. "I go to the galleries a lot in Providence."

He had demolished his burger. I still held two-thirds of mine in my hands.

"Can I ask about your ex-husband?" he said.

I made a *be-my-guest* gesture.

"Why did you marry him? You can give me the short answer."

I thought about Ted. "He was my first love," I said. "He

was really good at anticipating my needs, and I interpreted that as selflessness."

Jonah nodded. "And why . . . why did you get divorced?"

I took a swig of beer. "I found a diamond earring under the couch that wasn't mine," I said.

He winced.

"What about you?" I inserted the last wedge of my burger into my mouth. "Ever been married?"

"Came close once," he said. "A month after I asked her, she ran off with some doctor. Never did get the ring back."

"I'm sorry," I said.

"It took me a long time to get over it," he acknowledged. "But I'm not sorry anymore."

"Why's that?"

He shrugged. He looked through the crowd as if searching for a face, then turned and locked eyes with me. "I wouldn't be sitting here with you."

I picked up my pint glass and drained the last of my beer, trying to settle the lust that had suddenly coursed down my thighs.

Jonah flagged down the bartender and ordered us another round.

We went back to my apartment, and all I could think was that I hadn't had this much fun during sex since the yoga instructor I dated in grad school. Ted hadn't been a bad lover, just unimaginative. Jonah lingered, and it was delicious.

The next morning my alarm went off at 6:30, and I woke to find my bed empty. My heart clenched. Great, he's the revenge type.

I threw on my pink robe and went into the kitchen. Jonah was in the living room in his boxers, staring at the series of black-and-white photographs on the wall.

"Morning," I said, and a grin spread across my face before I could act casual.

"Why didn't you tell me last night that you take photos?"

"I don't do it much anymore," I said. "No time."

"You should make time," he said seriously. "These are really, really good."

I measured coffee into a filter. "Thank you."

"You must have taken classes in college," he said.

"A few." I dropped two pieces of bread into the toaster. "Toast and eggs okay?"

"Sure." He was still looking at the photo of Izzy. He turned toward me. "You don't believe me, do you?"

I didn't say anything, cracked four eggs into a bowl.

"Come here," Jonah said. He held out a hand, and I went shyly toward him. He took me on a tour of my photos, pointing out the light and shadow, the resolution, the focus I'd placed lovingly on each beautiful face.

The first photograph was of Mom and Bill four years earlier, at their twentieth wedding anniversary, when Bill had given Mom her sapphire ring. Izzy and I had planned a surprise party for them, a celebration of over one hundred friends and family. We held it at the Eastville Country Club, where their wedding reception had been. Mom was radiant in a lilac dress with flowers in her white hair, Bill smiling like a child in his polka-dot bowtie and narrow-shouldered suit jacket. Their heads were touching, their happiness tangible.

The next photograph was of Robert, sitting in an old leather armchair that used to be our father's, which still resided in Mom's living room. His two daughters were sitting on his lap. The lines of tension around his eyes and mouth betrayed his anxiety like finely drawn pencil marks, but there was a smile on his face that split the mask he often wore. The girls' faces weren't visible; they were looking up into his, adoringly, the way that only little girls can look at their fathers. My own father had held me in that same armchair; I could smell the cracked leather and his musky cologne.

Then Izzy, sleeping. All the energy and control my sister radiated while awake was hushed in the picture, her face quiet. Izzy had just given birth to the baby lying on her chest. Ivy clutched at Izzy's hospital gown with her little hand. I had faded out the harsh hospital lighting, so the scene was as softly illuminated as a Nativity.

The picture of James had been tricky. In photos he

always looked posed, and his poses came off as angry or falsely jubilant, both of which I found disturbing. I had finally taken the perfect photo at our cousin's birthday party. James was playing basketball with all the guys in the family, ranging in age from ten to sixty-five. For once, James wasn't playing for keeps; he passed the ball to the kids and cheered on his uncles. The picture captured him high-fiving Eli, the birthday boy, who had just turned ten. James's smile could light up a room; his eyes were distant, but not glittering like glass the way they were when he'd had too much to drink. He looked like the little boy he'd been, grown up.

The last photograph was of Amber, taken at her doctoral graduation. I had captured her face, framed by the mortarboard perched on her head, as she hugged her mom. Amber had been the first in her family with a college degree, and now she had a PhD in education. Amber was grinning, her eyes closed, the trace of an earlier tear etched down the side of her face.

Jonah noticed the things I had tried so hard to do, and a wave of emotion rolled over me: hope, and trust, and something else that moved beyond petty interest and lust, something like caring.

And for the first time I realized how significant it was that I had never been able to take a photo of Ted that satisfied me. He ducked whenever he saw my camera, chastising me for wasting time and money on a frivolous hobby.

There had been so many clues.

That night I woke in the dark to a pounding on the door, jerking awake as if I were free-falling from an airplane. I rolled over and squinted at the clock: 2:32 a.m.

The pounding continued. Mouth dry, heart beating in my throat, I slid out of bed and grabbed my phone in one hand, punching in 911 but not dialing yet. With the other hand I reached into my closet and grabbed a two-by-four left from when I'd installed new shelves.

I flicked on the stove light, tiptoed to the door, and peered through the peephole. There was a man standing with his back to the door; after a moment I grimaced, realizing that he was urinating over the side of the porch. I was about to press the send button on my phone to call the police when he turned around.

"James, what is the matter with you?" I shouted, flinging open the door as my brother raised his fist to resume pounding.

"Sorry," he slurred, giggling as I pulled him into the apartment and slammed and locked the door. "I couldn't get a cab."

My voice shook with outrage. "I can't believe this shit, James. What are you, seventeen years old? You're pathetic."

James had collapsed onto the couch. His knuckles were bleeding, and he smelled of alcohol and urine. After a moment, he started snoring. Fuming, I double-checked the locks on the front door then stormed into my bedroom and locked both that door and the bathroom door that adjoined into my room. I lay back in bed, adrenaline and anger pumping through my body.

Too furious to sleep, I watched the minutes and hours tick by: 3:16; 4:42; 5:07. Around 5:15 I dropped into an uneasy sleep, waking stupefied at 6:30 when my alarm went off. Pulling on my robe, I went to brush my teeth. Opening the bathroom door into the great room, I dropped my toothbrush in shock.

James was gone, and my front door was wide open.

I sprinted to the door, slammed it shut, and locked the knob and the deadbolt. I crouched by the front window and squinted through the blinds, my pulse pounding in my ears. No sign of my brother or, thankfully, anyone else. I was about to collapse on the couch when I noticed the other tokens he'd left behind: a pint glass half full of vomit on the coffee table and a smatter of bloodstains on my white couch. I forced down the bile in my throat.

I went to the closet, pulled a plastic bag from my stash, and dropped the glass of vomit into it. Cinching my robe tighter, I yanked open the front door and dropped the glass into the trash can at the bottom of the porch steps. The morning was already steamy. God, I was sick of summer.

At that moment my neighbor, Luis, came out of his apartment onto his porch, locking the door behind him. "Hey, Laura," he said. "Are you okay? Doug and I heard someone trying to pound down the door last night. We were about to get up when it stopped. Then Helen said this morning she was out walking and your door was wide open!"

Trust Helen to notice something like that and do nothing but gossip. "Yeah, sorry for the disturbance," I said. "My brother got into a little trouble."

Luis nodded knowingly. "Okay, well, if you ever need anything, just give us a call."

"Thanks." I went back inside, slamming the door. I winced at the bloodstains, the lingering acrid smell of vomit. I had a voicemail from Bill, letting me know he'd be cooking brunch on Sunday as usual, and that he was expecting my other siblings to be there as well. Good—maybe that got me off the hook for not stopping by this week. "And your mother would love it if you could come for Mass," he said. I sighed and went to get dressed for work.

Chapter 5

James

On Friday I'm working a roofing job with Benny. The afternoon sun is brutal, sapping my strength as I install shingle after shingle. "You get home okay last night?" he asks.

I'd forgotten I'd seen him at Lazy Joe's. I think about it. "Sure," I say. I scan my memory. "I crashed with Laura."

I did crash at Laura's, right? I should probably call and thank her. If it were Izzy I'd have to send a handwritten thank-you note on cardstock. But then I'd never dream of showing up at Izzy's uninvited. I pull my phone from my pocket, even though we are definitely not allowed to have phones on the roof, and hit Laura's speed-dial key. It rings twice and goes to voicemail. Ugh. Screening my calls, of course.

"Hey Laur," I say. "Thanks for the other night. You really helped me out." I hang up, but something's nagging. I probably did something to her. It gets hard to keep track sometimes.

It's three o'clock, about time for a water break, I figure, when my phone buzzes. Maybe Laura's calling to say all is well. But it's Ava. My heart starts pounding. "Hey," I say. "Is Jeremiah okay?"

"Yes," she says. "He wants to ask you something."

"Hey, Dad," he says. His voice sounds nervous.

"Hey, J. How's everything going?"

"Fine."

Benny is gesturing to the ground. I hold up one finger—just a *minute*.

There's an awkward pause. I can practically see Ava nodding encouragingly. "I just got a letter that I was nominated to join the Junior National Honor Society this year," he says.

My mouth drops open. "Wow, J, that's great! Congratulations!"

"Yeah," he said. "The thing is, I have to do all this stuff to actually get accepted, and one of the things I need is service hours."

Jeremiah goes to the hoity-toity private Catholic

school that Rick went to; Rick got him to apply for a bunch of scholarships that made it affordable, though I'm kicking in a little extra on top of child support for the uniform and stuff. Jeremiah is so much smarter than I am, smarter even than Ava, and we want him to go to a good college.

"Anyway, I'm helping out with a Habitat for Humanity build this weekend," he says. "And . . . they need more adult volunteers who know carpentry and stuff."

"That's fantastic," I say without hesitating. "I can show you a few tricks of the trade."

"Mom said I should ask you."

I chew on my lip. "I'll still come anyway."

"Okay," Jeremiah says, sounding more resigned than excited. "Mom'll e-mail you the details. It starts at eight tomorrow morning."

That night I'm so afraid I'll sleep in that I set three alarms and don't even go out. I jerk awake all night, checking the clock. I finally drop into a really deep sleep around 5:30, so when my first alarm goes off at 7:15, it has to swim through several levels of consciousness before it wakes me up. I shower and dress and get in my truck. The early-morning sunlight is a pale lemon color I rarely see. I stop at Dunkin' Donuts and get a large coffee with milk and sugar and a couple dozen Munchkins. Maybe the Munchkins are overkill, but I want the kids to like me.

I pull my truck up to the address Ava sent me, which is in Kingstown. The e-mail encouraged us to bring our own tools, suggesting at least a hammer. I get out of the truck and sling my tool belt around my waist, leaving the extra set of tools I brought for Jeremiah in the truck until I get the lay of the land.

The street is narrow and one-way, and I park a few houses down. It's easy to tell which house it is, even though there's no number visible. It's in pretty rough shape. The front room is completely open, though there's a new wood frame up. The houses are small two-story deals, probably three bedrooms, with small front yards and long, narrow backyards. I can hear a crowd around back, so I walk down the gravel driveway, which is jammed with SUVs.

The backyard is littered with junk and supplies: rusting car parts, a few spare tires, piles of lumber and boxes of nails, a new bathtub wrapped in cellophane.

There's also two long tables, one covered with sign-in sheets and flyers held down with rocks, the other laden with OJ, coffee, and a glass platter holding cheese Danishes from La Patisserie, a French bakery in Newport. Two black men stand by the back door, one wearing a tool belt and an unmistakable air of authority, the other talking emphatically, waving his hands. A knot of well-dressed white parents stand by the tables. A group of five or six students are talking in the middle of the yard. Jeremiah is the darkest one there. He spots me and says something to the group, who all laugh, then breaks away to come toward me. The other parents swivel their heads to watch him as he crosses the yard.

"Hey, Dad," he says and reaches out to give me an awkward sideways hug. "Thanks for coming."

"No problem," I say, stifling a yawn.

His eyes fix on the pink-and-orange box of Munchkins I'm carrying. "Doughnuts! Thanks! Kelsey's mom brought these weird cheese things that no one likes." He takes the box from me and leads me over to the tables. He opens the box, selecting two chocolate doughnut holes and cramming them into his mouth.

"Mrs. Donnelly, this is my dad," he says to a short blonde woman who's clearly in charge of the student side of this enterprise.

"James Keene," I say, holding out my hand.

She shakes it warmly. "It's so nice to have you," she says. "Jeremiah says you do some carpentry work."

I nod, unsure whether to feel awkward or proud. "Mostly roofing," I say.

"Perfect." She shows me where to sign in. "Let's introduce you to Cole, who's heading the project," she says, walking me over to the black men. Tool belt guy is Cole. His close-cropped hair is graying. He's shorter than I am, but his stockiness seems to make up for it. His handshake is firm. The other guy is the homeowner, Avery.

Cole shakes my hand, eyes my tool belt and dirty

fingernails appraisingly. "Can I put you in charge of drywall?" he asks.

"Sure," I say. "I've got a drywall screw gun in my truck."

"Good. We got some screws around here somewhere." He looks around, then at his watch. "Okay, everyone, huddle up," he calls to the yard at large, and the kids and parents gather around him in loose concentric circles. "We'll be in three groups like we were last Saturday, but this week group three will get to use power tools."

"Sweet," Jeremiah mutters, high-fiving the lanky guy next to him.

"You'll be installing drywall in the front room with Mr. Keene," he says.

I try to think of the last time I was called Mr. Keene. High school? Maybe in the courtroom during my DUI hearing.

"My group, meet me upstairs," Cole continued. "Mrs. Donnelly's group, you're in the kitchen again."

Everyone begins to disperse. I drain my coffee, my stomach alive with nerves again. Cole tells me the drywall is stacked in the front room, then turns and walks into the house.

Jeremiah, the tall kid, and a dad assemble around me. I've never instructed anyone on doing anything. At work sites I'm always the lowest guy on the totem pole. "Okay, guys, through here," I say, leading them to the front room.

"We'll do the ceiling first," I say. "Who's got a tape measure?"

The dad does, but the boys come up empty. "J, why don't you get my tool box out of the truck," I say, tossing him the keys. "There's another tape measure in there."

"I'm Alex," the tall kid says. "Thanks for letting me borrow some tools. My dad's a lawyer. He'd much rather pay someone to fix something than try to do it himself. I don't think he even owns a hammer."

"No worries," I say, my spirit lifting.

We work for two hours, finishing the ceiling and two of the walls, then I give the kids a water break. Jeremiah and Alex start horsing around at the lemonade cooler in the kitchen, where Mrs. Donnelly and a few girls are painting the cabinets yellow. The boys' horsing around increases in volume and exuberance in front of the girls.

"Oh, to be young," Ray says. Ray's son is upstairs spackling with Cole. I follow his line of sight and see he's not looking at the boys, who are scuffling in the corner, but at one of the girls, who is stretching on a stepladder to reach the top of the wall with her paintbrush. I move around in front of him to block his view, sipping my sickly sweet lemonade. "What do you do, Ray?" I hate the question myself, but anything to distract him from ogling the ass of a fifteen-year-old girl.

"I'm in real estate," he says, pulling out his phone. "I sell dreams." He winks at me, and I try not to vomit.

He probably knows Ted; it's a small town, and real estate is one of those professions where everyone knows everyone. I don't want to ask, because then I'll have to explain that he's my ex-brother-in-law and that he's a douche.

"I'm waiting to hear back from a client, excuse me." Ray ducks into the backyard.

I try not to feel awkward standing there alone. I want to call my group back together, but it's only been three minutes and I told them they could have ten.

I strike up a conversation with Mrs. Kenny—"Call me Nicole," she says—and find out she doesn't work. I don't know anyone who doesn't work at all. Even Izzy, who takes care of her kids full-time (and they are a full-time handful), still takes accounting clients, especially at tax season. Then it occurs to me that Julia doesn't work (though again, with the full-time parenting thing). Then again, she's such a bitch, she's sort of in her own class of human being.

After a quick lunch of subs and chips and another hour installing drywall, we're done for the day. It's only 1:30. I'd normally just be showering.

I find a broom and sweep up the front room out of habit. Nicole smiles at me as she passes by. "I hope you'll come back," she says. "We'll be here again next week."

"I'll see what I can do," I say. I dump the dustpan of debris into a trash can and lean the broom against a wall. Through the dining-room window, which still has stickers on it, I can see Ava's Mercedes idling in the street.

I go out the back and down the driveway. Jeremiah's

standing at the Mercedes, talking to Ava through the open window. He turns and high-fives Alex again; they must have gotten permission to hang out for the rest of the day. Jeremiah turns and sees me, and his face lights up. It hasn't lit up like that for me in a few years now.

He comes toward me, unstrapping the tool belt from his waist. "Thanks, Dad," he says, holding it out to me. "For everything."

"No problem, J."

"Think you can come back next week?" he asks. "Everyone really liked having you here."

"I have to check some things on my calendar," I say. "I'll let you know, okay?"

"Sounds good." He shrugs and walks away.

I wave to Ava as Jeremiah and Alex get in her car. I get into my truck and drive home, a swarm of emotions thick in my chest.

Chapter 6

Laura

On Friday night I was getting ready to go out to dinner with
Amber when Jonah texted and offered to take me to the beach on
Monday after work.

I'm in! I texted back, smiling.

I put my phone back on the speaker dock and blasted U2.
I was straightening my hair when I heard "Wrecking Ball."

"Izzy," I groaned, then picked up.

"Laura, honey, can you do me the biggest favor ever?"
Izzy was using her wheedling voice.

"No," I said. "No freaking way." Izzy called me for
"emergency" babysitting once a month.

"Laura, *please*. Sam and I are going to a benefit. Our sitter
just canceled, and it'll look bad if I'm not there. I'll owe you
huge."

My temper flared. This happened once a month. "Do you
even *have* a sitter? Or is she a figment of your imagination?"

"Of course we don't want to ruin your weekend," Izzy
said in her fake-injured voice. "But Sam's boss bought out the
table, and it'll be insulting if there's an empty seat—and you
know all the law firms are downsizing right now . . ."

I hesitated.

My sister pressed her advantage. "*Please*, Laurlie. Just this
once."

Half an hour later, instead of sipping martinis in Newport, I was
making popcorn for Ivy, who was six, and Isaac, four. Ian, nine
months, was asleep.

I snuggled on the couch under a pile of blankets to watch
Trucks for the third time in as many months, a fresh-scrubbed,
pajamaed kid on either side of me. Per our tradition, I held the
bowl of popcorn on my lap so they each had equal access. The
popcorn was my special recipe, one that had once subdued a
decade of Eastville tantrums. I brought a bag of kernels with me,

popped it in a pot on the stovetop, and drizzled the fluffy globes with olive oil, garlic powder, and Parmesan cheese. Of course the tantrum-taming days when my popcorn gave me the edge over every other babysitter in town were long over. Being an aunt was much more fun than babysitting: I had a little more authority and respect, but mostly I loved my niece and nephews with a tenderness that had never entered into the realm of my feelings toward my spoiled babysitting charges. I pushed away a nudge of guilt over the hurt in Amber's voice when I'd canceled on her and crammed some popcorn into my mouth.

As the big race approached onscreen, both kids ran around the couch chanting, "Go, go, go"; the room seemed to fold in on itself and rematerialize in a different reality. Out of the corner of my mind's eye I could see the daughter I'd dreamed of for years sleeping in Ted's arms while I snuggled next to them.

My niece and nephew climbed back onto the couch. "Aunt Laura, you never cry at movies," Ivy said, twisting to look up at me.

"I'm just glad they won," I said. I wiped each of my eyes with my pinkie finger and willed them to stop watering.

"But you've seen this movie a *million* times."

"True." I had no other excuses to offer. "Let's see what's on Nickelodeon." I clicked over to cable and found an episode of *iCarly*.

"I hate this show," Isaac mumbled, burrowing under my left arm.

"You picked *Trucks*," I said. I shifted the bowl of popcorn to the coffee table, a few unpopped kernels sliding around the bottom.

Isaac was asleep by the next commercial break. He got cranky if he slept too long on the couch, so I hoisted him onto my hip, his legs wrapping automatically around my waist, his head lolling on my shoulder. My arms tightened as I ascended each step—*ten, eleven, twelve*—glad that Izzy was so obsessively neat that there was never anything to trip over in the hallway. In the boys' room, Ian was sleeping soundly, his scrunched face illuminated by the Spider-Man nightlight. I shifted Isaac's weight to my right arm and dipped to the left to tug his bedspread and tightly tucked sheets down. I deposited him into bed, and he curled around his stuffed dinosaur. I tucked him in and kissed his temple, then I moved to check on Ian. His cowlick coiled perpendicular to his head; I smoothed it out of habit and went downstairs, pressing down a wave of emotion.

Ivy had put on the Disney channel and fallen asleep. I changed the channel to *The Bodyguard* and went to the kitchen to pour a glass of wine. I didn't usually drink when I was with the kids, but I felt both exhausted and keyed up, simultaneously wishing I could go home to bed and dreading the moment when Izzy and Sam returned to resume possession of their children.

I woke to the rumble of the garage door opening, my neck stiff against the back of the couch. Kevin Costner was guarding a politician while Whitney wailed, "*I will always love you.*" The credits rolled.

Sam came into the den, his bowtie untied and his collar flapping open. "Thanks," he mouthed as he picked up Ivy and took her upstairs.

I untangled myself from the pile of blankets and stood, my left foot tingling. I carried my empty wine glass into the kitchen. Izzy came in from the garage barefoot, her heels dangling from her left hand. Her mascara had bled slightly, making the circles under her eyes appear darker. She sat at the island and nodded at the open bottle of Shiraz. Understanding and, for some reason, obeying, I went to the cabinet, got another glass, and poured a healthy measure of wine for her, sliding it across the counter until she could reach. I lifted the bottle again to refill my own glass.

"Haven't you had enough?" she said.

I stared at her. "You get mean when you drink."

Izzy's face hardened. "I do not."

"You do," I said. "You're like Dad. You get *mean*. And I think what you meant to say was, 'Thanks for saving our night.'"

Izzy waved a hand. "You love saving the night."

"Actually, I don't," I said. "I had plans, and now Amber is pissed at me."

Izzy raised an eyebrow. "You do what you have to do for family."

"This is crazy," I said. "This wasn't an emergency."

Izzy looked at me like I had three heads. "Of course it

was. Our sitter canceled. We had to go to this event or Sam could lose his job."

"Sam is not even *close* to losing his job," I said. My voice got louder of its own accord. "You just couldn't bear having people think you aren't *perfect*."

Izzy sniffed. "You're hysterical."

"I am *not* hysterical," I said. "I am fed up with you guilting me into doing whatever you need me to do."

Izzy yawned. "I can pay you next time, if you want."

I stared at her. "Oh my God," I said. "You really don't get it at all."

"Get what?" She looked at me quizzically, took a slug of wine.

"You have no idea how selfish you are," I said softly.

My sister's eyes bugged out. "*Me?* Me, selfish? Who's always been the golden child who could do no wrong? You. Who has always had the easiest time in our family? You. And when I need a little help—"

"Iz, you exploit the fact that you know I'll do anything for you."

"Don't get all therapist on me," she snarled. She was breathing hard, her face was red, and her hair was slipping out of its updo. "I'm the one who holds this family together. I don't know why the three of you are so *ungrateful*."

This was the point in our argument where I usually caved. Usually, I would say she was right and apologize, just to maintain the status-quo peace, just to get out of the conversation.

My sister stood there, waiting for me to play my part.

"Next time, please give me three days' notice if you want me to babysit," I said.

Izzy recoiled as if I'd slapped her. "This is insane," she said.

"Actually, it's not," I said. "It's actually a pretty reasonable request. See you later." And I left.

My hands shook on the steering wheel as I drove home.

I texted Amber on Saturday morning to see if she'd let me treat her to breakfast. She texted back, *Fine*, which meant she was still mad at me. I knocked on her door with my elbow at 9:30, holding a vanilla latte in each hand. Amber answered, her purse on her shoulder. Usually she'd let me in and we'd talk while she got herself together. But today she took the latte wordlessly and followed me to my car.

Elcy's Cafe was housed in an old train station, and we used to stop there in the afternoon when we were in high school to study or goof off, eating scones and drinking coffee. Occasionally we saw girls from Blessed Mother, our Catholic high school, still wearing the same uniforms: navy plaid skirts, green sweaters, and penny loafers. They usually pulled it off with their shiny hair and smoky eyeliner in a way we never had.

Back in high school I'd dragged my old camera around, taking what I perceived to be "artsy" photos: the sun on a leaf, an old bike leaning against a deserted building. I'd walk to the convenience store to drop the film off at the 1-Hour Express, then be crushed every time when the pictures didn't turn out well. They were usually overexposed. But I'd done a series of black-and-white photos in Elcy's that were by far my best high school work. I wondered if I still had the negatives somewhere.

We walked into the cafe, the bell on the door jingling over the whir of the milk being steamed and the hum of the brunch crowd.

The walls were painted a sunset orange, and mismatched tables and chairs squeezed into every possible space. A line straggled in front of us along the lit pastry case. We sat at the only empty table, the ceramic tabletop doubling as a chessboard.

"Remember when we used to play checkers with the chess pieces?" I said.

"Yeah." Amber smiled. "When we should have been doing Latin translations." Her smile fell. "I'll go order. You want the pancake special, right?"

I nodded. I watched as Amber walked across the cafe to stand in line; every head turned to watch her. She was wearing a jean skirt and a pink-and-purple tank top that matched a pink scarf tying back her hair. I watched Amber talking to Cara, one of the baristas we knew, both of them laughing.

She came back with two mugs of coffee, her face grim again.

"Amber, I'm sorry."

She makes a face.

"It'll never happen again," I said.

"You're kidding yourself."

"No." I sighed. "I asked Izzy to give me more notice. Next time she does this, I'll turn her down."

"You hate disappointing people," she said. "I just don't know why it's easier for you to disappoint me than your sister."

That stung. Because it was true.

"She practically raised me," I said, struggling to put it into words. Mom had gone back to work full-time when Dad died. "But it's like she's never satisfied, no matter what I do."

"Why can't you let it go? You're thirty-two years old. Why does her approval matter so much to you?"

"I don't know," I said, "but it does."

Cara arrived with my pancakes and Amber's omelet.

"How are things with Brian?" I asked tentatively.

A small smile tugged at the corners of her mouth. "Good, I think," she said. "He took me windsurfing last weekend."

"That sounds fun," I said.

"How's Jonah?"

"Hang on," I said. "I wasn't done."

She sighed. "Just don't therapize me, okay?"

"I wouldn't dream of it," I said, refusing to let my feelings be hurt. "Tell me more about him."

"What do you want to know?"

"What kind of man is he?"

Amber smiled again. "You ask the weirdest questions."

I forked a triple bite of pancake into my mouth.

Still, she considered my question in a way that let me know she was happy I'd asked. "I feel like he's the first actual adult I've ever dated," she said. Her eyes focused on the wall behind me, as if she were seeing something else, her face soft. "I know that sounds weird. But it's like, all the other guys I've known are teenagers in grown-up bodies, you know?"

"Yes," I said, thinking of James.

"He's not afraid to talk to me. And I mean, he doesn't act like the talking is what he has to give me in exchange for sex."

"I am so happy for you," I said, smiling. Amber had dated a lot of idiots. I would of course reserve judgment on Brian until I met him myself, but he was possibly a non-idiot.

"Okay, your turn," she said.

"I know what you mean, about the not-being-afraid-to-talk thing," I said. "Jonah confronted me about how I'd left his place so abruptly last weekend. He didn't let me off the hook. It wasn't like he picked a fight," I said. "It was like he exposed this issue that would otherwise have festered. I mean, in any other relationship I've been in, it would have festered, because I'd want to pretend everything was fine and the guy—"

"Ted," Amber said.

"And Ted would have been oblivious to how he was feeling about it. Or he would have made a joke, because that's how he dealt with tension."

We finished eating, and I left a few dollars on the table. "Want to walk around the farmers' market?"

The market was in the next parking lot over. Twenty or so tents shielded fresh produce, homemade cheese, organic wine, and fresh bread from the boiling sun. Heat rolled across the blacktop in waves.

"How are your parents?" I asked. "I miss them." Amber's parents had moved back to Ghana a few years ago to care for her grandmother.

"They're doing well," she said. "I miss them too. I think I'm going to go over there for a few weeks at Christmas."

"That'll be nice," I said.

"How's your mom?" Amber took a toothpick sample of cheese from under the first tent.

"I'm not really sure," I said. "I've kind of . . . been avoiding going over there. I called a few times, but you know Bill. He never complains about anything. But we're all doing church and brunch tomorrow. I can't skip out on that."

"Is *everyone* going?" Amber asked.

"Yeah."

"That'll be . . . interesting."

We looked at each other and burst out laughing.

"Unpredictable might be a better word," I said.

"Volatile."

"Riveting."

"Tense."

"Want to come?"

Amber laughed. "No way. I get my fill of Keene family togetherness on Thanksgiving."

"Fair enough, though you should see us when you're not there. The level of craziness just ticks up a couple notches."

"I can only imagine."

We laughed again and meandered into the produce tent. I popped a peach slice in my mouth, where it promptly burst with sweetness on my tongue. I started gathering a few peaches into a plastic bag, squeezing them lightly to find the ripest.

"How's work?"

I sighed. "Fine. It feels weird after my client dying."

"Are all your coworkers walking on eggshells?"

I smiled. "No. That's the thing. They're all super blunt about the whole thing. Like, *Do you want to talk? Have you been seeing Marisa?*"

"Have you? Been seeing her?"

"*Yes*," I said.

"Don't get all pissy," Amber said. "Your mother has a degenerative disease, and one of your client was murdered. I'm glad you're seeing your therapist."

"Me too."

Chapter 7

Laura

On Sunday morning I stood outside church as if perched on the edge of a high dive. I hadn't set foot in Our Lady of the Sea since graduating eighth grade, except for weddings, funerals, and the occasional christening (which for a Catholic family don't count as church). The four of us had all attended kindergarten through eighth grade there. I could see myself and my brothers traipsing up the hill in our ugly gray wool uniforms and saddle shoes, me in third grade, James in sixth, Robert in eighth. Izzy was already at Blessed Mother and took the bus; the rest of us were jealous, especially in winter.

I arrived a little late and sat in the pew behind everyone, feeling like I'd been put in detention. Robert twisted around to wink. His eyes were glassy; he must have come straight from work. Julia and the girls were conspicuously absent. James sat next to Robert. Just seeing the back of his head made me angry. Izzy and Sam and the kids sat on James's other side, dressed to the nines.

I inhaled a whisper of incense, my mind stilling. No matter how many times I'd been to this church, every single time made me think of my father's funeral. I'd cried beforehand, wanting Daddy, and Izzy had shushed me angrily, telling me Daddy wasn't coming back. I kept crying, thinking she meant I did something wrong, and she abandoned me in my room in disgust. Finally Robert came in, put his arm around me, and told me it wasn't my fault. He asked if I could try not to cry during the funeral, because it would upset Mom. I'd nodded seriously. And sat on the hard pew for what seemed like an eternity, conscious not to swing my feet like Daddy had taught me, pressing my tears down and down. Later, when Mom had come to tuck me in, I'd asked her when I could cry again. She'd hugged me tightly and told me to cry whenever I needed to, and she'd held me and we'd cried together.

Mom seemed agitated now. She shifted in her seat and murmured through the homily. She was silent during the responses she'd known for years. At one point she turned around and beckoned me close. She whispered, *"Sanctus, sanctus, sanctus Dominus Deus Sabaoth."* I nodded and patted her hand.

Halfway through Mass, she took off the sweater Bill had put around her shoulders to ward off the subzero A/C temperature. She was wearing a blue top and a flowery knee-length skirt. I watched her left arm snake up into her sleeve. When her right arm did the same thing, I lunged forward, grabbing the hem of the shirt and trying to tug it back into place.

"I'M GOING SWIMMING!" Mom bellowed. "YOU CAN'T STOP ME!" The entire church turned as one toward us: Mom's shirt around her neck, her threadbare bra encasing her sagging breasts, me half-crouching behind her. She thrashed against me with surprising strength.

The priest announced the offering, and people were distracted, digging for their giving envelopes and dollar bills. Bill and I hustled Mom out of church, her arms pinned to her sides in a ridiculous blouse straitjacket. She was flailing against us for the first several feet as we held tightly to her arms then suddenly became dead weight; she almost fell to the floor. Robert hustled to our aid, and James ran ahead of us to get the door. Izzy and her family stayed in the pew.

We got Mom home, where she continued to be ornery, pacing and muttering.

Robert, James, and I set about making brunch. Robert moved around the kitchen like a zombie. I refused to even look at James. He was cracking eggs into the frying pan while I measured pancake mix, oil, and milk into a bowl. I turned to him to get three eggs and found the blue Styrofoam carton empty.

"Dammit, James! I need three eggs for the pancakes!"

"You didn't say anything," he said. "I'm standing right next to you."

Robert was frying bacon on the back burner. "Laura, we'll make some toast. We'll have enough food."

I pushed the bowl away, slopping pancake mix onto the backsplash of the counter. "Go ahead, make excuses for him."

"Laura, chill," James said. "I'll walk to the store and get a dozen eggs. It's no big deal."

"You ruin everything," I said, stalking from the kitchen.

I went into the living room and stared out the bay window. I couldn't believe I'd overreacted so spectacularly. *Someone has to make him see*, I thought, not knowing exactly what I wanted him to see. I knew only that I was tired of pretending James's actions didn't affect me.

I heard the side door open and bang shut—James going for eggs. It opened again, and I could hear Izzy and Sam bickering and the kids shouting. The smoke alarm went off, which happened when anyone cooked in the kitchen besides Mom. I stood looking out the window for a long time. I heard James come back, the sound of someone beating the eggs into the pancake mix.

"Breakfast," Robert called ten minutes later. I heard Ivy and Isaac stampede into the kitchen. I followed reluctantly, avoiding my family's eyes. Bill led grace, which my family chorused in a dull, rote chant. "Bless us, O Lord, and these thy gifts which we are about to receive from thy bounty, through Christ our Lord, amen."

Dishes of pancakes and eggs and bacon were passed up and down the table. Everyone talked around Mom and me, the two problem children of the day. I found it somewhat peaceful, albeit strangely lonely, to eat an entire meal with my family without speaking once. Bill made everyone laugh again by saying that Mom had been channeling Mrs. George last night, screaming obscenities.

The doorbell rang. "I'll get it," I said, jumping up from my seat and striding through the porch room, where a Red Sox game was playing for no one, and opened the side door.

Ted was standing on the path, as if afraid whoever answered the door would strike him if he stood too close. He was wearing knife-pleated khakis and a pink polo shirt. From my vantage point at the top of four brick stairs, he looked shorter than I remembered, and his sandy hair was definitely longer. His shoulders were jammed up near his ears, and new worry lines framed his eyes and mouth. I hadn't seen him since our divorce had been finalized in March.

I wanted to close the door in his face, but instead I stepped outside and closed the door behind me. My family didn't agree on much, but since he'd cheated on me, they had agreed to hate Ted with a single-minded intensity.

"What are you doing here?" I walked down the steps gingerly, leaving five feet between us.

"Your lawyer wouldn't give me your new address," he said.

"I wonder why," I said. My body was reacting to Ted strangely, as if he were a substance I simultaneously craved and was horribly allergic to. My heart pounded, my fingers grew cold. A buzzing sound grew in my ears.

"I was showing a house nearby," he said. He closed the distance between our bodies in two steps and placed a hand on each of my upper arms, drew me forward, and kissed me deliberately on the cheek. "I'm sorry about your mom, Laura," he said. "Is there anything I can do?"

"No," I said. "How did you even hear about that?"

"Mrs. Jenkins," he said, referring to Mom and Bill's neighbor. "I ran into her at the A&P yesterday."

I didn't say anything.

"Listen." He shuffled his feet. "I'm sorry about everything. I know I screwed up. It was the biggest mistake I've ever made, and I've been regretting it ever since." He looked at me. "Do you think we could try again?"

I stared at him. I sat down on the stoop of my mother's house. Ted had come here with me for Thanksgivings and Christmases and Fourth of July barbecues for five years. I'd fled here after I'd left him. But for a moment I imagined what it would be like to accept his offer of help. We could pick up where we left off; we could start a family. My heart recoiled from all the damage he'd done, yet I wanted to run into his arms and forget the last year of our lives. I don't know how long I would have sat there if the door hadn't opened again.

"Ted." Bill closed the door behind him, moving onto the top step with a crunching sound. The concrete was chipping.

"Sir." Ted inclined his head toward Bill respectfully. "I heard that Katherine wasn't well," he said.

I cringed at his use of my mother's first name.

"I was in the area—" Ted said.

"Thanks for stopping by," Bill said.

"I just wanted to check on Laura—"

"She's not for you to worry about anymore," Bill said.

I stood up and put my hand on Bill's arm. "It's okay," I said. I turned toward my ex-husband. "Don't do this again, Ted. I don't want to see you."

He flinched slightly, then nodded.

I went inside and walked up the stairs to my childhood bedroom. I lay down on my old twin bed, on top of my worn yellow comforter, and curled into a ball.

The room hadn't changed much. Izzy and I had shared it until I was five, when Dad died. Then Mom had moved Iz across the hall into her old sewing room, shifted the sewing things into her bedroom. I had the sense, at five, that the crowdedness in her bedroom made Mom feel less lonely. Izzy's room had a big-girl bed and makeup and a vanity that had lights all the way around the mirror. Whenever she let me—and sometimes when she didn't—I spent all the time I could in there.

The sunlight moved across the wall as morning turned to afternoon, and still I didn't move. I could hear Robert and James and Bill shouting at the Red Sox game on TV.

The door of my old room creaked open. At some point I'd rolled over and was facing the wall; I didn't move, didn't even open my eyes. Someone sat on the edge of the bed. I smelled Izzy's perfume.

"Bill told us Ted stopped by," she said. "Are you okay?"

I didn't want to talk about it, so I didn't say anything.

Izzy sat down at the foot of the bed and put a hand on my ankle, which was odd because she never touched me unless the situation demanded physical contact. "I'm sorry. I haven't really been there for you this year. Especially considering all the times you've saved by ass with . . . *emergency* . . . babysitting."

I cracked a smile, cleared my throat. "Thanks. That means a lot." Coming from her, it did.

"Is there anything I can do?"

I opened my eyes, stared at the yellow wall. "Just give me a break now and then, okay?"

"Yeah." She got up, the bed creaking in protest, and left the room.

That was our version of a sisterly heart-to-heart, and it actually felt pretty good.

I went home, grabbed my camera case from its perch on my coffee table, and got back in the Caddy and drove to Easton Beach in Newport. It was crowded with sunbathers. I dropped my keys into a pocket and left everything in the car, carrying only my camera bag.

The sun glimmered on the ocean like liquid gold. I walked north along the beach, thinking. I climbed up the short hill behind the beach and sat down in the dune grass, hoping that stilling my body might still my mind. I sat for a long time before I unpacked my camera from its case. I sat for an even longer time, the weight of it familiar in my hands. The bottom left corner was scratched from the time Ivy had dropped it. The shutter button was faded gray from the number of times I had pressed it.

When I finally raised it to my face, peering through the viewfinder, it was as if I'd been living underwater for years and finally risen to the surface and remembered that I was supposed to breathe air. The whole world looked different through the camera lens. The water came alive, changing color as the sun and clouds shifted, trailing light and shadow in their wake.

The landscape was beautiful, but it was the people that drew me in through the viewfinder. The thrilled smile of a high school girl as her boyfriend reached for her hand. The indignant shriek of a little girl as her brother dumped a bucket of water over her head. The joy of a woman licking an ice-cream cone.

I stayed on the beach until the sun began to set.

On Monday I got to work by 8:30 as usual, even though I didn't have a client until ten. I went to the break room to refill my thermos with coffee. I used this thermos every day, but today the sight of the GW seal raised a lump in my throat. I had loved having so many like-minded friends in my doctoral program. My first-year roommate, Lacey, had introduced me to Ted, whom she had known at American. They had a crew of undergrad friends in

DC for the first year I was there, but one by one the group began relocating, moving home to be closer to family, taking lucrative job offers in New York and San Francisco. Ted and I had gotten together when his college girlfriend moved to France.

Two weeks before my graduation, just after I'd turned in my dissertation, Ted and I threw a party at our Capitol Hill apartment. I had last-minute party jitters for two days beforehand as I bought guacamole and tortilla chips and stocked up on beer and wine and cheap tequila. What if no one came? What if everyone came and no one had any fun? But from the moment the first guests arrived—a mismatched group that included one of his frat brothers and the guy's girlfriend, who was still in college, and one of my colleagues from the clinic where I'd done my externship and her husband, who had two kids—Ted had a drink in everyone's hand and was making connections between them they never would have found themselves. His frat brother's girlfriend had grown up in West Virginia and gone to the same high school as my colleague's husband. My thesis adviser lived on the same block in Georgetown as his boss. At three in the morning we were blasting Bon Jovi and singing at the top of our lungs when two cops knocked on the door and sent everyone home. Ted knew one of the officers—had in fact sold him his newly built house in Woodbridge—so we got off without a fine.

We'd had so much fun in DC. Ted was a fun magnet: He always knew the newest restaurant opening, the free gallery night, the cocktail party at the W where he talked us past the bouncer even though we weren't on the guest list. The problem was that my friends had become Ted's friends, and that intertwining made it impossible for me to pick up the phone and call any of them now.

"How are you doing?"

I turned around and saw Kevin standing in the doorway. "Hey," I said. "I'm okay. Elaine was so sweet to come to the funeral with me."

He smiled. "She is sweet."

"It happened to me a few years ago," he said. "One of my clients killed himself."

I took a sip from my thermos. The Keurig coffee was lukewarm and weak.

Kevin came in and leaned against the counter. "I just kept going over and over his last few sessions. I second-guessed every word I'd said to him. Maybe I should have tried being tougher instead of just listening. Or maybe I should have reiterated that he call my emergency number if he was thinking about hurting himself. That last day, if I had just been more encouraging . . ." He sighed. "You can drive yourself crazy," he said.

"Macy didn't kill herself," I said. I plucked a chocolate doughnut from the pink box on the counter.

"I've never seen you eat something from the break room before," Kevin said.

"Yeah, well, I'm doing a little stress eating," I said, sinking my teeth into it.

"Listen, Laura, it's not your fault. You can't blame yourself."

"Who said I'm blaming myself?" I said. "I'm not blaming myself." I got up and stalked to my office, unsure why I was venting on him.

The rest of the morning was just as strange. At ten o'clock I saw Alana, a college student whose crippling anxiety was affecting her social life and her grades. At 11:15 I had Ned, who seemed to participate in the therapeutic process because it sounded cool, rather than from any deep place of needing to heal or wanting to change. He exhausted me the most, because he wanted me to tell him what to talk about. I had to explain for the millionth time that he had to have a stake in his own process if he wanted to see any results. My words sounded oddly hypocritical to my own ears. Maybe I should take my own advice.

My last appointment of the day was with the Porters at 12:30. Colleen had agreed to Vince's demand that they see me together for eight weeks, after which she could file for divorce. It was their third session, and they spent most of it arguing about whether they should be seeing me at all.

I left work at two o'clock, feeling like I was cutting school. Maybe I should stay and finish my client notes. I half-turned to go back inside, but the sun was warm on my arms, and I had hardly been to the beach all summer.

I drove home and put on my green polka-dot bikini, twisting this way and that in front of the mirror. My stomach was taut from all the Pilates videos I'd been doing, but it was fish-belly white. I sighed. Well, it would have to do. I slathered on sunscreen, dropped a black cotton dress over my head, and drove to the beach.

I walked down 13th, carrying my straw tote on one shoulder and my beach chair on the other. Hordes of tourists swarmed in front of Flo's, carrying trays of hot dogs and burgers and jockeying for space in the shade of umbrellaed picnic tables. A line snaked out the door of Twisters, the sidewalk full of kids clutching melting ice-cream cones and cups heaped with Italian ice. When I reached the beach I stood on the sand, letting the warm grains sift through my toes. A group of shirtless guys to my left was playing volleyball. Dozens of people sunning themselves on towels and beach chairs spread out on either side of the tall white lifeguard stand. I pulled out my phone and called Jonah; his phone went to voicemail. I sighed. I didn't really feel like slogging through the sand with all my stuff to look for him.

"Laura!" I turned to my left. Jonah was waving from the center of the volleyball players. As I watched, the ball arced toward him and he jumped to spike it over the net into the sand. His team clustered around him, chest-bumping and giving high-fives. Both teams dispersed and he ran toward me, grinning. God, he was so tan he looked like a Greek god. I looked like a pale alien in contrast.

"Hi," he said. He kissed me.

"Hi. Thanks for getting me out of the office."

He smiled. "Want to play?"

"I'll sit this one out," I said. I was not coordinated in any sports that involved balls.

"I'm just kidding. I told them I'm not playing anymore."

"Really? Why?"

He looked puzzled. "Because I invited you to the beach, and now you're here. Why would I spend my time with a bunch of sweaty guys?"

"I don't mind if you play," I said magnanimously.

He nodded. "Uh-huh. Women always say stuff like that. 'I don't mind.' But you do mind. And that's fine. Because we're on a date."

I laughed. "Okay. I'm glad you want to spend time with me."

"Just let me get my stuff."

He jogged back over to the sand court, picked up a backpack and a beach chair, shook his head and laughed when one of the guys asked him something, jogged back to me. "They want to meet you," he said. "I told them they had to wait until we'd been on more than three dates. Let's go." He held out his hand, and we walked down the sand toward the water. "Where do you like to sit?"

"It's your beach," I said.

"I usually sit as far from all the people and as close to the water as I can get," he said. "But it's more walking."

"I'm fine with walking."

We set up camp with our feet in the water, our bags hung on the back of our chairs. It was quiet, the breeze occasionally bringing us snatches of people talking and kids playing.

"How was your morning?" Jonah asked.

"Okay," I said.

He smiled. "Tell me one thing about it," he said.

I couldn't say anything about my patients, so my options were severely limited. *My coworker was trying to be helpful and I bit his head off?* I wanted to tell him something real. "I worked in the break room for a little while," I said, "because I kept expecting to see my client who was killed walk through my office door."

He reached over and squeezed my hand.

"How was your morning?" I said.

"Won three games, lost two," he said. "Not bad, but usually we crush them. Mondays are off days, though."

"You play every day?" I said, incredulous.

"On all my days off. There's a bunch of us—me and another guy from my floor, couple of bartenders, lifeguards. People who don't work the standard 9 to 5."

We were quiet for a while, staring at the waves. I wondered if the silence was a good sign—we were comfortable with each other—or a bad sign—we didn't have enough in common. I closed my eyes.

"I haven't dated in a while," Jonah said.

I opened my eyes. "Me neither."

"Do we have to have the conversation? About being exclusive?"

My mouth turned upward of its own accord. "I'm not really into the sleeping-around scene."

"Me neither. So I can call you my girlfriend and you won't be offended?"

"Not offended," I said, smiling for real.

"Okay then," he said, and leaned his head back again and closed his eyes.

It had been a long time since I'd started something new. Change usually scared the shit out of me, but this felt different. This felt . . . refreshing.

Chapter 8

James

I had fun at the build last week, but the fear starts creeping up again Friday around quitting time. I'm tired, and I don't want to wake up early again tomorrow. Even I don't see that as a worthy excuse for disappointing my son, but in the meantime I need a little reward for working all week. I try to drink responsibly—a few glasses of good Scotch—so I won't be hungover.

As soon as I wake, I know something's wrong. The light is too bright.

"Fuck." I pick up my phone and peer blearily at the screen: 10:30. "Fuck!" I throw the phone across the room. It hits the wall and falls to the floor, the screen cracked.

I try to hurry; I'm already late but still move slower than molasses. I pop four Advil, make a pot of coffee, shower.

I arrive at the build three hours late, doughnut-free. I fill my thermos with lukewarm coffee from the coffeepot in the kitchen. Jeremiah avoids my gaze when I walk through to the front room. He and Alex are nailing up the last piece of drywall. His anger is palpable.

Cole gives me a mock hard time—"What, you stay out too late?"—but the other adults, who probably guess that I *did* stay out late, and that it's not an isolated incident, meet my eyes less frequently. I supervise Jeremiah and Alex hanging drywall in the basement. At lunch I close myself in the only working bathroom, which is hardly big enough to turn around in, and splash my face with cold water. There are no towels, and the toilet paper is the cheap kind that shreds when it comes into contact with water, so I rub my face dry on the sleeve of my T-shirt.

I need to find Jeremiah and make him talk to me. I open the bathroom door and find him standing in the hallway. "Listen, J, I'm sorry I was late. I overslept." I smile weakly.

My son's face is stony. "Yeah."

"I said I was sorry," I say, and I can feel my hackles rising. "What else do you want from me?"

"I want you to leave," Jeremiah says, still not meeting

my eyes. "I should have known better than to invite you to this. You're embarrassing."

He slides past me into the bathroom, closes the door in my face. I slip back through the house, light a cigarette the second I'm out the door. I get in my truck to smoke with the window rolled down. When my cigarette goes out, I can't muster the courage to go back inside; I start the truck and drive away.

I meet up with Dean and Eddie at the Irish pub on Saturday night. We drink, we go outside to smoke, we play darts, we shoot pool. But mostly we drink. Dean just leased a new Acura; he lets us sit inside it before our smoke break. It has a sunroof and a moonroof. I'm nauseated with envy. Eddie's saving up to buy his girlfriend an engagement ring. She wants two carats on a platinum band. He's been saving for a year now, but he goes out six nights a week, so I don't know how far along he can possibly be.

I'm not saving for anything, which I guess is a good thing, because I don't save well. I don't have the saving gene. Or the achieving gene. I'm fine being mediocre. I sleep better at night.

Nights like this, though, I start to wonder whether everyone who looks at me just sees a *loser*. I drink more when I get like this, get a little more aggressive with the darts, with the girls I approach, with my friends.

I drink more, because otherwise I won't sleep at all.

Chapter 9

Laura

I had offered to take Mom to her doctor's appointment. Other than Sunday brunch, I hadn't dropped by the house since before Mom's fall. I missed *wanting* to drop by (mostly to talk to Bill). Now every visit was fraught with the fear of what Mom would say or do.

I let myself into the house and found Bill in the kitchen. He looked exhausted. "How's the home aide working out?" I asked, sitting at the table next to him.

He shook his head. "Could be better."

I waited.

"Your mom bit her," he said. "She left and is refusing to come back. Understandably."

"Mom *bit* her?"

A small smile turned his lips upward. "Your mother wanted to leave the house, ah, in the nude, and the aide was blocking the door." Mom ambled in then. "Katherine didn't like that too much."

Mom sat down placidly at the head of the table, staring into space. It was as if she wasn't in the room with us at all.

Bill put a hand over his face. "I hate . . . taking away her freedom."

I was surprised. Of all the things I thought he would hate—having his wife not recognize him, the fact that he would grow old as the sole caretaker not only of her ailing body but of their memories, the fact that Mom bit her nurse—his choice surprised me.

"What's new with you?" he asked.

I smiled. "I'm seeing someone. One of Mom's nurses, actually. Jonah."

Bill's face lit up. "I'm so happy for you, my love. I want to meet him."

I made a face. "You have met him."

"You know. In this capacity."

"So not ready for that yet," I said. "But I'll let you know when I am."

"Good."

"Is it time for school?" Mom asked abruptly. Her hands were in her lap.

I looked at Bill. "Get some rest," I said. I stood and held my hand out to Mom. "Yes," I said. "It's time for school."

I kissed Bill goodbye.

"You can still come pick her up for church on Sunday?" he asked, phrasing the reminder as a question out of courtesy.

"Sure." Bill was going fishing with friends.

"Thanks."

I drove with Mom to Our Lady of Fatima to see Dr. Pindar.

Mom seemed surprisingly at ease in the labyrinth of hallways in the medical center. She used to get upset ("Why do they have to make all the corridors look exactly alike?"). Today she followed placidly behind me.

The office was bright and cozy, decorated in shades of blue: navy carpet, cerulean curtains, sky-blue sofas. I'd never seen real couches in a medical doctor's office. They usually had those connected chairs, which were awkward no matter how plush. We waited alone in the front room for a long time. The receptionist apologized for the delay but didn't offer an explanation.

Mom looked around her every few minutes and asked, "Where are we?"

"At the doctor's office, Mom," I said. Again. And again.

She turned to look at me after the fourth iteration. "And who are you?"

I could feel a headache starting behind my eyes. "Laura. Your daughter."

Mom's face suddenly split into a lovely smile. "You are?"

I smiled back at her. "I am."

She took my hand, then resumed humming.

I'd brought a book but couldn't concentrate enough to read a single sentence. I checked my phone instead. Jonah had texted: *How's it going?* He knew I was in the building. I wrote back, *Waiting.* My phone buzzed: *Dinner tomorrow night?* I smiled. *Sure.* It buzzed again. *I'll pick you up at 7. Wear walking shoes.* Thank God I had something to look forward to.

"Mrs. Keene?"

Mom didn't react. I looked up at the receptionist, who was smiling.

"The doctor is ready for you."

"Come on, Mom." I stood and held my hand out to her. She took it, pulling on my arm as she heaved her small frame out of the chair. Her hand was frail as paper encasing brittle bone.

"Laura?"

"Mom?" I turned, hope leaping in my chest.

Her eyes were focused and bright. "You're beautiful," she said.

Tears pricked my eyes. "Thanks, Mom," I said. I don't think Mom had told me I was beautiful even on my wedding day. It had been Bill who'd said it, tears welling in his eyes, as I walked carefully up the steps into the church vestibule to take his arm.

"Keep taking care of them," she said.

"Of whom, Mom?" Mom rarely remembered my name since her fall; she never remembered my profession.

Her eyes slid away.

"Mom. Take care of whom?" I wanted her to validate the choices I'd made. I was tired. Tired of caring so deeply.

"The children," she said.

My heart fell. Unreasonably. I couldn't bank on the fact that anything she started to say would stick around long enough for her to finish the thought.

Dr. Pindar stood as we were ushered into his office. The desk and bookcases were mahogany, gleaming in the sunlight pouring through the windows. The chairs were leather with brass studs and heavy wooden arms. *This is the kind of office Robert should have*, I thought suddenly, and the vehemence of the thought surprised me.

"How are you doing, Mrs. Keene?"

I leaned forward. "She's been doing okay," I began.

Dr. Pindar held up his hand. "Laura," he said, and I was surprised he remembered my name, "I'm very interested in your take on how your mother is doing. But let me see if she'll talk to me first, okay?" His lilting accent and gentle tone were meant to remove the sting from his words, but I still felt chastened. Of course he wants to talk to her. You should have known that.

Dr. Pindar smiled at me and turned back to Mom. "Katherine?"

She smiled. "Yes?"

"How are you feeling?"

She nodded. "Yes."

God, why had I tried to jump in? I would never have done that three weeks ago. It helped to take myself out of the role of Mom's daughter and see the situation as I would professionally. How would I reach a patient whose memory and mind were so inconsistent?

"How's Bill doing?"

"He's fine," Mom said.

I'd tap around her shell and see if I could get any kind of reaction.

Dr. Pindar leaned forward. "How's the new home aide working out for you?"

Mom's face darkened. "I hate her," she said.

There it is.

After her appointment I took Mom to lunch, gave Bill an update, and went home feeling secretly relieved to escape.

On Friday I got home from work and collapsed on the couch. I had planned on cleaning my apartment, but that wasn't going to happen. I should at least do laundry. I dragged myself up and put a load of whites in the washer. As I pulled down the bottle of fabric softener from the shelf in the hall closet, my gaze fell on a set of boxes next to it. I left the softener where it was and pulled the boxes down.

The top box was white, and I knew it contained wedding photos; I put it back. The other three boxes were brown and held every photograph I'd ever taken of which I was not horribly embarrassed. I carried them to the couch. The first box was filled with prints that had all been taken during college. Beautiful objects were in shadow. My friends posed with frozen smiles on their faces.

Senior year I'd taken a yearlong photo class with a

visiting professor from RISD: Lawrence Bigby, a Pulitzer Prize-winning photographer. We'd all called him Bigby. He had taught us that for a photograph to be beautiful, the subject of it didn't have to be objectively lovely—the light did. I opened the lid of the second box.

There was a beautiful collection from Christmas, senior year of college: close-ups of the Nativity scene outside Our Lady of the Sea, so carefully framed that the silent figurines appeared almost alive. A series from Christmas dinner that belonged in an issue of *Gourmet*: a fat, perfectly browned turkey and a luscious pink ham, green bean casserole with fried onions, homemade cranberry sauce in its antique china dish.

The photos of people appeared as they became drunker and more malleable subjects: Bill with his arm draped loosely around Mom's waist, face tilted upward in laughter; Izzy leaning toward Sam, her engagement ring sparkling on her left hand as she looked at him with smoldering, sex-now eyes; Robert whispering in Julia's ear in an unguarded moment of intimacy. That had been the first Christmas he'd brought her, and he'd proposed a few months later. None of us had liked her. I closed my eyes and remembered how alone I'd felt that Christmas: Everyone had someone; James had his drinking, a dark companion that hovered by his side at all times, even if he didn't have a beer in his hand; I had only my camera. So I'd used it as a way to be alone with my family at Christmas and still participate. And now the fruit of that lonely participation was evident: I had uncovered things in my family I never would have seen otherwise.

Bigby's gravelly voice came back to me now. "Laura," he'd said, "you are very good." His praise was so rare that my class had stared at me, open-mouthed. For the rest of that year he'd been harder on me than on anyone else, and I'd worked harder than the rest of them.

I put the photos next to me on the couch and took a deep breath. Discovering that I was a better photographer than I'd thought was like getting divorced and finding out that my world didn't end: Both were about locating strength inside myself that I hadn't known I possessed.

I didn't know what to do with that information, so I set about cataloging the photos by year. I was immersed in this task when there was a knock on the door.

Jonah was wearing jeans and leather flip-flops and a purple Phish T-shirt. He tried to peer over my shoulder. "Cleaning?"

"More like making a mess. Let me get my bag."

I brushed my hair, swiped my lips with gloss, slung my purse over a shoulder. "Ready."

Jonah was looking at the photos, then looked at me. "You could bring your camera, if you want."

I considered him for a moment. "You don't mind?" Ted had refused to go anywhere with me when I had my camera in tow.

"Nope."

I picked up my camera bag and followed him out the door, locking it behind me.

"You know," he said as he walked toward his car, "I read in a pop psych book that cleaning out closets is a sign that something in your life is changing."

I grinned. "That so?"

"Yep."

We climbed into Jonah's tiny, rusted Bug, which was surprisingly clean inside. Jonah shifted into first gear and roared off.

"Where are we going?"

"You'll see."

He tuned his phone to the Phish station on Pandora, sang along to every song.

We drove north toward Providence, the skyline razor-edged against the blue sky like cutouts in a popup book. He parked in a tiny gravel lot that made me glad his car was so old, and we got out and started walking. He reached for my hand. I could hear music.

"WaterFire?" I asked, and he nodded. I grinned. "I haven't been in years."

Providence was famous for WaterFire, an art installation of bonfires on the three rivers that crisscrossed the city.

"I thought we'd have dinner first," he said, "and then we can watch the fires being lit."

"Sounds good to me," I said.

He took me to a vegetarian restaurant, and we shared sweet potato and black bean burritos, a quinoa salad, and a pitcher of sangria.

The shadows lengthened as twilight approached. I could smell the wood smoke as the braziers were being lit. When we turned a corner, the river spread out before us, the twinkle of firelight playing on the surface of the water. "Wow," I sighed. "It's beautiful."

Jonah kissed me on the cheek. "It is."

Sunset painted the sky with streaks of purple and pink and the music swelled in volume, blaring from sets of speakers along the waterfront. We meandered, holding hands, pausing when I saw a good camera angle and stopped to frame a shot. I crouched beside Jonah sometimes, catching his profile lit by the bonfires, delighted with his willingness to let me shoot him. "I'm having fun," I said.

"I'm glad," he said.

We walked in silence for a little while.

"You seem lighter today," he said. "I mean your spirit . . . it seems lighter."

I considered this. "I feel lighter. I had this moment when I took my mom home after her doctor's appointment yesterday. I just realized, this is the way things are, you know? I can't change them. So I might as well do my best to enjoy the time I spend with her, even if it doesn't ever go the way I want it to. So I think that acceptance has helped a lot."

Jonah nodded. "That makes sense."

We walked along the river for a long time before turning back, the firelight flickering as far as we could see. In college I'd gone to camp in Scotland with Amber one summer, through her church. I'd been terrified to go. And on the last night we'd had a bonfire on the beach and I'd sat with my new friends, whom I felt I'd known forever. We'd laid back in the sand and looked at the stars, and anything had seemed possible. That was how I felt tonight.

When Jonah pulled up to my apartment, he turned to face me. "I had a great time," he said, the car still in idle.

"Me too," I said. "Not good enough of a time to come in, though?"

He sighed. "I have to work early," he said.

"I guess I have to be okay with that."

"Guess you do."

He kissed me, cradling my face in his hands. "Maybe I can spend the night next week sometime."

"I'd like that," I breathed.

So I went inside alone. I tried to remember the last time I'd wanted to have sex after a date and the man in question had gone home instead of coming inside. Never?

With my excess energy, I put away all my newly organized photos. I straightened the hall closet and Swiffered the kitchen floor.

I kicked off my jeans and got in bed, restless. I pictured Jonah's face, imagined his lips on my neck, as I slid my hand inside my underwear. The first stroke was enough to make me moan. Ted had always hated when I made a lot of noise during sex; he was afraid our neighbors would hear—through our walls, the side yard, and their walls. Now my next-door neighbors, Luis and Doug, probably *could* hear me—but I knew they'd be happy for my good fortune, so I let myself go. My fingers slid in and out and my breathing grew heavier. I felt my orgasm building in a crescendo of nerve endings tingling, and I moved a little faster, moaning. I came with a loud "*Yes!*" and whispered Jonah's name as pleasure washed over me, circling my wet fingers on the soft skin of my inner thigh.

I slept like a baby that night.

The next night Jonah called me at 7:30. "I have good news," he said.

"Oh yeah?"

"Yeah. My shift tomorrow got canceled."

"And why is that good news?" I said, but I couldn't keep the smile out of my voice.

"Because you can come over and I can cook a delicious dinner—and by cook, I mean order in from Bernardo's—and we can . . . spend some quality time together."

"Mmm," I said. "What if I already had plans?"

"Cancel them," Jonah said.

"Lucky for you, I didn't," I said. "I'll be over in a few minutes."

Jonah coughed. "Give me half an hour," he said.

"So you can get the other girl out of your apartment?"

Jonah sighed. "If you must know, since I work twelve-hour shifts, I leave all my dishes in the sink, drop my dirty scrubs on the floor, and don't take out the trash."

"I'll be there in half an hour," I said.

I picked up a bottle of tequila at the liquor store, then went next door to the A&P for grapefruit juice and frozen strawberries.

"What's this?" Jonah said when he answered the door and I came in with my purchases.

"Just my world-famous recipe for strawberry-grapefruit margaritas," I said. "I assumed you had lime juice."

"In the fridge," he said, kissing me and letting me inside.

"So why are you off tomorrow?" I asked, putting the bags down on the kitchen counter. "And where's your blender?"

"Under the sink," he said. "I already fulfilled my quota of weekend days, but someone else was short."

"You have a quota of weekend days?"

"Yep. Have to work a minimum of two weekend days a month."

"Yikes," I said, pouring a generous measure of tequila into the blender. I added a handful of frozen strawberries and some grapefruit and lime juice.

"You don't measure?" he asked.

"Nah."

"I would not have guessed that about you."

"Guessed what?"

"That you weren't a stringent recipe-follower."

I added some ice and pressed the "Blend" button, holding down the lid. "So, you think I'm just a boring follow-the-rules kind of girl, huh?" I said.

"Not boring," he said, coming up behind me and wrapping his arms around me.

I poured us each a margarita and we clinked glasses. "Cheers," I said. His face was very close to mine. Jonah lifted his glass to his lips and drank the entire thing in six long swallows.

"Long day?" I said.

"I wanted to get on to more important things," he said, pushing me back against the counter and kissing me.

"My margarita's melting," I said as his lips moved along my neck.

"I would drink it quickly if I were you," he said, his breath tickling my chest. He peeled the straps of my tank top and my bra down my shoulder and licked my nipple. I shivered. His tongue was cold.

I downed the margarita, and he picked me up and crushed me against the wall.

"Lucky you're wearing a skirt," he said, inserting a thumb in the leg of my underwear and drawing it down.

"Not luck," I said, staring into his eyes.

He crushed me against the wall again, undoing the button on his jeans, and I wrapped my legs around his waist and gasped as he thrust into me. "I like it when you make noise," he said, and I moaned again.

He carried me to the bedroom. "Isn't this better than going home alone like last night?" I whispered in his ear.

Afterward he got up and walked out of the room.

"Where are you going?" I said, my mouth cottony.

"Be right back," he said, and he appeared a minute later with one glass and the margarita pitcher. He poured it to the brim, then handed it to me. I took a long sip, handed it back to him, lay back on the bed.

"You changed your sheets," I said. I could smell fabric softener.

"In case I had a female guest," he said. "You make a strong margarita."

"That's the way I like them," I said, taking the glass back from him and finishing it.

He poured another. "Tell me something," he said. "Something real. Something I don't know about you."

"I was pregnant last year," I said, the words coming out before I could think them over.

Jonah stared at me.

"When things with Ted . . . unraveled, I left him and went to my mom and Bill's." Goosebumps rose on my arms; I rolled myself under the sheet. "And the next night I was taking a bath and there was blood in the water and . . ." I couldn't finish.

"Oh, honey," he said. He gathered me into his arms. "I'm so sorry."

"Sometimes I see her," I said into his chest. "She would have been four months old." I took the full glass from him and took several icy swallows. "Your turn."

"I'm adopted," he said. "I was born in Chicago," he said. "It was a closed adoption. I don't know anything about my birth parents."

I interlaced my fingers with his.

"My mom always wanted children, but she couldn't get pregnant. She said I was the light of her life. My dad left us when I was six. My mom said they had problems in their marriage. But I always thought it was because of me. I don't think he really wanted me."

We made love again, forgot about dinner until almost eleven, and it was so late we had to order Chinese food for delivery because we were both way too drunk to drive. We devoured sesame chicken and shrimp lo mein in bed, the sheets tangled around our legs, and fell asleep.

The morning light was an anvil behind each of my eyelids.

My mouth was slimy and tasted like something dead. I rolled out of Jonah's bed, opened his top bureau drawer, and slid a white T-shirt over my head. I went to the bathroom and drank some water from the sink faucet, swished and spat. My head weighed about twenty pounds.

I walked barefoot to the kitchen and poured a cup of coffee from the full pot. Thank God. There was a Post-It on the counter: *Went to get breakfast, 9:15.* I squinted at the clock: 9:30. My stomach rumbled. I hoped he was getting pancakes, my preferred hangover food.

My phone was dead, so I took it back to the bedroom

and connected it to Jonah's charger. I leaned back against the headboard and sipped my coffee, feeling the caffeine start to penetrate the pounding in my head. My phone buzzed with three voicemails. Really? Hardly anyone left me voicemails anymore. I clicked over and saw they were all from Bill, and my heart plummeted.

"*Shit.*" It was Sunday. I should have been at Mom and Bill's two hours ago. "God *dammit.*" I called Bill.

"Laura! Are you all right?" His voice was panicked, not angry, and that only made me feel worse.

"I'm so sorry," I said.

"Where are you? I went to your apartment, but your car wasn't there. I was afraid something happened."

"I'm at Jonah's," I said, a little defensively.

There was silence on the phone.

"I'm so sorry," I said again. "I—Jonah had off unexpectedly, and my phone died so my alarm didn't go off—"

"I have to go," Bill said, his voice distant.

"Can I come now?"

"The guys left to go fishing hours ago, and if we don't leave now we'll be late for church," he said, and hung up.

Bill had never hung up on me before. He had never been angry at me before. I took deep breaths, trying to calm down, but I could feel my face going all red and blotchy. I got up and splashed cold water on my face, but I couldn't meet my own eyes in the mirror.

There was a rattle of key in lock and Jonah came into the apartment. "I got pancakes," he called.

Chapter 10

James

On Sunday I get to Lazy Joe's around 12:30. I haven't been here in a few days. Gerry slides me a beer. Dean comes in a few minutes later. We're just getting a little pick-me-up before we leave. We're driving to Boston to see the Red Sox play the Mets.

"Hey, man," Dean says, staring out the plate glass window. "Isn't that your sister?"

I scramble to my feet and see Laura walking toward the bar. She looks like hell. Shit. *Mom died.* I fumble for my cell, see a missed call from Bill, and my guts freeze over.

I walk toward the door as she walks through it. Her hair is in a ratty ponytail and she's still wearing her sunglasses even in the dimness of the bar.

"Hi," she says.

"Is it Mom?"

"No," she says, her voice hoarse.

I squint; my sister is hungover, and I'm confused. I guide her to the stool next to mine. "You want a beer?"

She turns her head toward Gerry. "Club soda, please."

"Laura, what's up? You drink too much last night?" Dean's voice is overly loud.

"Dean, go have a smoke," I say.

"I'm good," he says.

I turn and glare at him. "Go have a smoke."

Mercifully, he turns and walks outside.

Gerry sets a glass in front of Laura, who pokes the straw at an ice cube a couple times, watching it bob up and down. She pushes her sunglasses on top of her head. I have never seen her like this. I'm a little scared.

"I did something," she says. "Something stupid."

"Okay," I say.

She doesn't look at me. "I thought you might . . . understand."

"Whatever it is, I'm sure it's not that bad," I say. I mean, seriously. What could *Laura* possibly have done?

"I was supposed to stay with Mom this morning while Bill went fishing."

"Okay." I try not to draw out the word in a *that's it?* sort of way.

"I went to Jonah's last night, and we drank a lot, and my phone died—"

"Who's Jonah?"

Laura stares at the bar. "Oh, God."

"What? Just tell me."

She picks up the glass and presses it to her forehead. "He was Mom's nurse when she was in the hospital."

I strain my memory. Mom had a male nurse? I didn't notice. "Oh. Well, whatever. I'm not Robert. I don't care who you date."

"I didn't even remember until two hours after I was supposed to be there."

This still sounds like no big deal to me, but I can feel my sister's pain as sharply as if it were my own. I signal to Gerry for another beer.

"Bill's really mad at me," she says, her voice breaking.

I put my hand on top of hers where it's resting limply on the bar.

"I just—I don't want to be near Mom," she says. "I know that makes me a terrible person. I took her to see the doctor the other day . . . and it was just so *hard*."

"I know."

"No," she says. "You don't know. Mom *loves* you. She's always calling you honey and making you a plate of food when you show up at their house still drunk on Sunday morning. But she doesn't *talk* to me. I go over there for brunch every goddamn weekend, and it's like she won't talk to me. I don't get it. She's my mother. Bill and I aren't even related, and I feel so much closer to him. It doesn't make any sense to me."

I don't meet her eyes, because she's getting close to something, and maybe I should just tell her. But instead I say, "Laura. Of course Mom loves you. Don't be crazy."

She shakes her head. "I know. Of course she does." But she doesn't meet my eyes. She lifts her hand from under mine and props up her forehead. "What do I do now?"

I sigh. "You give it a few days. Then you go over there and apologize."

"I feel like I'm going to vomit."

I inch my stool away from hers a little.

Laura smiles weakly. She finally takes a sip of her club soda and her face puckers.

I inch back a little more.

Laura fishes the lime wedge out of her drink and puts it on the thin napkin, where it bleeds a circle of wetness across the thin paper layers. "I made margaritas last night."

I laugh before I can help myself. "Everything makes so much more sense now," I say. "God, your margaritas are strong."

She closes her eyes. "I know."

"And they generally instigate some good sex."

She smiles, her eyes still closed. "I know."

I'm surprised; I had thought her eyes would fly open and she would swat me on the arm and blush. The knowing smile on her lips is a little TMI for me. "You want to go to the diner, get some lunch?"

She shakes her head. "No, I should go home and take a nap." She stands up. "Thanks for . . . you know."

"Yeah, no problem."

She hugs me then looks out the window, where Dean is smoking what must be his third or fourth cigarette and talking to a blonde chick wearing only a bikini.

"I'll walk you to your car," I say.

The relief on her face makes me laugh again. I walk her to the old Caddy; she kisses me goodbye and I feel full of an emotion I don't understand. No one has ever come to me for help before.

On the way to the game, Dean and I stop at the liquor store and fill our flasks with cheap vodka. My flask fits easily into my cargo pocket. I take a few swigs out of the bottle in the car as Dean parks in the cheapest lot. It takes us about fifteen minutes to walk to the stadium.

Fenway is a mass of red and white. We walk all the way

around the stadium to the bleachers in the outfield, where Tier 5 seats are only twenty dollars. We prefer to spend our money on beer. Still, we're so segregated from the rest of the crowd that it's a little funny. Like we're in a different social class.

On the way to our seats, we each buy a hot dog and two beers. They don't send the beer vendors through our section, though we can see them, like yellow-shirted bees, swarming in the lower sections across the field, where tickets go for up to 175 dollars for the privilege of sitting close enough to the players that you can see them spit without looking at a TV monitor.

The game starts slow as usual. I never get real interested until inning five or six, when the exuberance of the alcohol begins to take over. Dean and I swig from our flasks, chasing the cheap vodka with Bud Light. One game last year they ran out of Bud Light and we had to drink Bud Light Lime. Nightmare. It tastes like it was flavored with air freshener.

Our fellow bleacher sitters are mostly families, church groups, and Scout troops. They clap politely when the Red Sox make a good play and don't boo when the Mets score. Boring. But I catch sight of two cute girls sitting three rows ahead of us and one section to the right. They're both wearing tiny jean cutoff shorts with mesh crop tops that show tan, toned abs punctuated with dangling belly rings. They're standing, facing toward us, talking to two guys in the row behind them. All four of them are wearing Mets paraphernalia. I nudge Dean in the ribs and nod toward the girls.

He sighs. "Mets fans," he says.

"You can't have everything in life."

On our next trip to the concession stand I buy two Bud Lights for myself and two Bud Light Limes. I snag a ten-year-old and give him five dollars to carry the Limes down to the girls. He does it, gesturing toward us when the girls take the beers. They turn and Dean and I hold our own beers up to toast to them. The blonde nudges her friend and smiles. The brunette shouts, "Red Sox suck!"

Dean tenses a little next to me, but I kick him in the ankle. "You can't have everything in life," I say. "Not every chick you meet at a baseball game is going to root for the Sox." I drain my beer, feeling philosophical.

That lasts until the girls finish their beers and don't even come up to say hi to us. I mean, how rude is that? A guy buys you a beer, doesn't that at least obligate you to talk to him? I mean, what the fuck, are manners totally dead?

The Mets score twice, and the girls and their guy friends cheer obnoxiously.

My phone rings and it's Robert. I pick up, even though a distant voice in my head warns against it. "Hey."

"Hey. Have you heard from Laura today? She's not answering her phone, and I wanted to make sure she's okay."

"She's fine."

"How do you know? Did you talk to her?"

"Why the fuck would I say she was fine if I hadn't talked to her? You think I just make shit up?"

A guy sitting in front of me with his two daughters turns and glares at me.

There's a short silence. "Where did you see her?"

"She stopped by to talk to me."

"At your apartment?" Robert's voice is incredulous.

"At the bar," I say grudgingly.

"Oh." The comprehension in his smug voice makes me want to hit someone. "Did she say what happened? Bill wouldn't tell me; he just called me back to say she was fine."

"She got drunk with her boyfriend last night and her phone died," I said. It occurs to me that Laura always covers for me, but it's too late to offer her the same courtesy. The words are out of my mouth and I can't take them back; now I feel bad, and it just adds to the low simmer of annoyance in my gut.

"I didn't know she was dating anyone."

"She's dating one of Mom's nurses." God, what is wrong with me? I bang my forehead against the heel of my hand. I need to get off the phone.

Silence again.

"You know, the male nurse," I clarify, in case Robert is getting weird ideas that divorce has turned our sister gay.

"I would have stayed with Mom this morning myself," Robert said, with the air of someone not wanting to deal with the information he's just been given, "but I'm on call, and I haven't slept in two days."

What the fuck—did Bill ask everyone else to stay with Mom this morning? No one's asked *me* to do anything.

Not that I would have wanted to do it, but they could have the decency to pretend I'm a member of the fucking family.

There's a roar as the Mets hitter cracks the ball straight toward us. "I gotta go," I say, and hang up. "Come on, get it!" I yell at Victorino. The tip of his outstretched glove catches the ball, which lurches, drops to the ground, and rolls away from him. "What the fuck is your problem, you idiot!" I yell.

Dean is shouting, "Lo-ser! Lo-ser! Lo-ser!" There are more glares coming our way now.

I collapse into my seat, take out my phone, scroll through Facebook. Anything to distract me from that horrible play.

Jeremiah's at the top of my feed. *Mets up 3–1 against the Red Sox! Go Mets!* captions a selfie of him and Rick, both wearing Mets caps. Below that there's a selfie of Jeremiah and Ava, their backs to the field. They're sitting right behind first base. Like, practically on the damn field. My whole body goes numb.

The Mets score another run; the girls turn around in unison, and each gives Dean and me the finger. "Yeah, fuck you very much!" I yell.

"Yo," the guy in front of me says. "Watch your language."

I lean forward, get in his face. "Excuse me? It's a free country. I'll use whatever fucking language I want."

The guy takes his two daughters by the hand and leads them out of the row.

"This game sucks," I say.

"What happened to 'You can't have everything in life,' dude? You were all zen like twenty minutes ago," Dean says.

"Nothing," I say resentfully. I refresh Jeremiah's page and see that he's tagged in one of Rick's posts. *Enjoying a day in Fenway with my favorite fellow sports fan, Jeremiah Perry.*

Dean gets up. "Want another couple beers?"

"Yeah. Thanks."

I'm watching the Mets girls shaking their asses to "Hey Ya" when movement to the left catches my attention. I see my seat neighbor standing in the aisle next to my row, pointing me out to two security guards. "Sir," one of them calls down the row. "Could you come with us, please?"

Naturally, I weave down the row in the opposite direction.

And slam straight into one of the guys my Mets ladies have been flirting with all game. "Hey, asshole, where you going?" he says, grabbing my arms.

"Dude, do *not* touch me," I say. He's got a good six inches and fifty pounds on me, but I'm scrappy. I twist my body against his hands, which are pinning my arms to my sides.

But his friend is there too. The security guards are scrambling across my row toward us.

"Get your hands off me!" I yell.

The shorter guy, the one who isn't holding me, has a huge mole on his chin. "I banged one of the girls already in the men's room," he says. "So quit sending them beer."

I wish he'd get a little closer so I could head-butt him. "You deserve each other," I said. "Mets guys are douches, and Mets girls are hos."

Mole guy hauls off and throws a punch, but I twist away from his friend with my mad ninja skills and duck. His arm swings around and he's off balance; I dart around him and slug him in the face.

I feel better immediately, like the poison that's been building in my bloodstream since I saw Jeremiah's Facebook post is leeching out of me with the impact of my fist on bony nose cartilage.

Mole Guy is screaming, blood pouring out of his nose, and the three of us are being hustled up the aisle by the security guards, everyone staring at us with horrified, titillated interest, like we're a live reality TV show. We are dragged past the concession stand and Dean grins at me goofily, holding up his almost-empty beer bottle in an admiring toast.

The wannabe cops go through the motions of asking us what happened, but they don't really care. They tell us they're ejecting us from the stadium, warn us that we could have been arrested for disorderly conduct. They drag us all toward Gate B. People look at me, past me; I'm not bothered, although my hand is starting to hurt like hell.

But then a face stands out in the crowd, staring at me: Jeremiah. I lock eyes with my son; I open my mouth to call his name, but he looks past me, turns around, and walks in the opposite direction. And all the air really does go out of my body, as if I really had been punched in the gut.

Out of the park, I go to Copperfield's to wait for Dean. My sneakers stick to the floor as soon as I walk in, the place smelling like sour beer. I get two Bud Lights and press the back of my aching knuckles to one, down the other.

I can't stop replaying Jeremiah's face: the recognition, the shame, the blank disregard.

PART II

Chapter 11

Laura

By Monday afternoon I was exhausted from trying to focus on my clients instead of obsessing over my failure. At 12:30 Colleen and Vince came into my office holding hands. That was new.

They sat down on the couch, their thighs touching. Vince looked at me, a challenge in his eyes that didn't match his relaxed posture. "Is it true you're divorced?" he said.

"Excuse me?" I said. I sat up straighter in my armchair.

"You heard me."

"My marital status is not really relevant in this context," I said slowly.

"You don't wear a ring," he said.

Colleen was staring at her lap, running her thumb along Vince's index finger.

"Why is this important to you?" I said.

"I bring my wife here, trying to convince her not to leave me, and our therapist is a woman who left her husband," he said. His face was twisted as if he'd smelled something rotten.

"Where is this coming from?" I said, looking at each of them. I willed myself to stay calm.

Colleen still wouldn't meet my eyes, but it was she who spoke. "We ran into our real estate agent last night at The Wharf," she said.

Ah.

"Ted Clark," Vince said, and for some reason in this context Amber's words from when she'd first met Ted echoed in my mind: *Never trust a guy with two first names.* "He asked how we were doing, we got to talking, we had a couple drinks."

"I left to go to the bathroom," Colleen said to the carpet.

"Ted was going on and on about what a great couple we were, asking if we were going to start a family, saying we'd be great parents," Vince said.

Of course he was. Ted had obviously sold them their

oceanfront condo, and couples in baby mode would need more space.

"And I cracked. I told him we were having problems, we were seeing a therapist, and he asked who. Then the whole story came out. He was very classy about it," Vince said, jutting his chin forward. "Didn't say a single bad thing about you. Said you were right to leave him. Said he'd made too many mistakes for you guys to start over. That you were a great therapist, and we were in good hands." Vince leaned forward, his eyes boring into mine. "So why didn't you tell us? Why didn't you tell us you were *biased*?"

I concentrated on controlling the heat threatening to suffuse my face. If I lost my temper, they'd never trust me again. If I undermined Ted, Vince would probably walk out. I cleared my throat. "I don't discuss my personal life during therapy," I said. Vince opened his mouth, but I held up a hand. "But I will make an exception for you, this one time, if it will help you to trust me."

Colleen glanced up at me from under her eyelashes.

"I value the therapeutic process too much to allow something someone said about me derail you," I said. "What do you want to know?"

"Why did you leave your husband?" Vince said, his voice aggressive. Colleen closed her eyes.

"Because he cheated on me," I said.

Vince deflated. "Oh."

"I'm not saying that every married couple in which a spouse cheats needs to get divorced," I said, working hard to keep my voice even. "But in our particular circumstances, it was not something we could move past."

Vince was turning a little red. "I'm sorry," he muttered to the carpet.

"Let's talk about you now," I said, sliding my feet out of my sandals and tucking them under me, feigning ease. "What changed this week?"

I got in the Caddy and started driving the opposite direction from home. I rolled all the windows down and blasted the radio. I was pissed at Vince Porter, but mostly I was pissed at Ted.

Half an hour later I U-turned to head back to my apartment. I needed a run: a hard, fast run. Too much adrenaline pumping in my veins.

I was driving down Second Street when I saw a sign for something called The Box. Under the name it proclaimed, "WE DON'T MAKE LIFE EASIER, WE JUST MAKE YOU TOUGHER." A pair of stenciled boxing gloves hung over the word "tougher."

I turned the Caddy into the unpaved parking lot, gravel flying as I braked hard. Two beefy guys came out of the cinderblock building, their T-shirts soaked with sweat.

I walked inside. The floor was concrete, the fluorescent lights buzzing and flickering over two empty boxing rings. A row of punching bags being pounded by young men lined the back wall, adjacent to a mirror flanked by shelves of dumbbells. The smell of body odor hung thick in the chalky air. The whole place was the complete opposite of the sterile gyms I hated, which were filled with tiny women running nowhere.

There was no front desk. I walked down the length of the room, spotting an office in the corner. A short, muscular woman with a long braid stood amidst stacks of paper and filing cabinets.

"Hi," I said, false bravado making my voice strong. "Do you have a beginner's class?"

She looked me up and down. "In twenty minutes," she said. "First class is free. We don't sell pink boxing gloves because this is not kickboxing."

"I sure as hell hope not," I said.

I changed into the sneakers and running clothes I kept in my trunk.

The class consisted of me and three college-age guys with Kate as our instructor. She started by teaching us how to wrap our hands. "Boxing is not just learning how to throw a punch," she said. "It's about discipline, strategy, and speed."

She led us through a warm-up and then began demonstrating the basic moves. Practicing step-drag and pivots, left jabs and right crosses, I felt the tension knotting up my shoulders, throat, and neck loosen and flow out of my bloodstream like poison being drawn from a wound. Sweat streamed into my eyes and I grinned like an idiot, even as my arms shook while I tried to eke out one more push-up.

I was exhausted. And being physically exhausted instead of mentally exhausted was a relief.

I called Bill a few times during the week, wanting to stop by. "Your mom's been a little . . . ornery," he said. "I'll let you know when it's a good time. I think for now we should skip brunch on Sunday." He was cordial, but our once-easy closeness was strained.

Jonah proved a more than willing distraction. He stayed at my place Saturday night after his third shift, conking out at eleven. But I was grateful, because his presence made the prospect of Sunday morning feel bearable.

When I woke up I brought two mugs of coffee and the paper into my room and got back in bed with Jonah. I gave him an overview of the incident with the Porters and my follow-up phone call with Ted, who had been apologetic. He'd actually made me laugh a few times on the phone. He always could make me laugh.

"How did you find out?" Jonah said. "That he was cheating on you?"

"I was vacuuming the den one afternoon, and I found a

diamond earring under the couch that wasn't mine."

The paper was strewn across our laps. He set his coffee mug down on the night table and looked at me. Jonah had a way of listening with his whole body. I could feel his attention like another presence in the room.

"I recognized the earring. We'd been to dinner at The Wharf a couple weeks before with some of his coworkers, and I remembered Chloe wearing them."

"What did you do?"

"I packed two suitcases, and when he got home I was sitting in the kitchen with the earring on the table in front of me. He started crying as soon as he saw it."

"I couldn't imagine cheating on you." He encased my hand with both of his. "Did he say why?"

"He was afraid of being a dad," I said.

Jonah kissed the side of my head.

I didn't tell him about my trip to The Box—I'd gone twice more that week, bought a one-month intro membership—and I had no idea why.

I guess I just wanted one thing that was only mine.

On Monday night, alone in my bed again, I woke to the shrill ring of my apartment phone. I stumbled out of bed in the dark. Mom was the only one who ever called this number; I had transferred it from my house after the divorce only because she had complained she'd never be able to memorize another one. I squinted at the green glowing numbers on the microwave as I passed it: 2:13 a.m. I snatched the phone out of its cradle. "Hello? Mom?"

"Please come," Mom said.

"Mom, are you okay?" I sprinted into my bedroom and dressed: jeans, bra, T-shirt, sweatshirt. "Are you hurt?" Silence. Then: "Please come. Please." Her voice broke and the line went dead.

I ran for the Caddy and made it to Mom's house in six minutes, a record.

Izzy had made me a copy of Mom's key when they'd had

the locks redone. I hadn't thought I needed one, since they hardly ever locked the doors except at night. "Don't be ridiculous, Laura, everyone needs a home key," she'd said, handing me a copy still attached to its white cardboard mounting with a black plastic tie.

I unlocked the side door and ran through the porch, through the dining room, up the stairs. "Mom?"

The only light in the whole house was a small pool coming from the left of the stairs: the master bathroom. The bed was empty. Mom was kneeling in her long white nightgown on the carpet next to the seam of bathroom tile. Her eyes were closed, and she was rocking back and forth. "Mom," I said, crouching down behind her. "Are you hurt?" She looked at me with blank eyes then swiveled her head to look forward. I followed her gaze and saw Bill lying on his side, the cherry bathroom rug bunched under him. A half-sob, half-scream strangled in my throat. I leaped toward him, rolled him onto his back. He wasn't breathing. I laced my fingers together and began chest compressions. I looked around frantically for the phone, saw it at Mom's knee. I stretched my leg out and managed to scoop it toward me with my foot, dialed 911.

"911, what is your emergency?"

"My stepfather—he's not breathing!"

"How long since he stopped breathing?" the woman asked, brisk and efficient.

"I don't know! My mother called me—I just got here—I'm doing CPR!" In graduate school we'd been taught to modulate our voices, to speak in measured tones, especially during moments of conflict or pressure. My voice broke out of its trained boundaries and skittered all over the register.

"Okay, ma'am, we're sending an ambulance. You stay calm. I'll stay on the line with you."

"Tell them I left the side door open," I said. "They should come upstairs. I can't—I can't leave him." I was out of breath as I pumped my interlocked hands again and again on Bill's chest.

Five minutes later a fist pounded on the screen door, the aluminum rattling in the door frame. My whole body convulsed, but I kept pumping until three EMTs appeared in the doorway behind me. I paced around the bedroom as they worked over

Bill's body, shaking out my wrists.

Two of the EMTs loaded Bill onto a stretcher and wheeled him from the room. His face was crumpled and gray.

"Ma'am," one of them said. "We're taking him to the hospital now."

"What hospital?"

"South County."

"Can you take him to Our Lady of Fatima?" It was always easier when Robert could pull strings.

The kid nodded. "Yeah, if you want us to. Will you be riding with us?"

"No," I said. "My mother . . . isn't well. But my brother is a surgeon at Fatima—I'll have him meet you there. Robert Keene."

He nodded again.

"I couldn't feel a heartbeat," I said.

"We'll keep working until we get him there," he said. "Does he have an insurance card or other information we should have?"

I rifled through the nightstand and, wonder of wonders, found a packet of papers that had a copy of Bill's insurance card and a complete medical history. I gave them to the EMT and he walked out of the room. I checked the clock: 2:45.

I sat down on the edge of Bill's side of the bed. Amazingly, Mom had fallen asleep. I took Bill's cell phone from the nightstand, where it was charging, and scrolled through to find Robert's number. I dialed it on the house phone.

"Hello," Robert said, his voice hoarse.

"Robert, it's Laura."

"What's wrong? Is it Mom?" He was immediately alert.

"No. It's Bill . . . Mom called me . . . he collapsed . . . they're taking him to Fatima now. I didn't want to leave Mom . . ." My voice trailed away.

"I'll go now. I'll call you when I know something." He hung up.

I went downstairs and made a pot of coffee, turned on the TV. I wasn't hopeful, or fearful. I was numb. At 3:32 the phone rang and I looked at the screen: Robert. "Hi."

"Hey, Laurlie."

I knew without him saying, knew from the heaviness in his voice.

"Bill's gone," Robert said.

I felt anger flare up in my gut. I hated when people said "gone" when they meant "dead." Or "passed away" instead of "died." Bill wasn't gone. He was dead, and there was a huge difference.

"He had a hemorrhagic stroke," Robert was saying. "A blood vessel burst in his brain. He was DOA. There was nothing you could have done."

"Right," I said quietly.

"Are you okay there for a while?" Robert asked. "Since I'm here I thought I'd do some paperwork, so I can come over there in a few hours."

"Sure," I said. "I'm fine. I'll be fine." I had never been less fine, but Robert coming over wouldn't do anything to change that.

I hung up. I knew what I had to do next. I had just never dreaded anything more in my life.

I walked upstairs slowly, went into Mom and Bill's room. Mom was snoring gently. I sat down on the bed and Mom woke up, her mother's instinct taking over. "What is it, sweetheart?"

My eyes welled. Mom never called me "sweetheart." "Bill died," I whispered, my voice thick.

Mom sat up, looking at the empty half of the bed.

"You found him in the bathroom," I said. "Remember? You called me. He had a stroke, Mom. He's dead."

Mom lay back down, staring at the ceiling. She fumbled around in the covers until she found my hand. "Why don't you try to get some sleep, sweetheart."

I couldn't imagine sleeping, but I went to my room and lay down on the narrow twin bed anyway. After a long time I fell into a doze. When I jerked awake it was 6:30, dawn creeping around the curtains with soft pink light. My neck and shoulders and wrists ached. I went to the kitchen and poured myself a cup of coffee from the pot I'd made hours ago, which tasted stale and burnt. I lifted the phone from the counter as if it weighed ten pounds and dialed Izzy's house, one of the only numbers I still knew by heart.

"Hellooo?" A giggle.

"Hi Ivy, it's Aunt Laura. Can you put your mom on, please?" My voice sounded normal, and that made it strange.

"Aunt Laura, why are you at Grandma's house?"

My throat tightened, and I cleared it a few times before I could speak. "Just a sleepover, sweetheart. Get your mom, okay? It's important." I stood at the sliding doors, staring out at the dunes.

There was a rustle and a clunk as Ivy set the phone down, then an earsplitting "MOM!" After an interminable minute, Izzy picked up one of the extensions.

"Hello?"

"Iz, it's me."

"Ivy, HANG UP THE PHONE!" Izzy yelled; I could hear the *iCarly* theme song playing through the other phone. Another rustle, a click.

"Laura, what's up?" I could hear my sister's distraction.

I had never done this before, never called someone I loved to tell them someone we both loved was dead. Right now, in her own sphere of the world that seemed light years away from my own, Izzy was going about the routine of a regular morning. All I wanted was one more normal morning, because it seemed to me now that I might never have a normal morning again.

"What is it?" Fear shrilled Izzy's voice. "Is it Mom?"

"No," I said. "She . . . she called me in the middle of the night, and she didn't say anything except 'please come,' and I came over—"

"What happened, honey?" Izzy had never spoken to me so gently.

"Bill," I said.

"He fell again getting out of bed?" Bill had broken his ankle two years ago. He'd claimed that he'd tripped over their ancient cat, who had since died, but Mom insisted he had just been clumsy.

"He's dead," I said.

Silence. "He's . . . dead?"

"Yes."

"Oh my God. What *happened*?"

"He had a stroke. I did CPR—I called the ambulance;

Robert met them at the hospital—but he was dead." My voice thickened on the word "dead."

"Honey," Izzy said. "I'm sure you did everything you could."

"I did. I really did."

"Okay. I have to . . . take the kids to camp. And then I'll be over. Okay? Did you talk to James? What about Eric?"

Shit. I had totally forgotten about Eric. Bill's son. "I'll call them." I forced the words out of the hollowness of my aching body.

"You need anything?"

I squeezed my eyes shut. They were dry and burning. "Can you stop by my apartment and pick up my cell phone?"

"Yes."

"I'll see you when you get here."

"Okay. Hey, Laur?"

"Yeah?" I was mentally prepping for my conversation with James.

"I love you."

"I love you too, Iz."

I dialed James. "I'm coming over," he said, his voice froggy with sleep. "Who's there?"

"No one. Well, Mom, obviously."

"Are you kidding? Izzy and Robert aren't there?"

"Izzy's dropping off the kids at camp. Robert met Bill at the hospital—he's coming over soon."

James was quiet. "What do you want for breakfast?"

"Breakfast?" I couldn't imagine eating.

"Never mind, I'll get a little of everything. Love you."

I called Kevin on his cell and told him I needed the week off. He was warm and understanding, and I couldn't get off the phone fast enough.

I poured more coffee, then walked through the living room into my father's old study. My mother still wrote Christmas cards and checks here at his antique cherry wood desk—or had, until recently. I sat down, déjà vu creeping up my spine. I was never allowed in this room as a child. My father's rotary phone still sat in the corner of the desk, unplugged. I used to sneak in and play with it, pretending I was his secretary, that he was still alive. "No, I'm sorry, Mr. Keene isn't in," I'd say politely through the mouthpiece to no one, then hang up and dial the numbers, waiting for each turn of the circle to rotate backward before moving to the next one. Bill would find me and drag me out to play in the yard, where my mother wouldn't scold me.

I opened the top right-hand drawer of the desk and pulled out my mother's leather-bound address book. I took a deep breath, turned to the "N's," and dialed the number for Bill's son, Eric.

He answered on the third ring; it was two hours earlier in Texas, and I'd woken him. I felt bad about that—strangely, worse than about the news I was delivering. I told him and he was silent for a long time. "Eric?"

"I'll fly up today," he said. "How's Aunt Katherine taking it?"

"I'm not sure," I said.

"Grief will do that to a person."

"Yes," I said, "and she has Alzheimer's."

"She does?" Eric was surprised. "I'm sorry." A heavy silence resonated through the phone line. "I have to go . . . book a flight. I'll text you the info. Were you going to meet with the funeral home today?"

"I guess," I said. I could barely think one minute into the future.

"I'd like to be there," he said. "If you make the meeting late in the afternoon, I can probably make it."

"I'll see what I can do," I said, feeling a surge of annoyance. Why should we go out of our way to accommodate Eric? It wasn't like he'd ever done anything for Bill.

I hung up the cordless phone with a shrill beep. I'd forgotten that Eric called Mom "Aunt Katherine." I remembered they'd tried the same with us—to call Bill "uncle"—and Izzy and Robert and James had refused. "He's not part of our family," Izzy had said. Mom had been upset, but Bill had hushed her. He told Izzy we could call him whatever we wanted. "Bill, then," she'd said decisively, and at that time, stepfathers were as uncommon as calling any adult by their first name. Once when he caught me as I fell from the monkey bars, I'd whispered, "Thanks, Dad," and his smile was so infectious that I'd laughed and said it louder:

"Thanks, Dad!" Izzy had heard me and her glare turned me to stone. She didn't say anything then, but that night when I was in bed she'd stood over me and said, "Bill is not our father. Don't you forget it. You had a real father, and now he's gone."

I wondered now if Bill had a copy of his will at the house. If he did, it would be in this room. I rummaged through the right-hand desk drawer. Under sheaves of papers, a checkbook, and a box of pens, I saw a packet of photographs caught under the bottom of the drawer. I lifted the wooden edge carefully and pulled it out. For some reason a strange foreboding rose in my chest, my fingertips thudding with the strength of my pulse. I opened the packet and took out the first photo. Bill and my mother at a party, their heads close together, the energy between them unmistakable. Their faces were young, unlined; the black-and-white photo made them both look like movie stars.

The screen door on the opposite side of the house opened with a whine then slammed shut. "Hey," James called, his deep voice carrying easily.

"Be right there," I called back, shoving the photo into the envelope with the others and tucking it carefully under the drawer detritus. I picked up the address book and went to the kitchen. James was unloading bags onto the table. He turned and hugged me tightly. Over his shoulder I could see an orange-and-pink Dunkin' Donuts box, a brown paper bag from Einstein Bagels, and a white plastic bag I recognized from the Short Stop. I tore into that one and pulled out a paper-wrapped sandwich. My mouth filled with saliva at the scent of bacon, egg, and cheese. James sat down and selected a cruller from the box of doughnuts, broke it in half, and dunked it in his coffee. "Laura, I've been meaning to tell you—"

I pulled the garish doughnut box toward me, picked out a Boston cream. Wasn't grief supposed to suppress the appetite? I took a deep breath, a big bite of doughnut. *Let yourself feel what you feel*, I coached myself.

"I'm sorry about that night I crashed with you."

My eyebrows lifted of their own accord. "Do you need something?"

He stared into his coffee cup. "No, I don't need anything. I mean it. I'm sorry."

I rubbed at my left temple. "Okay." I finished the doughnut, licked each finger, stared at the table.

A high, warbling voice sang from upstairs. "*Morning has broken, like the first morning, blackbird has spoken, like the first bird . . .*" Light footfalls on the stairs. Mom came into the kitchen, humming. "Did Bill go out and pick up breakfast?"

I looked at James. I couldn't do it again.

The kitchen door burst open. "I got bagels," Izzy said.

Chapter 12

Laura

Izzy drove Mom and me to the funeral home in her minivan. When we parked, Eric got out of a dark sedan with Florida plates.

Izzy looked at me. "I thought his flight didn't even land until three," she said, an accusing note in her voice. The only appointment we could get was at three, and we'd expected Eric to be late.

"That's what he said." Let the games begin.

Eric was taller than I remembered. He had dark hair, Bill's blue eyes and straight nose. He leaned down to hug me. I could feel his shoulder muscles through his flannel shirt. "I got on standby for a nonstop flight," he said.

"Great," I said, then mentally kicked myself. *Great*? Flying across the country because your dad died is never great.

I watched as Izzy kissed him stiffly, and Mom embraced him like he was her long-lost son. "Eric," she said.

I couldn't help rolling my eyes. She hadn't seen him in four years, and it was his name she remembered.

The funeral home was dark and cool, with a burgundy carpet and the heavy smell of overripe roses. A short blonde woman met the three of us in the lobby and shook hands with a subdued smile. "Laura, we spoke on the phone," she said. "I'm Jenna." In spite of my surroundings, I felt like I was meeting a friend. I was perversely glad I had a one-up on everyone else; Jenna knew my name. "And you must be Mrs. Keene," she said, shaking hands with Mom.

She turned to my sister. "Izzy?" she said.

My sister nodded mutely.

"And you are?" she said, turning to Eric.

"Eric Norman," he said, pumping her hand as if he'd just won something.

"Bill's son," she said, nodding. "In here, please. We're waiting for a few more?"

"Our brothers will be here soon," Izzy said. There was an awkward pause as we all registered that Izzy didn't include Eric under the heading of "brother."

James and Robert arrived, both doing a slight double take when they saw Eric. We seated ourselves in a semicircle at the round table—no one seemed to want to sit too close to Jenna—and I found myself in the center chair. Mom and Izzy sat to my right, Robert, James, and Eric to my left. A gold lamp perched on the corner of the desk behind Jenna, bathing her in a pool of warm light. A paperweight shaped like a bird sat in the corner of a bookshelf. I seemed only able to absorb tiny details, as if the part of my brain that tied everything together had stalled.

"I'm so sorry for your loss," Jenna said.

We all seemed to sag at her acknowledgment of our pain and confusion. Unspoken in the air was the surprise we all felt that we were sitting here with Mom, planning Bill's funeral, instead of sitting here with Bill, planning Mom's.

Jenna began to walk us through the details. We decided to hold visiting hours on Thursday and the funeral at Our Lady of the Sea on Friday morning. "Father Munroe can meet with you this evening to plan the Mass," she said. "And he'll ask if a family member will be giving a eulogy."

Eric's face was wide open with grief. My brothers and sister wore closed, poker-faced expressions, as if to say, *Let us show you how New Englanders do this.*

"I'd like to do the eulogy," Eric said, looking at me.

I had assumed that I would do the eulogy. Of the four of us, I was clearly the closest to him. I hadn't counted Eric at all.

"I thought Laura would do it," James said, an edge in his voice. "She was the favorite, anyway."

"It's okay," I said, even though it wasn't. "Eric is Bill's son."

I had lost the only father I'd ever known, but I didn't have the rights a daughter would have.

The conversation moved on. Eric chose a flower arrangement of white carnations in the shape of a cross, with a lurid swath of red roses across the front. Robert agreed to provide Jenna with details of Bill's life for the obituary. Izzy volunteered to create photo boards.

"Do you know whether Bill wanted to be cremated or buried?" Jenna asked.

For some reason, everyone looked at me. I started to stammer, as if I were in high school trying to answer a math problem.

"Bill and I have a plot together at Holy Sepulcher," Mom said.

There was an intense silence.

"No," Izzy said, patting Mom's knee. "Mom, you're being buried with Dad."

Mom shook her head resolutely. "Bill and I have a plot together," she repeated.

"I can actually double-check right here," Jenna said, her French-manicured fingers tapping on her laptop. "I have access to the cemetery's internal site."

She tapped again, then chewed on her lip. "This is showing that Mrs. Keene actually has purchased two plots, one with Robert Keene and one with William Norman."

"Right," Mom said. "And I'm being buried with Bill."

"Mom," Izzy hissed. "You don't know what you're—"

"She's being buried with our *father*," Robert said to Jenna.

"If Aunt Katherine says—" Eric began.

"Do us a favor," James said, "and stay the fuck out of it."

I leaned over to Mom. "Buried with Bill?" I said.

She nodded.

I made eye contact with Jenna and nodded too. Jenna bobbed her head, made a note, and slid a binder of casket options across the table. Mom and I made the rest of the decisions in ten minutes while my siblings continued to argue among themselves.

Father Munroe came to the house that evening at five o'clock to plan the funeral.

We gathered in the kitchen. Sun streamed through the sliding glass doors, which opened onto the stone patio. Beyond that were the dunes.

We sat ourselves around the huge cherry kitchen table, which was scratched and dented with thirty years' worth of family dinners. After listening to my siblings argue about readings and hymns for half an hour, I wanted a run, a drink, and a bath—in that order.

"Hang on," Izzy said as Father Munroe left. "Robert got the will from Mr. Peterson."

Robert shifted uncomfortably in his seat. "Billy can come by tomorrow to walk through it with us," he said.

The rest of us called the family lawyer Mr. Peterson. Robert had played golf with him once at a fundraiser six years ago and still considered himself on a first-name basis.

"Don't be ridiculous," Izzy said. "Just tell us the highlights."

Her eagerness made me a little nauseous.

"Okay," he said, and sighed. He pulled a sheaf of papers out of his briefcase. "The worth of Bill's estate goes to Eric," Robert said, shifting in his seat.

"All of it?" James asked.

"Yes."

Awkward silence.

"What about the house?" Izzy said. "Or does it just stay with Mom until—"

"No," Robert said. "She signed it over to him two weeks ago."

"So we split it?"

"Not exactly," he said, pushing his glasses up the bridge of his nose. "The house has been entrusted to Laura."

Everyone looked at me.

"What does that mean?" I said.

"It means that . . ." Robert cleared his throat. "It means that Laura is the caretaker of the house."

"She *owns* it?" James said.

"That can't be right." Izzy snatched the will from Robert's hands.

"She owns it," Robert said. "Now . . . if she decides to sell, we would split the money evenly among the four of us"—his gesture left Eric out—"with a fifth equal portion for Mom's housing arrangement."

I owned . . . the *house*?

"We should put it on the market right away," Izzy said. "Real estate has been recovering, and you never know what can happen in this economy—"

"Izzy, get real. This is *oceanfront property*. Its value will only go up," James said.

"Well, I just think it would make everything cleaner," Izzy said, sniffing. "And then we can get Mom situated . . . somewhere."

Everyone looked guiltily at Mom, who was staring at the ceiling, humming.

I owned . . . the *house?*

"Well? Laura?" Izzy's voice was abrasive.

"No," I said.

"No, what?" Robert took off his glasses, pulled a square of silk from his pocket, and began to clean the lenses.

"No, I don't want to sell the house," I said. "At least not right away. But give me a goddamn minute to think."

"Laura," Izzy said urgently. "We could *really* use this money." Her face was fevered, needy.

The habit of doing whatever my sister wanted ran so deep that I very nearly said, "Yes, let's sell it." But I caught the words just in time, pushed them back inside. "I'm not going to make a decision now."

"This shouldn't be *your* decision!" she fumed. "This is insane. We're a family. It's a family decision."

I stood up. "Apparently not," I said.

Eric was smoking a cigarette on the patio. I hadn't even noticed him slip out.

He nodded toward the kitchen. "What's going on in there?"

I collapsed onto the low wall, the stone warm through my jeans. "Mom signed the house over to Bill a couple of weeks ago, and he left it to me. If I want to keep it."

Eric whistled. "Can't imagine that went over well."

I snorted. My throat burned from the cigarette smoke. "He left you all his money," I said.

Eric sat down next to me. "Damn," he said.

"What was it like?" I said. "Growing up without him?"

Eric lit another cigarette, the clink and spark of his

lighter the only sound in the muggy evening air. "I hardly knew him," he said, placing his lips around the filter of the cigarette and inhaling deeply. "Mom never liked when he came around, or he would've done it more often, maybe. She was mad. Had a jealous streak, especially when he married your mom. Wouldn't let him in the house. Wouldn't let him take me out even when he flew to Texas to see me. I loved her, you know? So I took her side. He didn't deserve that. He was always kind to me." Eric leaned an elbow on his knee and put his hand over his face.

I thought he was shielding his eyes from the sun until a tear dripped off the edge of his chin. I put my hand on his jean-clad knee. The smoke from the cigarette clutched in his fingers twined around us, and I didn't mind at all.

My siblings and Eric went home after a meal of lukewarm lasagna someone from church had dropped off. Everyone, including me, assumed I would stay with Mom again.

Mom and I watched the news, then reruns of *Friends*, and I helped her to bed.

I padded back downstairs in my bare feet, feeling a surge of energy: I was half-eager and half-terrified to look at the photos again.

The house settled in around me, large and empty without Bill. I'd forgotten how few of the windows had curtains or blinds; my mother preferred the bare glass, and the darkness outside seemed to suck the light from every room. The office loomed before me, a still-dark cave, fear and anticipation thrumming through my veins. I sat down again at my father's desk. James wasn't going to interrupt me this time.

I pulled out the stack of photos and studied Mom's and Bill's faces, alight with love. My grief, which felt too big for my body, was suddenly superseded by a wave of irrational jealousy. I was jealous of Mom and Bill's marriage. They'd made their vows and kept them. Mom would mourn, a mourning fractured by her memory loss, but she could find peace knowing that Bill had died loving her. I mourned my marriage, while Ted went around in the world sleeping with other women and ruining my reputation with my clients. It wasn't fair.

I flipped over the photograph. *For you to remember our night, darling,* was scrawled on the back, and a date: *December 3, 1980.* My brain did the math without my consent: seven years before my father's death. Three years before Bill and my mother supposedly met at a neighbor's party and became friends. Eight and a half months before my birthday.

I shuffled through the rest of the photos, anger building in my heart. They seemed innocuous: a beach covered in snow, the facade of the Denmark Hotel, a young man playing a Steinway piano. But set against the photo of my mother and my stepfather dated seven years before my father died, they seemed to tell a story that I could barely imagine, a story that had been hidden from all of us—a story that was in danger of being lost entirely.

That was what I'd seen, looking at the photo this morning. In Bill's younger face, his straight nose and wide-set eyes had looked familiar in a different way. Like mine.

He'd left me the house.

And the knowledge I'd been trying to suppress under a tidal wave of sadness and confusion and anger burst forward: Bill was my father.

I stood and picked up the antique phone and threw it as hard as I could. It crashed through drywall and landed between the struts, shiny gold wallpaper hanging limply around it. "GODDAMN IT!" I screamed so loudly that I felt flesh tear in my throat.

I fell to my knees and screamed again, this time a wordless cry of anger.

It wasn't fair that Bill had died, leaving me alone with my mother. It wasn't fair that I had never been able to call him Dad. It wasn't fair that he had died while still angry at me.

I lay there on the floor, curled into a ball, for a long time.

Finally I seemed to wake to myself as if from a nightmare, though I hadn't been sleeping. It was still dark out, the whole first floor still blazing with all the lights I'd turned on. I sat up slowly.

Mom was standing in her nightgown in the living room, looking out the bay window.

My sinuses were congested, and my whole face throbbed as I took a deep breath. I picked up the photo of her and Bill, staring at their faces. My mother was wearing a cocktail dress with a huge flower appliqué on the shoulder; Bill was wearing a pinstriped suit. A chandelier and a Christmas tree sparkled in the background. I felt both joy and revulsion at their obvious happiness. I picked up the picture gently, irrationally afraid of smudging it, and walked toward my mother.

"Mom," I said.

She turned, unsurprised, as if she'd been waiting for me. The window reflected our image back to us against the dark outside. I wished there was a curtain I could close so no one could see us. I felt exposed.

I held the picture out to her.

"The night we met," she said, laughing a tinkly laugh that wasn't my mother's at all. She took the photo from me, cradling it in her hands. "He looked so good that night. It was the Jenkins's holiday cocktail party."

So that part of the story had been true.

"Izzy had the flu and Robert had caught it from her, so he offered to stay home with the kids." She laughed again. "And that was unheard of! It was the first time he'd ever been home alone with the three of them. James was just a baby."

I felt like I might throw up again, but I couldn't move.

"Bill was visiting from Texas, came with his sister. He had a son and he wasn't married, and they weren't so open-minded about it all in the South. He wanted to start over somewhere new, so he was scouting out whether he'd like it here. But he didn't tell anyone that." My mother looked at the photo again and smiled lasciviously. "The moment we saw each other we knew. Just the sight of his face did something to my nether regions." She giggled. "And when he got his hands under my pantyhose, my Lord! I hadn't known I could feel so much. I never even knew what an orgasm *was*! Up until that point, at least."

My face flushed and my stomach contracted. I talked to my patients about sex all the time, but hearing my mother talk about orgasms felt worse than sixth-grade Sex Ed with Sister Agatha.

Instead I took the photo back from her, stuck it back in

its flimsy paper envelope. I strode through the dining room and the kitchen and threw open the sliding door. I paced the porch, the humid air like a wet washcloth held over my nose and mouth, choking me.

I'd often wished Bill was my real father. But having my wish come true on the day he died felt cruel.

And under the grief crept another emotion: anger.

Why hadn't they told me?

Chapter 13

James

I can't believe Bill's dead. I wasn't expecting this shit.

I feel good about myself in one way—I was the first one to show up for my sister yesterday. And Mom, not that she notices this crap anymore. But my family's always kept score, and I'm one up. For once.

I'm crawling out of my skin after the funeral planning meeting, so I leave the house. In the truck I call Ava.

"Hey, James, can I call you back?"

"Um," I say, my voice croaky. "It's kind of important."

A small sigh. "Okay. What's up?"

"Bill died," I say, unable to do any preamble.

"*What?*" Her shock is palpable. "What happened? Oh my God. I'm so sorry."

"He had a stroke. Early Tuesday morning."

"Your poor mother. How is she holding up?"

Right. Because I haven't told her that Mom is sick. "Not too good," I say. "I sort of didn't tell you she was in the hospital a couple weeks ago. She has Alzheimer's."

I expect her to be angry at me for not telling her sooner. "What a hard time for your family," she says instead. "When's the funeral?"

"It's on Friday at ten. Do you think Jeremiah could come?"

"I'll take him out of school," she says. "I can come to the Mass, but then I have to get to work. Can you bring him home?"

"Of course," I say. She hardly ever lets me bring him home since they moved in with Rick. I think she's worried that one time I'll get out of the truck and pound Rick into the pavement. I won't say I haven't fantasized about it.

"Okay. Well, I'll see you Friday. Let me know if I can do anything."

"Yeah," I say.

Being in my head is so monotonous. I drive to Lazy Joe's and order a double whiskey and a pint of beer. I lift the glass of whiskey and breathe in the fumes. I throw the glass back and gulp it down. I set the glass down and pick up my pint, drink it in six long, delicious swallows.

Your stepdad is dead, the one guy who challenged you to stop drinking, and all you can do is drink. You're a loser. You're never going to amount to anything. You're going to drink through your paychecks until you die, never be able to buy a house, never be able to retire. You probably won't live long enough to retire anyway. You're a drunk, and you're never going to be anything else.

I'm going to collapse from the weight of the voices.

I drink until I get thrown out. I sit on the curb for a while because I can't walk straight, and after some length of time, a few minutes, a few hours, I start walking home.

On Thursday afternoon the ring of my phone wakes me up. Izzy asks if I can pick up Mom for the funeral tomorrow.

"Can't the aide drive her? Isn't that what the aide is for?" I say. I have a headache and I'm nauseous, and I do not want to talk to my sister.

"We're paying the aide until eight a.m. You'll need to get to the house by eight. Mom should be showered and dressed and everything."

"And why can't we pay the aide for the whole day?"

"James! You're not even putting in any money, and the rest of us don't have unlimited funds. It makes no sense to pay for an aide when Mom will be with us all day. It's not like she needs constant medical care."

"I can kick in some money," I say, my voice sullen. I really can't afford it, but being in debt is better than being seen as an asshole by my siblings.

"Don't be stupid, of course you can't," Izzy says. "Just do this for me, okay?"

There's no refusing Izzy.

I get up and shower, then walk to Lazy Joe's to get my truck and drive to the liquor store to buy a pint of vodka. I get back in the truck and drive around aimlessly. I consider driving to Newport to see Ava; luckily I haven't started drinking yet, so

I'm smart enough to put this out of my mind. I go to the movies, the air-conditioning like balm on my sweaty face, the vodka secured in my back jeans pocket. I sit in the back and sip the vodka. I can't believe Bruce Willis is still doing action movies.

I think about going back to Lazy Joe's, don't want to be around people. I hit the Burger King drive-thru in Narragansett for a couple of Whoppers, drive next door, and pick up another pint of vodka.

I end up in the back parking lot of Our Lady of the Sea. There's a tiny chapel at the back of the building, very austere, where the Eucharist is on display for adoration twenty-four hours a day. It's nearing nine o'clock, and the chapel is empty. There are no candles, so the lights are dim, illuminating three wooden pews, a simple stone altar, the monstrance made of dark clay. I come here sometimes, against my will, it seems, because it's quiet enough for me to think. I don't mean the external quiet. Something about this room makes the clamor inside my head quieter. My friend Brad bragged once about losing his virginity in here when we were in ninth grade, and I punched him in the face. What an idiot.

I sit in the third pew, close my eyes. I left the vodka in the truck.

I never liked Bill much. He would never mind his own business, never let me be. It started when he married Mom. I was twelve, and suddenly he was coming to all my seventh-grade basketball games. I felt his eyes on me, challenging me to play harder. "Engage your work ethic, James. You have it in you, I know you do." I didn't like feeling pressured. I'd been content to be mediocre, because that's the kind of player I was, the kind of kid I was. I was a decent point guard. I made Cs and Bs in school. My teachers knew my dad had died, didn't push me. Mom was busy keeping us fed and clothed, paying the mortgage.

Bill pushed me, and I resented him for it. I was comfortable not being pushed.

I quit basketball after eighth grade.

I never liked Bill much, but I respected him. He bailed me out of jail twice without even telling Mom. I was at Rhode Island Community, barely passing my classes. But after the second time, he told me he would never help me again unless I quit drinking, and he never did. If it were up to him, I wouldn't even be allowed in the house. I know it. I'm probably the only thing Mom and Bill ever fought about.

But Mom always let me in, and Bill didn't give me the silent treatment like Izzy and Robert did. He always treated me civilly, but he didn't avoid the subject of alcohol around me, either.

I envied Brad's family growing up. He had no curfew. He was never punished for low grades or calls home from the principal about fighting in the schoolyard. Actually, he boasted that his parents told off Sister Agatha when she tried to call. Brad was even wilder than I was, started showing up to school drunk when he was twelve.

Brad killed himself our junior year of high school.

I close my eyes and lean back. The chapel is so small, I can rest my head against the concrete wall behind me.

It was a Tuesday morning when Father Mahoney, the principal, asked to see me and Fran and Leo in the office. I remember it was a Tuesday because the Patriots had beat the Steelers the night before and I wanted to lord it over Brad, whose dad was from Pittsburgh. I walk down the hall with a bounce in my step to show everyone sitting in class that I don't care.

I'm wondering what I'm supposed to have done wrong this time.

Father Mahoney is sitting behind his desk, his face stern as usual, but there's a twitch in his right eye that I've never seen before. "Gentlemen," he says, gesturing for us to sit in the three wooden chairs in front of him. We stand in front of our chairs until he sits down, then we sit.

He clears his throat, the skin around his Adam's apple squinching against the black-and-white collar. "Gentlemen," he says again. "I'm afraid I have some very bad news."

The three of us exchanged nervous glances. Father Mahoney's eye twitches again. "Brad O'Leary died last night."

We stared at him.

"He, ah . . . he hanged himself in his garage."

The Steelers lost, I thought improbably. *Did he seriously kill himself because the Steelers lost?*

"It seems that he had . . . an altercation with his father

earlier in the evening."

Then Father Mahoney told us to go back to class, that he would make an announcement to the school at lunchtime.

I went back to math class. I stared at my textbook. An image of Brad's purple face, eyes popping out, swam above the equations.

It didn't occur to me to cry. It didn't occur to me to walk out of school. I just checked out of my body.

I got paged to the office again at lunchtime, and Bill was waiting for me. His jaw was set and his eyes were glittering. He put his arm around me and walked me to his truck.

I leaned my head on the dashboard and cried—huge, wracking sobs that shook my entire body—his arm tight around my shoulders.

In the chapel I lean forward, rest my head on the back of the pew in front of me, open my eyes and find they're full of tears.

Chapter 14

Laura

I was helping Izzy clean Mom's house on Thursday morning when Amber arrived. She handed me and Izzy each a large iced vanilla latte and gave Mom a black coffee, mouthing "decaf" at me. Her own iced mocha was half drunk, the whipped cream melted into chocolate-stained clods.

"Let's sit outside," I said.

"You go," Izzy said, sucking down a third of her latte in three quick gulps. "I want to finish cleaning the windows." She was holding a squeegee that was dripping dirty water on the kitchen floor.

"Mom?" I said. "Want to sit on the patio with us?"

"You go ahead," Mom said vaguely. She was sitting at the table, an unopened book in front of her.

"How are you doing?" Amber said as we pulled the heavy iron chairs away from the table and sat down.

The metal was cool against my thighs, even though the sun was already hot and the air was thick with humidity. I closed my lips around the green straw and swallowed some cold, sweet coffee. I felt a little nauseous. "I don't know," I said. "I really don't know. I feel like I'm living someone else's life. It's totally surreal. Like, part of me is here helping Izzy clean. And part of me is trying to wrap my head around the fact that I'll never talk to Bill again. And part of me . . . is somewhere else." I pulled the silver heart charm on my necklace back and forth along its chain.

"I haven't seen you wear that necklace in a long time," Amber said.

"Bill gave it to me when I turned eighteen."

"I know." Of course she did. Amber had come to dinner with us on my eighteenth birthday, at a nice Italian restaurant on the beach that had since gone out of business. My hand closed around the silver heart. It was warm. Goosebumps rose on my arms despite the sun. "I let him down," I said, staring at the table. "He was mad at me when he died, and now it's too late for him to forgive me."

Amber dragged her chair closer to mine and put her arms around me. "I'm sorry," she said.

A rush of emotion washed over me. Gratitude: Amber didn't lie and say, "Of course he forgives you," because she couldn't know that. Grief: Bill was really gone. Fear: What would happen to Mom, to the house? I closed my eyes and took three deep breaths; the wave seemed to recede, leaving behind it the detritus of a viselike headache and a bone-deep exhaustion.

We sat in silence for a long time, Amber not feeling the need to fill it with words that would make her more comfortable. She simply sat with me while I took small sips of sweet coffee and stared at the wet rings the cup made on the wrought-iron table. After a while I said, "How are things with Brian?"

Amber smiled. "Really good," she said.

"Tell me."

"He took me to the Cape last weekend to meet his family," she said.

My eyebrows lifted. "Wow! This is starting to sound serious."

Amber's face was soft as she smiled into the middle distance. She wasn't smiling for my benefit. She was smiling because she couldn't stop herself. "It is serious."

"How did the weekend go?"

"It was really fun. His family is lovely. I mean, I'm sure they'll get on my nerves at some point, but they're really welcoming. We had a barbecue our first night there . . ."

I watched my friend's face become more and more animated, and I thought, *She's going to marry him*. I considered the thought, noting a faint trace of envy and a stronger wave of joy attached to it. But I was detached from both emotions, because there was no room in my body for anything but grief.

After lunch that afternoon, Mom and I sat at the kitchen table
while Izzy whirled in and out of the room, a dervish leaving not
chaos but order in her wake.

"Laur, run down to the basement and grab me that box
of glasses behind the bar, okay?" She left the kitchen without
waiting for an answer.

I hadn't been down the basement in years. I left the
kitchen and turned right into the dining room, seeing that she'd
already moved the chairs into other rooms and laid a tablecloth
on the long oak table for the buffet. I opened the door to the
basement slowly; it resisted sliding across the carpet. I flicked
on the yellow light and descended the wooden steps, footfalls
echoing.

The staircase was in the middle of the room, the air
cooling as I descended. I reached the bottom, staring at the
black-and-white-tiled floor expanding around me. The pool table
to my left was covered in a white drape like a cheap Halloween
ghost costume. I stood still, feeling a tingling in my fingers and
a chill in my spine from the cool air, breathing in stale cigarette
smoke from decades-ago parties. I walked behind the staircase,
where there was a bar that could serve both sides of the room.
I stepped behind it and squatted down to look for the box my
sister wanted.

When I was six I'd been playing behind this bar during
a party. I couldn't remember what the occasion was; it couldn't
have been Christmas, because Dad was still alive. I was wearing
a pink party dress and, having gotten kicked out of Izzy's room
where she was playing MASH with her friend Sheila, had sought
refuge down here. The basement had been empty when I'd come
down, but after a few minutes touching all the liquor bottles,
listening to the clinking sounds they made against each other,
I'd heard heavy footfalls down the wooden steps above my head.
Daddy was talking to someone.

"We're underwater on the house," he'd said, and I'd been
confused. Our house was definitely not underwater.

"You need a big win," the man said. His voice was unfamiliar.

"Put a nickel down for me on Saturday's race," Daddy said.

"I need the money up front," the man said.

"Dammit, Roy! You know I don't have it."

I shifted on the upended crate I'd been sitting on. There was a hush, then footsteps, and Daddy's face appeared over the bar. "Go back up to the party," he said to the man. "I'll bring you another scotch."

The man retreated upstairs and Daddy lunged toward me; he grabbed my upper arms and shook me. "Don't you ever tell anyone what you heard," he said, his breath hot in my face.

I never had.

He had died three months later.

James had offered to get Mom ready for the funeral. Or he'd been pressed into service by Izzy.

Robert had offered to pick up the aunts who didn't drive.

I had offered to drive the photo boards over to the church, even though Jenna had said one of her staff could do it. I wanted to be alone before I met my family at the funeral home to say goodbye to Bill.

Izzy hadn't offered anything. "It's hard enough to get my family ready to be anywhere at 9:30 in the morning," she'd said.

When I woke up alone in my apartment, I closed my eyes, feeling Jonah's weight on top of me. I wanted him with me and I didn't. I clutched the heart pendant on the necklace I'd taken to wearing even to bed.

I got up, put on my one black dress, drove to Our Lady of the Sea.

I parked in the back lot behind the old gym. The school building crouched low at the base of the main parking lot, huddling against the hill as if for warmth. The church loomed ahead, the 1970s triangular vestibule in sharp relief against the gaudy pink-and-purple sky. The facade was of stone inlaid with stained glass so dark I couldn't make out the patterns.

"I can't believe you're gone," I said to the humid air inside the Caddy.

I got out and pulled the photo boards from the trunk. When I reached the church, I pulled hard on a brass door and almost fell backward when it opened easily; the doors were lighter now that I was an adult. The vestibule floor was slippery, and my heels echoed on the marble.

I set up the three boards in the vestibule then climbed the three flagstone steps and opened the glass door into the sanctuary. A priest I didn't recognize was on the altar blessing the Eucharist. Fifteen or so worshipers were scattered in the front pews for the end of the eight o'clock Mass.

I walked slowly to the farthest corner of the church, which was shaped inside like a demented trapezoid. I tucked myself into the shadowy corner of the last pew and sat close to the white wall. I lay down on the polished wood, breathing in familiar scents of furniture polish and incense. I let my right arm hang down, grazing the cool linoleum.

When I was ten years old, the meanest girl in school had accused me of not having a father.

"I do too," I'd said, stamping my foot.

"Not a real father," Sally Rollins sneered. She loomed over me on the dusty hill of the playground, the battered climbing equipment hulking in the background.

I'd used the phrase with Marisa, a field day for her. "A real father," she'd said, her voice as neutral as the blank walls of her office. "What does that mean to you?"

Real meant belonging. A real father picked you up from ballet class, bought you a corsage for the father-daughter dance, and didn't get angry when you cried because he wouldn't let you camp on the beach all night with the older kids until you turned eleven.

Bill did all those things.

But there was some element of biology too, wasn't there? Part of that belonging was a physical tie, like being out with your dad and seeing your homeroom teacher and having her tell you on Monday how much you look like him, and you rolled your eyes but were secretly pleased.

Our family had never been the family I wanted. In college

I was homeless one Thanksgiving. Mom and Bill went to see Eric in Texas, Izzy was married and eating with Sam's family, Robert was on call, and James was in jail for assaulting a police officer.

My roommate found out the day before the holiday that I had nowhere to go. I'd feigned indifference, flipping through *Vogue* on the bottom bunk. Bridget's face had shut down briefly—with pity, I thought, and pity was useless to me—and she went out into the hall. I could hear her murmuring into her cell phone. When she came back, she tucked a strand of red hair behind her ear and said, "Pack up. You're coming home with me."

Home. I wanted to go home, was angry I couldn't, but any home was better than our matchbox dorm room.

Thanksgiving at the Ryans' was out of a movie: a big red-headed Irish Catholic family. Bridget was the youngest of six, and four of her siblings were married with a kid or two of their own. Dinner was chaos as the family laughed and pushed one another for a spot at the buffet table so covered with platters of food that the tablecloth was completely obscured.

No one fought.

My jealousy of Bridget's family ate me up inside. I loved being with them and also hated it, because it was a testament to everything I would never have.

The organ at the front of the church boomed. Grief flooded through me, so strongly I feared I would drown in it. With my right hand I gripped the edge of the pew, and with my left I gripped my right elbow, tight across my body, holding on to myself until the tide receded. And what was left in its place when the waves rolled back, exposing what was underneath, was something even uglier: self-pity. Bill had left me, and we hadn't made up from our fight. He had left me alone with my guilt.

My body vibrated in time with the organ. I'd lost two fathers now, and my mother was stealing away from me at a pace I couldn't fathom, to a place I couldn't follow.

Chapter 15

Laura

I didn't hear a word of Eric's eulogy. I sat in the pew next to
Robert, hands in my lap, feet planted on the shiny tile floor, as if
I were about to receive my first communion. The church around
me laughed and sighed and sniffled. Eric's face was by turns
animated, downcast, wet with tears. Not a single word he spoke
entered my ears.

I couldn't stop thinking that it should have been me up
there. It should have been me sharing Bill with the people who
loved him best. Eric had seen him twice a year. I had grown up
with him.

During communion I watched family, friends, and
strangers parade past me. No one looked at us except for Amber,
who gave me a huge smile. I smiled back.

The organist was already playing. My brothers, Eric,
and three of Bill's fishing buddies lifted the casket onto their
shoulders.

I walked behind Eric, my arm linked with Mom's.

Eric's fingertips on the wooden casket were square and
his nails broad. Like Bill's. Like mine.

I rode to the cemetery with Jonah. He cut ahead of the traffic by
swerving out the side driveway, then reached for my hand. "God,
your hands are freezing." He lifted my hand to his mouth, blew
on my knuckles with warm breath, cradling my hand to his lips
with his warm palm.

I laid my head back against the headrest, closed my eyes.
My heart was pounding.

"You look really pale."

In that moment I missed Ted acutely. Ted had known me
long enough to know that when I didn't want to talk, I wouldn't
talk, and no amount of cajoling could get me there. He would
know to let me be until I was ready. I craved our easy silence.

Jonah drove the rest of the way to the cemetery without

speaking. When we arrived, I got out of the car. He walked around and met me in front of it, grasped my shoulders. "We're new at this," he said, gesturing to the space between us. "I want to know how I can support you."

I looked to my right. The funeral line was arriving.

Jonah kissed my cheek and, unbidden, the thought came to me: *I'm falling in love with you.*

Loving Jonah felt like the last straw of emotion. It landed on me as devastating. I wasn't ready to love again. Loving hurt too much. I pulled away from him. I just wanted to be alone.

"Laura?"

I looked up at the sound of my name, spoken in a low female voice. The day before, without consulting any of my siblings, I'd dug out the phone number for Macy's sister and asked if she could sing at Bill's burial. I reached my right hand out to Dina, but she brushed past it and enveloped me in a hug, then went off by herself. The breeze carried snatches of her vocal warm-up back to me. I sat down on the grass and breathed in the scent of fresh dirt, and I realized in my bones that Bill was gone. He was dust. The sun was shining, glinting off the contraption that would lower the casket into the ground. A mountain of dirt covered with green carpet was piled next to the open grave, which was blocked off with thin elastic. In a sudden frenzy I stood up and yanked at the green tarp until the mound of dirt stood there as what it was: a mound of dirt, the dirt that would cover over my father's casket. The rounded toes of my black pumps were coated brown. I bunched the tarp up as small as I could make it and hid it behind a gravestone a few feet away. Then I sat back down by the yawning grave. My dress was wrinkled, and flecks of dirt glinted on the black material.

Jonah came and sat next to me on the grass. I didn't acknowledge him, didn't speak, and when he covered my hand with his own, I stood up and walked toward my family.

The mourners arrived and clustered around the grave, a flock of ravens. Dina took her place at the head of the grave. I felt a prick in my finger and looked down. I was holding a red rose and had squeezed too hard; a drop of blood welled on the pad of my index finger. I was standing between Izzy and Robert. Mom was on Izzy's other side. I couldn't seem to register any other faces, though I saw more than one person looking askance at Dina. Besides Amber, who my family had known for years, she was the only person of color in a sea of pasty white faces. Father Munroe nodded to her, and Dina opened her mouth and began to sing.

> I went back home, my home was lonesome
>
> Missed my father, he was gone.
>
> All my brothers, sisters crying,
>
> What a home so sad and lone.
>
> Will the circle be unbroken
>
> By and by, Lord, by and by?
>
> There's a better home a-waiting
>
> In the sky, Lord, in the sky . . .

Next to me, Izzy sniffled and grabbed my hand. I tried to remember the last time she had voluntarily held my hand. I must have been five or six, when she would help me cross the street.

I had absolutely no reaction to the song. No goose bumps. No tears. No sudden epiphany that Bill really had loved me, even if I'd let him down. No voice of Jesus whispering in my ear that all would be well.

I'd been prepared to deal with an onslaught of feeling. I was not prepared for the numbness that had settled onto my skin like being tarred and feathered. There was a barrier separating me from the outside world, and I had no idea how to start penetrating it.

The casket was lowered into the grave. We filed past and threw our roses on top of the shovelful of dirt someone must have ceremoniously scattered on it. Ashes to ashes, dust to dust. Or something.

I couldn't be with Jonah right now. I climbed into the back of the gray limo with Robert and the girls, James, Jeremiah, and Mom. Izzy had left the burial early with Sam to prepare the house for guests. As the limo pulled away, I saw Eric standing at the open grave, alone, his shoulders shaking.

I listened to my brothers talk. I watched Jeremiah playing *Angry Birds* on his phone. Mom was folding a music sheet from the funeral program like an accordion. I watched the creases form and reform. My mother and I were like those parallel folds—running adjacent to each other, never touching.

The familiar rooms of the house were full of people. I was accustomed to them being empty and quiet. I left my family at the door and went through the porch with my head down, nodding when people spoke to me, avoiding eye contact and conversation, until I reached the dining room where the food was laid out.

I couldn't remember the last time I'd eaten. The salty smell of cold cuts and the fresh, yeasty smell of bread turned my stomach. I poured coffee into a Styrofoam cup, pasted on a half smile, and slipped into the kitchen and out the sliding doors. The clouds threatened rain, and my cousin Mary was the only person outside, smoking a cigarette and arguing with someone on the phone. She waved and rolled her eyes at me as I slunk by, jealous. Smokers were lucky. They had a built-in excuse to hover on the fringes of any social gathering.

I saw Jonah's Bug inch down Edgewater, searching for parking. I walked quickly down the patio steps, up the familiar sandy path to the beach, dunes and sprigs of grass obscuring my view of the water until I rounded the corner. I slipped out of my pumps and hooked my fingers into the heels, squishing my toes in the warm sand. The wind was out of the northeast, the sea iron gray and choppy. Piles of gray clouds rolled above me. The beach was bleak and all but deserted. I walked a little ways, feeling the sea spray on my cheeks, then sat down Indian-style at the base of a dune, tucking my dress under my thighs. I drained my coffee, even though I didn't want it, and scooped sand into the cup so it wouldn't blow away.

I had been sitting there for a long time when I saw Ted walking toward me, barefoot in his suit, carrying a small paper bag. He sat down next to me, burying his feet in the sand next to mine. Of course he'd known where to find me. And he would've left his shoes at the top of the path. I'd always told him someone could just come along and take them, but he'd never listened. He passed me the paper bag.

"Congee," he said.

Tears welled, my throat tightened, and my nose filled with mucus. But the tears didn't fall. When I was pregnant and nauseous all day, congee was the only food I could eat. I pulled the plastic container out of the bag and peeled off the lid. The aroma of chicken and rice rose with the steam, and I breathed it in, filled with hunger, if one could be filled with something defined as a lack. I dug the plastic spoon out of the bag and began to eat the soup, which was salty and bland at the same time, exactly how I liked it. I ate every bite of it, lifting the container to my mouth to drain the last drops. I licked my lips, salty and oily, and took a deep breath. I put the empty container, soup spoon, and my coffee cup into the paper bag.

We sat and watched the sea rolling in and didn't talk, and it felt like nothing had changed. But everything had changed.

Finally Ted sat up a little straighter. "How have things been?"

I told him about Mom's diagnosis, about the late-night phone call. I told him about the photograph and the will. It was a relief—even more of a relief than I imagined crying would be, though my eyes still burned with unshed tears.

Ted shifted so that his right hand was a foot or so from his body, ostensibly to lean back. But I knew him, and I knew he was inviting me to sit closer. Against my better judgment, I scooted inside the crook of his arm. He wrapped it around me and his fingers traced the soft skin at the inside of my right elbow. He turned his face toward me and inhaled deeply, his nose in my hair. His exhalation tickled my ear and my pelvic muscles tightened. I was exhausted and let my body sink into his, releasing muscles I hadn't known were flexed.

"Let me take you home," he said.

Dimly, I knew I should go back into the house and find Jonah, help Izzy clean up, help put Mom to bed later. But I was drunk with exhaustion, and my apartment was empty and quiet.

"I don't want anyone to see," I said.

He bit his lip.

"I mean, see me leaving already," I amended, though I also didn't want anyone to see me getting in the car with him.

Ted smiled now, his ego soothed. "Walk down to Thirty-first," he said, gesturing with his chin down the beach. "I'll come pick you up."

I walked down the beach slowly, feeling lonely.

Ted picked me up at Thirty-first Street where it dead-ended into the dunes. I got into his navy BMW and closed the door. I closed my eyes and felt the buttery leather against my thighs, smelled the new-car smell that never seemed to fade and the cologne Ted had worn since I'd met him.

The last time I'd been in a car with Ted had been the week before I'd found Chloe's earring under the coffee table. We'd been to a wedding of one of his coworkers. Chloe, I remembered now, had been at that wedding. I wondered if it was before or after they'd had sex on the couch in our den.

I'd been bored at the wedding, drank more 7 and 7s than I'd meant to. On the way home I'd been insanely horny, blood zinging through my veins fizzy as soda. I'd loosened his tie during the drive, slipped it over his head and around my own neck, unbuttoned his dress shirt, unnotched and slipped off his belt. We'd made out from the car to the house like teenagers; he'd fucked me against the wall, on the coffee table, and then we'd both finished in bed, so spent and satisfied we fell asleep without showering.

"Laur?"

"Yeah."

"Where am I going?"

We weren't going home. He didn't even know where I lived. I'd withheld that information on purpose, and now I was giving him directions: Down to Main Street, hang a left; it's that little apartment complex off Ocean.

I had forgotten how quiet his car was. The only hint that we were moving was a slight flutter in my belly. Ten minutes later

I opened my eyes. We were outside my apartment. "Thanks,"
I said. I leaned over and kissed his cheek. His eyelash brushed
my nose. Desire thrummed through me. I swallowed. *Divorced,* I
reminded myself. *He cheated on you. And you are falling in love with
Jonah.*

But Ted slipped his hand around to cradle the back of
my neck and pressed his lips gently to mine, and my resistance,
already shaky, crumbled. I got out of the car and unlocked my
front door, led him into my bedroom and let him make love to
me. I wasn't so far gone in my grief or neediness not to recognize
how especially tender he was, nor to notice that he did all my
favorite things. I lay in his arms, naked under the covers, closed
my eyes, and tried my very best not to feel anything.

Chapter 16

James

I'm angry at everyone. The stupid limo driver who didn't even bring any booze. It's a fucking funeral, for Christ's sake. My hands are shaking. Izzy is being a bitch. Ava didn't want to leave Jeremiah with us for the afternoon, even though she'd already agreed. "I have a bad feeling," she'd said. Fuck her bad feeling. Everything's fine, except that Bill's dead.

I'm just pissed off. There's a bar at the house—Robert's idea. He might dress different, work different, but he's like me on the inside. He had no more desire to get through this day without a drink at the end of it than I did.

Jeremiah and I ride in the limo back to the house, where my crappy truck is parked behind Robert's Jaguar. I bolt for the side door of the house, grab a bottle of Johnny Walker Red when the bartender's not looking, pound upstairs to my old bedroom. I sit on the hard bed and take a long swallow. My hands don't stop shaking until the fourth or fifth swallow. Fortified, I tuck the bottle in the corner and go downstairs. There's a film between me and the world, a cotton cloud, a barrier invisible to everyone but me.

I pop a stick of gum into my mouth and make the rounds, freezing my face into a somber expression. I kiss old ladies (neighbors, friends of Mom's) and young women (friends of Izzy's and Laura's). I swipe a glass of wine off an end table in the living room, avoid the waxy lipstick smudge on one side of the rim, drain it.

I set the glass discreetly on the windowsill behind me. The living room is crowded with black-clad men and women, but I wouldn't call them mourners. What the fuck's a mourner anyway? It makes me think of sallow faces and gruel dinners. Celebrate life, I say. I head to the bar for a beer; it's been half an hour since the last drink I got from the bartender.

Ted comes over to me in his pinstripe suit. Dork. Laura's boyfriend is here somewhere too, the nurse. This must be real fun for him.

"Seen Laura?" he says, not bothering with a hello, as if we're still related.

"Nope." I have no desire to help him with anything.

He's still talking. The air is thick and stuffy. I nod a few times, drain my beer, the carbonation settling my stomach. Ted gives a jocular wave, and the impulse to slug him across the face rises up, my fist clenching. He's so fucking *happy*. He really is! He's happy Bill died, because it gives him a gateway to Laura that he's going to exploit.

I feel like I'm suffocating.

People start looking past me instead of at me a few drinks later. There's fear in their eyes. But they're just jealous, jealous that I'm finding oblivion.

Darkness falls. The crowd disperses. Mom must have been put to bed, because I haven't seen her in hours. Hope someone gave her a tranquilizer. Then again, her lack of memory just might serve that function on its own. I go upstairs to check on the bottle of Johnny Walker Red; it's gone. Someone must've swiped it. Bunch of savages in this town.

I find Jeremiah in the basement shooting pool with Jonah. I watch my son cuing up for a tricky diagonal shot, watch him drop the 13 into the side pocket, easy as dropping change into a bucket.

"Nice shot," Jonah says.

"Shouldn't you be with my sister?" I say.

"We can't find her," Jeremiah says. "Maybe she needed to be alone." He chews his bottom lip. "Aunt Laura was real close to Bill."

"Let's go, I'll take you home," I say to Jeremiah, careful to enunciate.

Jeremiah snorts.

"I told your mom I'd bring you home tonight. It's not my weekend."

My son looks me squarely in the eye. The anger there— almost menace—frightens me. "You're trashed, Dad. Like I'd get in the car with you. What do you think I am, stupid?" His eye roll makes him look so much like Ava that I want to cry. He drops another stupid ball into another stupid pocket. "Uncle Robert said he'd take me home."

Anger floods my body with heat. I can feel my face warming, my armpits sweating. I wheel around and stomp up the wooden stairs, search through all the rooms for my brother. I finally spot him coming in the side door. He sees me, avoids my eyes, his gaze flicking quickly past. I charge toward him. "You think I can't drive my own son home?"

"Easy, James." He steps back, his eyes darting right then left. He's cornered, knows it. "It's been a tough day. It's no big deal if you had one too many." He clears his throat, his chest puffing out slightly as his self-righteousness gains ground. He claps a hand to my shoulder. "I'll take Jeremiah home. You can sleep it off here. Izzy's staying with Mom. You can have our room, like—" He stops. He's about to say, "like always," knows it'll piss me off. He smiles the half-certain, half-superior smile I always get from him, sidesteps me, and leaves the kitchen.

I stand there, knowing what will happen next, watch it play out before my eyes exactly how I imagined. Robert must have called down the stairs to Jeremiah, because my son walks through my line of vision, framed by the kitchen doorway, through the dining room and into the porch. It's too loud for me to hear but I imagine the porch door shutting quietly—he doesn't want to say goodbye to me.

I slip out the kitchen's side door. The August night is heavy and humid.

Robert's Jag purrs to life and the lights flick on. He must have given Jeremiah the keys.

My truck has three huge white splashes of bird shit on the dash from the sprawling tree under which it's parked. The Jag, in front of it, doesn't have a spot on it, and suddenly my rage boils over. I fly down the short hill where we used to sled when we were very small, down the street to the corner. I throw open the driver's side door and slide into the Jag, the soft leather smell enveloping my senses.

"Dad, what the hell are you doing?" My son's face pales in the glow of the interior lights.

"Showing you how fine I am to drive." I put the car in gear and pull forward. Jeremiah struggles with the handle to open his door, but I step on the accelerator. Dimly I realize I've blown a few stop signs.

"Dad, c'mon, please . . . I'm sorry if I upset you . . . please just let's go back, we can talk about it—"

I'm having fun testing how smoothly the Jag pulls tight corners, the centrifugal force pinning me to the seat. I turn onto Route 1, play chicken with a UPS truck.

"Dad, come on; please take me back."

My eyelids are heavy now, so I spin a U-ey at the next light. But something's not right—the lights glowing through the windshield are white, not red; horns are blaring in a cacophony of sound, headlights bearing down on us from all sides as tires spin and grab for purchase on the pavement. But the sensation that cuts through all the others is my son's voice crying out in fear—"Dad!"—before a smashing of glass and a burst of pure energy that throws me against the door.

Chapter 17

Laura

The phone rang and woke me up, again, and my first thought was that Mom must be dead this time. *No,* I thought, still mostly asleep. *Not so soon.*

I untangled myself from Ted's body and fumbled for my cell. Thirty seconds later I was pulling on clothes, shaking Ted awake. He mumbled and rolled over. I turned on the overhead light.

"Ted! I need your keys."

He sat up, blinking, taking in my fear. "What's wrong?" He stood and put a leg through his suit pants.

"I don't need you to drive me; I just need your keys."

He pulled his keys from the pocket of his pants, cupped them in his fist. "What happened?"

"James was in a car accident. With Jeremiah." My worst nightmare.

"I'm driving," he said, and all I wanted was to get there. We made it to the hospital in eleven minutes, at 11:42. Ted pulled up to the ER; I opened the door before he'd stopped.

"Wait," he said. "I'm coming in."

I shut the door. "No."

The window rolled down. "Laura, come on."

I stopped, my voice breaking with frustration and fear. "Ted, please listen to me this one time and just go home." I turned and ran through the sliding doors. Goose bumps prickled on my arms as I walked under a blast of A/C and through the second set of doors. I headed for the stairs and jogged up three flights to pediatrics. Ava and Robert were sitting alone in the waiting room. It had been Robert who'd called. Ava's face looked like the air had been let out of it. My brother looked angry. My knees nearly buckled as I walked toward them. I lowered myself into a chair across from them. "How's Jeremiah?" I was afraid to ask what I wanted, which was, "How are *they*?"

Ava crossed her arms over her chest, the manicured nails of her right hand digging into the skin of her left bicep, and stared over my left shoulder. I turned to see what she was looking at. There was nothing there.

"They're running some tests, but he's going to be okay," Robert said, his voice flat.

I balled my hands into fists. I hadn't entertained the idea of Jeremiah *not* being okay.

"He has a broken femur, his right arm's broken in two places. Broken rib. They're doing a CT because he probably has a concussion."

I had to force myself to keep breathing, in through my nose, out through my mouth.

"Tell her why," Ava said.

Robert swallowed; I could see his Adam's apple bob. "James ran a red light and swerved into oncoming traffic, and a car struck them on the passenger side."

"I want to know where the fuck the two of you were when you let your brother get behind the wheel blackout drunk with my baby in the car." Ava's voice was low and mean.

Where was I? Fucking my ex-husband, naturally. Cocooned in my own pain.

"I was going to take Jeremiah home," Robert said.

"Didn't work so well, did it?" Ava said.

"He stole my car! I gave Jeremiah the keys to start it while I said goodbye to everyone; James got in the driver's side and took off."

Ava and I digested this for a moment. I was stunned. She looked one degree less angry.

"Coffee for everyone!"

The three of us looked up to see Ted walking toward us, wearing his white button-down shirt and suit pants, a Styrofoam tray of four coffee cups in his hand.

Ava and Robert turned to me in one motion, eyebrows raised.

I didn't wish I could disappear, exactly. I actually wished I had never been born—that Laura Keene had never been born and grown up to become such a colossal idiot as I felt like right then. I buried my face in my hands, not bothering to greet him.

Ted took no notice of his less-than-warm reception. He sat down next to me, offered a coffee to Robert (who took it and set it on the table next to him) and to Ava (who ignored him). He put the tray on the floor between us, slurped at his own cup with indecent pleasure. He stretched his arm behind me on the seat. I felt frozen in place with misery and anger. I'd brought at least this misery on myself. Ted had always been incorrigible, and I'd given him an inch. I could practically feel the smugness radiating from him, could practically see the daydreams of us getting back together flitting through his mind.

"Ava, where's Rick?" Ted asked.

I'd been afraid to broach that question, and here he was asking it straight off. The man had no subtlety. It was what made him such a successful real estate agent.

"Business trip." Her head was turned away from Robert, away from us, toward the hallway where the doctor would come when Jeremiah's tests were done.

Ted nodded. "Cool. Where?"

"Hong Kong."

Ted turned to me. "So how's James doing?" He grinned. "It had to catch up with him sometime, right?"

The air seems to deflate as the three of us, connected by our grief and anger, regarded the buffoon who had somehow wandered into our midst.

Robert sighed. "He has a concussion and a broken shoulder."

"That's it? Man, he got off easy this time."

Ava and Robert stood simultaneously.

"Laura." Robert jerked his head toward the nook by the elevators. I followed him. When Ted made to stand up as well, I fixed him with a glare that froze him to his chair. Ava went to the bathroom. Robert turned to me.

"Izzy?" I said.

"With Mom."

"Right." I closed my eyes.

"I'll spring for an aide for tomorrow and Sunday so you and I can get some rest."

"Thanks. I'll put in some money."

"Whatever." Robert punched the elevator down arrow. "Ted?"

"Stupidest fucking mistake I've ever made," I said, and

the venom in my voice surprised me. "What floor's James on?"

Robert shrugged.

"You haven't seen him?"

He turned his eyes to me, and I flinched at the anger in them. "I don't want to see him. I'm done. You should be too. Don't let him take advantage of you. Like he always does."

The elevator dinged and my brother got on the car. "And for God's sake, do something about Ted."

I went back into the waiting room and sat next to Ted, not because I wanted to but because I couldn't think of anything else to do. He passed me a cup of coffee, and I accepted it this time. I took three long sips—it was almost cold—and slouched down in my chair until I could rest my neck on the back of it. I nodded off for some length of time, and when I jerked awake my neck was stiff as concrete. I sat up, rubbing at it. Ted was watching *Judge Judy* and, without moving his eyes from the screen, reached over and began to massage the back of my neck with his left hand. It felt so good—the only necessary thing in that moment—that I closed my eyes in gratitude. When I opened them again, I noticed a figure standing in the hall to our left, diagonal from me, watching us.

Jonah was standing there staring at me, and I felt exactly the way I did the time James knocked me out of the dogwood tree in the backyard when I was eight; I fell on my back and the breath rushed out of me, and I couldn't seem to make my lungs inhale again. I brushed Ted's arm away and stood to go to Jonah. To his credit, he didn't walk away. He stared at Ted until I got close to him and then slid his eyes, not to meet mine but to stare past me, and said, "Who's hurt?"

"Jeremiah," I said. "James was driving."

Jonah's face flickered. "Is he going to be okay?"

"Yes," I said. "But it's pretty bad. What are you doing here?"

"Got called in. I'm sorry about Jeremiah. He's a good kid." His eyes flicked to the left again. "And him?"

I reached for his hand and he stepped back.

"He was with you when you got the call?"

My face was wooden.

Jonah crossed his arms. "I came to the funeral lunch, but

I couldn't find you anywhere. What did you do, take him upstairs to your room?"

I couldn't look away, although the pain in his eyes was unbearable to see.

"I was falling in love with you," he said, his voice quiet. "Thanks for saving me a lot of time, I guess."

My brain stalled. "Was?" I said.

Ted came up behind me.

Jonah looked from me to Ted. "Was," he said.

"Everything okay?" Ted said, slipping an arm around my waist.

I shook him off. "Go. Just go."

"How will you get home?" he asked, his voice carrying an undercurrent of lasciviousness.

"Just fine without you," I said.

His whole body slumped a little. "Well, call me tomorrow and let me know how everyone is."

Lying would have made the hideous moment end faster, but I couldn't do it. "I'm not going to call you."

Jonah was still standing in front of us. My shoulders twitched; I was practically writhing in my discomfort.

"What do you mean, you're not going to call me? I thought we were—"

"What, Ted? Getting back together? Picking up where we left off?"

Jonah spun on his heel and walked away. I chased after him, grabbed the sleeve of his blue scrubs. "Jonah, wait."

He stopped but did not turn toward me. I walked around his body until we were facing each other.

"You just said it yourself," he said. "You think we can just pick up where we left off?"

Mercifully, Ted was gone when I turned back to the waiting room. Ava came back and sat with me, her right elbow leaning on her knees, her right hand covering her face. After an interminable amount of time, a doctor approached. "Ms. Perry?" She stood up, her face pinched.

The doctor said some things I couldn't process, then led us toward Jeremiah's room.

Walking into that hospital room was the hardest thing

I'd ever done. My spirit was so raw. I had no strength left.

Jeremiah lay inert in the bed, his frame small against the white sheets. His right arm was in a cast from wrist to shoulder. His right leg was encased in a contraption of metal hoops and wires and suspended in traction. The right side of his face was bruised. And those were only the injuries I could see. Ava approached the bed, placed a hand on the rail, staring at her son's face.

She turned to look at me, and I held my arms out, but she put up a hand to stop me, covered her nose and mouth, shook her head. I was suddenly so nauseous I thought I might throw up.

"Tell him," Ava said, then stopped. "Tell him that if I ever see him again, I swear to God I'll kill him."

I believed her.

I went to the nurse's desk and gave her James's name. She gave me his room number, reminded me that visiting hours were long over. I told her I'd come back tomorrow, then took the elevator to the second floor.

James had the room to himself and occupied the far bed, staring out the window. His left arm was in a sling. His right wrist was handcuffed to the bed rail. A bruise bloomed on his left temple. It was 2:30 in the morning, but he turned to look at me. His eyes were lost and scared. "No one will tell me how he is," he said.

I sat down. I pulled up the camera roll on my phone, and showed him the picture I'd taken of Jeremiah's face: his right eye swollen shut, scrapes and bruises marring his beautiful skin.

James closed his eyes and picked up his head and pounded the back of his skull into the hard pillow, over and over. "I am such a fucking loser," he said. "I am such a fucking waste of space."

"For God's sake, James, this is not about you. Stop feeling sorry for yourself, for once in your goddamned life."

"I can't," he said, crying pitifully. "I can't."

"You almost killed your son," I said, finally meeting his

eyes. He flinched. "Ava threatened to kill you, and Robert never wants to see your sorry ass again."

My brother started crying in earnest, and it really was pitiful, like a wounded animal keening out its death wail. My heart was bursting with pain. I pushed my patients like this all the time, but to push my brother when he was already broken was almost more than I could bear. I didn't know if he could take it. I knew only that I'd always let him off the hook too easily.

I took a deep breath. "If you want—and only if you want—I'll get Mr. Peterson in here to talk through your options. I think if you agree to go to rehab, and finish it out, you won't have to do that much jail time."

"I can't afford rehab," he croaked.

I swallowed hard. "I'll pay," I said. "On three conditions."

He looked at me, waiting, his mouth twisted.

"You never try to contact Ava or Jeremiah, until Ava says you can. Which might never happen."

James stared straight ahead. The TV was playing a PBS cooking show on mute.

"You don't contact any of us until—and *unless*—you finish rehab." My voice broke. "We need a *break*, James. We need to heal too." My hands were shaking.

"The third thing is, this is it. If you drink again, I don't want to see you. I won't give you anything. This is the last time."

"Ava used to say that all the time."

"Have I ever said it to you?"

His face crumpled. "No."

"I mean it. Take it or leave it."

A vein pulsed in his bruised forehead. "I'll take it."

Mr. Peterson came in at nine o'clock on the dot. I was standing at the window, staring out at the gray landscape. I was past exhaustion. Mr. Peterson was growing old now, with salt-and-pepper hair, a large nose, and oversize glasses. He was carrying a worn leather briefcase. I walked toward him and kissed him on the cheek. "Thanks for coming." I resumed my post, leaning against the low windowsill.

"Of course." He sat down in the chair on the left-hand side of James's bed. "How are you feeling, James?" he asked kindly. He'd represented James more than once.

"Been better," James said.

"Yes, I imagine we all have," Mr. Peterson said. "I'll get right to it. Since this is your second DUI in five years, the penalty has ratcheted up," he said, pulling out some papers. "You're very lucky, really. Jeremiah just turned thirteen. If he'd been under thirteen, or been more seriously injured—any kind of permanent damage, I mean—you'd be looking at a minimum of two years' jail time."

James closed his eyes.

"As it is, I think I can get you the minimum—ten days' jail time—if you complete rehab afterward."

"Okay," James croaked.

"Now, you won't be locked in—that is, you can leave rehab any time. But if you do, you'll likely be sent back to jail for up to a year."

My brother nodded.

"I'll make the arrangements then," Mr. Peterson said, standing. "You'll be released directly into police custody, I think. They'll set bail, and we'll wait for your arraignment. A few more weeks and you'll go to trial. We'll plead guilty to get you the minimum sentence."

I walked Mr. Peterson into the hall. "Thanks for coming," I said again.

"You're welcome."

"It'll be the last time we call you about James."

He smiled sadly. "I hate to say it, but I've heard that before," he said.

"Not from me," I said, and the steel in my voice surprised me.

He nodded. "Let me know if there's anything else I can do to help."

I watched him leave, then called Izzy to come pick me up.

Her minivan arrived outside the hospital twenty minutes later.

"My car's at Mom's," I said.

Izzy ignored me and drove to the pier. She parked and we

both got out, Izzy clutching a white paper bag from Monty's. My sister didn't look well. Her white baseball cap had sweat stains on it—the kind of thing she usually threw out. Her skin had a grayish tinge to it, and because she wasn't wearing makeup— in itself very unusual—the blue circles under her eyes were prominent.

The pier was lined with food vendors and dead-ended at Wonderland. The rides looked overly bright in the morning sun. We walked through a throng of joggers and cyclists to the far side of the pier and sat on the bench that bore a plaque with our father's name. Seagulls cawed and wheeled above us. The ocean crashed against the shore. The waves looked high; a storm was coming.

We sipped coffee in silence. Izzy pulled out a doughnut, passed me the bag. My doughnut was perfect: dusted with cinnamon sugar, crispy on the outside and doughy on the inside. I ate the whole thing in three bites and sat sucking the sugar from my fingers. I waited for her to question me about James. I was so bone-deep weary that I had no words. I felt as if a bomb had exploded next to me and I carried the reverberations in my marrow.

The wind off the water was stiff and cool, the salty smell of the ocean overpowering.

"Dad used to bring us here on Saturday mornings," Izzy said.

"Did he?"

"You don't remember?" she said. "I guess not. You were little."

"Why did he stop?"

"I don't know. He was . . . different the last few years of his life. Angry." She took a sip of coffee. "This whole thing reminds me so much of Dad dying."

"What do you remember?" I said. Izzy never talked about Dad's death.

"Everything," she said. She pulled out another doughnut, took a delicate bite. "I remember Mom telling us he had cancer. She waited until after dinner, and we were all asking why he wasn't there. She wanted us to eat, she told me later. She hadn't been able to eat all day. Anyway, she told us he had cancer, and that he wasn't going to get better. Robert and James started crying. And you just said, 'So he's going to die?' You were very serious. You didn't cry until later."

I remembered that night. I remembered thinking that if Daddy died, maybe Mom would pay more attention to me. I sighed. I'd thought for a while now that she'd been too busy to give me the attention I craved. But it had started before Dad died.

"Mom took me to see him the day he died. She thought I was old enough to handle it. Mrs. Jenkins was watching you guys, and she took me to the hospital. I was so scared. Dad couldn't talk. He just put his hand on my face. And then—that night, he died. I was still awake when Mom came home, and when I saw her face I knew." Tears dripped from the corners of my sister's eyes. She linked her arm in mine. "Are you okay?"

"No. Not even close." I turned to look at her face in profile, the face I'd idolized my entire childhood. "Are you?"

She shook her head, didn't look at me. "How's James?"

"A mess." I wiped a tear from the corner of my eye. "I told him I'd pay for rehab if he promises not to contact any of us unless he finishes." I dragged the frayed cuff of my sweatshirt under my nose. "Don't yell at me. I can't take it."

"You did what Robert and I couldn't," she said. "Thank you."

We sat in silence for a moment. "Bill was my father," I said.

Izzy went very still.

"The night he died, I found this packet of photos. There was one of him and Mom, dated for 1980. Mom confirmed they had an affair." I winced. "In graphic detail."

"I should've seen it before," she said. "You have his eyes. His hands."

I didn't say anything else.

Izzy sighed. I'd expected screaming. "I'm glad," she said. She cleared her throat. "I was a bitch to you about Bill when we were young. I feel bad about that now."

"Don't say anything to Robert, okay? I want to tell him."

She shrugged. "If you really want to."

We kept sitting there, immobilized. "I slept with Ted," I said.

Her eyebrows rose so high they almost disappeared into her hair.

"And Jonah saw him at the hospital."

Izzy put her arm around me and pulled me close to her so that my head rested on her shoulder. "Yikes."

"I really fucked things up this time. I did to Jonah exactly what Ted did to me."

She hugged me tighter. "I love you."

"I love you, too." Exhaustion lapped at my body, the fatigue setting in with a heaviness in my feet and legs. "Can you take me to get my car?" We walked to the van. "Are we telling Mom about the accident?"

"Robert already did," Izzy said. "He came over this morning."

"Who's there now?"

"One of the aides."

The van was dark and musty after the fresh salt air. We drove in silence. When we pulled up outside the house, we saw Mom in her robe and nightgown walking up the dune to the beach. I closed my eyes. "I'll help you get her back in the house," I said. "Can you deal with the rest of it?"

"Yeah." Izzy's voice was grim.

We hurried after Mom, who was walking steadily toward the ocean, shedding clothes as she went. I picked up her white satin robe and her socks as we trailed along after her. "Mom," I called. Izzy broke into a run when Mom lifted her blue cotton nightgown over her head and dropped it into the foaming water. She was wearing only threadbare white underpants, her wrinkled breasts pale in the bright cloudy light. Mom's scream was bloodcurdling as Izzy grabbed her wrist.

"Who the hell are you?" she shouted. The crowd of beachgoers stared.

I tucked the clothes under my arm and ran to Izzy's aid. We wrapped the wet nightgown around Mom's chest, then each hooked one of her arms around our shoulders and started dragging her up the beach.

"Let me go! Let me go! *Help!*"

Still we dragged, her wet feet making long tracks in the sand.

When we reached the house, I turned to Izzy. "Get the aide to help you put her to bed, then call the agency and have her fired."

Izzy nodded.

I locked the door behind me and went home and fell into bed, where I slept for twelve hours.

I waited until eight o'clock on Sunday morning to call Amber. She came over immediately, wearing a ratty pair of high school gym shorts and a T-shirt and carrying a container of chocolate chip cookies. She set about making tea. I lay down on the couch with a cookie and bundled myself in the afghan my grandmother had crocheted for me. Mom's mother had crocheted each of us an afghan when Mom was pregnant with us. Mine was the prettiest: pale yellow, intricate stitches, tassels. I couldn't remember my grandmother at all. She had died when I was two.

My brain, normally so tightly wound in its relentless patterns of frantic thought, was quiet. It seemed to be hiding from the emotions that lay in wait somewhere in my body, as if my mind were prey to the stalking grief and had to use evasive tactics to ensure survival.

Amber set two mugs of green tea on the table.

I told her everything: about being Bill's daughter, about sleeping with Ted after the funeral, about the confrontation with Jonah at the hospital, about Jeremiah's injuries, about the ultimatum I'd given James. "They'll have transferred him to jail," I said. The mug of tea clutched between my hands was almost cold, but I drank it anyway. "I don't know what to do now," I said.

"You're doing what you need to do," Amber said. "Grieving." She patted my knee. "It's going to take a long time. You've been through the *wringer*."

A strangled laugh escaped from my throat. "I really have."

I realized then that I was supposed to work the next day, and that I couldn't. I couldn't even face a phone call; I texted Kevin and asked him for three more days off. I texted Marisa and asked if I could see her tomorrow, since I'd missed my appointment yesterday.

Amber sat with me on the couch for the rest of the day. I had a strange desire to watch Christmas movies, even though it was only August, so we did.

Chapter 18

Laura

Next day I approached Marisa's office with trepidation. Normally I went into a session with a set topic in mind I wanted to explore—say, how my aversion to conflict enabled James's alcoholism—as if I were constructing an argument for an undergrad psych paper. I was way too messy to do that today.

When I entered the office Marisa walked forward and hugged me. I sagged into her body for a moment before straightening up and plopping into a chair.

She looked at me, waited. I gave her the quick sketch of everything that had happened.

She half-smiled in sympathy. "How are you managing?"

I opened my mouth to say something about how angry I was at my brother. "Jonah told me at the hospital he was falling in love with me," I said. I didn't mention that he'd said, "was." Past tense.

Marisa nodded.

I felt surprised. Was I really *that* girl? Whose family was in shambles, who was grieving, and who wanted only to talk about her boyfriend?

"How did that make you feel?"

"Depressed," I said.

She waited a beat, and when I didn't continue said, "Why?"

"Because I realized the day of the funeral that I was falling in love with him. And that afternoon I had sex with Ted."

"Why did you have sex with Ted?" Her voice is without inflection, without judgment. A simple, probing question.

"I don't know."

She waited. It was her job to make me think about things I didn't want to think about. I stared out the window, wishing I could walk away from my life.

"Laura, I'm not judging you. I'm just asking a question."

"I'm judging myself."

"Why don't you tell me about it?"

"I am a total fucking idiot." I hated how much I sounded like James.

"No, you're not," Marisa said gently. "You're human."

"I slept with him because he was *familiar*," I said, spitting out the word.

She nodded. "Any other reasons?"

"I don't know." I closed my eyes. "I'm tired."

"Could one reason be that you were afraid of loving someone else? Afraid of getting hurt again?"

"I don't know. Maybe." Yes. I leaned all the way back in the chair, the hug of the pillows erasing my peripheral vision. I'd never relaxed so deeply in this office, and that in itself felt unnerving.

"So what are you going to do?"

"About what?"

"About Jonah."

My face creased with incredulity. "Nothing. I screwed up. That's it. I have to get over him now. I finally found a healthy relationship and I intentionally sabotaged it." I swallowed hard. "I'm an idiot."

"This doesn't have to be it."

I sat up, restless. "Let's talk about something else."

"People apologize and make relationships work after events like this all the time. The only question is whether the relationship is worth saving."

I made a noncommittal sound in the back of my throat.

"Just because you didn't want to stay married to Ted after he cheated on you doesn't necessarily mean you couldn't make a relationship with Jonah work after cheating on him."

"Yeah, okay," I said. "That sounds crazy."

She changed tacks. "How are you feeling about Bill's death?"

"Alone." I said the first word that came to mind, something I was always encouraging my clients to do and rarely did myself.

"Tell me more about that."

"I feel like he left me alone with my mother," I clarified.

"Ah."

"It's like my mother is there—but not there," I said. "Since she got sick, I can see her, I can talk to her, but a lot of the time she's somewhere else. And the thing is . . . that's how she's always been with me."

"What do you mean?"

I struggled to put it into words. "It's like my seventh birthday. It was the summer after our dad died, and Mom didn't even bake me a cake. She baked cakes for all our birthdays. And she gave me this Barbie that wasn't even wrapped. I was trying to sit on her lap, and she got up and started doing the dishes." I felt my throat closing. "And then Bill came in the kitchen door with a chocolate-frosted cake from Bella Bakery, because he knew it was my favorite."

"How does that memory make you feel now?" Marisa asked.

I plucked a tissue from the box on the side table and blew my nose. "Like he spoiled me because he knew I was his daughter."

"And how did it make you feel about your mother?"

I blew my nose again. "Like she was so busy holding our family together that she was never emotionally available to me."

"That's not a feeling, Laura. That's an analysis. How did that make you *feel*?"

I closed my eyes. Scared. Lost. "Unwanted," I said.

Marisa nodded. After a few minutes of silence she said, "Do you know when you're going back to work?"

"Thursday."

Her eyes widened. "This Thursday?"

"Yes."

"You don't think it's early?"

"No," I said, nonplussed. "What am I supposed to do, sit around alone and cry?"

"Grieve," Marisa said. "Spend time with your family. Take care of yourself."

I sighed. "You think I should quit my job?"

"I'm giving you options of how you could spend your time if you chose a course different from the one you're currently taking. And of course you could take a leave of absence rather than quitting." Her mouth twitched. "Quitting is such a final act." She knew I hated to quit anything.

"I'm better when I'm working." I looked down at my hands in my lap, circled the base of my left ring finger where my engagement and wedding rings once sparkled.

"How do you know?"

"What do you mean?"

"Have you ever chosen *not* to work?"

"No," I said, my voice scornful. "I can't just take a break. I need the money. And . . . that's just not what we do. You push through, get on with things." I forced a smile. "It's the New England way."

Marisa smiled. "Just think about it."

I looked at the clock; I was itching to get out the door. "Okay," I said. "I'll think about it." My tone was a petulant child's saying, *Yeah, yeah.*

I went back to work on Thursday as I'd planned. Fifteen minutes into my first session, I wondered if Marisa had been right.

My patients' pain landed on me as if I had no skin, no bones protecting my vital organs. Their pain amplified my own pain. My throat swelled and my eyes stung. Minute by minute I scolded myself to toughen up.

When Leo left at two o'clock, closing the door behind him, I took out my files and sat at my desk, leaning my forehead on my hands. A tear dripped off the end of my nose onto the keyboard of my laptop.

I closed my eyes. I saw Macy sitting on the couch across from me, her eye swollen shut. I smelled Bill's cologne. I felt Jonah's lips on mine. Grief rolled over me in waves.

There was a knock on my door. I reached for the tissues on the corner of my desk, dabbed at my red eyes. "Who is it?"

"It's Kevin. Can I come in?"

There was no way I could hide the fact that I'd been crying, so I gave up trying. "Yes."

He came in and sat in the chair opposite me. "Hi."

I cleared my throat. "Hi."

"I wanted to see how your first day back went."

I laughed a little. "I think it went okay for my clients. But it didn't go so great for me." More tears leaked from my eyes and I swiped them away.

Kevin sat there, his right ankle crossed over his left knee. "You've been in my thoughts," he said. I could feel his empathy as viscerally as if he'd put a hand over mine.

"I can't do this," I said, staring at my hands. "I thought I could, but I can't."

"What do you need to do?" Kevin asked.

It was the perfect question. I gathered my shredded sense of self around me. "I need to take a leave of absence." After a long moment, I looked up at him.

He looked steadily back at me. "Then let's make it happen," he said.

"Really?"

"Really." He shifted in his seat. "How long do you need?"

I swallowed, my mouth suddenly dry. "I don't know. I don't even know what I'm doing right now." I rubbed my palms together. The skin on the back of my hands was dry and cracked. "Six months?" It seemed such a long time that I was tempted to halve it.

Kevin nodded. "Let's check in then and we can see how you're doing, if you need more time."

I had no idea what my life would look like in six months. "Thanks."

"We'll miss you."

"Yeah," I said. "I'll . . . miss you too. I'll put together my client files for you."

"That would be great."

I didn't want to come back, so I sat in my office for two more hours, bringing all my client notes up to date, making sure their files were in meticulous order. I locked them in my desk drawer and slid the key under Kevin's door. I was the last one in the building, so I turned out all the lights and locked the door behind me.

I spent most of the weekend in bed watching Netflix on my laptop. In the fifteen seconds between one episode ending and the next beginning, the twin tragedies of losing Bill and having driven Jonah away threatened to suffocate me. My throat and chest felt constricted as if I had suddenly developed claustrophobia.

I picked up my phone to call Jonah every few hours, but the anger on his face when he'd said, "You think we can just pick up where we left off?" stopped me. The fact that I knew exactly how he felt—rejected, wounded, used—doubled my anguish.

I thought about calling Ted. We were on the same level now: cheaters. I'd turned to him at a moment of weakness, and he had been what I needed in that moment. But then I remembered what an idiot he'd been at the hospital, and I burrowed deeper under my comforter.

I ordered a Hawaiian pizza for dinner Saturday night. Ted had introduced me to Hawaiian pizza; before that I'd been a plain-only kind of girl. I didn't even like pepperoni. Growing up, we'd order a pepperoni pie that incited Izzy, James, and Robert to fight over every slice, and a plain pie that Mom, Bill, and I would have to ourselves. But the salty ham and sweet pineapple of a Hawaiian pizza, plus the shaved slices of fresh Parmesan that Ted would add at home, became an addiction. We finally set a boundary: pizza only one night a week. Everyone at Station Pizza knew our order when they saw our number on the caller ID.

I recognized the delivery boy by sight when I opened the door, still in my white cotton pajamas.

"Hey," he said. "It's $15.50. Fran threw in some Chunky Monkey."

I gave him $20, refused change. When the pizza guy also knew your favorite Ben & Jerry's flavor, it was both a blessing (I now had dessert) and a curse (evidence that people I barely knew could see how pathetic I was).

I flicked on the TV, not even bothering to change the channel, opened the pizza box on my lap, and started eating the first slice over it, my fingers immediately slicked with grease.

The picture of Mom and Bill from their twenty-fifth anniversary kept drawing my gaze away from the TV. Bill's face was luminous. I set my slice down on top of the rest of the pie, set the box on the coffee table, wiped my hands on a napkin, and took the photo off its hook. I stood there, holding it in my hands, for a long moment, then brought it over to the couch and hid it face-down under a throw pillow next to me.

Thursday was my birthday. I was thirty-three.

Izzy, sensing that I would have stayed in bed all day, called on Wednesday and informed me that she was cooking me dinner at her house, and that Robert and Mom were coming over. "Oh, and Amber's coming too," she said.

"Okay," I said dully. "Did you tell Amber to bring her boyfriend?"

"He's out of town on business, apparently," Izzy said. "I didn't even know she was dating anyone. She brought it up." Izzy cleared her throat. "I was thinking maybe I could call Jonah and invite him, if you gave me his number—"

"No."

"If you two could just talk, I'm sure you could—"

"No. Stay out of it."

"Fine." My sister blew out a breath. "Be here at 6:30."

Izzy could make even birthdays feel like a chore.

Still, the dinner was nice. Sam grilled chicken and corn on the cob, and Izzy made cucumber salad and peach sangria.

Last year Ted had taken me to Aruba for my birthday. The previous Christmas he'd signed us up for a scuba diving class at the Y, and we got certified in time for the trip. We spent the entire week lying on the beach drinking pina coladas, making love in the huge bed enclosed by sheer white curtains, and scuba diving in the clear sea, marveling at the vibrant coral reefs, the technicolor fish. I missed being married. I missed belonging to someone. I missed having someone plan my birthdays who actually knew what I enjoyed.

But I took that thought back as the kitchen lights darkened and Izzy came out onto the deck, holding a chocolate-frosted birthday cake from Bella Bakery, lit with thirty-three candles. The sun was low in the sky behind the trees, darting through the green leaves with sparks of radiant light. The faces around me were illuminated in the candlelight as my family sang "Happy Birthday" to me. But the absence of Bill, of James, of Jonah, even of Ted, seemed to yawn in the space between me and my family, separating me from them with a gulf of uncrossable pain.

After we all ate cake, Sam went to put the kids to bed. Amber stood to go. "I have to pick up Brian from the airport," she said, kissing me goodbye.

"Mom, want to watch TV with Ivy?" Izzy said, and I had a bad feeling that I was about to be ganged up on.

She settled Mom in the living room and came back outside with a full pitcher of sangria. She refilled each of our glasses and sat down next to Robert, both of them across from me.

I looked from one to the other. "What's up?" I'd told them last week that I'd left work and they had been surprisingly supportive, but I wondered now whether they'd reconsidered this position and planned an intervention.

"Well," Robert said. "Here's the thing."

I hated when people said "Here's the thing."

"My lawyer and Julia's are still negotiating, but given the amount of child support I'll likely have to pay, plus lawyers' fees and paying both the mortgage on the house here and the house on the Cape, plus rent on my apartment, I'm not going to be able to contribute to an aide for Mom much more than an hour or two a day."

Izzy cleared her throat. "And I'm in the same boat. Money's really tight these days."

"Right," I said. "Of course." And I had just taken a leave of absence and committed to paying for James to go back to rehab.

"Mom still has plenty of money in her retirement account," Izzy said. She'd been doing Mom and Bill's finances for years. "But Bill had term life insurance and it was up five years ago, so there's no payout. She has enough income for years to come, but it would burn through really fast if we put her in a nursing home."

Robert and Izzy exchanged glances, and Robert continued, as if they'd planned this tag team. "The way we see it, we have two options," Robert said. "Either we can sell the house and put the money toward Mom going to a nursing home, or you can move back in and take care of her." He coughed into his fist. "And I want to make it clear, Laura, no one expects you to move home and take care of Mom. You have your own life. But since you seemed so hell-bent against selling the house last week, we thought we'd bring it up as a possibility. Unless, of course, you can think of a solution that Izzy and I haven't."

"Right," I said again. "Can I have a couple days to think?"

Robert glanced at Izzy. "Yes. But we should decide soon."

"Fine." I stood up. "Iz, thanks for the dinner. I really appreciate it."

"Well, don't forget your cards," she said as I kissed her and Robert goodbye. "I put them on the counter next to your purse. And I wrapped the last two slices of cake for you."

I drove to the beach at Thirteenth Street, where Jonah had taken me a few weeks ago. I walked down to the jetty and sat on a rock, facing the ocean, watching the water turn aqua in the sunset.

The first birthday card was from Amber and contained a gift certificate for a massage. The second was from Robert and held a check for $50. The next card was from Izzy's family and contained a check for $50 and two folded up drawings, one of a robot shooting a laser gun from Isaac and one of two girls holding hands, with a border of purple flowers, from Ivy.

I held the last unopened envelope in my hands, as if weighing it. The flap had been folded into the envelope instead of licked and sealed. This was from Mom, all right. She had always been a germophobe.

The card displayed a picture of a cupcake pierced with a lit pink candle. Inside the Hallmark text read, *Hope your day is sweet.* Under that Mom's careful penmanship said: *Happy birthday! Love, Mom.*

The sense of letdown was incomprehensible. No money, no gift, not even a personalized message—not even my *name.* I wondered if Izzy had bought the card and asked Mom to sign it just before dinner.

Bill would never write me a card again. Last year he had written on both sides of the card, then on the back, about how proud he was of me, and how much he loved me. Bill had always been the pushover, the softie, the one to tear up at graduations and weddings. Mom had always been unsentimental.

But it still hurt.

Darkness was falling now, the four words in Mom's upright cursive becoming harder to read.

I stood up, my knees creaking, and went home.

On Saturday afternoon I went to see Mom, pausing on the brick walk to the porch door. I missed Bill grilling steaks on the patio. I closed my eyes. I could practically smell the char of steak, the smoky scent of charcoal.

An idea had been growing in my mind all day, an idea I couldn't believe I was considering. I let myself in the house, where I found Mom and her aide, Caitlyn, playing cards in the kitchen.

"Hi, Mom." I kissed her on the cheek and sat down. Mom had warned me years ago that I should never consider it acceptable to kiss her on the forehead.

"Hello," Mom said, not naming me, not looking up from her hand. "She's cheating."

"I'm not," Caitlyn said, sighing. "I'm just *winning*."

"Good for you," I said.

I sat and watched my mother play cards, her brow furrowed, her eyes deep in concentration as a chess player's. Mom pulled her score up and up and up, eventually beating Caitlyn by sixty points. We'd grown up playing Shang-hai, and Mom hardly ever lost. Her two brothers and three sisters had all been card sharks. Family parties had degenerated into fierce, silent card games, with the winner—often Mom until they started on poker—crowing victoriously, not a shred of grace visible.

Watching Mom in her element, despite the fact that she'd barely acknowledged me, seemed to reinforce the decision that had been making itself in the back of my mind. When she finally looked up I said, "How are you today?"

She blinked. "Who are you?"

"Laura, Mom. Your daughter."

"Humph," she said.

"How about a nap?" Caitlyn said.

"TV," Mom answered, and they left the kitchen.

I slid the screen door open and went down to the beach. I walked for a long time.

When I returned to the patio I sat on the low stone wall. The air was warm and soft as cashmere. The rustle of waves soothed me.

I went back into the house, walked through the kitchen and into the porch, where Mom was asleep in her armchair. Caitlyn was watching *Access Hollywood* and tapping furiously on her phone. I walked through the dining room, where we had held more family parties than I could remember. The living room, where I'd celebrated every Christmas morning of my life.

I sat down on the bottom step, curled a hand around the banister spoke. I couldn't lose this house. Not now. Not when I'd already lost so much else.

I'd decided. I was moving home.

Chapter 19

James

They let me out of the hospital on Sunday. A cop picks me up and takes me to the police station for processing. They book me, take fingerprints, and put me in a holding cell. There's another guy in there, reeking of alcohol, dead asleep on the bench.

Mr. Peterson arranges for a bail bond, has me out before five p.m.

I go home and sit on my futon. I avoid it for a while—the thing I know I have to do. I watch TV, jouncing my leg up and down uneasily. Flick through the channels: wrestling, baseball, golf, and back again. When the sun is setting in purple streaks through my living room window, which cracked last winter from a kid's icy snowball and which the super still hasn't fixed, I get up from the couch. I dig out all the alcohol I have in the house: a six-pack of Yuengling, two half-empty handles of Jack, a fifth of Belvedere, five mini bottles of flavored rum I got at a promotion last weekend, and a bottle of red wine. I remember that there's a red box in my closet containing a Macallan rare cask whisky that I've been saving for a special occasion. I suck in a deep breath, try to forget it's there.

I open all the containers, their lids spinning on the countertop. Then I dump the contents of the bottles, two at a time, into the sink. The beer fizzes in that glorious white foam I love. The alcohol splashes out of its bottles, tangy and sharp. The wine stains the sink red. I toss the bottles into a garbage bag with a heavy clinking and carry the bag downstairs and out back, drop it into the recycle dumpster. The dark alley smells like piss and stale beer.

For the next six weeks I live as a miserable hermit.

Benny only lets me work three days a week, which is barely enough to cover my rent. It makes sense; I'm going to jail in six weeks, and if he gave me more days he'd have to hire someone to replace me. After work I go to the high school track. At first I walk, lap after lap. Three weeks into this routine I can jog without shooting pain in my shoulder, so I do. A week later

I'm running two miles a day.

I come home and drink can after can of diet soda and chain-smoke. I sleep less than four hours a night.

The four days a week when I'm not working I can barely make it out of bed. I don't sleep; I just lie there stewing in my own juices. I watch Netflix. I feel sorry for myself and the mess I've made of my life, and I punish myself for what I've done to Jeremiah.

The arraignment is uneventful.

The trial, finally, is on Friday, September 19. I get a haircut, put on the cheap suit I wore to Bill's funeral. I plead guilty. I have to turn myself in to prison two days later, so I pack up all my stuff and move it into a storage unit.

I haven't had a drink in forty-two days, but even I wouldn't call myself sober. I'm a dry drunk.

I've been arrested plenty of times before, but I've never done time. I've never had to strip naked and put on the orange jumpsuit, to give up the only possessions I had left: the clothes on my back. I wish I'd spent less time the past few weeks running and more time lifting. I feel puny. Weak. I know better than to think that weaker animals get protected by the pack. Weaker animals get picked off from the pack and eaten alive.

It's only ten days, I tell myself. My legs are shaking as the guard unlocks a cell and I step into it. The clang of the door closing, the grinding of the lock turning, starts tears in my eyes.

"Hey," I say to my cell mate, a beefy guy with a long goatee, who's lying on the bottom bunk. "I'm James."

He doesn't look up, doesn't acknowledge that I've entered the twenty-by-twenty space.

"I usually at least get a first name before I spend the night with someone," I joke. He keeps staring into space. Ooookay. "I'll take the top bunk, then." I swing myself up onto the bed, lie on my stomach, press my fist hard into my mouth.

I squeeze my eyes shut and breathe in and out through my mouth, try to think of something neutral. I can't think of anyone or anything from home or I'll lose it. I start reworking my fantasy football lineup. I've got Eli Manning starting QB. Everyone wants Malcolm Smith starting outside linebacker this season, and even though I prefer to do the opposite of what everyone else would do, I like him too. He's starting.

My breathing starts to slow down as I consider who I want for tight ends for the game on Sunday. Do they even have a TV in this place? Shit. I haven't missed a Sunday football game since . . . shit. Since the last time I got arrested and was in holding for thirty hours.

Clanging in the hall.

"We go out to the yard?" I say.

Silence.

"Hey man," I said, "this is like being in solitary."

Silence.

I consider whether I can survive ten whole days without anyone to talk to. It's only been an hour, and I already feel like I'm losing my mind.

In the yard I stand near the fence, shoulders hunched, trying to maintain a posture halfway between pushover and threat.

A couple of guys approach diagonally. Big, Latino, with bulging forearms covered in tattoos.

I look away until a shadow falls across my face.

"Hey man," one of them says.

Suddenly I panic. Maybe this is their spot at the fence. Maybe I'm about to get pounded into the ground.

"Whatchu in for?" the closer guy asks.

"DUI," I say. The spit in my mouth dries up. My mind is racing in circles like a hamster on a wheel. Am I supposed to ask what he's in for? Or is that rude? How the fuck am I supposed to last ten days in here? I'm already fried from all the stress.

The first guy puts a hand on his chest. "Robbery." He points at his buddy. "Assisted robbery." He laughs, a big bellow of a laugh.

I can feel the rest of the yard watching us.

"Musta been your second offense," the guy says. "Unless you had a really shitty lawyer."

I clear my throat. "Second offense," I confirm.

"You need anything in here, you let me know," he says. "Name's Diego."

He reaches out a hand. I hesitate, then take it.

Dinner is a million times worse than the high school cafeteria. I sit at a table two seats down from Diego, at the corner. Easily defensible. He doesn't have to talk to me if he doesn't want to. I glance around surreptitiously, mimic the posture I see everywhere: hunch over the plate, shovel food in my mouth like a Neanderthal.

"Where you from, James?" Diego asks.

"Eastville."

Diego whistles. "Fancy."

I snort. "Not my part of Eastville."

Diego grunts. "My cousin mows lawns in Eastville. He says it's *all* fancy."

"Well, it's nicer than Central Falls," I joke. Central Falls is a shithole.

Diego and his buddy exchange dark looks.

My jaw goes slack. Fuck. I just insulted the one person in here who is talking to me.

Diego looks at me for a long moment, and I'm afraid he's going to punch me in the jaw. Then he grins, points at me. "You should see your face," he says. He and his buddy high-five, laugh.

I try to swallow, but my mouth is bone-dry.

"We're from East Providence," he says.

"I'm sorry, man," I say. Central Falls has a large Latino population. Why do I say such stupid shit?

"It's fine, it's fine," Diego says easily. "So, James. You got a family? Anyone waiting for you out there?"

Jeremiah's face, terrified in the white glow of headlights just before the crash, swims before my eyes. "I dunno," I say.

"Sounds about right," says Diego.

Back in the cell I have to take my first shit in front of another man. My face burns with humiliation.

I don't sleep at all that night. It's like all of my nightmares come true. The impact of the crash. The clang of the bars. Jeremiah's terrified face. Laura's disappointment. My father's belt on my back. The first time I made Mom cry. And the second, third, and fourth times.

The night seems to last forever, especially because there's no clock and no light. Only darkness.

Finally, finally, finally there is clanging in the hallway. Light comes on. "Shower," says a guard.

There are ten stalls, all delineated by three tile walls and a flimsy, clear plastic curtain. At least we're not all under the same couple showerheads like in the movies.

I squirt shampoo into my right hand and suds up my hair one-handed—my shoulder still hurts if I raise my arm above my head. I'm working the scratchy washcloth around a nub of soap when I hear the scraping of metal hoops—the curtain drawing back—and feel cold air across the back of my body. I turn and see Diego standing there, naked.

"What the *fuck*, man?"

Without a word Diego grabs me and pins me to the wall with his huge forearm, water still running down over us. I'm kicking, yelling, trying to throw a backward punch. I land an elbow in his chest, but it doesn't stop him. I'm powerless. I try twisting underneath his arm, but it's no use. His arm is like an iron bar pinning me in place and he's got more than a hundred pounds on me. I struggle, yell. A dizzying blow to the side of my head and my vision whirls and pops. His other hand parts my buttocks and his dick rips into my ass. I'm crying like a baby now, begging him to stop, but the thrusting continues painfully until I feel a stream of hot liquid issue from his dick. He releases me and is gone before I can turn around.

I stand in the shower, watching blood and thick white semen circle down the drain.

I don't speak or shower for the next nine days.

I get out of prison on Wednesday, October 1, the first date of the new month a mere coincidence. It doesn't feel like a fresh start. I doubt anything will feel like a fresh start ever again.

Mr. Peterson picks me up from the West Warwick Correctional Facility with the duffel bag I'd packed and left with him. He drives a Lincoln MKZ: buttery leather seats, powerful engine, an airlock so tight I can't tell we're in a car, even when we're doing eighty miles per hour north on I-95 toward Central Falls. Mr. P is humming along with jazz on the radio. He hasn't said a word to me, and I'm grateful. I was afraid he'd try to make conversation.

After half an hour he gets off at exit 29. Only a few turns later we arrive at the Central Falls Rehabilitation Facility, which sounds so similar to the prison I just left that I feel the gorge rise in my throat as we drive past the blue-and-white sign and down the long gravel driveway lined with twiggy trees. It has officially turned fall since I've been in prison, and orange leaves flame against the sky.

We pull up outside a low white building that looks like a converted Holiday Inn. Mr. P puts the car in park. I wait a beat, intending to follow his lead, until I realize he's not getting out of the car. The trunk pops as I get out, and I retrieve my duffel and close the trunk with a soft thump. I know I should thank him, but I also know I won't be able to bring myself to do so. Still, I approach the driver's side to at least shake his hand through the window. Instead the car pulls away, so quietly I hadn't even heard the engine shift back into drive.

I check in and, instead of feeling grateful that I don't have to trade in my clothes, that there are no bars on the wide, no dirty windows, I feel angry—like I'm still in prison, but no one wants to admit it.

I want to die.

The schedule on my desk, printed on purple paper,

informs me that my group meeting starts at 4:30. At quarter to five I'm lying in bed staring at the pockmarked drop ceiling.

I hear a heavy tread striding down the hall; the walls are paper thin. A knock sounds on my door. I don't answer.

The door opens and a huge black guy fills the frame. I scramble to my feet as he steps inside. With the light on his face I see that his eyes are kind, but that doesn't change the dominance I associate with his posture. A huge, inky tattoo of a dove in flight spreads across the right side of his throat, as if it's about to fly up across his face.

"Meeting started fifteen minutes ago," he says. His voice is deep; the gentle note is unfamiliar. "Or you can go back to prison," he says, stepping back into the hallway. "Your choice." He glances back at me. "Though you don't look like ten days in the joint agreed with you."

I follow him downstairs.

The layout of the place is pretty basic: The second floor is all single bedrooms, women in the east wing, men in the west wing. We're not allowed to fraternize with members of the opposite sex, so you need a key card to get into your wing. (Like that would stop anyone from having sex if they wanted to.) The first floor is devoted to meeting rooms, with a rec room at the far end of the east wing. The rec room holds a TV, a shabby pool table, and a couple of worn couches that look like they belong in a frat house. The best thing about the rec room is that you can see water from the east-facing windows—the small pond across the grounds. The water is the only thing that makes me feel calm.

Fear of prison is the only thing forcing my compliance.

After breakfast on my first morning, which is at 7:30, we sit in a circle in one of the meeting rooms. The walls are white cinderblock and the floor is blue linoleum. It smells like stale coffee, and it's colder in here than it is outside. One of the other counselors is facilitating a discussion about our dependence on alcohol, how it shapes our decisions, distorts our thinking. I wonder if alcohol is really my problem. Alcohol doesn't distort my decisions. It fuels them.

I skip lunch and go to the chapel, not because I'm seeking solace or time with God, but because I can't stand spending any more time with the losers in my group. The chapel is strange; the stained-glass windows are so dark and opaque, it might be nighttime. The front set of pews face each other instead of facing forward. I sit on the left side, my back against the wall, under the statue of the Blessed Mother. The statue is different from any other I've ever seen. Mary's skin and eyes are dark, and instead of standing impassively with her arms at her sides, palms facing outward, she is breast-feeding the infant Jesus. A smile rises to my lips as I imagine the prudish shock of Sister Mary Frances, my sixth-grade teacher. Still, I liked the image of Mary going about her business, feeding her kid like it was no big deal.

I sit there for a long time, and a thought falls into my head. I've been James the screw-up, the drunk, for so long that I can't imagine being anyone else. If I didn't drink, I don't know who I would be.

I refuse to shower for the first couple days, but finally give in and shower at eleven p.m. on Friday, when the bathroom is empty. There are doors to each shower stall, but no locks. I choose the shower farthest from the door and jump if I see movement through the foggy glass. I go to breakfast every morning and attend morning meeting. There are about twenty-five of us, plus assorted staff. Then I go to my small group, with four other guys. Our leader is Marcus, the black guy with the dove tattoo. I eat lunch by myself. The afternoons are a repeat of the mornings, with an individual counseling session with Marcus thrown in.

My goal is not to learn the tools of living a sober lifestyle. My goal is to figure out how to live the way I want to without ever going back to prison.

On day 5—twenty-three days to go—I skip breakfast and get to morning meeting late. All the seats in the back are taken, so I slouch to the front, slump into a metal folding chair. We spend most of our days sitting in rooms while earnest staff try to get us to bare our souls to a bunch of other drunks. You'd think they'd spring for some nicer chairs.

Afterward Marcus walks outside with me, offers me a cigarette. We light up, inhale, blow smoke in tandem. I am consumed with self-pity. Marcus finishes his cigarette, stamps it in the butt holder, and turns to me. "Start participating, or get out. You're wasting everyone's time, including your own." He hasn't threatened me, exactly, but I feel threatened.

That afternoon I go to group, and when it opens I say, "Hi, I'm James, and I'm an alcoholic." They are the first words I've spoken in two weeks.

"Hi, James," the group says in unison.

"I, um, I was just in prison for a DUI," I say. My heart is pounding and my mouth is dry. I can't believe how hard this is. "I don't want to go back to prison." I can't bring myself to say anything else that's true, and I can't bring myself to lie in front of so many eager faces.

The next day I'm sitting in the rec room at 12:30. It's lunch time, but I want to be alone.

I feel a presence behind me and twist around to see Marcus standing there. "Get up," he says.

I get up.

"C'mon. Lunch."

"Not hungry." My stomach growls in spite of myself.

"Feeling sorry for yourself won't help anything."

I roll my eyes. I can't believe this guy.

"Let's go. I'll take you off-site, get you a burger."

"I'm not allowed—"

"You are if you're with me."

The promise of not having to endure the shitty cafeteria is tempting. "Okay."

Stanley's is full of guys in jeans and sweatshirts with calloused hands, joking with their buddies, complaining about the rain. I used to be one of them. Marcus orders two double cheeseburgers for himself and one for me. At our red-checked table, which is covered with a fine film of grease, he shakes salt onto his fries. "I figure I gave up booze, might as well enjoy as much salt as I want."

I pick up my burger.

"Hang on, Baba Looey," Marcus says. "I'm gonna say grace." He bows his head and closes his eyes. "Heavenly Father, thank You for all that You have blessed us with, and thank You for this food." He opens his eyes and inserts a fry into his mouth. "Okay. Eat away."

I eat in silence, ravenously. I don't want to talk. I don't want to be in my own skin.

"So what's your deal?" Marcus says, slathering two salty fries in ketchup and folding them into his mouth.

"Here under protest."

"Because you don't have a problem, right?"

"I said yesterday that I do." I reach for my soda, slurp down half of it in three long, satisfying straw pulls.

"Since you won't tell me, I'll have to make it up," Marcus says, attacking his burger now. Every bite chomps out a quarter of it. "Had a rough time in prison, I'd guess."

I don't say anything, but my leg twitches and my foot strikes the metal leg of my chair.

"You've always been misunderstood. Parents divorced, maybe. Had a kid with your girlfriend. You just couldn't give her what she needed, so she left you for someone who could. You work when you have to. You could stop drinking any time you want, you just don't want to." Marcus chomps another quarter of his burger, chews. "You're arrogant and you did something, something real bad, that's eating you up inside. Am I close?"

I fight to keep my face composed. Is it what I did to Jeremiah that's eating me alive? Or what happened to me in prison?

"What's it gonna be, James? You gonna stop living in denial?"

Marcus seems perfectly comfortable having this one-sided conversation. He picks up his second burger, drains his Coke with a loud slurping sound. My plate has been clean for several minutes now.

"Let's go."

I'm waiting for him to demand some kind of pledge from me, am surprised when he doesn't.

We get in his car, and I realize the truth is this: No one cares what I do any more. No one.

That night after dinner I'm in my room, and the loneliness gets real bad. It almost has a face. I can smell it in the musty sheets on my bed, smell the self-pity as it billows around me. I want to call Laura. I want to call Ava. If I don't get a couple shots of whiskey in me soon, I think I'll drown in pain.

The door bangs open. Marcus stands there, taking up the whole door frame, blocking most of the light from the hallway. "C'mon," he says. "Play you at pool."

If I stay alone any longer, I might start screaming. I get up and follow him down to the rec room.

On day 8—twenty days to go—I finally speak during small group. I've heard all the guys' stories by this point—the guy who spent his teenage daughter's college fund on scotch and gambling; the guy who hit a cop and went to jail for a year; the guy who tried to kill himself; the guy who woke up one morning and realized he had pushed away everyone he cared about and was alone except for his drinking.

I can't tell them anything *too* real. "My stepfather died suddenly a few weeks ago," I say. "My mom has Alzheimer's, and he was taking care of her. I don't know—I don't know who's going to do it now." I sniff hard. "I got trashed at his funeral. That's partly why I'm here."

"Thanks for sharing, James," Marcus says.

I'm angry because I've never been able to change. What the fuck makes me think I can change this time? But every time I want to bolt I see the image of Jeremiah's bruised face burned into my retinas.

I still don't give a flying fuck for the other people here. I don't want to waste energy or time fixing anyone else. I just want to figure out how to fix myself.

The rage is a tower so tall I can't see the top of it.

On day 10 I enter small group feeling murderous. There's no particular reason except that I slept horribly the night before. I kept reliving the car crash, hearing Jeremiah yelling "Dad!" feeling the bone-crushing impact of the SUV slamming into the passenger side door of Robert's Jag, jerking awake with a half-scream.

Lou is going on—and on, and on—about discovering his Higher Power. I hate this whole line of talk. "The Great HP," Marcus calls his. Rehab is full of the Higher Power shtick. It annoys the shit out of me, in part because they won't even call it God and be done with it (and who would have thought that the Catholic Church would seem like a straight shooter in comparison to any other group?). But no, AA has to go and conceal what they really mean by using the New Age-y term "Higher Power," when all they want from me is to say I believe in God.

"And it occurred to me—when I was awake in prison for more than forty-eight hours because I was too afraid to sleep— that my Higher Power is sleep," Lou was saying.

Nods and smiles. A couple guys break into grins.

"I mean, it's something I surrender to every day. It's a place where I can rest. We all need sleep, just as we all need a Higher Power. It restores us to sanity. That was the entry point for me."

A quiet, self-satisfied atmosphere falls over the group.

I can feel anger itching at the back of my throat. "Sleep as a Higher Power?" I say. "Give me a fucking break."

"James," Marcus says, a warning in his voice. He points to a sheet of chart paper on the wall that spells out our group norms, the first of which, written in Marcus's messy handwriting, is "Be kind," and the second of which is "Don't offer your opinion or advice on what anyone else says."

"I just can't keep sitting here and listening to this bullshit," I say, standing up, the anger coursing through my veins now like poison. "If I'm going to stop drinking so I can stay out of prison, I need something *practical*. Not all this stupid Higher

Power bullshit." My rant is losing steam now because I said "bullshit" twice, but that just makes me angrier. "You are all so fucking naive."

The faces around the circle, who had been looking at me with bland disinterest, start to display anger, and their indignation fuels my aggression.

"I hate this fucking place, and I hate all of you. I'd leave right now if it didn't mean I'd be going back to prison." I've stopped shouting; my words are even, cold, perfect in their furious precision.

"James." Marcus stands up, and I feel my anger drop a notch with fear as soon as my head has to tilt back to keep looking at his face. "I want you to leave this room right now, and don't come back until you're ready to apologize."

I turn and stalk out of the room, out of the building, into the chilly air. I stride down to the pond, kicking shredded brown leaves in front of me, my breath puffing. Halfway around the pond, I've worked myself into a pretty good lather when the cold starts to bite me in the ass. I'm wearing only jeans and a long-sleeved T-shirt, and it's probably forty degrees. Cold for October. My hands, which were red with anger inside, are now draining into a deathly pale white and are so cold they hurt. A sharp pain presses on my lungs as I push myself to walk faster, chafing my hands in front of me to warm them. I come to a clearing with a rickety picnic table. A small, twisted dogwood tree, already leafless, leans over the table. I step up into the cleft of the tree where the short trunk splits into three long arms, and I jump up and down as hard as I can, feeling the wood jar through my feet and knees and lower back, until the tree cracks into two broken pieces. I stomp on one of them until I have a club of dry, dead wood, and then I slam it into the remaining third arm of the tree until that branch cracks too, and all that's left is the hacked stump, the tree in pieces on the ground.

PART III

Chapter 20

Laura

Saturday morning was now like every other morning. There was
no sleeping in. There was no variation in routine.

I got up with Mom at six o'clock and drank coffee out
of my purple Scrivener's mug, the one kitchen item I hadn't left
in the boxes now stacked neatly in the corner of the basement.
The mug made me feel at home. Every day I washed it, dried it,
and put it back in the cabinet so it would be there the following
morning.

After breakfast Mom and I walked down to the beach
along the lip of the ocean. It was far too cold to go swimming,
but Mom still tried to make a break for the water. I held tightly
to her hand as she leaned her weight away from me, straining.

"No, Mom," I said, sighing. I threaded my elbow through
hers and kept walking into the wind, pulling her along behind
me.

After our walk we played cards then watched TV. At noon
I heated up some vegetable soup and we ate watching the news.

By the time Caitlyn arrived at one o'clock I was waiting
by the side door in my jacket.

On Sundays Izzy would bring the kids over or Robert
would come by with the girls, and we'd read to Mom or play
board games and eat chicken salad sandwiches for lunch. Life
was strangely empty of things I used to do all the time, like
picking up dry cleaning, listening to other people's problems, or
wearing anything besides jeans and sweats and sneakers.

It had taken three weeks to arrange everything, and I'd
moved home with Mom four weeks ago. We'd established a
rhythm, but it felt uneasy. Missing Bill was an aching absence like
an infected gum after a tooth is pulled or the itch of a phantom
limb. I kept swinging the limb around, knocking things off
shelves. Eric took to calling once a week, on Sunday afternoon, as
if he were in college and I were his mother.

I heard nothing from James.

The days were exhausting, and as the weeks marched relentlessly forward, my fatigue built on itself. I would have welcomed a day at work listening to other people talk about themselves. The isolation was the X factor I hadn't counted on.

The king bed I'd bought myself when I moved into my apartment took up way too much space in my child-size room. My old twin bed had been wedged across the hall in Izzy's old room; for some reason I couldn't bear to part with it. I'd unpacked all my boxes, but my room still felt temporary. I hadn't been sleeping well. I was grieving for the loss of my apartment, a little death. The house felt secretive to me now, as if it knew things I would never know.

One Friday night in mid-October, I lay staring at the ceiling for hours, finally dropping into a fitful doze around 2:30. At 4:45 I woke to the soft pad of footsteps on carpet. I dragged myself out of bed and went into the hallway. Mom was walking down the steps, her body thin and frail in her transparent white nightgown, her feet bare.

Though I hadn't made a sound, she swiveled her head with a mother's uncanny intuition. "Go back to bed, Laura."

I froze in the middle of the hall. Mom hadn't remembered my name in weeks.

She reached the bottom of the stairs and turned left into the dining room. I followed. I couldn't suppress the surge of hope that built in my chest: If she remembered my name, what else did she remember?

I found her in the kitchen and stood in the doorway, leaning against the frame. I watched, amazed, as Mom went to the fridge and pulled out a bag of Dunkin' Donuts coffee, opened the top right-hand cabinet and pulled a filter out of the package, placed it the basket of the Mr. Coffee, measured in four scoops of coffee grounds, held the pot under the tap and filled it halfway with water, tilted the water into the coffeemaker, placed it back on the burner, and flicked the "On" switch. Mom hadn't remembered how to make coffee in weeks either; last week I'd found her drinking hot water with Sweet and Low in it. I wondered what Izzy would say if she knew I was letting Mom have caffeine in the middle of the night, but I was so proud that I couldn't bring myself to refuse her a treat she seemed to have earned.

The coffee burbled in the background. Mom went to the table and sat down.

I walked around to the office, found the packet of photographs, and brought them back to the kitchen. I took out the second photo, a beach covered in snow, and laid it on the table in front of her. Her face broke into a smile.

"Robert was in New York on business," she said. "I left the kids with a neighbor for the night, told her I had to visit my sister in the hospital in Providence." She smiled mischievously. "I was pregnant with Laura. I knew she was Bill's from the beginning, but I didn't tell him right away. We rented a house on the beach. It was February. I had never had so much fun. We had a snowball fight, then went inside and made love by the fire for hours. I loved Robert for who he was, but I had never felt passion like that before."

The coffeemaker beeped three times to signal the coffee was ready. Mom stood and crossed to the cabinets, took down two white china teacups we never used, and poured two cups of coffee.

Mom sat, twisting her sapphire anniversary ring around and around her finger. She saw me watching her and smiled. "I want you to have this ring when I die," she said.

"Mom, you're not going to die," I said, my voice catching.

"Oh yes," she said. "Of course I am."

Kevin had arranged for me to continue seeing Marisa during my leave, for which I was grateful. On Saturday morning she surveyed me and said, "You look well."

"It's all the boxing," I said. Marisa was the only one I'd told about boxing; I'd been taking classes three afternoons a week and running and lifting on the other days. It was the only thing keeping me sane.

She nodded. "I want to talk to you about why you decided to move home."

My shoulders sagged a little. When I'd told her about my decision, her face had closed a millimeter, a camera shutter clicking shut. But she hadn't said anything—and I'd interpreted her silence as permission. She'd let me guide our conversation the past few weeks. "Okay," I said.

"I'm concerned that you're using moving home to care for your mother as a way to move away from your own pain."

I sighed. "I don't even know what that means."

"I think you do."

I did. I knew exactly what she meant.

"I don't want you to use your mother's need for care as an excuse not to grieve."

In that moment another moment unfolded. The week after I left Ted, I'd come home from work to Mom's house and found James at the kitchen table. There was a warrant out for his arrest for punching an off-duty cop in a bar fight.

I'd taken care of everything: called Mr. Peterson to escort James to turn himself in, arranged for a rehab to admit him when he was out on bail. I was about to go toss James's apartment for alcohol when Bill stopped me. "When you stop being busy," he'd said, "whether in three days or three years, your pain will still be there, until you deal with it."

I could hear his words in that moment, sitting in Marisa's office, not just in my mind but with my ears, my face, my skin. I looked at Marisa and felt like the shell I carried around was dissolving. If she was saying something Bill had said—Bill, who knew me better than anyone, who I missed so much I couldn't encompass the missing—then I could listen. I spent so much of my life weighing the motives behind what people said to me that it felt like a relief to trust her words, to trust the care behind them.

"I'm listening," I said.

"You're grieving for your father, your brother, your nephew, your boyfriend, your marriage. I'm just asking that you make time to feel all that pain, to work through it instead of skating over it. Ask for help."

Robert and Izzy came over for brunch on Sunday with the kids. Though I'd never liked Julia, and her absence was a relief, the pain on Robert's face hurt me. Sam was missing from the lineup as well. The table felt oddly empty.

"One more bite of eggs, Isaac, and then you can have a piece of candy," Izzy said.

"Athena, I'm going to count to three, and you're going to sit down and finish your fruit," Robert said.

"Laura doesn't have any children," Mom said, apropos of nothing.

I stood up and scooped more eggs onto my plate, taking deep breaths. When I sat down again, Mom was saying to Robert, "It's so nice to have company."

Robert glanced at me. "Laura's always here keeping you company, Mom."

Mom waved a hand.

"We've been walking on the beach every morning, haven't we, Mom?" I said.

Mom turned to Izzy. "Robert took me to lunch last week."

I glared at my brother.

"Mom," he said. "No, I didn't."

"*I* took you to lunch," I said. "We had club sandwiches at the Princess Diner." Mom kept looking at Robert. "Mom! Will you *look at me*!" All the kids fell silent and looked at me. My brother and sister exchanged glances. Mom was still looking at Robert.

I stood up, the cloth napkin Izzy had unearthed from the dining room falling from my lap. I went upstairs to change a load of laundry and was folding towels when Izzy appeared beside me. "Just leave it, okay?" I said.

"I just wanted to make sure you were okay."

"She won't *look* at me," I said. "When you and Robert are here, it's like I don't exist."

Izzy picked up a towel and folded it, the edges perfectly matched, the creases hospital-tight. She placed it next to the ones I'd folded, which now looked like they'd been done by a five-year-old.

"I don't know . . . how long I can do this," I said.

Izzy put her hand over mine on the pile of still-warm towels. "One day at a time," she said.

I shook myself back into motion. "Mom's been taking a nap after lunch lately. I'll go get her."

"Let Robert do it," Izzy said.

Half an hour later Mom was in bed and we were all gathered in Robert and James's old room, which had a closet full of toys and games for Sunday afternoons.

"Where's Sam today?" I said. I wanted to talk to my siblings privately, but we couldn't leave the kids.

Izzy was sitting on the floor with Ian in her lap, dangling a set of plastic keys in his face. "Golfing."

I pressed my lips together. Seriously?

"Which course?" Robert was sitting in Mom's old rocking chair.

"Daddy, it's your *turn!*" Athena said, tugging his attention back to their game of Mall Madness.

Robert pressed the button of the game's intercom. *Attention, mall shoppers, there's a clearance at the shoe store!*

My mouth moved in the shape of a smile. The game had been mine as a girl. I couldn't believe it still worked.

Isaac was pushing a dump truck around on the floor. He had always been able to amuse himself.

"Can we talk about Mom for a sec?" I said from the doorway. The floor was littered with toys.

"Ivy, give that toy back to your brother," Izzy said as Isaac silently fought his sister for the truck. "I'm going to count to three. One. Two."

"What about her?" Robert said.

"I'd like a night off every week," I said. "You know, go out to dinner."

"We agreed that Robert and I would pitch in for an aide three hours a day, in the afternoon," Izzy said. Ian threw his keys across the room then began to wail. Izzy forced her fingers into his mouth, winced as he bit down with his two teeth.

"Yes, so I can run errands and exercise," I said. "I need a

night of social time too."

"The rate is more expensive in the evening," Robert said.

"Aurelia, that's *mine*," Athena said, snatching back her game piece.

"No! Mine had the purple dress!"

A scuffle broke out, which Robert presided over by handing the purple-dressed cardboard piece back to Athena. "Aurelia, yours is blue." He pointed.

"I'm not asking for an aide," I said. "I'm asking for you two to help out."

Robert and Izzy exchanged looks.

"I've taken on the lion's share of Mom's care," I said. I took a deep breath; my voice was starting to waver. It always gave me away.

"That sounds reasonable," Robert said. "Iz and I can switch off."

"I don't know if—" Izzy said.

"We'll work it out." Robert cut her off, looking only at me. He smiled. "We're just glad you're doing this so we can keep Mom home for as long as possible."

"Has anyone heard from Ava?" I said.

Izzy set Ian on the carpet and stood up, leaning backward with her hands on her lower back. Robert was tapping his pink-dressed game piece along the mall floor, directing it into the shoe store to make a purchase.

"She won't answer my calls," I said.

"I'd leave it alone," Izzy said.

"He's our nephew," I said.

"Jeremiah was only in the hospital a couple of days," Robert said, looking up. "He should be out of the external fixation device by now, so he'll be doing physical therapy for a while."

I chewed my lip. Maybe I should just stop by and see him. I roused myself, thinking of the other thing I had to do. "Robert, can I talk to you?"

He looked at Izzy, who nodded. He followed me into the hallway and down the stairs, where we stood in the foyer by the seldom-used front door.

"How are you doing?"

Robert ran a palm over the stubble on his cheeks. "I'm tired." It was a mark of the growth of intimacy between us that he didn't ask what I was talking about.

"And Julia?"

"I don't know. She's still refusing to sign the divorce papers. Wants more child support." He sighed. "I just hope she'll accept the next deal so we don't have to go to court." He looked at me. "How are you doing?"

"I don't know," I said. "I made all these big decisions very quickly, and I can't quite figure out how I feel about them."

"Have you made up with Jonah?"

I shook my head. "He was so mad when he saw Ted at the hospital. I can't bring myself to call him."

"Ah," he said. "Well, I'm not really in a position to give relationship advice, but if I were . . . my advice would be that an apology can usually get you further than you think."

"Listen," I said, ignoring him. "I have to tell you something." I looked around, motioned to the living room. "Let's sit down."

Robert looked wary as he followed me to the high-backed loveseat.

I stared at my hands. "There's not really an easy way to say this," I said. "But I found this photo when I was looking for the will—" I pulled it out of my pocket.

Robert studied it for a moment. "So?"

"Turn it over."

He did. He became very still.

"Bill was my father," I said.

"When did he tell you?"

I shook my head. "He didn't. Mom did, before the funeral. She went . . . a little strange."

Robert laughed hoarsely.

"I mean, she was telling me about them having sex and stuff."

My brother buried his face in his hands, still laughing. After a time he stopped and considered me. "So, Mom cheated on Dad," he said.

"Yeah."

"And you're . . ."

"Your half-sister."

"Why didn't you tell me this sooner?"

I had no answer for that. "I was trying to deal with it."

"Well fuck." Robert stood up. "I guess that explains the house. Christ, Laura." He turned his back on me. When he looked around, his eyes were glistening. "Do you mind watching the girls for a little while? I need to clear my head."

I watched my brother's retreating back. "Sure."

Robert had actually taken the news better than I'd feared. James was the only one left I had to tell. He got out of rehab in two and a half weeks.

I had been prepared to get fed up with caring for Mom, which was definitely happening. I had been prepared to miss having my own space, which had happened the first night I moved back.

I had not realized I would be so *bored*.

There was nothing to achieve, nothing to win, nothing to earn. No one to give me the approval I craved. No one to praise me when Mom was being crazy and I was patient as a saint.

She wasn't sleeping much at night any more—usually just five or six hours. So I woke up tired, yoked to her sleeping hours of 11 to 5, and then spent the day hardly doing anything.

I felt exactly the way I used to feel during our yearly drive to the Cape every summer. We stopped going when Mom and Bill got married, but she still took us two or three summers after Dad died. The drive was less than three hours even with bad traffic, but as a five-year-old those hours stretched like an eternity, during which I always had to pee. I'd be wedged with James in the back seat of the station wagon, which faced backward, a laundry basket of beach towels between us, my trash bag of clothes under my feet so that my knees were jammed up near my chin. Even with all the windows down, the wind on the highway was hot. My thighs stuck to the ripped vinyl seat. After what felt like hours I'd ask, "Are we there yet?" No one would answer. Mom would turn up the radio volume. The car would slow, surrounded by traffic. I'd feel a buzzing in my legs. I couldn't sit still. Mom didn't pack books or games for the car; it was up to us to bring what we wanted. I had always brought a book, forgetting every year that I got dizzy after ten minutes of reading in the car.

Izzy and Robert loved to tell the story about the time I'd wet myself during that drive. It must have been the summer I turned four, because I hardly remembered it. I did remember the roar of Daddy shouting and, one of the few times ever, Mom shouting back at him. "Laura's just a little girl," Mom had said. "She's just a little girl." And we had pulled over and she had poured some water onto a rag she found wedged under her seat and cleaned me up and put me in a fresh pair of shorts from my trash bag. My underwear was all the way at the bottom, and I remember the uncomfortable chafe of the seam of my jean shorts against the top of my inner thigh the rest of the ride, which seemed to take forever, though Izzy swore it was only twenty more minutes.

That's how I felt on a daily basis now: like I was in a car going nowhere, with no opportunity to stretch my legs.

Once a week I checked my bank balance, my guts freezing every time I saw how much my savings account had dwindled. I had no money coming in, and after writing the check for James to Central Falls Rehab I wondered every day whether I'd made the right decisions. My expenses were minimal and my savings were high, but that didn't stop me from worrying. Ted had always been remarkably blasé about money—he was of the *there will always be more where that came from* tribe—but I'd never caught his carefree attitude. I'd worried about money when we lived in DC on his commissions and my tiny student stipend; I'd worried about it when we bought our house, which was well within our means and left us enough margin to keep saving; I'd worried about it when I was on my own again, and I worried about it now. The problem was that I had very little reasonable ammunition to lobby against my obsessive mind, because I wasn't earning any income.

So one Sunday, to introduce some novelty from my thought patterns that were growing as rutted as a well-traveled dirt lane, I got out my camera.

Mom was a much better subject than she'd been before, because instead of hiding her face she didn't acknowledge that I was photographing her. I took simple shots—of her eating lunch and playing cards. The act of taking photos worked its usual magic, which was simply to make me pay better attention to ordinary moments. The act of paying attention made them beautiful.

Mom had taken to slipping out the back door and heading straight for the ocean at every opportunity. Sometimes she even wore her swimsuit, presumably having changed while I thought she was using the toilet. We put a child safety lock on the sliding door, but that wouldn't guarantee anything for long.

Two nights after the installation of the child safety lock, Mom wet the bed. Izzy ordered a new plastic-lined mattress. I bought a pack of Depends.

Chapter 21

Laura

The hard workouts at The Box were so necessary. On Sunday, my rest day, I felt like crawling out of my skin. Sweat was the only thing that cleared my mind, as if the exertion were scrubbing it clean of grief and lightening the load of caretaking. As I grew physically stronger, I felt psychologically stronger.

Seeing Marisa had become a mental form of boxing. She sought my weak points and pressed her advantage. Instead of shutting down—fleeing the ring—I engaged. It was painful, but it felt like ripping off layers of crusty bandages, like pouring clear water over festering wounds. I was finding that things I'd kept in the dark for years, that had grown rampant in secrets and silence, couldn't survive in the light of day.

We unearthed old hurts: a high school boyfriend who had broken up with me for a mutual friend, and I'd pretended to be happy for them; the snubs and teasing I'd always endured from my siblings; the pain and confusion that had enveloped us after Dad died. Marisa pressed me to confront the grief I felt about my miscarriage. I still knew every day how old the baby would have been. I told her how sometimes when I was doing dishes or loading clothes into the dryer, I thought I heard a thin wail and my stomach dropped as if I'd forgotten about the baby—then dropped again when I remembered there wasn't a baby. We talked about how things had ended with Ted—who, since Bill's funeral, still called me a couple times a week. Sometimes I picked up just to have someone to talk to. He was kind and funny and listened to me more attentively than he had while we were married.

All the work I was doing on myself finally compelled me to call Jonah. I stood on the patio on Wednesday afternoon after a four-mile run, phone in hand, staring at his Google photo. Then I pressed my thumb to call him and lifted the phone to my ear. Two rings and it went to voicemail: screening my call. That was okay. It might be easier this way. I listened to his voice inviting people to leave a message, wishing them a wonderful day. "Hi, Jonah. It's Laura. I hope you listen to this message. I just wanted to tell you . . . how sorry I am." My voice wobbled, but I took a deep breath to steady myself. "I'm sorry that I slept with Ted. It was hands-down the dumbest thing I've ever done. And I'm sorry it took me this long to call you. You told me you were falling in love with me . . . and I never told you that I was falling in love with you too. I know this call is probably too little, too late. But I wanted you to know that I miss you. Okay. Bye."

On Friday after boxing I ran into the A&P to pick up a few things. My tank top was stained with sweat marks under the pits and boobs and my face was glistening. I didn't care; I felt free. Into the cart I tossed eggs and OJ and yogurt, a pint of Ben & Jerry's and two packs of Depends. I had to go next door for wine.

I turned my cart down the cereal aisle and saw Jonah standing in the middle of it, comparing nutrition information between Corn Pops and Apple Jacks.

He looked good; he must be lifting. The sight of his now-tight purple Phish T-shirt socked me in the gut. "They're both worth it," I said.

He looked up and smiled. I was tempted to say, "Hey, stranger," but imagined Amber's horrified face if I told her I'd said that, so refrained.

"Hey," he said. "I got your message." For a moment awkwardness swelled between us. "Thanks."

Thanks? Did that mean, like, *Thanks, I forgive you*? Or, *Thanks for acknowledging how much you screwed up*?

Before I could deconstruct this any further, Jonah's his eyes fell on the Depends and his face sagged. I was still clutching the handle of my cart when he dropped the cereal boxes to the floor and engulfed me in a sideways hug. I managed to let go of the cart and grip his left arm, my hands on either side of his elbow.

"I'm sorry," he said into my hair. And even though I was the one who was sorry, I knew he was sorry about my mother and I knew he understood how much pain I was in, and those two words meant more to me coming from him in that moment than they'd ever meant from anyone before.

After a long moment that I wished would stretch on forever, he let go. "Can I buy you a cup of coffee?" I asked, sure he'd say yes since he hadn't bolted when I commented on his cereal choices.

But he hesitated, biting his lip. "I'm kind of seeing someone," he said.

My eyes stung with tears, even though I was the one at fault. And I realized again, there in the A&P under the fluorescent lights of the cereal aisle, how much I loved Jonah, and that some mistakes couldn't be fixed. "I'm happy for you," I heard myself say. I smiled with a mouth that felt like someone else's, the muscles not working right.

"It was good to see you," he said.

I left my cart where it was and went home. Mom was shouting at Caitlyn, but I had another twenty minutes before her shift was up, so I got in the shower and stood under the hot water for a long time.

It was just Mom and I at dinner that night, eating baked potatoes smothered with broccoli and Velveeta. Robert and Izzy had been taking turns dropping by for dinner one night a week, in addition to the Wednesday nights when they traded off taking care of Mom. I think they sensed my loneliness, and they could see Mom deteriorating. But tonight it was just the two of us.

I poked at my potato listlessly. I'd been avoiding thoughts of Jonah for weeks, but tonight I let them wash over me. I thought of his face when he'd said, "I'm seeing someone else." He'd looked like he was trying to be happy—and failing miserably. I was sure that my own face had not looked like it was trying to do anything, except perhaps not to cry.

"Where's Robert?" Mom asked.

"At the hospital, Mom." I got up and poured myself a glass of milk. I hadn't drunk milk with dinner in twenty years.

"Is he sick?"

"No, Mom. He's a doctor, remember?"

She had cleaned her plate. She often forgot that she'd

eaten, her brain not registering that her stomach was full, so I tried to leave her empty plate in front of her as long as possible. "No he's not," she said irritably. "He's a banker. You think I don't know my own husband's occupation? I am mad at him, though. He hasn't been to see me for *weeks*."

I sat back down. I didn't know what to say. My presence never seemed to be enough for her.

Her face was puckered with irritation.

My phone buzzed from deep in my purse in the dining room. I dug for it, caught the call on the last ring. Jonah.

"Hi," I said, trying to contain my giddiness.

"Can we still get that coffee?"

I wanted to suggest a drink instead. Coffee was for old friends and first dates, but at that point I'd have gone anywhere with him. "Let me just find someone to stay with my mom," I said. "I'll text you, but it should be fine."

I called Amber, who had offered several times to stay with Mom so I could get out. I had yet to take her up on it. She agreed to come over, and I texted Jonah that I'd meet him at Scrivener's in an hour.

I convinced Mom to let me put a pair of Depends on her. Some nights it was such a struggle that I didn't bother, but I didn't want Amber to have to worry about anything bathroom-related. I took Mom down to the porch room and put on *Rudy*, one of her favorite movies. I ran the flatiron over the top layer of my hair and swiped on some mascara as the doorbell sounded. I let Amber in and gave her the rundown, as if I were a nervous mother leaving her child with a new babysitter for the first time.

I beat Jonah to Scrivener's, ordered a decaf skim vanilla latte for myself and a triple 2 percent mocha for him. It was open mic night, so the cafe was dark and filled with hipsters clutching guitars.

I sat down as far from the makeshift stage as possible, tapping my foot with nerves. Maybe he was just trying to let me down easy. But didn't he do that already? He was polite to a fault, though. I checked my watch. What if he was standing me up to get back at me?

Jonah walked in and caught my eye, smiling. My heart was hammering like a high schooler's. He leaned down and kissed my cheek, then sat down across from me. He took a sip of his coffee, the huge purple mug obscuring his face.

"I called you because things have changed," he said.

The bottom dropped out of my stomach.

"I'm no longer seeing anyone," he said, his green eyes piercing mine. "I mean, actually, I made that up earlier, trying to spare your feelings. The truth is that I couldn't believe you didn't call earlier. I'd told you I was falling in love with you. I thought you'd call right away so we could make up. Then I didn't want to see you ever again. Then you called, and I saw you, and I didn't know what to—"

"I meant it," I said. "I'm in love with you." I wanted so badly to add the word "too"—*I'm in love with you too*—but I didn't know if that was accurate. I shivered in the draft that swept across our table every time the door opened. It was cold for October.

He just sat there looking at me.

"I just couldn't forgive myself for what I did," I said.

"I forgive you," he said. "I want to put it behind us. Maybe we can go backward down the number line."

I stared at him. "What does that mean?"

He cracked a grin. "It's a Phish song." He drummed a little beat on the tabletop. "I'm trying to say that I want there to be an *us* again."

I looked out the window. The town turned off the streetlights at nine o'clock to save power. It was so dark outside that I could only see our reflection. "I'd like that," I said.

When I got home Amber was asleep on the couch under the blue-and-white afghan my grandmother had made for Mom. I turned off the TV and she stirred. "Hey," she said.

"Thank you so much for doing this," I said. "I'm sorry, I know you must be tired."

Amber struggled into a sitting position. "It's okay to ask

for help, you know," she said. "I was happy to do it. How'd it go with Jonah?"

"Good. We're back together." My smile escaped the sober face I'd been trying to maintain.

Amber smiled too. "Good. So what's the maybe-not-good part?"

I sat down next to her, still wearing my coat, my purse wedged under my arm. "He wants me to stop seeing Ted."

"Are you seeing Ted?"

"No."

"But?"

"I feel funny, saying I'll never talk to Ted again, just because that's what Jonah wants."

Amber didn't say anything.

"I mean, I did cheat on Jonah with Ted."

"Yeah." Amber's voice had the relieved air of *I-was-going-to-say-it-if-you-didn't*.

"And it's not like I want Ted still in my life."

Amber kissed me on the cheek and stood. "You don't need to figure it all out right now. Go to bed, get some sleep."

The weeks passed, full but uneventful. I thought of James more than I wanted to. Almost every day I was tempted to call him; Monday had been his birthday, and I had never not called him on his birthday. But I didn't want to know whether or not he was still in rehab. I'd told him he had to do it on his own, and I had to let him.

Chapter 22

James

After my outburst and my attack on the tree, I stay in my room for twenty-four hours. I come out only at the tail-end of mealtimes to grab a plate of food, which I eat in my room. I return the dirty plate at the next meal.

The truth is, I'm expecting Marcus to charge into my room at any moment and demand that I attend meetings. But I miss my one-on-one, I miss morning meeting, I miss morning small group, I miss afternoon meeting, and no one comes looking for me.

What finally drives me from my room after a solitary lunch isn't remorse or a burning desire to apologize; it's boredom. As I'm considering whether I'd be physically capable of sleeping *again*, I hear a soft knock on the door and my heart leaps in my chest. But before I can get up to answer, I hear Lou, whose room is next door to mine, say, "Come in!" Muffled voices, then two sets of footsteps walking down the hall. "Think someone'll jump down my throat again today?" I hear Lou say.

"I feel sorry for him," Tony says.

Before I can think too much, I open the door. "Hey," I say.

Lou and Tony turn, their expressions wary. "Hey, James," Lou says.

"Look, man, I'm real sorry about yesterday," I say. "To be honest, I had a real hard time in prison, and the thought of you finding God or your Higher Power or whatever while you were in there—it was hard for me to hear."

Lou and Tony stare at me, surprised; I'm surprised too. Lou holds out a hand. "Don't sweat it," he says as we shake.

We walk down to Meeting Room C together. Predictably, the other two guys and Marcus fall silent when I walk in with Lou and Tony. The two of them sit in their usual chairs. I stand in the doorway. "I'm sorry for my behavior yesterday," I say. "It was unacceptable. I'll—um—I'll try harder to follow our rules."

As I speak, I notice something remarkable. I hadn't been

sorry—or at least, I had been hell-bent on not being sorry—but as I say the words, I find that I *am* sorry, and that I *do* want to try harder.

Act the way you want to feel, I hear Laura's voice in my head. *Also known as taking the high road.* Bill's voice.

"What do you say, guys?" Marcus says. "Can we give James another shot?"

There's a murmur of agreement, and I sit down.

"Do you want to start us off?" he asks, looking directly at me.

I take a deep breath. "I always heard people say they went to rehab because they hit rock bottom. I never knew what that meant. I always knew I could go lower than I had. I've been to rehab twice, never finished." I close my eyes. "I don't know if I can finish this time. I don't know if I have it in me. I hate being here." I swallow, take a sip of water from the bottle I always carry. "But I'm here because I hurt someone I love very much, very badly. And I don't want to do it anymore."

During our one-on-one session on day 12 (sixteen days to go), Marcus gives me homework. My assignment is to have a ten-minute conversation with someone without talking about myself once.

"What if they ask how I am?" I say. "Do I ignore them?"

"No. You give them a one-word answer, and then you ask about *them* and keep asking. People like to talk about themselves. Piece of cake."

"I don't like to talk about myself," I say.

Marcus gives me a withering stare that reminds me of Ava. "What did Lou talk about during group this morning?"

I think. Nothing comes.

"Exactly." Marcus points a finger at me, as if he could physically touch this mental deficiency of mine. "You're so wrapped up in yourself. It's one of the things that makes you drink."

"I drink because I like drinking," I say stubbornly.

"And you keep drinking to numb your pain. Instead of

dealing with it like a grown-up."

I think of Bill's funeral.

"What're you thinking about?"

"How not normal it might be to spend your stepfather's funeral planning your next drink. Or does that qualify as thinking about myself too much too?"

Marcus's face spasms slightly. "It's okay," he says, his voice gentle. "It's okay as long as you realize your thinking is warped, resolve to work on it instead of getting stuck on what you've done wrong, getting depressed and primed for a drink." He taps his fingertips on the table between us. "See the difference?"

"Yeah." I get up to go.

"James."

"Yeah." I turn toward him. The office where we meet is so small that when Marcus stands, I'm almost afraid he's going to burst through the walls like the Hulk transforming inside a box too small for him.

"I'm proud of you."

I can't stop my face from smiling. "Thanks."

At dinner that night I sit with Lou and Tony. They were friends before coming here—but they're not the kind of friends that make you feel like an outsider. They seem cool. Laid back. They're both clean-cut, wear khakis and polo shirts every day like they're on a golf outing. Meeting them my first day had changed my idea of what an alcoholic looked like. I thought they were all losers like me—scruffy, broke, deadbeat dads who drank to cover their embarrassment that they weren't like Lou and Tony. But apparently clean-cut, rich, caring dads could be drunks too.

I spend the whole meal asking Lou questions—about his job as a VP with a bank, his wife, his daughters. I wonder suddenly if it was *harder* for Lou than for me to realize his life was falling apart. His life sounded beautiful, at least from the outside, whereas mine had always been a disaster. *Watch out*, I hear Marcus's voice in my head. *You might just be starting to learn empathy.*

My thirty-seventh birthday falls on day 13 (fifteen days to go; *I'm not even halfway?*).

I walk into breakfast feeling slightly nervous, afraid the group might break into song. Birthdays embarrass me. I don't want it to be a big deal.

But when no one looks up as I enter the cafeteria, I feel a peeling away of that delusion; underneath is a shattering disappointment.

I heap three pancakes on my plate. I've been putting on some weight since I've been here, but it's mostly muscle mass from the time I spend lifting in the afternoons. But it's my birthday, and I'm going to eat as many carbs as I want.

I sit down with Lou and Tony, open three plastic tubs of syrup, and empty them onto my pancakes. They don't wish me a happy birthday.

I feel my desperation growing as I sit through morning meeting, through small group. Aren't the people at intake smart enough to screen for birthdays? Don't they know that most of us are in here only because we've pissed off or hurt everyone we know out there?

By the afternoon I'm so miserable I blow off Lou when he invites me to play pool and go upstairs to sulk. In my room alone, I'm wishing for the thousandth time that I hadn't had to give up my cheap cell phone plan so I could stream some Netflix shows.

Marcus bangs into my room without knocking.

"We have to stop meeting like this," I say. You'd think I'd be relieved that he'd come to find me, but I'm just annoyed.

"C'mon. Emergency meeting downstairs."

"Leave me alone."

"I'll throw you over my shoulder," Marcus threatens.

I sigh and follow him, making a mental note to punish Marcus later by not participating in group.

As I follow Marcus into the community room, a cluster of people at the far end turn around and shout, "Surprise!" A large sheet cake rests on the table alongside the usual bottles of water and juice and cans of soda.

Since everyone's staring at me, I paste a smile on my face. "Wow," I say. "Thanks!"

Marcus shakes my hand. "Happy birthday, man."

They've done exactly what I thought I wanted, but I find as I cut myself a piece of chocolate cake that I'd rather be alone.

I realize then that maybe my misery has nothing to do with what's happening to me and everything to do with me, myself.

Day 21. Marcus and I are walking around the pond. I'm chain-smoking. He's trying to quit for the third time because his wife is pregnant. He convinced me to walk with him because the movement takes his mind off the nicotine cravings. He says. He doesn't ask me not to smoke. Which is good, because otherwise I wouldn't be hoofing it out here with him at all.

I feel better than I have in years. Not healthy, exactly. Not yet. But I feel as though I'm moving toward health. I don't know what it's about—I've been sober this long before, but I've never felt like this. Marcus says it's because I've opened up to connecting with people. I wish that weren't it. Because it hurts like hell. I've told a few friends in here more about Mom being sick, about Bill dying, about getting drunk at his funeral. I haven't told anyone yet about Jeremiah. I haven't told anyone anything about prison, except that one glancing reference I made when I apologized to Lou for being a jackass.

Marcus and I are talking about basketball, nice and easy, huffing a little as he sets a brisk pace. The weather's growing colder. My right hand holding its cigarette is chapped from the wind. The perimeter of the pond reflects the orange and red leaves, but the center is the same gray as the sky.

"What was it for you?" Marcus asks.

"What was what?"

"What drove you in here this time?"

My heart accelerates. I take a deeper drag off the cigarette. "My stepdad—"

"Don't lie to me, man." Marcus is out of breath. "If you

don't want to answer right now, it's okay. But I won't let you leave here until you do." He huffs a little, clutches at his chest, winded. "Let's stop here for a sec."

We pause at the rickety wooden picnic table next to the tree I destroyed. Marcus heaves himself onto a bench, leans back on the table. I step up onto the bench, sit on the tabletop, facing the lake, facing his back. "I got behind the wheel after the funeral," I said.

Marcus nods once. I'm glad I can't see his face. I feel like I'm in a confessional, a place I've avoided since I graduated from Our Lady of the Sea twenty-three years ago. "Jeremiah was in the car," I said, my voice breaking. "My brother was going to take him home—it was his car—but I got behind the wheel. After they told me not to. They all told me not to. But I wanted to prove how fine I was, you know? Jeremiah was scared. I tried to make a U-turn, take him back, but I turned into oncoming traffic. We were struck . . . on the passenger side."

Marcus shifts his body to look at me. "Did your son make it?"

My face crumples like a used tissue. "Yeah. But he was hurt pretty bad." I wish Marcus would turn away. He does, but he lifts a meaty hand and puts it on my knee, grips hard. He doesn't tell me it's okay, because it's not. And it's this absence of platitudes or any kind of letting me off the hook that calms me down. I have done terrible things. It's not okay. Getting sober doesn't make anything okay. But maybe if I can stick this out day by day, I can stop hurting the people I love most. Please, God, let that be true.

On day 27 I wake up and instead of being thrilled that I've only got one day left here, all I want is to stay here another twenty-eight days. Ironic. I think about all the times I've heard people say that God has a sense of humor and wonder if this is what they meant.

The prospect of going back to the world is terrifying. I don't know where I'm going to live. The only people I know will still talk to me are other drunks, and it's not like I can pull up a barstool and tell Dean and Eddie about my journey into sobriety. I talk it over with Marcus, and he just shakes his head. "You know exactly where you're going," he said. "You're just afraid. You're afraid to do what you know you have to do."

I've never had someone who knew me so well be so unflinchingly honest all the time. It sucks.

Today I'm afraid to write Ava a letter. When we had Family Day everyone was supposed to write a letter to one person they'd hurt, even if no one was coming. I hadn't invited anyone, per Laura's request, so I gave myself a pass on writing the letter as well. But now it's time.

I take a notebook and a pen to the table by the pond. It's cold today, and the wind is cruel. I don't have gloves, but I figure this will force me to write faster. *Dear Ava*, I begin, and I realize nothing could possibly make this go faster. I sit there on that cold bench and write about how sorry I am, one torturous word and sentence at a time. I write about how the prospect of one day earning the right to see her and Jeremiah again is the only thing that keeps me going on days when I crave alcohol so badly I can smell the fumes from memory, from thousands of hours studying the object of my obsession.

I have no idea how I'm going to do this. Finish the letter, leave rehab, stay sober the second I'm free again to go anywhere I want. I have no friends. No friends who will want me around when I'm sober, anyway. I write that at the end of the letter: *I have no idea how I'm going to do this, but because of you and J I'm going to try with everything in me.*

Chapter 23

Laura

On the Wednesday before Halloween, my door creaked open and I woke with a start, my adrenaline already pumping. "What's wrong?" I said. It was still dark out.

"Hi," Mom said.

"Are you okay?" I sat up and peered at the clock: 5:12.

"Are you okay?" Mom said, mimicking me. She was wearing her nightgown over a pair of navy slacks. Her feet were bare. She held out an empty mug. "Coffee."

I fell back in bed, staring at the ceiling. I did not sign up for this shit.

Mom sat at the foot of the bed and bounced up and down. "Coffee?"

I got up, my feet cold on the carpeted floor. My pedicure was chipped. I stuffed my feet into slippers and shuffled into the bathroom. Only twelve hours until Robert would arrive for my night off.

I brushed my teeth and washed my face and stumped downstairs. Halfway down there was a shatter of china breaking. I ran into the kitchen and found Mom standing over the shattered remains of my purple Scrivener's mug.

"What is *wrong* with you?" I said. "That was my favorite mug!" I pushed her backward a little, pointing at the table. "Go. Go sit down before you cut your foot."

She stared at me, uncomprehending.

I pointed again. "Sit!"

She sat.

I got out the dustpan and brush, trying not to cry. I was being silly. I could buy another one in town. Still, I didn't talk to Mom for the rest of the morning.

At noon I was spreading mustard on whole wheat bread for turkey sandwiches and heating up split pea soup while Mom paced the kitchen, whining that she wanted another cup of coffee.

"Of course you do," I said. "You woke me up at five a.m." But it was easier just to give in. I brewed a pot of decaf, making it extra strong so she wouldn't suspect the lack of caffeine.

I sat down at the head of the table, Mom on my left. I let my arm rest flat on the table, leaned my head on my upper arm. I thought about how Bill had made my relationship with my mother work. Now I knew why: I was their child. It was like my mother and I spoke different languages, and when Bill married her, I suddenly had a translator. An intermediary. And now that bridge was gone.

The microwave beeped, and I stood up to get our soup.

"I'm hungry," Mom said. "When are we eating?"

"Right now," I said. My voice was exasperated. Bill had never gotten exasperated with my mother, even when she was complaining about a situation she had gotten herself into against his advice. He was the epitome of patience. I was the epitome of frustrated daughter.

A knock sounded on the kitchen door as I carried two bowls of soup to the table, a potholder protecting each hand. Mom looked around as if she had no idea where the sound might have come from, and I smiled a little against my will. I worked one hand out of its potholder and opened the door without looking through the curtain. And found myself face to face with James.

"Did you lose your key?" I asked through the screen to cover my shock.

"No," he said, holding it up. "I just thought I'd let you decide whether to let me in or not."

Ava's words echoed in my head. *If I ever see him again, I swear to God I'll kill him.* I saw Jeremiah's face, pinched with pain. And I saw my brother standing on the doorstep, with the decency to let me decide if I wanted to see him. "You finish rehab?"

"Yes."

I stepped away from the door.

"Who's that?" Mom demanded, her voice querulous.

"Mom?" James opened the screen door and came into the kitchen, stood there holding his army green rucksack. "It's me, James."

She folded her arms and stared at him. "I don't know you."

In a way I could see what she meant. James had gained some weight back—his face looked fuller, his chest and arms more muscular. He looked well rested and smelled of aftershave.

"Mom, why don't you sit down so we can eat," I said. I didn't look at James but said, "You want a sandwich?"

"I'll get it," he said. He had put his bag down by the door and was carrying Mom's and my plates to the table. "You sit."

I took a few bites of my sandwich, my mouth dry as sawdust. James made himself a sandwich. He sat down next to Mom and bowed his head over his plate. I stared.

He looked up and shrugged. "Guy I was close to in rehab with always said grace before eating," he said. "I kinda got in the habit." He turned to Mom. "Mom, how have you been?"

She had finished her sandwich already and was eyeing his.

"She's deteriorated a lot," I said, keeping my voice low, as if Mom couldn't hear me.

"I have *not*," she said, glaring at me. "The doctor says I'm just fine. He gave me the all-clear to go to Europe with Robert. I need to finish packing. They say that Paris can be cool this time of year."

"Okay, Mom. That sounds great," I said.

She got up and left the table. I heard the TV turn on.

James and I sat in billowing silence for a moment.

"Why did you come here?" I asked.

"I wondered if I could leave my bag here while I went to see a guy about a room in a halfway house."

I shrugged. "I guess so. Whatever."

"Why aren't you at work?"

"I took a leave of absence." I took a deep breath. "I needed some time."

James's eyes widened. "But you love work."

"Yeah, I do." My voice cracked a little. "But so much happened at once. I couldn't . . . integrate it all, and stay healthy and present for my clients." I didn't say how much I missed them, how much I missed getting outside of myself. James had not earned the right to hear any of that.

"So . . . you're here for the morning?"

I looked at my plate. "I moved back in six weeks ago."

My brother's silence made me look up. He looked confused. "Why?" he said.

I could feel a headache tightening around my forehead. "We were going to have to sell the house to pay for Mom to go to a nursing home. I didn't want to do either of those things. We couldn't afford aides to keep her here. So I decided to do it."

"Why didn't you try to reach me?" His voice was empty of its usual anger, was instead concerned.

"You know why," I said.

James looked at me as if seeing me for the first time. "You're right."

"Wow, rehab really did change you." I leaned my head on my hand. "I'm sorry. Rough day."

"Do you want me to stay with Mom for a little while?"

"Caitlyn will be here at one," I said. "I'm going out for a couple hours."

"Okay," he said. "I'm going to go see about this room. When will you be back?"

"At four. Robert comes at five. I'd recommend coming somewhere in that window."

"I'll come back to get my stuff at four, then. Okay if I use my key?"

"Yeah." He walked to the door.

"James."

He turned.

"Happy birthday."

He smiled. "Thanks, Laur." He shuffled his feet. "You too. I mean, I know it was weeks ago, but—" But *I wasn't there* were the words he left unspoken.

"Thanks."

I hadn't had time to process that James was here before he was gone again.

When he came back at four o'clock on the dot, Mom was watching *The Real Housewives* of somewhere. She smelled like chlorine—Caitlyn had taken her swimming at the Y, since she only had bathroom trouble at night. I was sitting on the couch next to her reading *Emma*.

"How'd it go?" I said.

"Not great," he said, sitting down on the couch next to me. "They won't have a room for a couple of weeks." He sighed.

I waited, where before I would have jumped to make an offer.

"I'm going to ask you something," he said. "And if you want to say no, just say no."

I waited. Mom turned up the volume on the TV. I took the remote away from her and turned it back down.

"I'm *watching* that," Mom said.

"Mom, please. Just hold on." I looked back at James.

"Can I stay here with you and Mom for three weeks until my room is ready?" he asked. His voice was low.

"What would you do if I said no?"

"Borrow money from Dean to stay in a motel a couple nights, till I start working on Monday and can pay for it myself."

"Dean from high school?"

"Yeah."

"Have you been talking to him?"

Mom grabbed the remote back from me. "Let me *have* it."

James was looking between me and Mom. His gaze settled back on me. "No. But I'd offer him interest. He'd take me up on it, I know he would."

"I don't want you talking to him," I said. Dean had been involved in most of James's trouble through high school and college. I wished there was another alternative. "You can stay here."

"Thanks, Laur." He sighed again. "I really didn't want to have to ask you for anything."

Mom stood up. "I'm going out," she said.

"Okay." I didn't look up.

James stood up. "Where are you going, Mom?"

"Out," she said. "You can't come." She left the room.

James stared at me. "You're just—"

"She'll get halfway up the stairs and forget what she was doing," I said. I rubbed my forehead. "If I get one whiff of alcohol—"

"I'm clean," he said.

"You've said that before."

"This time is different."

"I hope so," I said. "I want to make two other things clear. Besides the fact that you obviously have to stay sober."

"I'm all ears."

"First, I'm still really angry at you, and I don't want you to think that everything's peachy between us just because I'm letting you stay here."

"Got it."

"Second, you're the only one who doesn't know yet that Bill was my real dad."

"He does know." Mom had come back and was standing in the doorway. "Because he's a drunk *and* an eavesdropper."

"Mom," I said through clenched teeth. "I'm talking to James right now."

James was staring at Mom. He dropped his gaze to the floor. "She's right. I did know."

My mouth fell open in shock. "What? How?"

"I overheard Mom and Bill talking one time. I don't know, I was maybe twelve. I was sneaking back in from smoking cigarettes with Brad O'Leary, and Bill was asking when they were going to tell you that he was your real dad."

I closed my eyes. "God damn it, James. Why didn't you tell me?"

"Because you were nine. Because Mom made me promise." He glanced at the doorway, but she'd disappeared. "She was so mad she was about to beat me." James sighed. "I listened."

My whole body felt wooden. James looked concerned. "I need to be alone now," I said.

James stood up without arguing.

I leaned my head back on the couch and stared at the ceiling.

I woke with a start to the sound of the porch door opening. Mom was playing with her knitting needles in the armchair. I leapt to my feet, staring wildly around. Robert must be arriving and I hadn't called to tell him James was here.

But it was Izzy who opened the door, shepherding Isaac and Ivy in front of her, carrying Ian on her hip.

"What're you doing here?" I said.

Izzy was too preoccupied to notice my tone. "Ivy just finished swim practice and we were nearby, so I thought we'd stop in."

The smell of chlorine intensified; Ivy's hair was still wet.

Isaac ran at me. "Can I have a cookie?" he asked as I gave him a hug, distracted.

"Sure," I said. "Iz, I have to tell you something."

Izzy nodded distractedly. "Okay. I have to feed Ian, and Isaac does need a snack." *Granola bar*, she mouthed at me. She had convinced Isaac that granola bars were cookies. "Let's go to the kitchen."

Before any of us could move, James walked into the room. I froze. James and Izzy stared at each other.

"Nuncle James!" Isaac hurled himself at James.

"Hey, buddy," James said, picking him up.

Ivy moved toward him a little more reluctantly, and James pulled her to him in a sideways hug. "Ivy, you're getting so big." She smiled shyly.

"My mom said you were going to be away for a long time," Isaac said. "Where did you go?"

"I went to a place where I could get better," James said, without missing a beat.

"Were you *sick*?"

"Something like that." He looked at Izzy. "Okay if I take them upstairs?"

Izzy shook her head. "Sorry, we're just stopping in. Kids, say hi to Grandma." We had all been ignoring Mom, who hadn't looked up from the tangle of yarn in her lap.

Ivy grabbed Isaac and dragged him over to say hello.

"Grandma will let you watch Nickelodeon if you ask nicely," Izzy said, and Ivy pounced on the remote. "Laura, can I see you in the kitchen, please?"

I followed Izzy past James. Ian started crying as she swung the diaper bag onto a chair and started digging for a bottle. She jammed the nipple into his mouth and turned her fierce eyes on me. "Explain."

"He just got out. He went to check on a room in a halfway house, but they don't have any openings for a couple of weeks. I told him he could stay here until then."

Izzy snorted. "Of course you did. You were always too soft on him."

I could feel my hackles rising. "Yeah, well, it was stay here or borrow money from Dean to stay in a motel. This is the first time he's finished rehab, and on my dime. I'd like it to stick."

"Wouldn't we all," Izzy said. She sat down and rubbed her eyes. "God, I could really use a cigarette," she said. She had stopped smoking ten years ago.

"It won't be for long," I said.

Izzy glared at me for a moment, but then her face softened. "He looks good," she said. "He put on some weight."

"He needed to."

"Yeah." Izzy sighed. "Well, I guess what's done is done." She looked down at Ian, who was sucking greedily on his bottle. "You still mad at him?"

I sat down next to her. "I'm freaking furious."

"Me too. And I have to say, my hopes are not high." She removed the bottle from Ian's mouth and patted him on the back. He let out a tiny belch. "You call Robert?"

"Not yet. This just happened."

Izzy whistled. "Well, shit."

At that moment the porch door opened and both of us tensed in our seats. "What are *you* doing here?" Robert's voice was mean.

Izzy and I jumped up and ran to the porch. Mom had moved to the couch with Ivy and Isaac. The three of them were watching James and Robert, who stood a few feet apart.

"Hi," I said, moving to stand between them. "James is here at my invitation."

Robert raised his eyebrows, looking past me at James. "What is he doing here?" he said again.

Izzy beckoned to her daughter. "Ivy, take your brothers upstairs."

We all waited as Ivy heaved Ian into her arms, took Isaac by the hand, and left the room.

"James is out of rehab," I said. "Which is great. And he's getting a room in a halfway house, it's just not ready yet, and he's staying with me and Mom until it is."

Robert stared at me for a long moment, and I found hope lifting in chest: Maybe he'd take the news as well as Izzy had. The volume of his voice a second later made James, Izzy, and me all jump. "Dammit, Laura! How many times are you going to let him walk over you?"

"Keep your *voice* down," Mom said from the corner.

We all turned to look at her.

She glared up at us. "I'm *working* here." She held up the needles and tangle of thread.

"It's only for a little while," I said to Robert, ignoring Mom. I could hear the pleading note in my voice.

"No," Robert said. "I want him out of this house." He pointed to the door for emphasis.

I looked at James. We were talking about him like he wasn't in the room, like he was Mom. But he didn't jump in, just looked at me. I turned back to Robert, my chin jutting out. "I'm the caretaker of the house. I'm caring for Mom. I get to decide."

"No fucking way," Robert said. "That is not how this works. Izzy, back me up. The three of us need to agree."

"*Ex*cuse me." Mom stood up. "I'll wash your mouth out with soap if you ever use language like that in my house again."

The four of us stared at her, chastened.

"Sorry, Mom," Robert muttered.

Izzy cleared her throat. "Laura's right."

I was so relieved and surprised, I started laughing. "Now there's a sentence I've never heard come out of your mouth."

Robert glared at me. "Stop laughing. This is serious. This . . . *idiot* totaled my car! He could have *killed* Jeremiah. And I want a say in whether or not he stays in this house."

James had been silent. I glanced at him now, gratified that he hadn't jumped in to defend himself. James looked at me. "He's right. I could have killed Jeremiah."

"No one's disputing that," Izzy said huffily. "But Laura's staying in the house, caring for Mom, and she gets to decide."

I thought Robert might turn and leave. He seemed to be fighting to control himself. Still pointedly not looking at James, he said, "He needs to be out of the house while I'm here with Mom. Mom and I are ordering in Chinese tonight, aren't we?" He didn't look at Mom either.

James left the room and came back a minute later with his jacket. "Laura, I'll be back after ten," he said. He stopped at the door and turned to me. "It was great seeing all of you. And I'm going to a meeting, not to a bar." He left.

Chapter 24

Laura

I was meeting Jonah at The Wharf at 7:30. It was only 5:30, but I needed to escape the house. I put on gym clothes, packed a dress and sandals and toiletries in my gym bag, and drove to The Box.

My body felt sluggish, like molasses was running in my veins, my head pounding. *What is* he *doing here? How many times are you going to let him walk all over you?*

I locked my bag in a locker and laced up my sneakers. Walked to the main gym, wrapped my hands, tugged on my black gloves. Warmed up in front of the mirror, step-drag pivot jab and weave duck right hook, dancing on the balls of my feet. The world receded. Step-drag pivot jab and weave.

I was pounding on the punching bag, no one to hold it steady, when Kate approached. "Want a sparring partner?" she asked.

I dragged the back of my glove across my forehead. "Sure."

I'd only sparred with her twice, and it had been humbling. I went back to my locker for my sparring helmet, which was of dense foam. Most boxers didn't use one, but I was vain. And I didn't want to explain bruises on my face.

Kate circled me in the ring, keeping up a steady stream of feedback. "Throw even if you're not sure you can land," she said after catching me in the shoulder, side of the helmet, and gut.

I threw an uppercut that she dodged.

"Short uppercuts, short hooks, long jabs."

She lunged toward me and I scampered out of the way.

"Step and pivot," she said. "Don't waste energy running all over the ring."

I pivoted, threw punches that didn't land, tried to keep my head moving. Sweat ran in rivulets down my face, stinging my eyes. Weave, pivot, jab, hook.

"C'mon," Kate said. "You gotta be faster than that. Don't be afraid to hit me."

I threw a long jab, connecting with her jaw and snapping her head back.

"Nice one," she said, grinning.

It felt good to hit someone.

By 7:15 I was showered and changed and drinking a glass of Sauvignon Blanc at The Wharf. The copper-topped bar stretched along one wall, with a seating area of high-top tables behind it. Bottles of unopened liquor lined shelves up to the ceiling. Mirrors behind the shelves reflected the autumn-pale faces of the patrons back at ourselves.

Jonah arrived, looking tired. He'd just finished his third shift of the week. "Hi," he said. He was wearing dark jeans and a green button-down that matched his eyes.

"Hi." I smiled.

He kissed me and sat down, looking at me. Then he reached over and took hold of the heart charm on my necklace, pulling the chain through so that the clasp sat at the back of my neck.

"Do you want another glass of wine, or do you want to sit down?" he asked.

"Let's sit," I said. The bar was crowded. I left fifteen dollars under the foot of my wine glass and climbed down from my chair. Jonah motioned to the hostess and we followed her upstairs. She seated us at a table by the dark window and handed us each menus.

"How was your day?" I asked, running my eyes down the menu even though I always ordered the same thing, linguine with clams.

"Not bad," Jonah said.

I looked up. He was staring not at the menu but out the window.

"Everything okay?"

"I'll tell you later. Are you ready to order?"

The waitress approached. "What can I get you to drink?" she said.

"Sam Adams," Jonah said. "And I'll have the seafood special."

I looked at him, troubled. Was he mad at me? "Sauvignon Blanc," I said when the waitress turned to me. "And I need another minute." She walked away. "Why can't you just tell me now?" I pressed.

"I'd rather not talk about it here," Jonah said. "And I'm hungry."

A busboy brought a basket of rolls and a plate with a swirl of whipped butter. Jonah took a roll, broke it in two, and slathered butter on the fluffy inside of each half. He crammed a bite into his mouth.

I thought over our last date, which had been three days ago. Everything had seemed ordinary; we'd had lunch and gone back to his apartment and had sex twice before I had to go home for the end of Caitlyn's shift. I'd left him a voicemail Sunday night; we'd talked briefly the night before.

Jonah put his hand over mine. "Laur, I've worked thirty-six hours in the past three days. I'm just tired. And I'm really, really hungry."

Relief flooded through me. I motioned to the waitress and ordered my linguine with clams.

Dinner felt rushed. We were silent most of the time. I wondered whether this meant we didn't have enough to talk about, reminded myself he was just tired.

"You're still coming over for a bit, right?" he said as the busboy cleared our plates. "Can we skip dessert?"

I smiled, immediately aroused. "Sure."

Jonah paid the check and I followed him to his apartment in the Caddy.

"I'm just going to change," he said as we went inside. There were empty takeout containers on the coffee table, a pair of plastic chopsticks protruding from one, and I could smell something sour from the trash. Jonah came out of the bedroom a minute later in boxers and a T-shirt. "You want a drink?" he called from the kitchen. I heard a clink as he took a bottle of beer from the fridge.

"Sure."

He brought two open bottles of Oktoberfest over to

the couch and collapsed onto it, still holding both beer bottles, leaning his head back and closing his eyes.

I plucked a beer out of his hand and took a long sip. "So, James is out of rehab," I said. I hadn't wanted to bring it up at the restaurant.

Jonah opened his eyes and looked at me. "Did he finish it out?"

"Apparently."

"Where's he staying?"

I blew out a breath. "With me and my mom."

Jonah whistled a slow, high-pitched whistle, then lifted his beer like it weighed a ton and took three long swallows. I watched his Adam's apple bob with each gulp. "I hope that works out for you."

"What's that supposed to mean?"

He looked puzzled. "What I said. I hope that situation works out."

"You don't think it will?"

He shrugged. "From what you've told me, James doesn't have the best track record at staying sober."

I opened my mouth to argue.

"Laura," Jonah said. "I don't want to fight right now." He got up and went to the kitchen for another beer. Mine was still nearly full. Instead of coming back to the couch, he went down the hall to his bedroom.

I sat there waiting for him to come back. When he didn't, I went to his room and found him sound asleep, the half-empty beer on his nightstand. I picked the bottle up and put a T-shirt under it, a makeshift coaster.

I went back to the couch and flicked on the TV, seething. My one weeknight off, and we'd barely talked at dinner. At quarter to ten I could still hear him snoring, so I went home with no sex, feeling like I was being punished for something.

Jonah called the next morning at ten. James was out; I hadn't asked where he was going.

I was half-tempted to ignore the call, but Mom was in a

good mood and I couldn't afford to pass up the opportunity. I left her doing a kids' word search at the kitchen table and went into the dining room.

"Hi," I said. I leaned against the wall by the window. The light was gray and muted, the sky thick with clouds. God, was it going to be cloudy for the rest of my life?

"Hey." His voice sounded gravelly.

"You just wake up?"

"Yeah."

I waited for him to apologize for last night, annoyed that he could sleep so late. Mom had woken me up at five again.

"Listen," he said. "I know you're going through a really hard time right now with your mom, and I know this whole thing with James really complicated everything."

"Yeah. James complicating everything is a bit of an understatement," I said, softening a little.

"But something happened at work yesterday, and I really needed you to listen to me. I know things are tough for you, but . . . we need to be there for each other instead of me always being there for you."

I felt winded: a punch to the solar plexus. "Ouch," I said reflexively.

Silence.

How I wished I could see his face. "I've been so wrapped up in myself," I said. "You're totally right. I haven't been there for you. I'm sorry."

"Thanks," he said, his voice softening. "I appreciate that."

"What happened at work yesterday?"

Jonah exhaled in a sort of grunt-sigh. "My ex came back."

My brow creased. "What do you mean, came back?"

"She, um, we used to work together," he said. "She left me for a doctor at the hospital. They moved to Miami. And yesterday she came back. The proverbial bad penny."

I felt jarred, like I'd been kicked in the face. My thoughts jumbled together, unable to coalesce. "I didn't realize she was a nurse."

"Actually, she's a doctor," he said, with a smile in his voice. "In this moment, I appreciate your unconscious sexism."

"So not the time," I said. I wondered what Robert

thought of her. "What's her name?"

"Whitney. Whitney Greer."

I pictured a tall woman with red hair and long legs in a black sheath dress and white coat. "How was it . . . seeing her?" My words were halting. I was trying not to get sucked into myself, which was exactly what Jonah had just asked me not to do.

"Painful. Confusing. Also really annoying, because I was having a good day."

I closed my eyes, leaned against the wall, and slid down to the floor. "I'm sorry. I totally understand."

"I know you do." His voice was husky again, but this time it had nothing to do with just waking up. "Can I come over tonight?"

I hesitated, just for a moment. He hadn't been over since I'd moved home. I felt weird about it, and even though we hadn't talked about it, he'd seemed to understand. "Sure," I said.

"Okay. I'll see you around eight."

"K. Bye."

I sat on the floor for a minute, hugging my knees. My shoulders were sore from sparring with Kate. I stood up haltingly, one hand on the wall, feeling off-balance. So Jonah's ex-almost-fiancée was back in town. Working with him.

I went back into the kitchen and found it empty. Mom was gone, the sliding door standing open.

Two hours later I was sitting with Mom and James in the kitchen. James had come home from a meeting and helped me search for Mom, who we found in the Jenkins's kitchen, having invited herself in for a cup of tea. "Just call me next time she drops by," I said to Mrs. Jenkins. "Please."

She'd smiled. "Will do," she said. "But Katherine was no trouble at all."

I was on my laptop ordering a ComfortZone watch, which housed a GPS locater. James and Mom were playing poker.

I called Robert, ostensibly to tell him about the locater.

"Good call," he said. "Thanks for doing that."

"No problem," I said, going back into the dining room. "Oh, and by the way. Do you know Whitney Greer?"

"Dr. Greer? Sure. She just came back to the hospital. Why?"

"No reason," I said. "What's she like?"

"Smart. Good doctor. I don't really know her very well."

"Is she pretty?" I made myself pause, even though I wanted to blurt out ten more questions.

"I know I'm supposed to say 'I don't know' when asked questions like this, but the truth is, she's very pretty. Why?"

"Well, I'm hopeful about this GPS watch," I said. "Could be worth its weight in gold."

"You know when people try hard to change the subject and it makes it even more obvious that they're changing the subject? Why did you ask about Dr. Greer?"

"Nothing. No reason. I'll talk to you later." I hung up, feeling like a twelve-year-old.

That afternoon I drove Mom to the last video rental store I knew of and rented *Roman Holiday*. After dinner I set the movie up in her bedroom and made her a bowl of popcorn. I had thought about buying the digital version on Amazon, but I would have had to play it on my laptop, and I didn't trust Mom with anything breakable.

Jonah arrived exactly at eight, clutching a bottle of wine. Thank God.

"Be right back," I said. I took the bottle into the kitchen and uncorked it, then rested my forehead against the cabinet that held the wine glasses. I was so tired.

"How was your day?" he asked when I returned to the porch room cradling two wine glasses by their bowls in one hand and the bottle in the other.

"Eventful," I said. I told him about Mom's break for freedom while I poured the wine. "I wanted to say again I'm really sorry about last night," I said. "Not having contact with a lot of people has made me more wrapped up in myself, I think."

"It's okay," he said, but it was just one of those things people say.

"So tell me about seeing her," I said. I couldn't bring myself to say her name.

"I don't want to talk about it right now," Jonah said. "Let's watch some TV." He put on a *Modern Family* marathon. After a few episodes he turned it off. "Everyone knew she was back before I did," he said. "It was like being in high school when someone sticks a 'kick me' note to your back or something. All the nurses on my floor were talking about me behind my back. I thought I was going crazy, but I was too busy to ask what was going on. Then I saw her coming down the hallway, talking to—him."

I rubbed his knee. "I'm so sorry."

"She didn't even have the decency to look embarrassed. She just gave me this huge smile, said 'Hi, Jonah,' and kept on walking. They were talking about a patient. *Consulting.*" He spat the word like a piece of gum. "She supposedly did some 'amazing' work in pediatrics in Miami, so at least I won't see her that much." He closed his eyes. "Not that the hospital is very big."

"Why did she come back?"

"They missed the *seasons*," Jonah said. "I heard her telling one of our nurses. Said they'd never realized how much they were Yankees."

I pictured the Kate Walsh lookalike in a black bikini by an aquamarine pool. I swallowed against a slight swell of nausea.

"How did it feel when you saw her?" I asked.

"I wanted to beat the crap out of someone."

"That's not a feeling," I said.

Jonah raised his eyebrows.

"Sorry," I said. "Therapist tactic."

"Well," he said, setting his wine glass down on the coffee table, "let's talk therapy, then." He leaned forward and pressed his lips to mine, pushing me back on the couch. I set my wine glass on the floor, wrapped my arms around his neck.

I led him upstairs—Mom's door was still closed, the movie still playing—and locked my bedroom door behind us.

We stripped off our clothes. I was riding him when we

heard the record player in my mother's room blare to life. Fuck. The movie must be *over*. "*You make me feel!*" Mom belted at the top of her lungs along with Aretha Franklin. "*You make me feel! You make me feel like a natural woman!*"

I was so aroused that I couldn't stop myself from coming, couldn't stop a half-scream of pleasure from escaping my mouth. My face was flushed with orgasm and shame. "Oh. My. God. I am so sorry," I said.

Jonah was shaking with laughter. ("*You make me feel!*" Mom sang.) "It's okay." He lifted his head to kiss my neck. "Don't worry about it."

I put on my robe, unlocked my bedroom door, and found Mom waltzing in the hall. I sighed, took her by the hand, and led her back into her bedroom. I turned down the volume on the record player, my pulse pounding my temples with anger and embarrassment.

"I love you," Mom said as I turned to leave.

"Just stay in here, please, Mom." I went back to my room without telling her I loved her too. I just couldn't get the words out.

On Saturday morning I left Mom with Caitlyn and went to see Marisa. The sky was iron-gray and the wind cold. Her office felt like a sanctuary to me now: a whole hour where I didn't need to worry about anyone but myself.

"How are you doing?" Marisa asked. A few brown leaves scuttled across the huge windows.

I thought about it. I gave her questions more weight now, considered my answers more deeply. "When my dad was sick, my mom took care of him for a few months before he died," I said.

This wasn't a direct answer to her question, not yet, but Marisa nodded along.

"I remember hearing Dad coughing late at night. Mom would hold a bowl up for him, and he would gag and spit this gross bloody mucus into it." I sighed. "She hardly slept at all. She kept packing us lunch, kept making home-cooked meals for dinner. Neighbors would stop by and call to offer help and she would turn it down. It was as if . . . she liked being in that role. She liked being the one everyone felt sorry for. She liked being the martyr." I crossed my legs, rubbed my arms. It was cold in here. "I don't want to turn into her."

Marisa nodded. "Did something happen that makes you think you're becoming like her?"

"No," I said. "But . . ."

"But what?"

"James is out of rehab," I said.

"Ah."

"He's staying with me and Mom for a couple weeks."

"How do you feel about that?"

"Confused," I admitted. "He's stayed out of my way so far. That's what's confusing. Usually he kind of takes over wherever he is. He makes everything about him." Which was exactly what I had done to Jonah on Tuesday night.

"And you don't know how to respond to him when he's not doing that?"

"Something like that," I said. "It's more like . . . like we were all in orbit around James for so long. Like he was a planet with crazy gravitational pull, and he pulled us along in the wake of his destructiveness. We all fell into place in our family because of him and how he was. And now I don't know where my place is. Because he's not pulling me along any more. When I'm not reacting to him, it's harder to know where I fit. Or something." I plucked a ball of lint from the sleeve of my gray sweater. I hadn't realized how few pieces of casual clothing I had. My wardrobe was stretched thin now that I wasn't dressing for work five days a week.

"How are you feeling about your mother?" Marisa asked.

I drew my hands in my lap closer together, hunching my shoulders as if against a strong wind. "This thing happened the other day."

"What thing?"

"We were eating breakfast. She knew exactly who I was. She was telling me about her plans for the day—which were delusional, I'll grant you that—but it was like she was reenacting an earlier period in our relationship. She was telling me about how she and Bill were going to the Cape for a long weekend, how she was putting together a fundraiser for the library. You know, stuff she would actually have done a couple years ago, stuff she would have told me about."

"And what happened?"

"I started telling her about my plans for the day. How I was going to take her for a walk on the beach, then we'd come back and I'd take some portraits of her. Then after lunch I was going for a run. And she just—she just zoned out of the conversation."

"That could have been a side effect of the dementia," Marisa said gently.

I shook my head in frustration. "No. It wasn't. Because she started talking over me about how she and Bill were staying at Robert and Julia's house at the Cape, how nice it was of them. She was still in the conversation. She just didn't want to listen to what I had to say. That's how it's always been with her. She won't just sit and *listen* to me for five fucking *minutes*." I rearranged myself in the armchair, pulling my left foot under me.

"Is she like that with your other siblings?"

I shook my head hard, rubbing my thigh. "No. They all take her for granted. Her attentiveness. Or they did, anyway. And I've always wanted to be close to her, and it's like she never let me in."

"Why do you think that is?"

I'd expected Marisa to counteract me, which is what my siblings had always done when I'd brought this up to them. "You're imagining things," Izzy would say. "Mom loves you," Robert would say. James wouldn't say anything, because I'd never confided anything to him until the day I'd let Bill down. Marisa obviously had no idea whether what I felt was true or not. But she had accepted the premise of my observation. And now I had to deal with the consequences. "I don't know," I said.

"Hazard a guess."

I looked out the window. It had started raining, the drops sliding down the glass like tears. "I think Mom felt guilty that she'd had an affair, that I was Bill's daughter." I'd been thinking about that for weeks now, thinking it without admitting that I was thinking it, and it felt good to put it into words and get the words out of my brain. "I think her way of managing her feelings was to keep me at arm's length. I'm a walking reminder of her moral lapse."

"I want you to try something this week," Marisa said.

"What is it?" I asked suspiciously. I had enough on my plate.

"I want you to talk to your mother about how you feel when she ignores you."

"She doesn't *ignore* me."

"Withdraws from you, then."

I rolled my eyes. "I can't predict when she's lucid and when she's not. And when she's feeling good, the last thing I want to do is upset her."

"It has nothing to do with her, really," Marisa said. "It has to do with you."

I didn't say anything.

"Will you at least try it?"

"I don't know," I said.

She leveled her intense blue eyes at mine. "I'm recommending this because I think it would make you feel better. If there's an avenue that might help you, and you choose not to at least try it, that's the definition of a martyr."

I dropped my eyes to my lap. "Fine," I said. "I'll try it."

On Sunday morning James left to go to his early meeting, so it was just Mom and I as usual. I couldn't say that was the way I liked things, but it was at least familiar. After breakfast I made Mom flip through the paper for an hour until the sun had risen properly. I showed her the packet of photographs again—her and Bill at the Christmas party, the snow-covered beach, the hotel, the piano player. She stroked Bill's face. "Pretty," she said.

"Do you know where this is?" I asked, flipping to the hotel.

"Pretty."

I sighed.

I took my camera with us on our walk, took some shots of Mom picking up seashells, gazing out at the water. The sun was low and white in the sky. When we got home I made us each a cup of tea to warm our hands. "Feel up to doing some portraits today, Mom?"

She smiled at me. "Yes."

Mom loved the camera now, loved preening and posing while I moved around her snapping photos. I set up a stool in the living room next to the bay window, arranged some lamps in front of it.

"I'll just go change," she said, and I smiled.

She came downstairs ten minutes later in the lilac dress she'd worn for her and Bill's twenty-fifth anniversary party. She wore the strand of pearls that had been her mother's and the pearl earrings that Dad had bought her on their honeymoon. She hadn't experimented with makeup today, thank goodness—sometimes she came down wearing red lipstick and bright blue eye shadow and gobs of mascara that took piles of cotton balls to clean off.

She sat on the low stool I'd found in the basement and posed for me. She threw back her head and mimed laughing, stared at the camera with what she clearly thought was an ingenue's gaze, then stood up to dance to music only she could hear.

I clicked the shutter again and again, moving around her, losing myself in the moment.

When she had sat down again and was staring out the window, ignoring me while I moved closer to her, adjusting the zoom and the filter, I started giving voice to my thoughts. "I like spending this time with you, Mom," I said. I moved in front of her to get the other side of her profile. "I feel like you're here with me. Even when you don't know where we are, or *when* we are, you're present."

Mom kept looking out the window.

"For a lot of my life I've felt like you weren't present with me." I let go of my camera and let the full weight of it hang from my neck. "It's like you don't want to let me in. And I've never known why." I leaned against the arm of the loveseat. "Like my senior year of high school. I had all these hopes that we would have more time together. Izzy and Robert were both gone and James was practically living at Ava's, and I thought, *Finally I'll have Mom all to myself.* But I didn't. That was the year you started volunteering at the library five nights a week. It was like you couldn't stand to be home with just me. Like I wasn't enough for you."

Mom turned her head and met my eyes. "Honey," she said, lifting a hand to stroke my cheek. "You were always enough for me."

Chapter 25

James

On Sunday night I get back to Mom's house around nine o'clock.
Laura's Caddy is here; she's pretty much always here from what I
can tell. The porch light is on and the house is quiet. I go around
to the patio and light a cigarette. I pull out my phone and dial
Marcus.

"Hey man," he says, picking up on the first ring. "How
you doing?"

"I'm okay," I say, but I'm not. I feel my throat thickening
as I suck hard on the end of my cigarette.

"First week's hard," he says. "Told you it would be. You
feel out of place."

"Does it get easier?" I ask, trying to keep the tears out of
my voice.

Marcus seems to be thinking. "I don't know about it
getting easier," he says. "But you get better at it."

When I enter the sliding door to the kitchen, the blue glow of the
TV is flickering from the porch. Laura's sitting in there, wearing
boxers and a T-shirt. There are black smudges under eyes where
her mascara didn't come off all the way. "Hi," she says.

"Hi."

Her eyelids are drooping.

"I never said thanks for sticking up for me with Robert
the other day."

She shrugs. "I'm still pissed at you. And I don't trust
you."

"Fair enough."

"And you knew. All these years you knew, and I can't
believe you never told me about Bill. He was my father and I
didn't get to have him, and you could have told me."

I lean against the doorway. "I know."

"How was it?" she says, clearly done with that
conversation. "Rehab?"

She's the only one who would ever ask me, the only one I'd ever tell the truth—except maybe Ava, and I'm dead to her now. "It was hell," I say, my voice croaky with tiredness.

She nods. "Yeah."

She doesn't ask me about prison, and she doesn't ask me if I think this time will stick, and for that I am grateful. It's a lot of work not to worry about that all the time. I fall into the trap of thinking, *I can't go my whole life without another drink.* I have to get myself to the space of *I can make it through today without drinking.* Or sometimes, when it needs to get smaller, *I can make it through this hour,* or *this minute.*

"I'm glad you're out," she says, leaning her head back against the couch. "I mean, I'm glad you finished."

I nodded, my throat swelling painfully. God, I hope I haven't turned into a total sucker. I need to do something with my body, so I walk into the room and sit on the loveseat opposite her.

"I got rid of all the alcohol in the house," she says. "And if I bring any in, I'll keep it in my room."

"You don't have to do that," I say, but I'm really thinking, *Thank God.*

She waves a hand to dismiss my feeble argument. "You've been going to your meetings?"

"Yeah," I say. "Do you want me to tell you every time I go?"

She thinks about this. "No. Do you have someone to keep you accountable?"

"My sponsor," I say. "Marcus."

"Okay then. How about I try just being your sister for once?" She smiles slightly, and I can see lines in her forehead that I don't remember being there before.

"Speaking of which," I say. "Why aren't Izzy and Robert helping more?"

"They switch off Tuesday nights," she says, not looking at me.

My mouth hardens. This is bullshit.

"It was *my* decision to move back in," she says, tossing her hair over her shoulder.

"I want to help," I say. "I start work tomorrow, but I can

stay with Mom a few nights and weekend days. Let's say Monday and Wednesday nights, and all day Saturday. Then you can spend some time with Jonah, go out with Amber, whatever."

Laura's looking at me like she's never seen me before.

"Fine. How about we do a trial run tomorrow night. If I don't set the house on fire, we'll make it a regular thing."

"Okay," she says. Her face isn't relieved. She looks suspicious.

"So," I say. "What else did I miss around here?"

She seems to ponder my question. "I mean, me moving back with Mom, obviously. I'm seeing Jonah again."

"I didn't know you had stopped seeing him."

She averts her eyes. "For a little while."

I don't press the point. I take a deep breath and get to what I've been afraid to ask for the past five days. "Laur," I say. "How is he?" I try to clear my throat. "Jeremiah." I mean to ask his name as a question, but my voice stumbles into a sob.

"He's still hurting pretty badly," she says. "The physical therapy is really painful."

I nod once. "Have you seen him?"

"I was going to go by this week and say hi," she says. "I'll let you know how he's doing."

"Thanks." I can't stop the tears this time; they well and spill, and I cover my face with my hands and sob.

Laura comes and sits next to me on the loveseat and puts her hand on my back. She doesn't tell me it's okay, but she sits with me until my tears spend themselves.

It's after midnight when I go upstairs and sit on my childhood bed, staring out the window I used to climb out of. I'm reminded of just how much I hate this room.

My rucksack and the three boxes I picked up from my storage unit are stacked neatly in the corner by the closet. I still can't bear the thought of unpacking.

Marcus told me that if I start feeling sorry for myself—which always brought on drinking in my before-life—I need to have a plan. It felt corny, but he helped me brainstorm a list, and

I unfold the crinkled sheet of paper now.

1. Do something for someone else.

2. Go to a meeting.

3. Read notebook.

4. Call someone who will tell you the truth.

I put the paper down on the bedspread, which is so flat I wonder if Mom ironed it, and go downstairs to Dad's old office. I open the closet door to find what I was hoping for: stacks of photo albums, all clearly marked with the year, and 8 × 10 envelopes of loose pictures stuck between the albums at chronologically appropriate intervals. I can practically smell Izzy's perfume oozing out of the organization. I pull out an envelope wedged against the right side of the bottom shelf and open it to find three 8 × 10 copies of the professional photo Izzy had done of the grandkids last Christmas. When I turn over the top photo, I see the name "Ava" written in the top left corner in Izzy's perfect cursive.

I go to the desk and pull the gold chain of the green lamp, which sheds a small pool of light that doesn't seem to reach any other corner of the room. In the middle drawer I find envelopes and stamps. I address the envelope to Ava, putting Mom's house as the return address. I don't put my name anywhere, but she'll recognize my handwriting. I'm so tempted to write something—to include the letter I wrote, which is still tucked in my notebook, or even just an index card saying only, "I'm sorry"—but she doesn't want me to contact her in any way. I'm not. I'm just sending something that was already hers, that she would've had already if I hadn't always been such a colossal fuck-up.

Self-absorbed, I correct myself as I lick the envelope and stick a few stamps in the corner. Don't want to fall into the trap of self-deprecation, which Marcus taught me is just another form of self-aggrandizement.

I sound like Laura, even in my own mind.

I open the front door and slide the envelope into the mailbox attached to the side of the house, leaving a corner sticking out.

In the morning, after sleeping only a couple hours, I get up to go to a meeting before work. My license is restricted; I can only drive to meetings, to work, and to do necessary errands like go to the grocery store. The interlock device they installed is weird. I have to blow into it—it's like a Breathalyzer—and the car won't turn on unless my BAC is 0. I blow into it now and start the engine. It'll be real fun picking up girls with this sucker. Then again, maybe I shouldn't be picking up girls. Since I could only take them to the grocery store.

Driving still feels strange.

I'm trying a different meeting today. I've been to meetings regularly before, mostly a couple years back when I was chasing a girl who got sober, but Marcus recommended I try a few I've never been to. Clean slate and all that. I'm nervous like I have been the past five mornings.

By the time I find the room, in the basement of the First Presbyterian Church on Front Street, I'm late, though I started out in plenty of time. I've been wandering around the church for ten minutes, first around the outside, looking for an unlocked door, then around the inside, looking for the right wing.

I hesitate at the door. Everyone inside is dressed for work, in suits and ties or skirts and heels. I'm wearing jeans and work boots. The Chair, a woman my mother's age with chin-length silver hair, looks right at me and smiles. Instead of indulging the impulse to turn and walk away, which has always been my response to the nerves jangling up and down my spine, I walk through the door and take a seat.

The meeting goes fine. Not great, not terrible. As I pour burnt coffee into a Styrofoam cup afterward, I think, *This is my life now.*

Tuesday morning I wake up at six o'clock and I feel so claustrophobic I don't think I can make it five more minutes without a drink, and even though I know I should sit with Mom and Laura for a little while, I must get out of the house. I drive to Dunkin' Donuts and get a large coffee then drive back to the First Presbyterian Church and sit in the truck listening to a tape of an AA speaker. Marcus gave me a set, laughing because he doesn't know anyone who still has a tape deck. But he hadn't thrown out his tapes, so I got lucky.

There's a tap on the window and I jump, slopping hot coffee down my white shirt. I turn to see a girl about my age, pale skin and blue eyes, and she winces as I dab at the stain with a napkin, succeeding only in spreading it further. "Sorry," she says. I roll down my window manually. "I was just going to tell you I'm opening up, so you can come inside if you want to." She points at the church basement door I had so much trouble finding yesterday.

"Oh," I say stupidly. "Thanks. I'll be right there." There's nothing I can do about the coffee stain, so I just wait in the truck like an idiot until she's inside.

The girl is setting up the coffee urn when I reach the room.

"I'm James," I say.

"I know. I saw you yesterday," she says.

I have no memory of her face. She has reddish-blonde hair, a mole above her lip, and dimples when she smiles.

"Penny," she says.

"Right. Hi."

"Want to grab the doughnuts for me? They're in the kitchen down the hall, in the left-hand cabinet. The one marked 'AA.' Obviously." She smiles.

"Sure." I get the doughnuts and, coming back down the hallway, hear another male voice in the room. Damn.

The guy, lucky for me, is in his sixties, with salt-and-pepper hair and a face as tanned and wrinkled as an old leather billfold. "Mike," he says, shaking my hand. His smile is irrepressible. What is it with these people? They always seem so damn happy. Penny seems a little more my speed—if only because she's not quite awake yet. She's holding a cup under the urn's open spout, coffee trickling in slowly as it brews. She sees me watching her and smiles. "Need my caffeine," she says.

"So. James," says Mike. "How much time you got?"

It reminds me a little too much of the question guys asked in prison. "Sober forty-two days," I say.

"Congrats. Just outta rehab?"

"By way of prison." I want Penny to know that, even though I'm talking to Mike, so she can decide now if she never wants to talk to me again.

"I'm just out of rehab too," Penny says. She still meets my eyes. She's not totally freaked out.

"Well, this is perfect." Mike is grinning hugely. "I'm starting a new AWOL group, and the last open meeting is tonight. Why don't you two join us?"

"Absent without official leave?" I say.

Mike guffaws, but even though he's so over the top, I can't help liking him. "Naw. Stands for 'a way of life.' Basically we get a group, usually people in early sobriety, and we all go through the Twelve Steps together. It's a commitment, for sure—usually takes a year, year and a half, and you gotta commit to coming every week. We can't move on from a step till everyone's done it. Even us." He grins. "The leaders, I mean. Me and my buddy."

There's a silence I find awkward as Penny and I don't jump to agree to join AWOL. Then she smiles shyly, her gray eyes lighting up, and says, "I'd like that. Can you send me the information?"

"Got a flyer right here." He whips a stack out of his pocket. "Got one for you too, James." He hands me one.

That night I end up at AWOL, mostly because I'm hoping to see Penny. Mike welcomes me at the door. I know three Mikes in AA already. This Mike is known as No Phone Mike, because he's the only person any of us know who doesn't have a cell phone. Even I picked up a cheap one my first day out of rehab. Not that anyone calls me.

The vibe is different from a normal meeting. Mike and his friend Bert stand up and explain the rules: There are three open meetings, of which this is the third. After that, we'll be asked to sign a contract stating that we will attend the group every week until it ends.

"Now let's get to know one another," Mike says. "Tell us three facts about yourself, including how long you've been sober. Don't make a big deal out of anything. Just tell it like it is."

So we do. It's the same as the other meetings I've been to: There's no common thread among us in terms of age, race, ethnicity, profession. The only common thread is that we cannot control our drinking, and we're finally ready to live a different life.

As much as AA feels tedious already, my first few times staying with Mom is even worse. It's worse than caring for a baby—not that I ever did that with any regularity—because she's not nearly as manageable, and not nearly as cute.

I purposely offered to stay with Mom on Saturdays because I get weird on weekends. In my before-life, if I wasn't working I was drinking, thinking about drinking, or recovering from drinking. If I'm committed to being with Mom, I figured I'd stay out of trouble. But still, it's hard as hell.

I make myself read my notebook while she naps in the afternoon. The notebook is a tool Marcus suggested we all use. He made us start one during small group one day, made us each show it to him during our one-on-ones. Basically it's a catalog of every stupid decision we ever made while drinking— every inappropriate person we hit on or slept with, every family member we hurt, every time we got arrested or thrown out of a bar or caused our partners, children, siblings, parents to cry. Then we have to write out an affirmation of ourselves for every stupid thing. I have 126 stupid things so far, and I'm still writing affirmations. It can be the same affirmation, but I get tired of writing *I, James, am a sober, upstanding guy*. Plus I feel stupid. So

I try to think of other good things I've done: the time I went to that build with Jeremiah, the time I helped an old lady change her flat tire on the highway, the time I was the first to show up for Laura and Mom when Bill died.

The stupid things remind me what's at stake. The affirmations are teaching me that I can be someone else.

I read the letter I wrote to Ava again and wonder if I'll ever be able to give it to her.

Chapter 26

Laura

On Sundays James went out for the day. I knew that staying with Mom all day on Saturday was hard for him, but I still felt lonely.

That morning he'd said he was going to a young people's meeting and then to see a movie. I was skeptical. While Mom was taking a bath, I opened the door to his room and stood there. The room was so neat, I couldn't tell James was living in it, except for the rucksack and boxes in the corner. I walked inside. Both beds were immaculately made, and while I assumed James was sleeping in his childhood bed—the one on the right, by the window—I couldn't tell for sure. The closet door was closed. The dresser and nightstand were bare except for matching blue lamps; I opened every drawer, and all were empty. I opened the closet: empty. I went to the army bag, loosened the drawstring closure, and rifled through the contents. Neatly folded clothes, a pair of sneakers, a bathroom kit, the AA Big Book, a Bible, a spiral-bound notebook. I got down on my hands and knees and lifted the bedspread. Nothing under the bed. Still, I lay all the way down on the carpet and pushed my head underneath the bed. Bedsprings, dust bunnies, and an unopened bottle of Macallan rare cask wedged in the corner of the box spring.

In mid-November her condition worsened, coinciding with the chillier weather, the darkening days. She treated James and me and Caitlyn as strangers hell-bent on torturing her. She grew more ornery in the evenings before bed. She left the house twice, once after a bath, so she wasn't wearing her ComfortZone watch. We had to call the police, who found her four hours later walking on the beach without a coat, two miles from the house. The next day she developed a cough and a fever. I called Robert, and he came over in the driving rain. We sat on the edge of Mom's bed together, Robert listening to her chest with his stethoscope, his face grave. He took her to the hospital, where they confirmed she had pneumonia.

Mom was in the hospital for three days. James and I did not acknowledge the fact that life was much easier while she was gone.

They released her when she was still too weak to walk; it was flu season, and they were overcrowded. We rented a hospital bed and set it up in the office so James wouldn't have to carry her up and down the stairs. Although Robert insisted that we needed to give the antibiotics time to work, give Mom time to regain her strength, I couldn't shake the fear that she'd never walk again.

"I really miss working," I said. "I miss my clients. I miss having that constant distraction from my own mind."

It was a Saturday morning, and I'd left Mom with James. She still wasn't walking.

"I even miss Kevin," I said, surprising myself. I felt around inside to see if that were true. It was. "I miss him because he was always pushing me to be a better therapist." I sighed. "Now no one's pushing me to be a better anything." That wasn't true, and I knew it. Mom pushed me every day to be a better person: more patient, more loving. It just wasn't a lesson I wanted to learn. Being more patient with Mom didn't have the same professional cache as becoming a better therapist.

I leaned back and looked up at the sky, which was thick with iron-gray clouds.

"I miss you," I said.

My butt was growing cold through my jeans. The earth beneath me was frozen and hard. I stood and looked down at Bill's tombstone. It was a plain granite rectangle, carved simply: "William L. Norman, 1949-2014." Next to his name was carved, "Katherine M. Keene, 1942-." I wondered if the year that would fill the empty space on the other side of the dash would be this year, or next year, or the next. I wondered if we should sand out her name on Dad's tombstone.

The hill was gray with dead grass and black and gray tombstones. I had brought an orange geranium in a green plastic pot. It looked lurid against the dull landscape, almost too bright to be allowed.

"That's what you were to me," I said out loud. "Almost too bright to be allowed."

I let myself imagine, for a moment, what life might have been like if Bill had lived. I'd still be working. I'd come over and help a few times a week. It would be hard, but not impossible. Jonah and I would not have the wedge of Ted between us.

James would probably still be drinking. Jeremiah would probably still be whole.

I sat up, wiped away my tears, and got in the car.

I drove to the hospital, parked in the lower lot, and walked through the covered breezeway to the medical building. I found the physical therapy suite on the third floor. It was a large open room filled with gym equipment and smelled of disinfectant and sweat. I spotted Jeremiah across the room doing leg presses with his right leg, which was shaking with the effort. A blonde woman stood over him, nodding her head.

I sat down in the waiting area. The perky receptionist smiled at me from behind her desk. "Can I help you?" Her teeth were impossibly white.

"I'm just waiting for someone," I said.

She nodded and went back to work, glancing at me now and then as if to make sure I wasn't causing trouble in the otherwise empty waiting area.

Ten minutes later Ava walked in. She stopped for a moment when she saw me, but she came and sat next to me anyway.

"Hi," I said.

She turned to look at me, her eyes full of fire. "I heard he's staying with you," she said.

I groaned inwardly. But this was just another difficult conversation, just another therapy session with a client who was coming to the sweet spot of dissatisfaction and anger with the way things were.

"Just for a couple weeks," I said. Which would be up in a few days. "He's clean." I cringed inwardly.

"He's been clean before," Ava said, looking away. Her voice wavered.

"It feels different this time," I said. "He says grace before meals and everything."

"It's going to take more than that to convince me."

"I know."

We sat in silence for a few minutes.

"Has he asked about Jeremiah?"

"Yes," I said.

She surveyed me. "He give you anything for me?"

"No. He's respecting that you don't want him to contact you. Isn't that different?"

"Hi, Aunt Laura." Jeremiah stood in front of us, leaning on his crutches. He was wearing a blue jersey T-shirt, a triangle of sweat staining the neckline. "I'd hug you," he said, "but I'm all sweaty."

I stood and kissed him on the cheek.

"How are you feeling?"

"Okay," he said. He looked at Ava, eyebrows raised, and she nodded once. "Mom and I usually go to the Princess Diner for lunch," he said. "Want to come?"

I smiled. "I'd love to."

The diner was small but bright, one wall lined with tall windows and the other covered with mirrors. Orange and brown paper leaves hung from the ceiling, and paper turkeys with bulbous crepe paper bellies and pert Pilgrim hats sat on every table. We ordered sandwiches, and Ava left to use the bathroom.

"How's my dad?" Jeremiah asked.

"He's okay," I said. "Sober." Please, God, let me not be lying to my nephew right now.

Jeremiah nodded.

"He misses you," I said. "He feels terrible. The guilt—it's eating him alive." I hadn't realized that last part was true until the words were out of my mouth.

"That doesn't change anything, though," Jeremiah said. "I still have to do physical therapy three times a week if I want to walk normally again."

I swallowed. "Yes. I know."

"I want to see him, though," he said, leaning forward.

"You do?"

"Yeah. He's still my dad, you know? I mean, I'm pissed at him; don't get me wrong." Jeremiah's face contracted. "But I don't, like, want to kill him or anything." He looked out the window. "Not like my mom," he said, under his breath. "Can you help me?"

"I don't know, 'Miah. Let me think about it."

Ava came back from the bathroom and I sipped my water, trying to hide my face. I'd promised her to keep James away. But my duty was to my nephew, wasn't it? He was the one I was related to. But Ava was his custodial parent. I kneaded my forehead. Why did I always seem to have a headache?

That night I was checking e-mail on my phone and saw one from Amber: a forward from a listserv for RISD. *Thought of you—check out #2,* she'd written at the top. *Xo, Amber.*

The e-mail announced a series of grant and fellowship opportunities in the arts. The second item was for the Gillespie Prize, a photography prize judged by Lawrence Bigby. I felt my heartbeat accelerate when I saw his name, remembering his voice from all those years ago: *You are very good.* The winner would have their portfolio displayed at a local Providence gallery. The deadline was four weeks away.

I thought of the photos I'd been taking of Mom. I had a lot of work to do.

Things were easier in some ways and harder in others now that Mom wasn't mobile.

Things were easier because Mom wasn't going anywhere. She'd recovered from the pneumonia, and her muscle tone was good. So it wasn't that she physically couldn't walk, Dr. Pindar explained, but that she'd actually forgotten how. "We see it often in later stages of Alzheimer's," he'd said. "And the pneumonia weakened her considerably. Still, she could regain her ability to walk. It does happen."

"How often?" James had asked. Though his words were a challenge, his tone was respectful rather than sullen.

Dr. Pindar's face had sagged slightly. "Not often," he'd conceded.

Things were easier because I could shower without

fearing Mom would make a break for the outside world in her underwear, snow fluttering around her slowly bluing skin. Though sometimes when I turned off the water, I heard her shouting for help. After racing down the stairs a few times, dripping wet in my towel, I learned that she didn't need help—she just wanted company. She was lonely, I realized, even when she was only alone for five minutes.

Things were harder because all movement involved a wheelchair. Getting her in and out of the wheelchair was exhausting. I'd never noticed how many places still weren't handicap accessible. And even though we always got good parking spaces now, I took Mom out less and less.

Sunday morning after breakfast, I went upstairs to get my camera. I sat on the loveseat in the office, where Mom was sitting up in bed watching *Planet Earth* on the TV we'd brought down from her bedroom.

I was approaching my portfolio for the Gillespie Prize differently than I would have in college. In school I would have sketched out what I wanted the finished series to look like, then tried to take those exact shots. Instead I kept my camera with me every day, and I tried to take fifteen or twenty shots a day. The hardest part was the fact that I spent so much time with Mom, it was hard to see her in a new way. And seeing something in a new way was what photography was all about for me.

Still, after a few hundred pictures, my ideas about the series started to take shape. It was about her decline into memory loss, but it was also about the moments when she bubbled back up into life.

My favorite so far was a black-and-white of Mom laughing. She loved to watch *The Three Stooges*; she, who had always had a sophisticated sense of humor, suddenly loved slapstick. The photo was a close-up, Mom's head thrown back, howling with laughter, and James in the background, smiling at her instead of at the screen.

Chapter 27

James

"I saw Jeremiah last week."

Laura lets that quiet little bomb drop on me Monday night. We're sitting on the couch watching TV, both exhausted. I think Laura would be downing a glass of wine if I wasn't here.

I want to get up and leave the room. I want to ask a million questions. I want to change the subject. I want a drink. "How is he?" I say.

"He wants to see you."

Warmth spreads through my body as I imagine hugging my son. "What did you tell him?" Laura is such a responsible person that I'm positive she shut him down, though I'm sure she did it skillfully.

"I told him I'd talk to you."

"You did?" I feel a strange mixture of shock, pleasure, and anger. "Why did you do that?"

The intensity of my voice surprises her. "I thought you'd want to see him."

"Of course I want to see him." It takes effort to keep the sarcasm out of my voice. I get sarcastic when I'm angry. Or sad. Or embarrassed. "But Ava most definitely does not want me to see him."

Laura's eyes slide away from mine. "I thought you . . . deserved it. I could, you know, set something up."

"No." The vehemence in my voice causes her to flinch. "If I'm going to have a shot at not hurting people just by being myself, I need to live by the rules," I say. "Can you find a way of telling Jeremiah how much I want to see him, but make it clear that we're not going to go behind Ava's back?"

Laura nods.

"I'm going out for a drive."

She opens her mouth.

"I'll stop at the store on the way home," I say. "What do we need?"

"Milk."

I breathe into the stupid interlock device, start my truck, drive. There's a lookout, just south of town, where I used to take girls. Feels like a lifetime ago. You drive down a dirt path and you're on a cliff overlooking the water. It's not like the middle of nowhere or anything, but you can still see more stars than you can near our house.

Our house. Since when had I started thinking of Mom's house as my house again?

The lookout is deserted. Ava and I used to come here all the time.

I get out of the truck, even though the wind is sharp and biting, and sit on the hood, lean back against the windshield, stare at the stars.

On Tuesday I get a call from my buddy that my room at the halfway house will be available in three days. He asks if I still want it.

Part of me is relieved. I'd love to get out of my stupid childhood room. I'd love to be able to work overtime, help pay for a nurse, because the truth is that caring for Mom is ridiculously hard. I don't know how Laura was doing it alone, day in and day out, with no hope of Mom ever getting better—only the surety that she will get worse. Sometimes that knowledge threatens to suffocate me.

On Thursday I come home from my meeting and find Laura in the kitchen eating breakfast. I pour a cup of coffee and sit down across from her.

"Laur," I say.

"Yeah." Her eyes had been drifting shut.

"Why don't you go lie down?"

"I'm fine," she says, propping her chin on her hand.

"Listen," I say. "That room in the halfway house is available starting Friday." I take a long swallow of coffee, sigh with relief. "God, I always forget how bad AA coffee is until I have the real stuff again."

My sister smiles wanly.

"I want to stay here," I say. "If you want me to. Just

until—" I can't finish the sentence.

"I do want you to," she says.

The unspoken words hang between us: *just until Mom dies.*

"I'm going to tell Robert when he comes tonight, then," I say.

"I can do it."

I shake my head. "No. It has to be me."

"That is 100 percent fine with me. Your funeral." She winces. "I mean—"

"I know what you mean. It's okay." I stand up. "I gotta go to work." I clear my throat. "Laur. Thanks for letting me stay."

"Thanks for staying. I know it would be easier to go."

I can hear the gratitude in her voice. I leave the kitchen.

I never showed up for my family before. I'm paying for it now.

I try calling Robert three or four times that morning, as I'm driving to work, on my breaks. I want him to come pick up Mom a little early so I can talk to him. I leave a voicemail and send a text to that effect.

He doesn't come early. Laura's already left for whatever it is she does—yoga, maybe, though she's getting pretty muscular from yoga. I'm going to AWOL.

"I have dinner reservations at 5:30," he says when he comes in the door and sees me leaning against the counter, counterfeit casual.

"I just need five minutes," I say.

Robert nods once, sits down at the head of the kitchen table without looking at me. "What?" He gives the impression of being not so much a participant in the conversation as a captive audience.

"I'm sorry," I say, moving to sit two chairs down from him.

"For what?" His aggression is peeking out now, and I can feel mine pulsing through me in response. Our aggressions usually slug each other a couple of times. They get bigger, rather than smaller, with confrontation.

"I'm sorry for all the ways I've hurt you. I'm sorry for the stupid, horrible toast I gave at your wedding. I'm sorry for all the times I laughed at you when we were growing up and you were trying to be the man of the family. I'm sorry I wrecked your car. And I'm sorry for how badly I hurt Jeremiah in the accident, and how badly I hurt you."

Robert looks at me. "That it?"

There's so much anger in his gaze that I flinch. "No. Um. I'm staying for a little longer. In the house, I mean. Laura and I talked, and we decided it's best—"

"For you? You always do what's best for you, James. And Laura always lets you walk all over her because she's too nice to see through your bullshit. Well, I'm not. You think that thirty-second speech and a couple weeks helping out with Mom can right all the wrongs you've done? It can't. I don't want you here, and that's not going to change."

He leaves the kitchen, finds Mom watching TV. I hear them leave from the porch door. I sit there in the dark alone for a long time.

On Thursday morning I'm sitting in my truck outside Dr. Steve's office. He was our pediatrician. He's my father's second cousin, or something like that, so he'd show up at big family parties. Laura was afraid of him—as soon as she saw him coming in the door in his suit, she'd hide her face in whatever was nearest (Mom's skirt, the side of the couch, a doll).

I loved him. Sitting with Mom in the waiting room, I'd look around at all the other kids and think, *Bet Dr. Steve doesn't come to your Christmas parties. Bet you can't even call him Dr. Steve. Bet you have to call him Dr. Lovato.*

The clock in the truck says 9:30. I want to turn the truck back on and drive away, but instead I get out. I open the office door and the smell hits me between the eyes: antiseptic and something in the wood family, like a roomful of tongue depressors. The plastic toys are faded but stacked neatly in the corner. The room is empty. I go to the window, where a young nurse sits behind the glass, talking on the phone. She sees me and holds up one finger. I take my phone out of my pocket and tap it a few times. I have nothing to look at—no texts, no new e-mails—but I don't want her to know that.

When she hangs up she slides the glass panel aside and stands up. "The child's name?" she says briskly.

"Um," I say. "Dr. Steve is a family friend . . . he agreed that I could come in because I don't have a general practitioner right now . . . I just need a quick test done . . . he said he'd do it for me."

The nurse is looking at me with confusion, or pity, when Dr. Steve opens the door behind her and steps into the office.

"James," he says in his deep voice. "Come on back."

I open the door from the waiting room and meet Dr. Steve in the hallway. He motions me into the second exam room on the right, the one with pink bears and blue elephants on the walls. This was always my favorite room.

"You could have just mailed me the script for the blood test," I say.

He closes the door. I'm still standing. Awkwardly.

"It's no trouble at all. I'll draw the blood here; that way it's quick and easy," he says. "Sit down."

I sit on the exam table, the paper crinkling beneath my jeans. My heart is beating fast and my mouth is dry. "I really appreciate your doing this," I say. "I know it's kind of . . . irregular." Awkward, awkward, awkward.

Dr. Steve is sitting down on his rolling stool, and this is what I was afraid of: He wants to talk. "Tell me what happened."

"I, uh, well. I was in prison. I'm sure you heard. And while I was there I was . . . raped." It's only the second time I've said it out loud. I swallow again, feeling like there's a walnut stuck in my throat. "Anyway, I just want to be sure . . . you know. I want to make sure I don't have HIV." Voicing the fear that has been gnawing at me for weeks is like pulling a twenty-pound dumbbell out of my chest and laying it at Dr. Steve's feet. He seems to sense this, because it moves him to action.

"Given the circumstances, I think that's a good choice." He rolls the stool over to a cabinet and takes out a syringe. "Let's find out, then."

I roll up the sleeve of my shirt, and he swabs the inside of my arm with sharp-smelling antiseptic. Snaps on his gloves.

"Squeeze," he says, handing me a stress ball. He inserts the needle. Quick pinching sensation.

I look away. I'm not squeamish, exactly. I don't mind blood. I just don't like seeing a needle sticking out of my skin.

"I'm going to run a full STD panel," Dr. Steve says, capping one vial and inserting another. "The results should take less than two weeks. I'll give you a call as soon as they come in."

I take a deep breath. "Thanks."

"Of course." I feel him remove the second vial, pull out the needle and replace it with a wad of gauze.

"Pressure," he says. "How's your mother?" he asks, turning away and putting labels on the vials.

"She's . . . okay," I say. I never know what to say when people ask. *'Not so well, but thanks for asking'? When she doesn't throw things, it's a good day? 'Sometimes I wish she would just die so our lives would be easier?* "Okay" is the easiest response.

"Give her my best," he says. "And your siblings of course."

"Sure," I say.

"You're a free man," he says, gesturing to the door.

"Don't I have to pay?" I ask. I had told him I didn't have health insurance.

He waves a hand. "I'll take care of it."

"I'd really rather—"

"James." He claps a hand on my shoulder. "Please. Let me take care of it."

"Okay," I say, feeling uneasy. I walk outside, blinking in the bright sunshine.

Resisting the bottle of whiskey under my bed makes me feel strong. I know this is stupid, and that it'll make me feel strong until it doesn't—at the point when I'll give in to it and be back where I started. Still, I don't tell anyone it's there. Laura would kick me out, which is maybe what I secretly want. Marcus would drive to the house and empty it himself.

I talk to Marcus on the phone a couple times a week. I've never had a friend I could talk to that often—or, for that matter, *wanted* to talk to that often. It's a relief to share some small part of my life with someone who understands. I guess this is why some people go to therapy.

When I tell Marcus that I'm making my living situation a little more permanent—or as permanent as things can be in this uncertain world, I joke—he's silent for a long beat.

"I thought you'd be proud of me," I say, hurt. So few people have ever been proud of me. It's something I crave like alcohol.

"I'm proud of you for sticking with your family," he says. "I know it can't be easy."

"Yeah," I agree, glad for the small amount of validation.

"But I'm concerned too—about how difficult your living situation is. The stress of it, I mean. At this point, anything that detracts from you putting your full energy toward staying sober is a concern. You still going to AWOL?"

"Yeah," I say, an edge of annoyance coloring my voice. "I signed a contract."

Marcus sighs. "You did. I'm glad you're going. You ask that girl out yet?"

I smile despite myself, and it feels good. "Naw. Don't want to make things at AWOL complicated if it goes south."

"That's good. It's good to protect that group for yourself. For your recovery. But that doesn't mean you should run away from how you feel about someone, either. You can ask her on a date. You don't have to sleep with her right away, start your twisted bad habits."

"Yeah." I feel a swooping in my gut. When was the last time I'd asked a girl out when I was sober? Had I *ever* done that? Maybe to my senior prom. Maybe not even then; my memory was hazy.

The Friday before Thanksgiving I'm at a jobsite in Westerly, putting a new roof on a clapboard house. From my perch, one leg slung on each side of the roof apex, I can see the Pawcatuck River glinting in the distance. A black SUV pulls up to the curb and a bald guy in a suit gets out, approaches Benny. I have a bad feeling.

Benny calls up to me. "James! Come on down."

My bad feeling intensifies as I wave and start down the ladder.

"He's from, I don't know, like the government," Benny says. Benny's always been real good with words. "Checking all my workers, like making sure they have papers and stuff."

"And you are?" the guy says, looking at a clipboard.

"James Keene," I say.

The guy pulls a manila envelope from the clipboard and hands it to me. "You've been served."

I'm sitting with Mr. Peterson in the kitchen, late-afternoon light slanting across the patio but leaving the kitchen in shadow. Laura walks in, an empty water glass in her hand, stops on the threshold. "This can't be good."

Mr. Peterson smiles at her. "Good to see you, Laura."

My sister comes into the kitchen and fills the glass from the Brita pitcher in the fridge. "It's always good to see you as well," she says, darting a reproachful glare at me.

"Ava's suing me," I say.

"Oh."

"Not surprised?" I'm annoyed, because this did take me by surprise, and the more I think about it, the more I realize it shouldn't have.

"No, I'm not surprised," Laura says. "But don't go getting all defensive and pissy. It's not like I talk to her behind your back or anything."

"Except for the time you went to see her and Jeremiah at the hospital."

"How is that behind your back? I meant, I don't go talking to her about you. I *do* go visit my nephew sometimes."

We're close enough again to snipe like kids.

Mr. Peterson looks at Laura over the top of his glasses. She's standing by the counter, one foot drawn up to press against the inner thigh of her other leg. I can't believe how steady she is, standing like that. "You saw them at the hospital? Recently?"

She shrugs. "Last week. Jeremiah's in physical therapy."

Mr. Peterson turns to me. "You would never win this case in front of a jury, especially because you already pled guilty on the criminal case. I'll meet with her lawyer and find out how much she's looking for. But once we settle, I'd advise you to file for bankruptcy. You don't have any assets, and because you get paid in cash, there's no proof of income. If the bankruptcy is granted—and I think we have a solid case—the judgment against you would be dissolved."

"But what about Ava and Jeremiah?"

Mr. Peterson adjusts his glasses on the bridge of his nose, which is creased. "What about them?"

"If I declare bankruptcy, she won't get any money. Right?"

Mr. Peterson is looking at me like I'm an idiot. "Right. But you don't have any money to give her."

"Can't I set up a payment plan, or something?"

Mr. Peterson closes his eyes. "You don't have any assets. Given the extent of Jeremiah's injuries and the egregious nature of your negligence on the night in question, Ava would be justified in seeking damages upwards of fifty thousand dollars."

The number is like a punch to my solar plexus, but once I regain some breath, I say, "What if they garnish my wages?"

"James," Mr. Peterson is getting impatient now, "you don't have any wages to garnish. Your income does not exist to the federal government. Which is illegal, but you didn't bring me here to tell you that."

"I'll get Benny to put me on the books," I say stubbornly.

"Let me get this straight," Mr. Peterson says. "You want to settle, and you want to have your wages garnished until payment of the settlement can be made."

"Yeah."

I look past him to see my sister staring at me like she's never seen me before.

Mr. Peterson takes off his glasses and polishes them, then looks at me. "Why do you want to do this?"

I roll my eyes. I really hate this guy. "Because I screwed up royally. I acted irresponsibly, and because of that my son was in the hospital for four days and has been doing physical therapy ever since. He *broke bones* because of me. And I should pay for it, in more than just remorse."

"It'll be impossible for you to save money, to get a car loan, to pay a mortgage. I'm sure you don't want to be living here forever."

I laugh hollowly. "I can't even imagine next week, let alone where I'd like to live in a few years." That's not entirely true. I have dreams of saving for my own house. But Jeremiah comes first.

"You realize you're acting against my legal advice."

I shrug.

"I'll speak with Ava's lawyer and call you when I have a number," he says. He stands up, closes his briefcase, looks at me. "I didn't think you could change, but you've proved me wrong. Good for you."

When he's gone, I plunk my forehead down on the table.

I want it resolved quickly, and Mr. Peterson comes through. The following week, a few days before Thanksgiving, we settle the case for forty-five thousand dollars. Even though I know I'm doing the right thing, it doesn't make me feel too thankful. Benny is putting me on the books for the business and has agreed to give me more hours, which is the only good thing to come out of this: I can spend more time out of the house. Which makes me feel guilty. But relieved.

A judge will decide sometime in the new year how much of my wages will be garnished, and how long payment of the judgment will take.

I know the money will mean a lot to Ava, and I know she'll invest it in Jeremiah's college fund. Still, I try not to picture Ava, Rick, and Jeremiah sitting on a beach, sipping fruity drinks out of coconuts, while I'm living in my mother's house for the next ten years.

After brooding over my sudden debt I go to AWOL, as if to cement my place in Loserville. At AWOL we all did the first step together at the first meeting: we admitted we were powerless over alcohol. I'm feeling powerless over pretty much everything these days.

We've been on the second step for three weeks now. There are three atheists in the group—three out of twelve—and they are supremely resistant to Step Two: "We came to believe that a power greater than ourselves could restore us to sanity."

Yes, that's right, I have to admit I believe in a Higher Power. But despite my blowup at Lou back in rehab, I don't understand what the big deal is. I've always believed there's a God, even if I hate calling Him the Great HP. Whether or not He cares about the colossal mess I've made of my life is unclear to me. But something—my fear of prison, my friendship with Marcus, my desire for redemption after what I did to my son—has changed me. So I'm not disputing the Guy's existence. Seems to me you've got to be either way smarter or way dumber than I am to deny the existence of God. So I settle right back into the groove of the lapsed Catholic: God exists; I just don't do much about it. Except when I need something. Like now.

Last week Mike made a convincing argument. It was about how we've all had contact with something bigger than ourselves at some point. Maybe it was that infinite feeling you get when you're young and you're driving down the highway with your friends for the first time, and the knowledge suddenly smashes down on you that you can go anywhere, do anything, be anyone, and you're filled to the brim with possibility and anticipation. That's a power greater than you, he said. Or the time you were in total despair: when your mother died, or you did something so inexcusably stupid when you were drunk, and you were sobbing your eyes out in your room. And suddenly, for no reason at all, you stopped crying, and it was like someone was in the room with you, comforting you. That's a power greater than you, he said. Or maybe you played sports as a teenager, and you had that big game, and your team was functioning seamlessly—every pass, every play was executed perfectly, until your collective power gathered and multiplied and you all played better and better and you won the championship, and it might rank up there as one of the best nights of your life. That's a power greater than you, he said. And those things, they took you out of yourself, and you felt healed.

So two of the three caved, admitting to the existence of a power greater than themselves and that it could restore them to sanity. But the last one, Gil, is holding out, his jaw jutting stubbornly, his arms crossed in front of his chest.

Tonight I arrive in the basement of the United Methodist Church of Eastville, on Ocean Avenue, and sit next to Penny. Drunks are creatures of habit, and by the second week we'd all taken to sitting in the same seats as if they'd been assigned by a teacher. I'd showed up early the first week to make sure I could sit next to Penny.

As the meeting begins, Penny raises a hand. "I want to say something to Gil," she says.

Mike sweeps his arm to the left in a "be-my-guest" gesture. His smile is patient as ever, but I wonder if there's a kernel of anger or impatience buried down there. Sometimes I imagine I can see it in his eyes.

"I prayed for you every night this week," Penny says.

"Okay," Gil says, his voice sullen.

"If you can believe that, you can believe in a power greater than yourself. You believe that *I* believe in God, enough to pray for you to Him. That's a power greater than yourself. And it could help you." She looks sideways at Mike for confirmation.

The rest of us are tilting our heads one way, the other way, wondering if this can possibly be true. We're all gauging Gil's reaction out of the corners of our eyes.

"But why would you pray for me?" Gil asks, and for the first time, his voice is soft. Not just quiet, but *soft*.

Penny considers this question. We're all leaning in now, curious.

"Because I want you to have the assurance that I have," she says. "That you are loved by God. So I prayed that you might have that assurance." She lifts her chin. "I pray for all of you, but especially for Gil. Because I can't imagine trying to stay sober without believing in a God who cares deeply about me, and who wants the best for me."

We all sit in awe of Penny's generous spirit. At least, I do.

After the meeting I gather up my nerve and ask Penny out for coffee. She agrees, looking surprised but pleased. I stammer out an explanation about my restricted license, how I can only use it to run necessary errands, and ask if she'd mind driving then bringing me back to my car. I actually blush. She agrees again, without looking at me like I'm a loser. As I get into her Passat, I realize this doesn't count as a date. It's been so long since I had an actual date—anything more than drunken sex, really—that I've forgotten how to do it. But I think dates generally involve more advance notice, and me picking the girl up, and taking her out for something more substantial for coffee. I decide to think of this as a pre-date.

"So," I say as we sit down at Scrivener's with our mugs. She ordered a chai latte that smells delicious, like Christmas in a cup. Feeling the need to be manly, I ordered a black coffee that smells like tar. "What are you doing for Thanksgiving?"

Her eyes dart to the side. "You know, nothing much. What about you?"

I let my eyes roll a little, but put on a smile. "My younger sister and I are hosting, but our older sister's cooking. We live with our mom," I say. "She's sick," I add, wanting to make it clear that I don't live at home because I'm some kind of freak. "She has Alzheimer's."

"I'm sorry."

I wave a hand, not wanting to talk about it. "You're just hanging around?" Why am I pushing this?

She nods.

"If you want," I say slowly, "you're welcome to come to our house for Thanksgiving. I mean, it'll probably be full of family drama, because my mother is liable to say anything that pops into her head. Also, my brother's barely talking to me, and he just got divorced and he's bringing his new girlfriend. But the food will be good. Or at least decent. I mean, no pressure," I say. "But you're welcome if you want."

Penny smiles and her eyes light up, my favorite thing about her. "Really? I'd love that. If it's not too inconvenient."

I had not thought for a second that she'd say yes. "Of *course* not," I say, perhaps a little too forcefully. "My sister always cooks for an army. There'll be plenty of food." Izzy's going to have a field day with this one. "Let me get your number, I'll text you our address. We usually eat at six. I know it's almost late for Thanksgiving dinner, but growing up our stepdad hated eating dinner at like three or four in the afternoon like everyone else does." Stop talking.

Penny smiles again, and that stops my rambling. We drink our coffee and joke about Gil and Mike, and I can't believe my good fortune.

I wake up at 6:30 on Thanksgiving morning and go to my meeting. When it's over I wait in line for coffee then bump cups with Penny and Mike. Thirty meetings in thirty days: I did it.

Mom's awake when I get home, waiting for me. I can smell that her diaper is full.

The desire for a drink nearly overtakes me. It is a hunger so intense I can practically smell the fumes of a nice fourteen-year-old Glenlivet, can taste the delicious, oily warmth; can feel it warming all the way down my throat; can feel the numbness spreading from my chest and radiating outward. But let's be honest: At this point I'd settle for the house whiskey. PBR. The worst wine I've ever drank, which tasted more like rubbing alcohol.

I bite my knuckle, hard; my knuckles are red and chapped, and the pain clears my head. Enough. I'll smoke in a minute, but first I have to change my mother's diaper.

I thought this would get easier the more I did it. But it gets harder instead, harder every day. I thought at first maybe I'd enter into a sacred space of sorts, that the disgust would dissolve into a tender love. It doesn't. The gorge rises in my throat every time. I feel shame and disgust and anger welling up inside every time. To make things worse, Mom's shit stinks as bad as a newborn's and she's got diaper rash now that requires cream. Every time I do this I swear I'm moving out, I'll get a job and help pay for a nursing home, because this is just horrible.

But afterward, when Mom looks up at me, smelling of Butt Paste and baby powder, totally helpless, my heart thaws a little—melts like a glacier in Alaskan summer, actually—and I know I won't leave her. I know she'll die before I walk away.

I'm scared shitless about Thanksgiving dinner tonight. I have not eaten a holiday meal with my family sober since I was fifteen. If I didn't pass out during dessert, I was headed to the bar: oblivion either way. Tonight there would be no liquid courage to survive Izzy's and Robert's snide remarks, no oblivion to sink into like a black pool of blessed forgetfulness. No Bill, either, to crack jokes and tame tempers.

I'm on my own.

It's the feeling of absolute aloneness, powerlessness, the fear of having no recourse, that drives me to it. I sit on the floor by my bed, lean back, and pull the bottle of Macallan out from where it's been wedged in the corner of my bed frame for thirty days.

I've been sober for sixty-eight days.

The amber liquid shifts with mesmerizing beauty as I tilt the bottle back and forth. The white label gleams in the lamplight. I set the bottle on the nightstand, enjoying the soft thud as the heavy glass meets the wood. I reach out to unscrew the lid.

266

Chapter 28

Laura

On Thanksgiving morning I woke to a soft knock on my door. It was late—8:30. "Yeah," I said, struggling to sit up, my heart automatically accelerating.

"Laura, I'm sorry," James said through the door. "I'm sorry."

I felt a plummeting in my gut. "What's wrong? Is Mom okay?"

"Mom's fine. I need you downstairs. Please." There was a pleading note in his voice that terrified me.

I pulled on a zip-up hoodie over my pajamas and slid into slippers, wondering if I should bother to brush my teeth, deciding against it.

In the kitchen James was standing at the sink holding the bottle of Macallan I'd found under his bed, and my heart almost stopped. Then I saw that it was still full, unopened.

James's eyes were red. "I'm going to dump it out," he said. "I just need you to watch me."

"Okay," I said.

James stood there looking at the bottle for a long moment. I wondered if he'd have the strength to do this. I wondered if I'd have the strength to live with him if he couldn't do it.

James took a deep breath and held it, as if he were about to jump off the high dive. He unscrewed the cap and poured the whisky down the sink. He seemed to be careful not to splash a drop of it into the sink itself, but poured the entire stream into the garbage disposal. When it was empty, he ran the water for a long time before he took another breath.

I put a hand on his shoulder. "You did great," I said. "I'll get rid of the bottle."

"Thanks." His voice was a whisper. "I'm sorry I had to wake you up."

"I'll make coffee," I said, as he retreated from the kitchen. I brewed a full pot of coffee then went outside, despite the cold, and walked across the street to stuff the bottle into the bottom of the Jenkinses' recycling bin. When I came back I heard the sound of the porch door slamming. "Izzy," I groaned.

Ivy and Isaac were watching the Macy's parade and Izzy was clattering things in the kitchen, presumably having brought all her supplies into the house.

She started talking as soon as I entered the kitchen. "Sam has Ian," she said. "Took him to Monty's to get us doughnuts, but he has to stop by his sister's. He'll be here later."

I poured two cups of coffee and left the kitchen without saying a word to my sister. I knew she'd be so distracted that she wouldn't notice my silence. I took the mugs through the dining room, doubling back through the living room into the office.

James was sitting by the bed watching Mom sleep. I handed him one of the coffee mugs and sat down on the loveseat we'd dragged in from the living room.

"Thanks," he said.

"No problem," I said, closing my eyes and leaning my head back until it rested on the wall. "You nervous about Penny coming over?" When he'd told me he'd invited a girl for Thanksgiving—"we're just friends, I swear"—I had definitely gone easy on giving him shit about it. I might as well start making up for that now.

A crash came from the kitchen. "She's he-e-re," James said, ignoring my question, and we giggled.

Mom stirred in the bed. "Robert," she said.

"He'll be here later, Mom," James said.

"I have to tell him something," she said. "Tell him to pick up chocolate chips at the store."

"Okay, Mom."

I'd had to work to stop feeling hurt that Mom always asked for Robert. Especially because she often meant Dad.

Ivy wandered into the office and sat on the arm of the loveseat. Ivy was staring at Mom with a look on her face that was half-terrified, half-needy.

"You can go sit on the bed with her," I said.

She shook her head.

Mom drifted off to sleep again.

I lifted my right arm, and Ivy slid down onto the cushion

next to me, under my arm.

"She doesn't remember who I am," Ivy said, her voice small.

I tightened my arm around her. There was no way to deny it, though I'd give anything to erase Ivy's pain. "It's hard, isn't it?"

She nodded, her head pressed against my breast. I bit my lip to force back the tears suddenly stinging my eyes. "I think she does know who you are, deep down," I said.

James sat up slightly. He was still staring at Mom as if he could heal her if he paid enough attention, but I could tell he was listening.

"I think her heart recognizes you," I said. "I think it just can't communicate with her brain, or her brain can't communicate with her mouth anymore."

James stood up as the smell of feces suddenly overpowered the Glade lavender air freshener. Ivy wrinkled her nose.

"Let's go see if your mom needs any help in the kitchen," I said.

James closed the door behind us.

At four o'clock I was reading Mom a book when I heard a deep voice coming from the porch that wasn't Robert or James. For one heart-stopping moment I thought it was Bill. My gut plummeted when I remembered he was dead—but then it bounced back when I recognized Jonah's laugh. I ran through the dining room, already set for twelve plus Ian's high chair and found Jonah watching Nickelodeon with the kids.

"Hi!" I said, forgetting to tone down my enthusiasm.

His smile illuminated his eyes. He came toward me, wrapped his arm around my waist, and kissed me full on the lips. With tongue. A little tongue.

Ivy and Isaac did a *wooo*!

"Let's keep it PG," Izzy said from the doorframe, where she was hovering like a bat.

Jonah pulled away, grinning like an idiot. "Happy Thanksgiving."

I smiled. "Happy Thanksgiving."

He leaned around me to smile at Izzy. "I brought some apple pie."

She smiled. "From where?"

"Iz," I warned.

"Just asking."

"I baked it this morning," he said. "I mean, I bought the crust premade. But the rest of it I made."

I nestled myself under his arm. I loved this man.

"I've never been much of a baker," Izzy said. "Thanks."

Amber arrived half an hour later and dissolved even more tension, and I was filled with gratitude that mostly replaced my apprehension as we sat down to dinner.

Whether or not the food tasted good remained to be seen, but the table was beautiful. Izzy had brought out a fancy white tablecloth and bought new white tapers for Mom's crystal candlesticks. Platters of dark and white turkey meat, garlic mashed potatoes, green bean casserole topped with fried onions, snowflake rolls, stuffing, and cranberry sauce covered every inch of table space. Handwritten name cards told us where to sit. Izzy was at the head of the table, "just because it's closer to the kitchen," she said as we sat down. Her family was to her left. Robert and his date, Becky, were to her right, then Penny and James. James wheeled Mom into the room and lifted her into the dining room chair. I sat on Mom's other side, at the foot of the table, as usual, with Jonah and Amber to my right.

We all sat down, a little awkwardly, then looked at Izzy, unsure what to do next. She smiled. I had a horrible thought: *Please, don't make us hold hands and then go around the table and say what we're thankful for.*

She didn't. "Let's just say grace," she said.

We all crossed ourselves and mumbled grace.

We passed plates and serving bowls and loaded our plates. I portioned food onto Mom's plate, which she promptly ignored. The plate of snowflake rolls sat in front of her, and she spread roll after roll with butter and dribbled each with honey.

Finally James got up and took the rolls to the kitchen. No one said anything, not even Mom, who moved on to eating food from her plate.

The dinner progressed somewhat normally. Robert didn't say a word to James, or even look at him, a fact that became overt when he took pains to draw Penny into conversation. But that was to be expected. Robert didn't say a word about the fact that there was no alcohol, a decision Izzy and I had made out of respect for James and Penny, even though James had told me—before this morning—that it was unnecessary.

"How did you two meet?" Penny asked Becky.

Becky smiled at Robert. "I work at the cafe across from the hospital," she said. "I'm divorced now, and I work there a couple days while my kids are in school. Anyway, one day Mr. Triple-Nonfat-Latte asked me out." She patted Robert's knee.

"How old are your kids?" Penny asked.

Becky's smile grew even more radiant. "Parker is nine and Paul is seven."

"Are they with their dad today?"

"Yes," Becky said. Penny's voice had been so gentle that the question didn't seem nosy—it seemed to acknowledge the fact that Becky must be lonely without her children, and in bringing that to light, Becky seemed to relax.

Izzy, on the other hand, was tense. She complained through the whole meal about the food she herself had cooked—the turkey was too dry, the homemade cranberry sauce too tart, the mashed potatoes lumpy.

"But it looks like a magazine," Penny said, and the ring of sincerity in her voice seemed to embarrass Izzy into silence.

"Robert hasn't been to see me in months," Mom said, apropos of nothing. Her anger was palpable, and I felt my stomach clench. Danger ahead.

"I'm right here, Mom," Robert said, his voice hurt, leaning forward so she could see his face.

"Not you," she said, waving a hand. "You come to see me all the time."

That was an exaggeration. James glanced at me over Mom's head, and I could tell he was thinking the same thing.

"You mean your husband Robert?" Amber asked, looking up from her conversation with Ivy about the pros and cons of Ivy's first-grade teacher.

Mom looked at Amber disdainfully. "Who *else* would I mean?"

Mom's sarcasm would have been funny if she wasn't so upset.

Izzy, from her perch at the head of the table, leaned forward. "Mom, Dad's been dead for twenty-seven years."

Mom kept eating as if she hadn't heard.

We all took nervous bites in unison.

Mom was murmuring something into her plate. I put a hand on Jonah's knee, and he covered my hand with his. I could feel his empathy, could practically hear him telling me to relax. "Nothing is perfect," he'd say, as if I'd wailed what I was thinking, which was, *I just wanted this one day to be perfect, and if not perfect, then at least okay.*

"There was another one," Mom said. The rest of the table had gone back to eating and to side conversations.

"What, Mom? Another what?" I said quietly. James was talking to Penny and Becky about elements of good coffee, but I could see his ear cocked to Mom. We were like parents of a toddler—always alert, waiting to see what she'd do or say next. I stabbed a piece of turkey with my fork and dunked it in the pureed sweet potatoes (the turkey really was dry).

"The other one. The other man. With the kind face."

"Bill," I said. I took a sip of seltzer, which Izzy had brought in an attempt to be festive, and turned to look at Mom.

Tears were leaking down her face. She sniffed hard, drawing the gazes of the closer half of the table. "I miss him so much," she said. "He's forgotten about me."

Everyone was staring now, and I felt like screaming at them to look away. I took Mom's hand, feeling like I might drown in her grief.

At that moment there was a knock on the porch door.

"I'll get it," Izzy said, bouncing out of her chair.

She came back into the dining room, followed by Jeremiah.

The room fell silent. Jonah, who had been talking to Amber, trailed off mid-sentence in the sudden quiet, looking around for whatever had caused it.

"Hi, everyone," Jeremiah said. "Happy Thanksgiving." His

eyes were wide and uncertain.

James opened his mouth and a strangled sound came out. He stumbled out of his chair, took four huge, lumbering steps around the table toward Jeremiah, and grabbed him in a fierce hug.

Mom had stopped crying. "Amber," I said. "Can you come sit with my mom?" Of the nonrelatives, Amber had known Mom the longest. I stood up. "I'm going to set up dessert," I said. Izzy was hovering in the doorway to the porch, behind Jeremiah and James. "Why don't we three talk in the kitchen," I said, putting a hand on James's back. I propelled him and Jeremiah into the kitchen ahead of me, wishing there was a door I could close between the kitchen and the dining room.

James pushed Jeremiah to arm's length to get a good look at him. "'Miah," he said, his voice croaky. "I am so, so sorry."

"I know, Dad. I know."

James hugged his son again, crushing his cheek against the top of Jeremiah's head. I could see tears squeezing out the corners of James's eyes and felt my own eyes welling up.

"How did you get here?" James asked, pulling back to look at his son's face. He kept both hands clasped on Jeremiah's shoulders.

"I took a cab," Jeremiah said. "Um. Aunt Izzy paid for it. She, um, she told me to come. I thought she would have—would have told you."

The three of us turned as one to see Izzy, now standing in the doorway of the kitchen, watching us.

"Izzy," James said, steel in his voice. "Can you give us a minute alone?"

I turned to go too, but James said, "Laura. Stay, please." As if he needed a witness. Shocked, I realized that's exactly what he was thinking.

"Dad," Jeremiah said urgently. "I didn't know Mom was suing you. She didn't tell me. I overheard her talking to Rick." He took a deep breath. "I needed you to know that."

"Thanks, buddy," James said. He was still holding Jeremiah's shoulders, staring at his face hungrily.

Jeremiah was staring at the floor. "I really wish you hadn't gotten in the car that night, Dad."

A convulsion shook James's body. "I know." His voice was strangely steady. "Listen, 'Miah."

Jeremiah looked up into his father's face, his expression a mixture of anger and defiant hope.

"I have never regretted anything in my life more than getting behind the wheel that night. It was the worst mistake I ever made. I'd give anything to be the one hurt, instead of you. And I'm going to stay sober, for you, even if you never want to see me again."

"I do want to see you again, Dad," Jeremiah said, his voice low.

Robert appeared in the doorway and cleared his throat. "Someone should probably call Ava and let her know that Jeremiah's with us."

"I'm handling it," James said. His voice was tense, but the typical aggressive note was missing.

"Probably better if you don't call her, since she threatened to kill you," Robert said.

"Robert. I'm handling it," James said again.

"Like you handled it last time?" Robert said. "Like you handled it when you got behind the wheel of my car drunk and drove the wrong way down the highway and put your son in the hospital?"

"Robert," I said. "*We're handling it*. Why don't you go back and sit down."

My older brother wheeled on me, his eyes crazy. "I knew you'd take his side! I know he's tricked you into thinking he's changed! But men like him never change! He's a drunk, Laura. He's a drunk and a liar and—"

"That's enough," I said. "You help with Mom two nights a month. He's here with me, living in the mess of it, day in and day out. You just feel guilty because for once James is the better son, and it's killing you."

Robert stood there a moment, his mouth gaping open and closed. Then he spun on his heel and left the room, squeezing past Izzy and Jonah, who had approached the doorway. I heard him telling Becky they were leaving, shuffling for their coats, saying hurried goodbyes. They went out the side door without returning to the kitchen.

Izzy looked at me. "You shouldn't have said that to him. He feels bad enough about Mom already."

I was already regretting my words. I so didn't need Izzy jumping on the guilt wagon with me.

"How about I get Jeremiah some food," Jonah said.

"Great idea," I said. Jeremiah squeezed past Izzy into the dining room. Jonah went to the cabinet and got an extra plate, then followed suit. I heard him introducing Jeremiah to Penny. Great.

James turned on Izzy. "How dare you?" he said. "How *dare* you?"

Izzy flinched slightly, but her embarrassment seemed only to add fuel to her indignation. "It's Thanksgiving," she said. "I wanted us all to be together. I know you wanted to see him, so—"

"Of course I want to see him!" James said, his voice on the edge of yelling now. "He's my *son*! But his mother does *not* want me to see him. And since I'm the alcoholic, deadbeat dad who nearly killed him, I think his mother's wishes deserve to be respected!"

The house phone rang. Izzy and James didn't break eye contact, so I walked over to the counter to look at the screen. "It's Ava," I said.

James closed his eyes. "Can you tell her what happened, please?"

"Hi, Ava," I answered the phone.

"Is Jeremiah there?"

"Yes, he is, but—"

"I'll be there in twenty minutes," Ava said. "Keep James the hell away from him."

"It was Izzy's—" I said, but the line had gone dead. I hung up the phone. "She's coming," I said. "James, she told me to keep you away from Jeremiah." I felt a weight settling on my chest.

"Blame it on me when she gets here," Izzy said. "I guess we'll go."

"No," I said.

"What?" "No" was not a word Izzy heard from me often.

"I said no. You invited Jeremiah here, and you can spend time with him and have dessert with us until Ava gets here."

My sister squirmed.

"I'll wait upstairs," James said, and left the kitchen. I heard him saying goodbye to Jeremiah and giving Penny a short, apologetic explanation, then his heavy tread on the stairs.

I started a pot of decaf coffee and put Jonah's pie in the still-warm oven.

My nerves were frayed. I felt like I lived inside a giant trash compactor of tension. I'd been living in it for years, perhaps, but suddenly the walls were pressing in not just from the top and bottom but from the sides as well. The free space I had to live in was becoming smaller and smaller. And I wasn't alone in there anymore. Mom was with me, and James, and Jonah. The space was too small just for me, and I felt like I was going mad. I stood for a moment in front of the oven, warming my hands in the pocket of heat, because that was the only thing I could think of in the moment that might make me feel marginally better. I was so cold.

Jonah came into the kitchen and put an arm around me, kissed my temple. "How're you doing?"

"Ava's coming," I said.

"There's lots of people out there to diffuse the tension."

"There's no diffusing Ava."

"Well, let's cut her a slice of pie and hope for the best."

"I'm sorry this was such a mess. I should've known. I shouldn't have subjected you to it."

Jonah wrapped his arms around my waist. "Your family is definitely never boring. But don't worry. I don't scare easily."

I went back into the living room, where Penny was standing behind her chair, holding her coat. "I'm going to go," she said. "Thank you so much for having me." I didn't try to convince her to stay, but she let me wrap a piece of cheesecake for her to take home. "Tell James thank you for me," she said. I agreed.

The rest of us drank coffee (Izzy drank her herbal tea that smelled like stewed weeds) and ate pie and cheesecake and ice cream. The minutes ticked away, and finally the porch screen door opened, then the inside door, and Ava appeared in the dining room doorway. She stood there for a moment, taking in the scene: Izzy was spooning ice cream into Ian's mouth at the head of the table; Sam was playing "I Spy" with Ivy and Isaac; Amber and Jonah and I were talking; Jeremiah was sitting next to Mom in James's former seat. Ava exhaled quickly through her nose, bull-like.

"Ava! Happy Thanksgiving!"

All heads swung toward Mom in amazement.

Mom was holding her arms out. "Come give me a kiss."

Ava's palpable anger melted just a degree. She seemed to unfreeze from her spot, walked slowly around the table, and gave Mom a kiss. She crouched down until she was level with Mom's face. "How are you feeling, Mrs. Keene?"

"Oh, fine. Can't quite get around the way I used to, but I'm managing. James has been such a help."

Ava looked as thunderstruck as I felt.

"Mom." Jeremiah stood up. "I'm sorry. I just wanted to see Dad so bad. It's Thanksgiving." There was a pleading note in his voice. "You can ground me for a *month*." His tone indicated that he thought a monthlong sentence was overly long, but he'd be willing to endure it.

"Oh, I will," Ava said. She turned to me. "I changed my mind. I want to talk to James."

I considered checking her purse for weapons, then decided that might make things worse. "I'll get him."

I brought James downstairs, his face wary.

"There you are!" Mom said. "I was just telling Ava how I couldn't survive without you and Laura." Mom beamed at James in a way she had very rarely beamed at him before, ever. She turned to Ava. "Those two are just the loveliest."

James and I traded puzzled looks.

"That's great," Ava said. "James?"

The two of them walked around the corner and shut themselves in the office.

I would've given an arm to be a fly on the wall. "Want to take some leftovers home, 'Miah?" I asked instead. "I can make you a plate if you want."

His eyes lit up. "Okay!" He smiled grimly. "Rick is, like, a *health nut*," he said, wrinkling his nose. "Like, the turkey's organic, and he makes his cranberry sauce *without sugar*, and he doesn't eat bread, so we had *no stuffing* and *no rolls*."

"Wow," I said. "That sounds rough."

We set about clearing the table: Izzy packed up the food, Jonah and Sam washed and dried dishes, Amber took Ivy and Isaac and Ian to the porch room to watch a movie. I made Jeremiah a plate, half-filled with stuffing and a snowflake roll. "Think your mom wants one?"

Jeremiah considered this. "She does love Aunt Izzy's stuffing."

I took a second paper plate from the pantry and made a replica of Jeremiah's carb-heavy plate.

"What about Rick?" I said.

Jeremiah just shook his head. "He wouldn't be able to eat anything. He doesn't even eat butter."

"Some Thanksgiving."

"It wasn't so bad." He was quiet for a moment. "Did I mess things up?"

"No," I said. "I just think that your mom is very angry."

"Me too," he said softly. "But I love my dad anyway. Sometimes I wish I didn't. It sure would make things easier."

Ava came into the kitchen. "Jeremiah, honey, let's go."

Jeremiah picked up a foil-wrapped plate in each hand. "Thanks, Aunt Laura," he said, kissing me on the cheek. "Bye, everyone." He turned back to me. "Can I say bye to my dad?"

Ava stuck her head back in the door. "'Miah, now."

"I'll tell him for you," I said.

Jeremiah left. I sat down at the table.

James came into the kitchen. The movement halted for a moment, but he didn't say anything, so everyone resumed washing, drying, and packing away food. He came over to me. "Thanks."

I shrugged, not wanting to talk anymore. "You still okay to stay with Mom tonight?"

"Yeah. You should go."

"I am," I said.

Jonah turned to me from the sink, and I nodded. We made a speedy exit.

"Thanks for sticking it out," I said in the car. "I know it wasn't exactly a *Leave It to Beaver* family Thanksgiving."

Jonah took my hand. "I wouldn't have missed it," he said.

I snorted. "Well, just let me know how I can make it up to you."

He smiled a little. "There is something."

"Oh, yeah?"

Jonah turned down Main Street. "Come to the Phish concert with me the Saturday before Christmas."

I groaned. "I don't even like Phish."

"You don't have to like Phish. You just have to like me. Please?"

I took a deep breath. "Fine."

Jonah punched a fist in the air. "Yes! I'll get us tickets."

"Where are they playing?"

"Providence."

At least it was close.

Chapter 29

Laura

I woke up early the next morning. I never slept well at Jonah's.

I wrapped myself in a blanket and sat with my mug in Jonah's huge blue armchair, which faced the window. He lived on the second floor, so I had a great view of Main Street. Cars were already vying for street parking. The storefronts were lit in the blue darkness, their windows filled with snowmen and Christmas trees and Santa Clauses. I thought of the first Christmas that Bill and Mom had been married. They'd taken the four of us on the train to Providence to walk around the city and see *Home Alone* in the theater. I was nine, and it was one of my favorite Christmas memories ever. After the movie we'd gotten hot chocolate and walked down by the river, our breath freezing in white puffs before our faces. I wore the white earmuffs Bill had given me the previous Christmas. I'd walked between Mom and Bill, completely content, and even James calling me a parents' pet hadn't bothered me in the least.

Jonah kissed the top of my head, startling me. He tapped my temple. "I'd love to know what goes on in there."

"You'd have run away screaming the first time we met."

He snuggled next to me.

"I enjoyed Thanksgiving," he said.

I snorted. "Even the surprise train-wreck ending?"

He shook his head. "Could've been a lot worse."

"That is so true."

We sat in silence for a moment. My head nodded and I jerked awake.

"I've been thinking," Jonah said.

"Yeah?" I kneaded between my eyebrows; I could feel a headache coming on.

"What if we move in together?"

My eyebrows rose of their own accord. "You mean, I would move in with you?"

"Or I could move in with you. Or we could move somewhere else together."

The thought of Jonah living in my mother's house made my skin crawl. I liked having his apartment to escape to.

He studied my face. "Just give me a ballpark reaction."

"I'm . . . surprised," I said. "It feels . . . a little early." My nose felt stuffy, and I wondered if I was getting a cold. I didn't want to talk about this. I had barely gotten used to living with James and Mom. I wanted things to be easy and uncomplicated between me and Jonah, at least for a while. I wanted to go home and go back to sleep. I'd always slept better alone. "Can I have some time to think?" I said.

"Of course."

That afternoon I went to see Marisa.

She smiled when I walked in. "I was wondering when I'd see you again." I'd canceled my last appointment. "So, what's been going on?"

I began mentally to organize a recap of the past two weeks, then realized that was the easy way out. I felt around inside for the thing that was bothering me the most. It took a minute. "Jonah asked me to move in with him."

Marisa nodded.

"I can't." I shook my head vehemently to underscore my point.

"Why not?"

"I have responsibilities."

She waited.

I chewed on a thumbnail. "My mother. My family's house. Making sure my brother doesn't relapse. Keeping my family together."

"Sounds like a lot of burdens."

"Not burdens."

"Burdens you put on yourself."

"I'm the reconciler," I said. "I'm the glue."

"What happens if you let go?"

A weight settled on my shoulders and my heart turned to stone: heavy and unbreakable. "I'm afraid to find out."

"What's the rush? To make the decision? Did he give you

a deadline of some kind?"

I sat down again. "No." My voice was sullen as a teenager's.

"It sounds to me like it was just a conversation," Marisa said. "But you seem to be taking it as an ultimatum."

I stared at her, amazed. "Yes," I said. "That's exactly what I did."

I left Marisa's office feeling ten pounds lighter.

I slept all afternoon then went to The Wharf to meet Amber for a drink. I climbed to the second floor and took a seat at the empty copper-topped bar. A thick green garland hung with lights and red velvet bows was strung above the bar. The dark windows reflected the room like murky mirrors.

I heard the clack of heeled boots on the stairs and knew it was Amber. She appeared around the corner, grinning with her usual exuberance, wrapped in a suede coat with a fringed white collar and cuffs and wearing a huge faux fur hat. She kissed me on the cheek and began de-layering, draping her coat and bag two stools down from me, plopping her hat on the bar, sitting down and sipping the red wine I'd ordered. I noticed she was still wearing her black leather gloves.

"Cold?" I said.

She grinned at me again. "I have some news."

"Oooh, fun." I sat up straighter, trying to muster some enthusiasm.

"Brian asked me to marry him." She whipped off her left glove and waggled a ruby-and-diamond ring in front of my face.

I felt like I'd been clubbed in the face with a two-by-four, but I manufactured a smile and pasted it on my mouth. "Oh my gosh, that is amazing!" I gushed, standing and hugging her. "I am so happy for you!" I turned to the bartender. "Could we have two glasses of champagne, please?"

"The ring is from Brilliant Earth," Amber said, sitting down. "They do all eco-friendly jewelry, all responsibly sourced, conflict-free." Her smile was secret, knowing, thrilled. "I know we haven't been dating that long," she said, looking at me as if for approval. "You haven't even *met* him!"

No, I hadn't. But I had to remind myself this was not Amber's fault. She'd invited me and Jonah to dinner with her and Brian a few times. I'd always deferred, saying I'd love to when things with Mom got easier. But they never did, and now my best friend was marrying a guy I'd never even met. "I'm sure he's a great guy," I said.

The bartender brought our champagne. "Congratulations," he said to Amber.

Amber was holding her champagne in her right hand, a small smile on her face, watching her engagement ring as she tilted it back and forth in the light.

"Cheers," I said, holding my glasses up to hers until they clinked. "To your happiness." Amber took a sip of her champagne, but I tilted my head back and swallowed the glass.

My throat felt thick. Amber had been there the night Ted and I got engaged. She had been there for me when Izzy had thrown a tantrum while we searched for bridesmaids' dresses, and when James had gotten so drunk at my wedding we'd had to put him in a cab before the cake was cut, and when I'd called her, hysterical, after I'd left Ted. She had been unwavering through every peak and valley in my life. And I wanted to be the same for her. I was just so tired. I felt so lost.

"He's coming to Ghana for New Year's," Amber was saying, "so he can meet my family."

"That's great," I said. "And when you come back, Jonah and I will take you guys out to dinner to celebrate."

Amber smiled. She was radiant. "That would be so nice."

Act how you want to feel, I reminded myself. I wanted to be happy for my friend. I *was* happy for her; it was just hard to dig out the happy feelings from under the avalanche of care that weighed down my days.

"So tell me the *story*," I said, picking up my wine glass. "How did he propose?" I injected enthusiasm into my voice. It was my turn to be there for Amber. It just seemed that these days, it was my turn to be there for everyone.

The next morning I woke up in a fog of self-pity, which made me disgusted with myself, which did nothing to dispel the self-pity. I went downstairs and poured two mugs of coffee, took mine to the table.

James bounded into the kitchen and picked up the mug I'd poured for him. "Thanks."

I sat down at the table in his chair, which was closer than mine, and positioned my face over the steam.

"You look like you're trying to drown yourself in there."

"Wouldn't be so bad," I said.

"What's up?"

"Amber got engaged."

"That's great!" James sat down next to me at the head of the table, taking long gulps of coffee. I was amazed; mine was too hot even to sip. He studied my face. "It's not great?"

"It is great," I said. "That's the problem."

"You're feeling sorry for yourself."

I looked at him sharply, to see if he was making fun of me. His face was serious. "Yeah. It appears so." I took a tentative sip of coffee. "I don't *want* to feel sorry for myself."

"You should try doing something for someone else," James said. "Takes you right out of the sludge."

I opened my mouth to complain about the absolute injustice of James saying that to me.

"I know," he said, holding up a hand. "But that's what I learned to do when I want to drink. Do something for someone else." He wrinkled his nose. "I mean, I sometimes do that when I want to drink. I want to drink almost all the time. Sometimes I convert that energy into doing something for someone else."

"Oh." I stared at my left ring finger, where my engagement and wedding rings used to sit. I had loved seeing them there, loved that other people could glance at my hand and know that I belonged with someone. "Are you dating Penny?"

I'd expected him to be defensive, but James smiled a stupid-looking smile. "I think so."

"You *think* so? What are you, in middle school?"

He smiled again, instead of prickling at my tone. "That's what it feels like. Seventh grade. I don't know the rules any more. I kind of missed out on the normal dating rules."

"Well, asking someone if they'd like to go out on a date is a good first step."

He grinned. "Done."

"When?"

"I'm taking her to dinner tonight."

I leaned over and punched him on the shoulder. "That's great."

James stood up. "Thanks. Do something for someone else." He grinned. "Or you could wallow. I never discount the need for a good wallow."

"You're so happy lately," I said. I couldn't keep the envy out of my voice.

James stood there, holding his empty coffee mug, and looked at me. "I never knew what it was to be happy until I stopped drinking," he said. "I feel like I need to make up for all the time I missed, you know? It's like there was . . . I don't know, like there was cancer eating my soul, and now it's gone. I was like . . . haunted before. Or hunted. 'Hunted' is probably the better word."

"By what?" I said. I couldn't believe what I was hearing. James was the least introspective person I knew.

"By this horrible sense of my own inadequacy. That's why I was so much more fun after the first couple drinks," he said. "Because I could forget how inadequate I felt and just *be*."

"Do you think it's because of rehab?" I said. "I mean, what made it different this time?"

"I hit bottom," he said. He looked into his coffee mug as if searching for his next words. "I got raped in prison."

My mouth dropped open.

"I was so angry afterward," he said. "I had so many *feelings*, and I couldn't numb them with alcohol anymore. I had to feel them."

"Did you report it?" I couldn't even take in the information James was giving me.

He laughed bitterly. "No. The guards are in on it—on the power dynamic, I mean. They get off on that kind of thing. They have bets going when new guys come in."

I swallowed against the nausea that was rising in my throat. "James . . . if you want to see someone . . . I can recommend a few names—"

"I talk to my sponsor," he said. "He's been to prison, so he gets it. No offense, but I don't think that talking to a therapist who's never been through what I've been through would help me any more than that."

"Okay." I stood and gave him a hug. "I love you."

"I know." He patted me awkwardly on the back.

I felt overcome with guilt and sorrow: guilt for every sarcastic or sharp word I'd said to James since he'd been home, when he'd been through so much, and sorrow for the pain he must be living through. But underneath was something worse: anger. And not even anger on James's behalf—*anger that he'd told me*, anger that he'd laid one more burden on my stooped and aching back. And then I was angry at myself for being angry.

To get out of myself, I wanted to tell him something in return. I cast around for something personal enough. "I've been boxing" was all I could come up with. I watched James rinse his mug and put it in the dishwasher. Before he'd gotten sober, he would have left his dishes in the sink.

He looked at me. "So that's why you're so buff."

I flexed a bicep at him.

He whistled. "Good for you."

"You're the only one I've told. Except my therapist."

"Why?"

I shrugged. "I wanted one thing to myself, you know?"

"Yeah. Thanks for telling me." He plucked his keys from his pocket. "Seeya."

He left for his meeting and I went to the office to change Mom's diaper and to feed her breakfast. After what James had told me, it seemed ridiculous to feel the least bit sorry for myself.

But I still did. It was the *dailiness* of caring for Mom that was so hard. It was physically taxing. It was mentally unstimulating. And it was emotionally draining. That trifecta created an experience that was eating me alive.

But I could do it, today.

On Sunday night I let myself into Jonah's apartment with the key he'd given me. I'd tried—and mostly succeeded—not to freak out when I'd found it one morning in the blue coffee cup I used at his place. But I hadn't used it yet.

He was working all day, the third and last of his shifts this week. I set about assembling a pot of chili.

I turned on all the lights in the apartment so Jonah wouldn't be startled when he came home and found me. I sat down on the couch and flicked through the channels until I found an *NCIS* marathon. I wrapped myself in his navy blanket and fell asleep.

I woke to a touch on my shoulder. "Ah!" I shouted, jumping so violently I almost rolled off the couch. For a long moment I had no idea where I was, or who could be laughing at me so hard.

I untangled myself from the blanket and sat up, still breathing fast. Jonah was doubled over laughing.

"Hi," I said, swallowing hard, my heart pounding. "I'm sorry. I fell asleep!"

"I noticed," he said, grinning. "You also made dinner."

"I did," I said. I stood up and kissed him. "Welcome home. And I was worrying that *I'd* scare *you*."

We sat down to eat. "I've been thinking," I said.

"Uh-oh," Jonah said. "Is that a good idea?"

I fake-scowled.

"I'm kidding. I just mean that sometimes you overthink things and it drives you crazy."

"Ha," I said. "Like I ever do that."

He snorted.

"Anyway." I took a deep breath. "I thought a lot about your . . . idea that we move in together." I'd been about to say "proposal" and figured it was a bad word choice.

"And?"

"I don't think I'm ready right now." I stared into my bowl. "Right now, caring for my mom, it's kind of all I can do." I swallowed. "I don't think this stage . . . is going to last very long," I said. "And then I'll be ready to pour myself into our relationship more deeply." I raised my eyes to meet his. "Are you disappointed?"

He looked at me. "Yes," he said.

My heart fell.

"But that's okay," he said. "It's a good thing that I'm disappointed, Laur. If I weren't, it would mean that our moving in together didn't mean that much to me, and that's not true." He leaned over and kissed me. "I'm disappointed because I want the next phase of our relationship to start now. But I can be patient." He nuzzled my nose with his. "Thanks for being honest."

"You're welcome," I said. I was stunned that it had been that easy.

Packing my photos to send in for the Gillespie Prize was one of the scariest things I'd ever done. I remembered reading that J. R. R. Tolkien had said, about sending *Lord of the Rings* to a publisher, "I have put up my heart to be shot at," and that was exactly how I felt.

The fear was so great that I had to do one small step each day, starting a week before the contest deadline. The first day, I took my digital card to the camera store on Main Street to have prints made. The next day I picked them up. The third day I packed the prints in an envelope lined with bubble wrap, along with a CD of the digital versions. Day four I addressed the envelope and dropped it off at the post office, my hands sweating on the cold steering wheel. Something was wrong with the heat in the Caddy, and I hadn't had time to think about getting it fixed.

After the post office I went to Scrivener's for a chai latte and a vanilla shortbread cookie. The sugar made me feel slightly better.

December seemed to fly by, even though I wasn't working, wasn't going to any holiday parties, and wasn't Christmas shopping (I ordered all my gifts on Amazon). Nothing out of the ordinary happened except that more neighbors and old friends stopped by to visit Mom. Far from cheering her up, these visits seemed to make her angry. She spilled hot tea on herself, burning a patch of skin on her chest. She threw silverware. She shouted insults, usually at me or James, that were so pointed we started making Kevorkian jokes. Our jokes were so dark these days, I didn't share them with anyone, not even Jonah.

The week before Christmas, the temperature dropped precipitously. I'd arranged to host Christmas Eve dinner at Mom's so I could spend Christmas Day with Jonah's mother and stepfather. Jonah and I were going to the Phish concert in Boston on Saturday night. There was so much going on. I was anxious and cranky when Izzy picked up Mom to take her out for pizza with the family so James and I could take his pickup to buy a tree.

I hadn't been in James's truck in ages, and he needed me to drive because it wasn't a necessary errand. He showed me how to blow into the Breathalyzer contraption, which he disinfected first, before turning the key in the ignition. The seat was ripped and scratched at my thighs through my jeans. Rusty screws rolled under our feet as I pulled away from the curb. The center console was dusty, with chewed gum in wrappers and moldy coins rattling in the catchall space.

James was in an unusually good mood, singing along with "White Christmas" on the radio.

"You're full of Christmas spirit," I said. *Why aren't I?* was the question I left unsaid.

"I've been sober eighteen weeks," James said, grinning as I stopped at a red light. "I know it doesn't sound like much, but I've never made it this far before."

"James, that's great!" Even my pessimistic mind shut up for a minute, and I began to enjoy myself as we passed stores and businesses strung with lights already twinkling at five o'clock. I

pulled into the parking lot of the pool supply store, where we'd
bought our tree for as long as I could remember. Even the past
few years, I had gone with Bill to pick out a tree, just the two of
us, in James's pickup. This was the first time James and I had
bought a tree together in at least fifteen years.

We hopped out of the truck, our breath freezing in front
of our faces. My parka weighed about six pounds, but at least my
body was warm.

The tree guy we always bought from waved from the
end of a row of short Douglas firs. The air smelled of pine and
snow, though there hadn't been any snow yet this season. It was
coming, though. I could feel it in the dampness of the air, the
coldness of the wind. Our guy finished a sale with another family
and came jogging toward us. He'd looked the same since I was
a child: close-cut hair and goatee speckled with gray, red flannel
jacket, jeans, hiking boots.

"It's the Keenes," he said, grinning. "Saved you guys a big
one."

Bill always bought the biggest tree they had. And then
he bought strands of lights with huge multicolored bulbs and
proceeded to replace all the other colors until the entire strand
was red.

"Where's your dad?" he asked over his shoulder, as we
threaded through a crowd of families waiting in line for hot cider
and popcorn.

James looked at me, and I shook my head. He squeezed
my hand. "He died a few months ago," James said as we followed
the salesman down a quiet, empty row. "Stroke." The trees here
were gigantic—ten, eleven feet tall at least, some upwards of
twelve or thirteen. The aisle was deserted; it felt as if we'd walked
into a forest.

The man took his cap off and stood before the largest
tree in the lot, his head bowed for a moment as if in prayer. He
looked up at us, his eyes shining. "I'm real sorry to hear that," he
said. He cleared his throat. "I saved this one for you." He thrust
his gloved hand into the thick branches and pulled on the trunk
so that the tree was standing away from the fence on which it had
been leaning. He spun it around for us. There were no bald spots.
The tree was perfectly cone-shaped.

James and I were, strangely, still holding hands. "White Christmas" was playing again over the loudspeakers.

"We'll take it," James said, and the guy called for his coworker; the two of them slung the tree onto their backs, fed it through the net machine, and hoisted it into the bed of the truck.

He shook our hands. "Threw some of these in," he said, handing me a plastic bag. I pulled the two handles apart and saw five boxes of red bulbs.

Chapter 30

James

The week before Christmas I decide to do it: Act how I want to feel. I ask Laura if she'd be okay with me buying Christmas gifts for Ava and Jeremiah, since this counts as contacting Ava. She agrees.

Three days later I ask if she'd be willing to drop them off for me, without calling first. I'm sure Ava will refuse over the phone, and I'm sure she'll be polite if Laura shows up at the door. Laura nods. My sister has circles under her eyes so dark they look like bruises, like she's been in a fight. She has. We both have.

"I want to know one thing, though," Laura says, and I know what she's going to ask before she asks it, and I know I'm going to answer her even though I don't want to. "What did Ava say to you on Thanksgiving?"

There was a time when I would have told Laura to fuck off and mind her own business, but that time is past. We're in a war together, she and I, and we have each other's backs. I never knew I could feel that way about anyone, especially not anyone I was related to. It was an entirely differently level in my understanding of what family was. "She told me that she was, in her words, 'so fucking pissed' she's thought about how she would murder me and make it look like an accident."

Laura's eyes widen and she nods; I can tell she believes that Ava would say that. And follow through on it, if she decided that was the course of action to take. I'm gratified, because I believed her too, and I don't have to impress on Laura how deadly serious Ava was. "But she was also grateful that I settled the case. She said it was such a relief not having to go to trial and say terrible things about me to the judge. She expected me to do that just because I love to argue, she said. She was also grateful that I didn't take the easy way out and declare bankruptcy. She said she was marginally impressed that I had grown a tiny bit more mature." I let my mouth curl up into a half-smile. "And she also said that if I stay sober for a year, and I can get three people who aren't related to me to testify to my sobriety and my changed character, she would consider allowing me supervised visits with Jeremiah. Occasionally. Like, once a month." I drum my fingers on the table. "Still, that gave me hope where before there was no hope."

Laura nods encouragingly. "That's great! You should have seen her at the hospital. I was kind of afraid on Thanksgiving she might pull a gun and shoot you right there."

"Thanks, Laur."

She shrugs.

"So, only nine months of sobriety to go," I say.

"Well, a lifetime of sobriety," Laura says. "Nine months until you have to scrounge up some people to say some nice shit about you."

We both laugh, even though it's not that funny. We've been doing that a lot lately.

I give Laura the two small wrapped boxes.

"You going to tell me what you got them?" she asks.

I shake my head. "Not today."

She nods, as if expecting this answer, then gets in the Caddy and drives away.

I'm giving Jeremiah four tickets to the next Patriots game so he can bring a friend with Rick and Ava. I'm giving Ava a gift card to the Rejuvenate Spa in Westerly and finally enclosing the letter I wrote her on my last day of rehab. I spent more on the two of them than on all my other Christmas gift recipients combined, but I owe them the biggest debt, in every sense of the word.

I'm cleaning up the porch room when I hear breaking glass in the office.

I sprint through the rooms to find Mom lying in bed with her eyes closed. A pile of broken glass glitters in the carpet opposite the bed. It appears that Mom has thrown her water glass at the wall—with quite a bit of force. I heave a sigh and go sit in the armchair by the bed. "Mom. Are you okay? Are you upset about something?"

"Wasn't me," Mom says, barely moving her lips.

I start laughing, although my laugh sounds kind of like a bark and could be mistaken for a sob.

Mom opens one eye and surveys me critically. "You going to clean that up?"

I stop laughing, or almost-crying, or whatever it was. "I am," I say. "Unless you want to do it."

"No," she says. "I'm busy." She closes her eyes again.

When I was growing up, I hardly ever saw Mom sit still for ten minutes at a time, much less lie in bed for hours and days and weeks on end. It's like she's already gone, like the shell that's left has no right to look so much like my mother.

I clean up the glass with a dustpan and broom then vacuum the tiniest glinting pieces with the Dustbuster. (I can't believe Mom still has a Dustbuster and then can't believe it still works, but it does.)

I put the Dustbuster back in the hall closet and feel my phone vibrate in my pocket. I pull it out. Dr. Steve. My pits break out in a cold sweat. I consider ignoring the call—but then I'd just have to call him back. I close my eyes and answer. "Hello."

"James. Dr. Lovato."

His use of his last name makes me want to cry. I lean my back against the wall for support.

"Hi."

"I'll cut right to the chase: It's all good news," he says. "Everything was negative."

He's still talking, but my relief is so great that I sink down the wall until I'm squatting. *Thank God. Thank God. Thank God.*

I'm waiting in the kitchen when Laura comes home. She looks perkier than I thought she would and hands me a tin patterned with snowmen. "Jeremiah made cookies in Home Ec.," she says. "They're not bad. I ate three in the car." She smiles. "Jeremiah says thanks. Ava didn't say anything, but she didn't throw things or yell at me, so that seemed positive."

"Okay," I say. "I ordered Chinese."

"Great," she says. "You going out tonight?"

I nod. "With Penny. She's working until seven, so we're doing the movies and coffee. Because not drinking severely limits your entertainment options."

Laura looks thoughtful. "You could take her ice-skating."

I snort a little to cover up my amazement as I open the tin of cookies, which are sugar cookies shaped like snowmen and Santas and bells. The amazement covers both the fact that my son is old enough to know how to make cookies and that he wanted to give some of them to me. "I can't ice-skate."

"Sure you can. You used to Rollerblade. It's practically the same thing."

So an hour later I find myself, full of General Tso's chicken and Christmas cookies—which I had proudly offered to Penny to try, and who had properly gushed about them—wobbling around McNally's Ice Rink in Newport. Penny is holding my hand, her skating even and graceful. "I didn't know you could skate," I say.

She smiles. "This isn't skating, James. This is teetering." She tucks a section of hair behind her ear under her purple hat. "I used to take lessons when I was younger."

I let go of her hand. "Let me see, then."

Penny skates off at warp speed, passing me three times before I make it around the rink once. Her face is glowing. She skates to the center with the show-offs then skates backward in a small circle, throws her right leg out, and executes a dizzying spin.

When she comes flying at me and I catch her around the waist and she kisses me, there under the bright rink lights, I realize for the first time that I'm having more fun than I ever had drinking.

Chapter 31

Laura

The Saturday before Christmas, Mom and I had the house to ourselves. James was working.

The sky was low and gray, the ocean foaming with whitecaps, and snow was in the forecast. I made pancakes in my pajamas. I piled a tray with two plates, two mugs of coffee, silverware, and a squat bottle of Vermont maple syrup.

Mom was sleeping, so I sat in the armchair next to her bed and ate pancakes and drank coffee. I leaned my head back, my eyes wandering up to the light fixture on the ceiling. Mom had been staring at it so much, for reasons we couldn't imagine, that we'd removed the bulbs and used only the bedside lamps. The room had no windows except for two squares of glass set high in the corners of the east wall. They faced the sea but were too high up to provide a view. The room was therefore in perpetual semidarkness, except for two squares of light that moved down the wall in the early morning and disappeared as the sun traveled west. Sometimes I thought of the dim light as peaceful, but today I felt trapped; all I wanted was the artificial brightness of the mall, the office, somewhere normal and full of people.

Mom stirred and opened her eyes.

"Feel up to some portraits today, Mom?" I wouldn't hear about the Gillespie Prize for a couple of months, but taking photos of Mom had become an ingrained part of our routine.

She didn't say anything, but I got out my camera anyway.

It no longer seemed to matter as much whether the light source was good; what seemed to make the photos better or worse was whether Mom was at home or not. I was getting some great shots of her, the lamplight reflecting in her eyes, when she looked right at me.

"Laura?"

I jumped.

"Mom," I said, my voice tremulous. I collapsed into the chair.

"You know, Robert knew you were Bill's daughter," she said quietly, as if continuing a conversation we'd started before she'd fallen asleep.

I wanted to pull out the packet of photos again, to find out the whole story. Why the hotel facade? Why the piano player? But suddenly I realized that this *was* the whole story: not what each photo signified, but what my mother could tell me. So instead of rushing to get the answers I thought I wanted, I listened.

"He told me when he was dying, told me he'd asked Bill to take care of us. He wasn't angry with me in the end." She sighed. "I was sorry for hurting him. He was a good husband. But in the end, he was glad you were Bill's. Because it tied Bill to me, to us. Robert knew that Bill wouldn't abandon his daughter, so he could die in peace."

Maybe this was how you got what you needed in relationships—by accepting what other people could give instead of demanding something you wanted. But still, there was so much more I wanted to know. I leaned forward, the balls of my feet pressing into the metal bed frame. "Why didn't you and Bill ever tell me?" My voice quivered.

My mother looked at me, her eyes soft and wise. "He was going to tell you. He'd decided it was past time. He'd put it off all these years. He never wanted you to feel different from your brothers and sister."

"But I did feel different," I said. "I always knew there was something different about me. I thought I was a freak."

She reached her hand out to take one of mine. "We should have told you years ago," she said.

"The photos—was I supposed to find them?"

"I don't know why I saved them. They were incriminating, weren't they?" She smiled. "We should have done better for you, Laura, but it worked out all right in the end."

I'd always felt like I'd never had a proper father. What if I looked at things differently? What if, instead, I saw myself as lucky enough to have had two fathers?

She took my hand. "I'm sorry if I ever made you feel unwanted," she said.

"Mommy," I said. "Of course you didn't."

She smiled sadly up at the ceiling. "You reminded me so much of Bill. So much so that sometimes I couldn't look you in the eye. I'm sorry."

"It's okay," I said, sniffing hard.

She looked around. "Are those pancakes?" she asked.

I handed her the plate and watched her eat every bite of them, amazed. We'd been feeding her for a week now; she seemed to have lost the hand-eye coordination to lift a fork to her mouth. "I love you, Mom," I said.

"I love you too, Laurlie." She closed her eyes for a moment. When they fluttered open again, her expression was mischievous. "Want to go for a swim with me?"

I shook my head, smiling. "It's way too cold out for me. Or you," I said.

She sighed. "I used to love swimming in the ocean in the winter," she said. "I was all alone with my thoughts." She closed her eyes. "I think I need another nap," she said.

"I'll be here when you wake up," I promised.

She fell asleep.

The afternoon was uneventful. I read in the semidarkness. I watched Netflix on my laptop. I brought Mom lunch. When she fell asleep again around 4:30, I ran upstairs to shower. When I clicked off the hair dryer I heard the doorbell ringing. "Coming!" I yelled, pounding down the stairs. Jonah was standing on the doorstep, flakes of snow in his dark hair. Twilight had already fallen.

"Ready?" he said.

"Almost," I said. "Give me five minutes."

I ran back upstairs, finished my makeup, and got dressed. I could hear the door open and close and two deep voices talking; James was home. I noticed my own complete lack of anxiety that James would say or do something stupid in the presence of my boyfriend. And the complete lack of apoplectic anger because he was late or drunk, because he was neither.

Both were nice.

The men looked up when I came into the porch room.

"Hey," Jonah said, standing and pulling me toward him. "You look great."

"Okay, kids, don't stay out too late," James joked.

I kissed him goodbye.

"I'm leaving at seven tomorrow," he said. "Taking Penny Christmas shopping in Boston."

"No problem," I said. "I'll see you later."

The drive to Providence was slow with traffic. Jonah had the Phish station playing on Pandora and was mouthing the words to every song, his hand tapping out a rhythm on my thigh. I was feeling distinctly underwhelmed about the concert but tried to smile every time Jonah looked at me. *This is fun,* I told myself.

We parked at the Dunkin' Donuts Center and walked into the arena. Jonah was bouncing with every step and waving at audience members he knew from other shows.

"I need to hit the bathroom," I said.

"I'll get you a drink," he said, motioning to the concessions stand.

The line was long, but I walked past it and stood in the corner by the row of sinks. The bathroom smelled like urine and pink soap. The concrete floor was wet. I texted Amber. *I'm at the Phish concert with Jonah. Just want to be home in my pajamas.*

WhatsApp flashed a message: *Amber is typing.* Her reply came: *Suck it up, lady. You have an amazing guy, and this is a small price to pay.*

I smiled. She was right. I washed my hands and went out.

Jonah was waiting for me, a beer in each hand, talking to three other guys. Two of them sported scruffy facial hair and were heavily tattooed. The third was clean-cut and tall and made me feel less out of place. Jonah wrapped his arm around my shoulders, introduced me. They were talking about how long it had been since Phish had played Providence, boasting about who had seen the best Phish shows (Jonah argued for Big Cypress in '99). They debated what the set list might be and what bars people were going to after the show.

The guys dispersed and Jonah took my hand. "Want to

go find our seats?"

"Sure," I said, injecting enthusiasm into my voice.

A crash of drumbeats sounded from the stage.

"Unless . . ." he looked at me appraisingly.

"Unless what?"

"C'mere." He led me by the hand away from the arena, back toward an empty hallway. There were two single-room handicap bathrooms there. He led me into one, locked the door, pushed me up against the door and stuck his tongue down my throat. He unbuttoned my jeans.

I felt suddenly reckless and horny as hell.

He kissed me again, his hands cupping my breasts. He was kissing my neck, one hand under my shirt unsnapping my bra.

The sex was hot and quick, both of us coming in a matter of three sweaty minutes. The music crashed in the distance.

"I always wanted to do that," he said in my ear.

"They call me Fairy Godmother," I joked. I lowered my voice to a pseudo-sexy whisper. "I make dreams come true."

He held my gaze. "You do."

I looked away, embarrassed.

He pulled my chin gently to look into my eyes again. "You do." He cleared his throat. "I know you don't really want to be here," he said. "But let's have a great time anyway, okay?"

I smiled. "Deal."

And we did.

My alarm went off at six a.m. after less than four hours of sleep. James was making coffee when I got to the kitchen.

I had trained him not to talk to me in the mornings. All he said was "I'm going to an early meeting, working, and then taking Penny out for dinner."

I gave him a thumbs-up.

I brought Mom breakfast. She seemed a little more alert than usual. "Okay," I said. "I'm going to take a quick shower. I'll be back in ten minutes."

I took the baby monitor we'd started carrying around

into the bathroom, then showered and dressed at top speed. I went back downstairs and got a deck of cards from the coffee table cabinet. Mom couldn't remember how to play Shanghai, but she liked to touch the cards and move them around.

"Hey, Mom," I said as I came to the office entrance. "Want to play—" I stopped short next to the rickety sliding doors we never closed because they always came off the track.

The hospital bed was empty.

"Mom?" Fear cracked my voice. "Mom?" She hadn't walked in *weeks*. For every minute of those weeks, I had known exactly where she was.

The living room was empty, the dining room was empty, the porch and the kitchen were still and quiet.

"Fuck," I muttered.

The door to the basement was closed. She hadn't come upstairs. Then I saw that the kitchen patio door was open a crack.

In the snow I could see a single set of footprints leading away from the house. I shoved my feet into shoes, tore across the patio and up the dune path, my Chucks sliding in the slush that covered the loose sand. When I crested the hill, I saw the line of footprints leading straight into the iron-gray surf. I ran, my lungs heaving as the cold air pierced them, and the distance fell away below my feet.

At the lip of the water I stopped and scanned the vast expanse of sea, searching desperately for unusual movement, an aberration of color in the gray-and-white landscape.

Nothing. Nothing. Nothing.

Then something caught my eye. Far to my right, a figure holding the leash of a dog was bending over a shape huddled on the sand. I ran, watching the silhouette grow larger, saw the figure pull the dog back, raise a hand to an ear as if talking into a phone.

My brain tried and failed to make sense of the shape in the sand. I focused on a very small part of the image as I came closer and closer and recognized the blue veins and white knuckles of my mother's hand, her sapphire anniversary ring catching the weak sunlight.

The impressions of the next moments were like photographs in my memory, even as they were happening.

An ambulance driving onto the sand toward me.

Paramedics loading my mother's waterlogged body onto a gurney.

A police officer wrapping a silver blanket around my shoulders.

Back in the kitchen of my mother's house, Jonah appearing out of nowhere. A police officer asking me questions.

Izzy arriving alone. The house was full of neighbors and police officers, people I didn't even know. I was sitting by myself on the couch. Izzy sat down next to me and held me in her arms. She didn't say a word.

I didn't remember leaving the house, but when I found myself at The Box, standing in front of the bag, I was relieved. The fluorescent lights seemed impossibly bright.

I bobbed and weaved, ducked and jabbed. Jab. Right cross. Jab. The smack of my fist against the bag, the bouncing of my feet on the concrete floor. I went into the zone of no thinking, no feeling, only moving. Sweat and tears dripped down my face, and my arms were shaking when someone finally grabbed me by the shoulders. I spun, drawing my right arm back, ready to punch.

It was James.

He was crying.

He grabbed me into a rough hug. I didn't respond but didn't stop him, my fists in their huge boxing gloves hanging limp and heavy at my sides. I could hear a sound I couldn't make sense of: a high-pitched keening like the death wail of some primitive creature. It was James. And I lifted my hands to pat his back with huge gloved buffets. All I felt was adrenaline coursing through my body. As if I could still fight this off. As if I could still outrun it.

James pulled back from our hug and grabbed the sides of my face, shaking it a little. "The door alarm malfunctioned," he said. "That's why it didn't go off. It's not your fault. You know that, right, Laura?"

I nodded.

But I didn't believe him.

Chapter 32

James

I'm worried about Laura. She was heartbroken when Bill died, but this is something else. I think that, if we let her, she wouldn't get out of bed.

Mom's funeral is tomorrow, the day before Christmas Eve. When I was little I used to call it Christmas Eve Eve.

Penny and Lou and Marcus are coming to the funeral. I asked them to come to the lunch afterward too, which we're having at the country club like normal people, instead of hosting it ourselves. Izzy didn't even object. And no one said anything when I told the catering manager we'd have an open bar but that it had to be in a separate room. My friends will sit with me, and their presence will fortify me against the bottomless desire to get shit-faced drunk.

Ava is bringing Jeremiah. She called Laura to say so.

Mom had gone swimming. She'd remembered how to walk, and she'd gone down to the ocean and walked into the water. They say that many Alzheimer's patients have a period of clarity right before death. They told us that before. Laura didn't put it together when Mom talked to her that last day, and now she's really beating herself up over it.

The four of us write Mom's eulogy together, and Sam offers to read it. None of us are in a state to do it ourselves. But the process of putting it together, sharing our favorite memories, laughing and crying, is cathartic. Robert keeps sneaking out of the room, coming back smelling strongly of whiskey so that I'm tempted to give him the business card of the Central Falls Rehabilitation Facility.

The day after the funeral, I arrive at my morning meeting and find Marcus sitting in my usual seat. I drop into a chair next to him. He throws an arm around my shoulders, squeezes me into his meaty torso, lets go.

When the meeting opens there's an awkward silence. I'm

surprised. Usually we don't have enough time in the hour for everyone who wants to share.

I raise my hand. I hardly ever raise my hand.

"My name is James, and I'm an alcoholic."

"Hi, James."

"My mom died four days ago," I say. My voice breaks a little. Great. I'm not even close to getting out what I want to say. "She had Alzheimer's. My sister and I took care of her." I cough. "I mean, I helped my sister take care of her the past few weeks when I got outta rehab." I laugh a little. "Tell it like it is, right, Mike?"

Mike nods vigorously from across the room. People laugh.

"Anyway, the truth is, it was real hard taking care of her. I hated it." My voice is quiet now, but the wobble has straightened out of it. "I loved my mother. Don't get me wrong, or make me out to be a monster for something I don't deserve. But the thing is—the awful truth is—that part of me is relieved." A weight lifts off my chest as I say this. "I know it's terrible. But there it is."

After the meeting Marcus takes me to the Princess Diner for breakfast. It's is packed. I tell him I have to get to work. "We'll sit at the counter," he says, which seems unrelated.

Marcus elbows through the crowd at the door and we take the last two counter seats. The ceiling is hung with plastic green wreaths; plastic Santa and snowman figurines sit on every table. Red and green glitter sparkles on the floor and counters.

A willowy dark-skinned waitress spots us and waves. "Whatcha having?"

"Two number threes," he says.

She nods and disappears behind the line. She's so gorgeous she should be a model.

Marcus looks at me and laughs. "Close your mouth," he says. "That's my niece. She'll move our order up."

"What'd you order?" I ask.

He laughs again. "That's right, you change the subject," he says. "I got us the combo breakfast, two eggs, two pancakes, two strips of bacon. And they usually throw a slice of orange on there."

I'm starving. I haven't been eating much the past few days.

"I'm proud of you," Marcus says. "Admitting what you did in there."

"I figured people there know what it means to be a horrible son, so I wasn't as worried about what they'd think of me."

"What you said you're feeling—relieved—doesn't make you a horrible son," Marcus says. "Makes you human."

Penny and I are moving at a glacial dating pace. We kiss at the end of each date, and that's it. I am afraid of pushing her away. She has a history of bad relationships too, and she's afraid of making the same old mistakes.

We have plans to attend an AA New Year's Eve party together. Penny picks me up at nine.

The party is being held in the parish hall of the United Methodist Church of Eastville, where AWOL meets. We arrive to find the hall decked out with black and silver streamers and a disco ball projecting shimmering flecks of silver on the floor. A DJ is playing "Livin' on a Prayer," and a hundred sober drunks are jumping up and down, singing at the top of their lungs. We grin at each other and dive into the fray. When Bon Jovi is done belting, we snack on slightly stale barbecue chips, drink flat soda, and eat chocolate cake.

Penny and I kiss at midnight. It is the tamest New Year's Eve I can remember. But I feel hopeful, and that's something I've never felt on New Year's Eve before.

Weeks pass. Laura and I return the hospital bed, file all the paperwork. I can't *believe* how much paperwork there is. We clean out Mom and Bill's room, donate clothes and shoes, toss toiletries. Laura invites Izzy and Ivy over to choose jewelry from Mom's collection. She has Robert come to pick out pieces for Athena and Aurelia. The only thing Laura takes is Mom's sapphire anniversary ring, which she now wears on her right ring finger at all times.

I'm waiting for Laura to initiate talk of selling the house. Or maybe we can move out and rent it. I start looking at apartments on Craigslist so I'll be ready to escape at a moment's notice.

Winter is passing so slowly, I think I might be asleep. One of Benny's regular employees catches pneumonia, so I'm working six days a week now. Since half of every paycheck is going to Ava, I wear the same two alternating outfits each day: layers of all the sweaters I own. I'm going stir-crazy now, can't wait to get out of this house, but I feel tied to my sister. Obligated is a better word, because she took me in when I least deserved it. Obligation was what I'd always thought family was about—and that was why I'd always run from it before. But this was different. I love Laura; we went through a war together, and I don't want to leave her alone.

One morning in late February, I come back into the kitchen after smoking on the patio.

Laura's sitting at the kitchen table. "Those things'll kill you," she says as I stuff my cigarette pack into my pocket.

"Drinking would've killed me," I say, temper flaring. "I can only kick one deadly habit at a time."

"I'm just concerned about your health," she snaps.

"Maybe you should be more concerned about *your* health," I say. "When was the last time you boxed?"

She stares at me, her eyes large in her face, then gets up from the table and leaves the room. She *has* gained a few pounds, all around her waist, but her cheeks are still hollow. Still, I can't believe I said that. What the fuck is my problem?

I should probably go apologize right now, through her locked bedroom door. But I can't bring myself to do it. I wallow instead, turn on a football game. A few minutes later I hear her footsteps coming down the stairs. She passes the doorway of the porch room in workout clothes, leaves out the side door without a word. God, I can still be such an asshole.

When she comes back ninety minutes later, I meet her at the door. "I'm sorry. That was so out of line."

She shrugs. Her face is flooded with color and her hairline wet with perspiration. She looks healthy for the first time in months. "It was true."

"I need a timeline," I say. "For moving out."

Her eyes skitter sideways. "So pick one."

"What's *your* timeline?"

She sidesteps me. "I can't talk about this right now."

I call Marcus, vent.

"She's right. You pick a timeline. You've been there for her. Now you need to do what's best for you."

"I do?" I'm confused.

"Yes."

"I thought I was bound to other people, and all that stuff."

I can hear the smile in his voice. "You are. But you're also bound to choose wisely for yourself. What's the latest you can stay there?"

"April," I say immediately.

"So make plans to leave by the end of April, and tell Laura now."

"Okay." I hang up and e-mail three people about apartments.

I'm not well. But I'm still moving toward wellness. For the first time in my life.

EPILOGUE

Laura

On the last day of February, I got a phone call from a blocked number. "Hello?" I expected Kevin.

"May I speak to Laura Keene?" Not Kevin; an unfamiliar man's voice, husky and low.

"This is she," I said.

"Laura, this is Lawrence Bigby."

"Wow," I said. "Hi."

"I'm calling to tell you that you've won the Gillespie Prize."

I had been sitting on the floor of the office, sorting through papers from the filing cabinet that had stood in the corner for as long as I could remember. I lay back on the floor and stared at the ceiling. We had never replaced the bulbs in the light fixture, so the room was still cloaked in semidarkness. I closed my eyes against a brightness that had nothing to do with nonexistent light bulbs. "Wow," I said again.

Bigby laughed.

"I really don't know what to say," I said, feeling like every sucker on TV I'd ever seen surprised, only turned down about seventeen notches. "I'm honored." I wondered if he remembered I'd been his student, wondered if it would be awkward to bring it up.

"Your work will be displayed in a gallery in Providence, Exposure, starting with an opening on March 28," he said.

"Okay," I said, rolling to my side and scribbling the name of the gallery and the date on the corner of an ancient IRS envelope.

"We'll send you a formal invitation of course," he said, as if he could see what I was doing. "I just wanted to be the first to congratulate you."

"Thank you so much," I said, feeling like a complete idiot. I couldn't seem to put words to anything but a platitude.

"You were a promising student," he said.

My cheeks burned.

"I'm so pleased that you didn't hang up your camera."

When I set the phone down, the first person I wanted to tell was Mom.

I'd always told Mom good things first, because I always wanted her to be proud of me.

I walked around to the kitchen, slinging my coat on as I went out the sliding doors and down to the beach. The wind was raw and damp, but I found it invigorating. That day I might have found a blizzard invigorating. I walked down to the edge of the damp sand—the tide was going out—and sat down. I could feel the moisture soaking into the butt of my jeans, but I didn't care. This was where I felt closest to Mom. Not in church, not in her bedroom or the office where I'd spent months taking care of her, not at her gravestone, where I still went to talk to Bill. But here, by the ocean that had claimed her life. "Mom," I whispered. "We won."

Jonah hosted a dinner party in my honor at his place: James and Penny, Robert and Becky, Izzy and Sam, Amber and Brian. We drank champagne and ate shrimp and filet mignon and ginger-carrot soup and roasted asparagus. (I'd made the vegetables, because Jonah's idea of a perfect meal was a piece of meat on a plate, and maybe a dinner roll.) I stayed the night, and the next morning I went home.

Izzy had been trying to convince me and James to move out of the house so we could sell it. "Do you know how much it's worth?" had become her refrain. We hadn't told her yet that James was moving out in April.

I knew Izzy and Sam were hurting financially, and I felt bad. But I also didn't feel ready to give up the house. Not yet. Giving up the house felt like giving up on Mom. On the family I'd always wanted, the family Mom's illness had started to bring about.

Jonah had been exceedingly patient. He'd only brought up moving in together once in the months since I'd told him I wasn't ready.

I still wasn't ready. I didn't feel ready for anything.

On March 28 I arrived early at the gallery opening, alone.
Jonah had wanted to drive me, since I was spending the night
at his place. But I wanted to see my photographs alone, before
anyone else arrived. The gallery was in downtown Providence,
on a cute street filled with artsy shops and trendy restaurants.
The storefront was brick, with a black sign proclaiming
"EXPOSURE" in blocky white letters. A plateglass window
outlined in tiny white lights displayed a large gallery space with
blond wood floors and pale gray walls. Walls covered with dozens
of photographs of my mother.

I opened the door, a tiny bell announcing my presence.
A small brunette woman in a scarlet dress turned from the
glass-and-steel podium that stood by the door into the gallery
space. "We're not open just yet," she said, smiling. "But there's
a great coffee shop next door, and you can come back in twenty
minutes."

I cleared my throat. "I'm Laura," I said, walking toward
her with my hand outstretched. "Laura Keene."

"Oh!" Her eyes lit up, and she ignored my hand and
leaned forward to kiss me on the cheek. "Laura! I'm sorry. It is
so lovely to meet you. I'm Renee. I am such an admirer of your
work." I smiled. My work had admirers.

"I wondered if I could freshen up a bit. And then—" I
looked toward the doorway, which was a clean cutout in the wall,
my voice faltering.

"Of course! You want to see your photos before there's a
crowd in there."

I nodded.

"Well, just head on down the hall; the bathroom's to the
right. I'll be right here if you need anything." She smiled and
turned away to direct a young woman who was lining up glasses
of champagne on a table covered with a deep purple cloth.

The bathroom was barely big enough for me to turn
around it, but it was tastefully made up with a bowl-shaped sink
resting on a steel counter draped with more purple cloth. The
small mirror was framed by bare rose lightbulbs. I washed my

hands with lilac-scented soap, smoothed on lipstick. My hands were shaking.

I walked back down the hallway and stepped into the gallery space.

Mom's face surrounded me as I stood in the center of the concrete floor, smoothing the skirt of my gray silk dress. The photographs had been mounted and lit beautifully. They were all different sizes, all unframed. Nothing mediating the view. They were printed with a matte finish, so they didn't have that shiny quality that looked fake.

The photos showed Mom laughing, Mom kissing her teddy bear, Mom eating ice cream out of the carton, Mom's face contorted in anger. Mom sleeping, Mom preening in a pink feather boa, Mom hiding a mischievous smile behind a fan of playing cards. A black-and-white photo of Mom standing at the bay window in her nightgown, her hand pressed to the glass, the fog outside misting the landscape. Mom staring at a photo of Bill as if he were a complete stranger. Mom in her wheelchair leaving the hospital after her bout of pneumonia. Mom taking a bite of pancake from the fork James was holding to her mouth. Mom staring at the light fixture in her hospital bed in the office, her eyes vacant.

I'd worn waterproof mascara. I'd been prepared for an onslaught of emotion. But I felt strangely detached as I stood there.

Maybe it was time to sell the house. Jonah's apartment had plenty of room for the two of us.

Why hadn't I left yet? It wasn't that I couldn't leave the place where I remembered Mom and Bill best. Part of it was an attachment to my childhood—and living there again as an adult had made me remember things I'd long forgotten, for better or for worse.

In our house I would always know who I was. It was where I inhabited my first role: daughter. Now that I was no longer a daughter, I didn't always know who I was, where I belonged. I had always belonged at home, no matter what else was going on in my life. And if I let go of the house, I was afraid I'd be permanently relinquishing that part of myself.

Where would I belong next?

The answer came to my mind unbidden, and it wasn't a place but a person: Jonah. Jonah was where I belonged now.

The bell sounded above the door. My palms started sweating. My adrenaline was on a hair trigger. I rubbed my hands together, twisting Mom's ring around my finger, and walked into the small foyer.

Kevin and Elaine were standing in the doorway, hanging up their coats on the long coat rack.

I'd started back to work a few weeks ago. Ironically, it had been Marisa who'd suggested it, positing that perhaps I needed an outlet for my grief.

"You were the one who suggested I *stop* working," I'd said irritably.

"Yes," she said. "And now I'm suggesting you think about starting again."

Once I'd gotten home from my session, though, the thought of having something to do during the day that didn't involve cleaning out my mother's house felt like a huge relief. So I'd approached Kevin about returning to work. It had been close to the six-month mark of my leave of absence, anyway.

"We'd love to have you back," he'd said. "You can start part-time if you want, see how it goes."

I nodded. "That sounds smart." So I started back, just three days a week, seeing some of my former clients. I was starting to feel stronger again, if not exactly happy. Yet.

"Hi," I said to them now, starting forward.

Elaine hugged me tight. "Congratulations," she said.

"Thanks," I said, smiling.

Kevin leaned in to kiss my cheek. "It's so nice to see you smile," he said.

I made sure they got champagne, but found I couldn't enter the gallery room with them.

Jonah arrived, looking handsome in dark jeans, a blue button-down shirt, and a black blazer. He kissed me on the cheek. "I am so proud of you," he said. He stood by me as I greeted other guests. Then more and more people started to arrive, most of them strangers; still I hung back in the foyer.

My three siblings arrived together in what I hoped was solidarity. James had brought Penny, but Izzy and Robert were both alone.

I wondered if they were worried about what they would see. James was the only one who had seen the photos before, and then only the digital copies I'd shown him on my computer before sending them off. He took my hand as they crossed the threshold. "Come with us," he said. He was holding a bottle of cranberry juice and a program in the other hand. He'd told me months ago that one of his strategies at parties was to make sure both hands were always full. Made it harder to reach out and pluck someone's whiskey from their hand and pour it down his throat, he'd said.

The photographs started on the left-hand wall, and they progressed around the room in a timeline that matched Mom's decline.

"You can *see* it happening," I heard one viewer say, behind us, and I turned to see the picture they were looking at: Mom's eyes, looking to the left of the camera, lost, hostile, confused.

I *had* seen it happen, and that had been what I'd wanted to show. I felt vaguely satisfied. But the feeling was as if I'd eaten a good meal but was still desperately thirsty: I was satisfied that the art I'd set out to make had connected with an audience. But I was still an orphan, and the ache of loss had not released me from its jaws.

James reached the end before Izzy or Robert. Penny was clutching his elbow. The final photo was the only one where Mom was looking directly at the camera. She was grinning.

"This was the day?" he asked, taking my hand.

"Yes," I said. I'd taken it the day she died, right after she'd told me Dad had known I was Bill's daughter. Renee had let me add the photo to the gallery collection after I'd won the prize.

"She looks beautiful," James said.

"She does, doesn't she?" I smiled at my brother, and my heart cracked open. Most of the time it felt like it was wrapped in cotton, muffled from the world, a step removed from everything. Today it had been thrust out into the open, and the wind of reality was bracing.

I looked at Mom's face again, as James and Penny moved to the center of the room, away from the crowds circling the perimeter.

I looked at Mom's face and saw something new. She looked like herself. She looked like a woman who knew exactly what she was doing. Suddenly I knew, in the marrow of my bones, that it wasn't my fault that Mom had died the way she did. She hadn't wandered down to the beach, confused and alone. She had walked into the ocean with purpose. She had not wanted to die safe in bed, shriveled and diminished. She had wanted to die in the water.

I felt a hand in mine and was relieved that Jonah was at my side again. "I think Izzy needs you," he said in my ear.

Izzy was standing in front of the photo of Mom in her wheelchair leaving the hospital. "You said she'd never walk again," Izzy said, hugging me. I could feel her tears on my neck. "You said so. And you were right."

I had been right, sort of. Mom had never walked again, until she walked out of the office, through the sliding door in the kitchen, across the patio, up a sand dune, down the beach, and straight into the freezing ocean.

I had thought it was because I hadn't been there to stop her. But now I knew that she had been waiting—waiting for me to leave her alone, to leave her to die in the way she had chosen for herself.

A meaty hand closed on my shoulder, and I turned around. Lawrence Bigby was standing behind me. He looked exactly the same as he had in the summer of 2002, if a little heavier, a little grayer. He leaned forward and kissed me on the cheek. "Congratulations," he said.

"Thanks," I said. I could feel Izzy next to me, staring. "Mr. Bigby, this is my sister, Isobel."

Bigby offered his hand to her. "Please, call me Lawrence." He slid his eyes back to me. "*You* can call me Bigby."

I grinned.

Izzy excused herself and Bigby looked at me, his blue eyes

steely behind his wire-rimmed glasses. "You had a lot of talent as a student," he said. "But this work is on a whole new level. You really let the viewer in. Into your pain as a caregiver, as a daughter. Your pain and your joy. It's a privilege to witness."

I smiled. "Thanks," I said.

The gallery was growing warmer, filled with bodies pressing toward the walls for a better look. Robert motioned to me from the doorway, and I followed him down the chilly hall, where it was quieter. "What's up?" I said, rubbing my arms.

Robert's eyes were sparkling with tears. "I just wanted to thank you," he said. "For all you did for Mom. I couldn't do it. You'd think, being a doctor, I could care for my own mother, but I just—"

"Hey," I said, putting a hand on his arm. "We all did it. We all took care of her. I'm sorry about what I said on Thanksgiving. That wasn't fair. I've been meaning to tell you that for months."

"And forgiving James the way you did—"

"I chose to forget what he'd done for a little while," I said. "It took a lot longer to forgive him."

"You held us together, Laurlie. You got us through it."

"We got through it together," I said, and I meant it. "Come on, it's freezing out here."

We found Izzy by the coats. "Laura, I need to talk to you."

"Iz," I said, sighing. "This is not the time to talk about the house. Again."

She looked hurt. "I can talk to you about other things," she said.

You just usually don't, I thought.

"I just wanted to know if you and James wanted to host Easter at the house or if you want me to do it."

I rubbed at my forehead. "When is it?"

Izzy rolled her eyes. "Next Sunday."

Right. So I'd been a little out of things. "You can do it."

"Okay. Dinner at 4:30 then." She turned her attention to Robert. "You have the girls, right? Julia had them at Christmas."

Robert nodded.

"It's settled, then. I thought, ham and roast potatoes, for sure . . ."

I looked at the two of them, but I was no longer part of the conversation. I had stepped out of it, as if I were taking a photograph of them. Izzy was talking about pineapple stuffing; Robert was glancing at his phone.

A hand slipped into mine and I looked up to see Jonah. "Can I borrow Laura for a minute?" he said.

Izzy nodded, and Robert started typing with his thumbs.

"Thought you might need rescuing," Jonah said when we were out of earshot.

"Thanks."

By nine o'clock the crowd was thinning. I thanked Renee for everything, and she gave me a bottle of champagne, a silver bow tied around the neck. "Thanks," I said, touched.

Jonah came and took my hand. "Ready?"

"Yes," I said. "Let's go home."

ACKNOWLEDGMENTS

It takes a village to raise a book, and *Catchlight* is no exception. The journey of writing this book and bringing it into the world was many years in the making.

Thank you to everyone at Woodhall Press—Christopher, David, and Colin—for believing in this book and helping me bring it into the hands of readers.

Thank you to Phil Klay, guest judge for the 2019 Fairfield Book Prize, for choosing *Catchlight* as the winner. I am truly honored.

Thank you to my mentors at the Fairfield University MFA program—to the late, great Da Chen, Hollis Seamon, Nalini Jones, and most especially Rachel Basch, all of whom helped draw the best version of this book out of me. Many thanks to Elizabeth Hastings, Sonya Huber, and Michael C. White for their tireless work running this amazing program.

To my best friend and writing-partner-in-crime, Caroline Garnet McGraw, for supporting me forever and always in writing, business, and life.

To my parents, Joan and Fran Adams, and my sister, Brittany Adams Recupero—thank you for being my first and best captive audience and for encouraging my gift before I knew I had one.

To my children, Elijah and Jacqueline—thank you for making me a better mom and a better person every day.

To my husband, Simeon—thank you for believing in me more than I believed in myself, for calling me out when I'm being too hard on myself (always), and for always saying "yes" to my dreams. I love you.

And finally, to my readers. The world is full of demands for your time and attention. Thank you, from the bottom of my heart, for spending a little of both with me.

CPSIA information can be obtained
at www.ICGtesting.com
Printed in the USA
LVHW091209191020
669147LV00009B/180

9 781949 116182